AF673856

PERVEZ

Praise for *Mixed Marriage and Other Parsi Stories*

"*Mixed Marriage and Other Parsi Stories* is a gallery of characters, some sensitive, some prejudiced, some generous and some plain oddball. The stories in this collection provide an insight into a closely-knit community."

– *India Today*

"The emphasis in all the stories is on the narrative ... at times when she focuses on character interaction ... the story has depth and leaves an impact on the reader."

– *The Hindu*

"This collection is an honest evaluation of the realities that have transformed the secular Bombay of yore. By diagnosing the malaise, the author hopes the people of Mumbai will find their own antidote."

– *The Statesman*

"*Mixed Marriage* is not so much about people as about social and moral issuses which form the vortex of the anthology ... there are flashes of beauty ... *Mixed Marriage and Other Parsi Stories* is a mixed fare of reasonable achievement for a first-time author."

– *The Hindustan Times*

"The strength of her writing lies in her ability to use simple words to reinforce the basic theme of her story."

– *Indian Express*

PERVEZ

a novel

MEHER PESTONJI

HarperCollins *Publishers* India

First published in India by HarperCollins *Publishers* 2003
4th Floor, Tower A, Building No. 10, DLF Cyber City,
DLF Phase II, Gurugram, Haryana – 122002
www.harpercollins.co.in

This edition published in India by HarperCollins *Publishers* 2024

2 4 6 8 10 9 7 5 3 1

Copyright © Meher Pestonji 2003, 2024

P-ISBN: 978-81-7223-442-3
E ISBN: 978-93-6213-318-2

This is a work of fiction and all characters and incidents described in this book are the product of the author's imagination. Any resemblance to actual persons, living or dead, is entirely coincidental.

Meher Pestonji asserts the moral right
to be identified as the author of this work.

For sale in the Indian subcontinent only

All rights reserved. No part of this publication may be reproduced, stored in a retrieval system, or transmitted, in any form or by any means, electronic, mechanical, photocopying, recording or otherwise, without the prior permission of the publishers.

Typeset in 11/14 Classical Garamond at
Manipal Technologies Limited, Manipal

Printed and bound at
Manipal Technologies Limited, Manipal

FSC
www.fsc.org
MIX
Paper | Supporting
responsible forestry
FSC™ C043100

This book is produced from independently certified FSC® paper to ensure responsible forest management.

For
Shabana, Shehnaz and Suma
with whom I entered curfew-bound areas

Monsoon

Throughout the monsoon there'll be
Brave fisherfolk battling the sea
Defying each storm
to take a catch home

They're a part of
the rhythm of
the sea.

1

A crow's cawing penetrated the darkness of sleep. An ominous shadow fell on a prostrate figure as its raucous voice hammered eyelids, willing them apart. Pervez stirred irritably.

Her first image on opening her eyes was the beady black eyes of the crow staring insolently at her. "Shoo!" she mumbled, pulling the thick coverlet over her head. The cawing did not stop.

Suddenly she sat bolt upright. D-day was beginning with a solitary crow. She strode to the window hoping to find its companion in the bushes. No companion. The same crow had flown to the bush to resume its throaty caw amidst ashes that had been smouldering the day before. A shiver ran down her spine.

She started to dress, slipping into the denim trousers and jacket she'd ironed the previous evening. A suitcase stood ready near the door. When she was fully dressed she turned to the huddled figure on the bed. Her husband seemed as oblivious of her as of the crow.

The room was semi-dark. Shadows hid in corners, eerily elongating and retreating as a naked bulb outside swayed in the breeze. "Fred," she said, touching him lightly on the shoulder. He did not stir. "Fred, I'm leaving," she said louder. Still no response. Her shoulders sagged.

She stood by the window in the waxing light, straining her ears for the sound of the cab. Silence broken by familiar kitchen sounds. Her mother-in-law's throaty cough, shuffling feet, sticks being shoved under the woodstove. "Are you sure it's what you want to do?" came a low voice behind her.

She swung around to face him. "I thought you were asleep," she said.

"Sleep comes, sleep goes." A pause. "Are you sure you want to leave?"

"Yes."

Silence froze the space between them as firmly as a wall. After a while he asked, "Does mom know?"

"I told her last evening."

"So it's final?"

"Yes."

"What time is the bus?"

"I'm taking a flight."

"My-my... fly-ing ... Im-pressive ... Money comes, wife goes ... "

"That's not the way it is, Fred! You know that! Look I don't want to fight in the last few minutes. Let's go outside."

He had opened his eyes and was looking at her though he still hadn't moved. "Come here," he said in a voice that was neither a plea nor a command. She obeyed out of habit, sitting at the edge of the bed. His eyes settled on her breasts. She neither wanted to resist nor give in. Only to leave, without another fight.

He took an arm out of the coverlet and put it on her knee. "Do you really want to go?" he whispered, looking intently into her face.

"Yes," she choked, refusing to waver. Then there was the swish of wheels in the compound.

He swung out of bed, wrapping a towel around his waist. His mother stood outside, tears rolling down her cheeks. "You will come back?" she asked as Fred carried Pervez' suitcase into the cab. Pervez stood stoic through the older woman's embrace. Gently she extricated herself from her mother-in-law.

Fred's shoulders slumped as he formally held out a hand. She took it and drew close, resting her head against him. He kissed her forehead, she brushed her lips against his cheek, then they pulled apart.

As the driver revved up the engine, the lone crow stood sentinel at the gate. Scavenger searching for titbits. She closed her eyes to avoid a last look at the bush with ashes at its roots, keeping them tightly shut till the village was left behind. Then paddy fields stretched on both sides of the road all the way to the airport.

How much shit can the sea absorb, she wondered as the plane skimmed over the coast, a narrow strip of brown separating azure waters from deep green foliage. They were flying at great speed but she could feel no movement. Only shudders of the humming bird flying at the edge of land and sea. Shadow mirrored in water.

She could see movements on the beach. Ant-sized people. Trees firmly rooted to the east, waves enticing to the deep west. Kids played between the sea and trees. Shit washed away with shells.

Bullshit. Enough bullshit.

Impossible to expel the sea. It would lick shores in Bombay as it did in Goa. With fewer trees. She'd miss wandering barefoot over hot sand. And splashing toes in waves.

But there'd be Darius. And life on a different keel.

"Will you please get dressed!"

"Why?"

"You can't hang around in home clothes when there's a party in the house! People will think you're ... some poor relative ..."

Darius stopped short, grimacing. "I'm sorry ... I didn't mean that," he said, slipping an arm around Pervez. "These things slip out only when you get stubborn. But you have to get into the swing again. You went to more parties than I did in college."

"All that is history."

"Today will also become history. Now be a good girl and get dressed. People will start arriving any minute."

Reluctantly Pervez went to her room and shut the door, fumbling in the dark for the piano switch that would bring on the light. Her finger slipped over a wrong notch and she heard the creak of the fan starting up. She moved her finger left, blinking as the room flooded into light. Quickly, she strode to the window on the far side, put on the table lamp that gave her room a soft glow, and went back to the door to switch off the harsh overhead bulb. Its glass shade had broken two weeks ago when she had flung a duster at a cobweb trailing to the ceiling. She hadn't bothered to replace it.

A Bombay party after eight years. Apprehension congealed with anticipation. One part of her eager to make up for lost time, another terrified to encounter new worlds. In eight years she had changed. The city had changed. She had to forge new equations.

Aside from the naked bulb the room was well furnished. Two beds, two cupboards, a dressing table, a writing desk with straight backed chair and a springy chesterfield armchair. Dhun had wanted to throw out the old chesterfield when the drawing room was re-decorated but Pervez had rescued her mother's favourite chair by spiriting it into her own room. It was the same room she and Darius had used as children.

The rest of the furniture was untouched. Even the small table with a portrait of prophet Zarathustra that had been placed between the beds at their *navjote,* the thread ceremony that initiated Pervez and Darius into the religion of their ancestors, remained the same. Her lips puckered into a smile as she remembered her mother telling her not to touch the table on days she was menstruating and the smack Darius got for cheekily remarking, "Girls become dirty when they grow hair down there."

She opened the cupboard that had been Darius' in childhood. It was stocked with half a dozen stylish silk shirts. A few days ago Dhun had come to her room after Darius left for the office to invite her to the boutique she ran with a friend. "Come and choose some clothes," she said, "and don't worry about money."

Pervez declined. Before coming to Bombay she had decided not to accept favours from Darius or his wife. "I don't go to fancy places so I don't need fancy clothes," she said.

"Not fancy. Just decent," said Dhun.

"Aren't my clothes decent?"

Dhun screwed up her nose. "Alright for the village or beach … but Bombay?"

"I know I need better clothes," stammered Pervez, embarrassed by the sister-in-law she barely knew. "But I'll buy them … from … Colaba."

Dhun drew a deep breath. "Look Pervez, we entertain a lot. We want you to meet our friends. But we don't want you feeling awkward in good company," she said, examining a perfectly painted fingernail.

Pervez didn't know how to respond. In Goa she had known nothing but jeans, shirts and cotton kurtas. She felt physically and mentally comfortable in them, dismissing the silks and voiles of her growing-up years as dispensable. "I don't want to buy things I can't afford," she said at last. "I don't want to become a burden on Darius."

"That's sweet, but silly," said Dhun, rubbing her finger on the back of her hand. "My husband has only one sister so the least we can do is look after her." She paused, looking beyond the balcony towards a tiny fishing boat bobbing among waves. "Look, can I give you some shirts I don't wear any more? That'll solve the problem. Don't think of them as hand-me-downs. After all we are one family."

Pervez was aghast. She had never tasted condescension before.

The only shirt she liked was a navy blue and green geometric print, loose sleeves cuffed at the wrist. But a brown stain on its left sleeve made it unwearable. Two others had floral prints which she hated and one was an over-bright magenta. That left the brown with gold buttons or the white with red buttons. She could wear the brown with her white pants or the white with her brown pants. For though size didn't matter with loose shirts, it did with pants. And Dhun was at least four inches plumper than her.

Her fingers closed over the chocolate-coloured silk shirt. She took it out and placed the hanger on the notch of the cupboard's handle. Her white pants were fresh from the laundry. Laying them out on the bed she drew the curtains, stripped and stepped into the bathroom for a shower.

Twenty minutes later she stood surveying herself in the full-length mirror of the dressing table. Large limpid eyes stared back at her, running over her short pixie-like hair that barely needed a comb, over the mouth now smeared with red, and cursorily over her body. At twenty-nine she was a woman in her prime, breast tips pointed into dots against the soft silk flaring to hug her hips. She could not identify with the dolled-up image she saw.

Her hand on the doorknob felt clammy. She went back to the bathroom to wipe her palm on a towel. Taking a deep breath she clutched the doorknob and turned. To be greeted by six strange faces, the men standing up as she approached.

"Meet my sister," Darius was saying, stretching an arm towards her. "She's home after a long sabbatical."

She felt a dozen eyes pierce her skin, shredding it with blades. Did she pass muster as the sister of a successful architect? Polite faces gave away nothing but smiles. Empty smiles. Darius motioned her to a sofa, and as she sat down the men resumed their seats.

"Have you been studying abroad?" asked the woman beside her, introducing herself as Mona Desai.

"No ... I was married ... in Goa," stammered Pervez.

"Goa's gorgeous, isn't it? We spend a week at Aguada every Christmas."

"Yes, it is beautiful," agreed Pervez as Darius handed her a thin-stemmed glass of sherry.

Directly in front of her the seven-foot grandfather clock indicated nine minutes to nine. The ticking of the pendulum was inaudible over the hum of voices but in exactly nine minutes Big Ben, as he was affectionately called, would start his sonorous chimes and the room would fall to a hush till the last stroke stopped vibrating. "It's really a beaut," someone would remark at almost every party.

Darius agreed, pride swelling in his voice. "It's almost a hundred years old," he never failed to add.

"You're lucky to have such an heirloom."

"Well ... an eye for beauty kind of runs in the family," he'd say, trying to sound nonchalant. "My grandfather collected clocks, my parents left us their porcelain collection and I'm into contemporary art. Have you seen my new Souza? I got it dirt cheap from a dealer in Goa."

The buzz of conversation, mingled with the clinking of glass, would resume and rise as guests kept invading the room, muffling out the ten and eleven o'clock chimes. Big Ben ticked on, oblivious of being ignored. At midnight, as room occupancy dwindled, his voice would ring clear to the handful of stragglers left. "He's telling us to leave," someone would drawl as Pervez silently agreed. But she was now free to retire to her room with Big Ben's reassuring chimes penetrating the darkness every quarter hour, her unchanging link with childhood.

"Wun-derful to see you again, Dar-ius. I'm dy-ing to catch up with friends." Pervez gaped at the newcomer in a strappy red dress, skirt slit up to her thighs.

"Where have you been, Kavita?" smiled Darius, running an eye over her full breasts.

"All the fashion meccas of Europe, dah-ling. Paris. London. Milan," she replied, thrusting her bosom forward.

"I hope you'll be free for my fashion show in August," said Dhun, slipping herself between Kavita and Darius.

"Of course, dah-ling. How can I forget you introduced me to modelling! But my fees have gone up, you know ..."

Pervez felt a warm trickle on her ankle. The sherry had spilt. Embarrassed, she wiped it with a paper napkin. Her leg felt sticky. She looked up to find Darius had moved away.

"Damn dangerous publicity stunt," she heard him saying to someone in a rust shirt. "If that fanatic isn't put in his place he's going to set the country on fire."

"Advani is building up the Hindu vote bank," boomed Vasant Chawla, curly hair sprouting at the tips of his earlobes.

"At the cost of giving India a bad image," Darius' voice was sharp. "We're talking of globalisation, of attracting foreign capital ... and then we have a sati in Rajasthan, a politician going on a rath-yatra. The West will think we're going back to the Dark Ages."

"We're nearing the twenty-first century, my dear," drawled the easy-going Dilip Kanitkar. "How can anyone take a man who struts around the country in a Toyota disguised as a chariot seriously!"

Pervez looked from face to face, baffled.

"You must understand Hindu psychology," said Chawla, raising his voice. "Every Hindu worships Lord Ram as maryada purushottam, the ideal man exemplifying ideal conduct. Naturally his birthplace is sacred to us." He paused, puffing on a fat cigar. "Besides, someone has to put those Mussalmaans in place. First they divide our country, make their Pakistan, still want to be big boss here! And Congress party panders to all their whims. Look what they did with that Rushdie book. Muslims demand, Congress bans. Before any country in the world!"

"Have some cashewnuts, Mr Chawla," intervened Dhun, smiling her best smile.

"Certainly, most beautiful hostess," he leered, helping himself to a fistful. "Anything you offer I will happily accept."

"Now, now, Mr Chawla, stop being naughty," she preened.

"No respect for women, they have," he said, resuming his earlier tirade. "When Muslim gets tired he simply says 'Talaq, talaq, talaq', and takes another woman. They breed like rats. Soon Muslims will be more than Hindus in India. What do you say, lady from Goa?"

Pervez froze. She had no idea what they were talking about. "I don't know too many Muslims," she stammered weakly.

"If divorce were so easy, even I might have got married," interjected Ranjit Gandhi, the diehard bachelor.

"First become Muslim, then marry," advised Chawla. "Four-four wives you can have and after di-vorce no need to give money also."

"How many Muslims do you know with four wives?" intervened an icy voice. No one had noticed Iqbal Rahimtoola walking in.

"Hel-lo Iqbal-bhai, we were just discussing Congress government's appeasement policy," said Chawla, lightly slapping the newcomer on his back. "No offence. We are friends, no?"

The room was filling up. Vasant Chawla offered Nandita Rajan his seat and led Iqbal to the bar. Pervez noticed he was barely five feet tall. A few minutes after replenishing his drink he made a beeline for Pervez. "Can I join young ladies' gup-shup?"

"Of course, Mr Chawla," replied Mona, flattered by the attention of the tycoon.

"Why do beautiful ladies hide in Goa?" he asked, looking into Pervez' face. She squirmed as he squeezed himself onto the sofa. "Are you in Bombay for holiday?"

"No," she replied uncomfortably.

"Are you here for good?"

"I ... I think so ..." She saw his beady eyes sizing her up.

"What you are planning to do in Bombay?"

"I might start working ... Or studying ... I haven't decided."

"You are not a graduate?"

"I am, but—"

"Then I can give you job. Good salary, plus commission. Pretty face, good sales. Selling computers or soap. But I will put you in my hotel."

"Excuse me, Mr Chawla. Dhun is getting dinner. I must help her," said Pervez, escaping from the sofa but not from his piercing eyes.

Dhun was presiding over the dining table, shifting a crystal vase with red roses to a side table to make space for food platters. Her off-shoulder emerald green dress highlighted the auburn streaks in the cluster of tiny curls fanning her face, the expanse of fair skin between auburn and green attracting every male eye. Emerald green was complimented by blue-green enamel earrings and a choker whose oval pendant pointed to the cleft between her breasts, while a matching bracelet jingled at her wrist. As Pervez approached she waved her away muttering, "Keep Darius away from Chawla. They mustn't get into an argument."

Pervez hovered around the kitchen keeping a distance from guests with awkward questions. On what basis had this stranger offered her a job, she wondered, glancing suspiciously at Chawla's bald pate. What did a sales job involve? Could she handle clients as sophisticated as Darius' friends?

Putting on padded oven gloves she carried out large Pyrex dishes, sniffing cheese and shrimp aromas as she placed them on wooden coasters. Next followed crystal bowls of salad, her palate tingling in anticipation of the crisp blend of carrots and oranges, apples and potatoes with tangy mayonnaise. As platters emptied and plates filled, she was about to escape to her room when she felt a light touch at her elbow.

"Farhad! How good to see you!" she cried, looking up into a clean-shaven face with deep-set eyes.

"You look great, Pervez!"

"So do you! How've you been? What are you doing? How are your parents?"

"Cool it! One question at a time. But first meet my wife, Anaita."

A flicker of disappointment skimmed over Pervez' face, but she turned to the woman in a pink crepe skirt beside Farhad with a smile. "Hi, I'm Pervez. We used to hang out together in college."

"I've heard so much about you, Pervez."

"Good or bad?"

"A bit of both."

"Let's hear the bad stuff first."

"Only about your eloping with that *makapau.*"

"Makapau!" Pervez burst into laughter, almost choking on her drink. "I'm hearing that word after ages! What's the other slang Parsis use for Goans?"

"Teewaas," smiled Farhad.

"Of course! *Teewaas* and *makas*! I went and married one and everyone was shocked."

"Want to hear the good things now?" asked Anaita.

"Are there any?"

"Sure. About how you flew bras from the college flag pole ..."

"Wasn't that a scream!"

"Farhad can't remember why you did it."

"Because some professor was trying to impose a ban on sleeveless clothes! So six of us took it on ourselves to protest. I'm glad you think it's among the good things you've heard about me." Pervez was beginning to enjoy herself. "Do you guys really want to sit here? Why don't we just go into my room and catch up."

The two women sat on the bed, the food on their plates barely touched as they chatted animatedly. Farhad made himself comfortable on the chesterfield, lively eyes darting from one attractive woman to the other. The silk shaded table lamp filled the room with a warm glow. Though Pervez chatted with Anaita, she was intensely aware of Farhad. And the memory of her first kiss.

Pervez double-skipped down the stairs without waiting for the elevator. Thu-dump, thu-dump, thu-dump. Right foot before left. Seven steps. A square landing. Another seven steps topped by a dusty window. Another square landing. Then the last seven steps before the second floor.

They lived on the third floor of Sagar Mahal towards the end of a six-kilometre curved boulevard facing a bay whose waves rose from far out in the Arabian Sea. At the southern end of Marine Drive stood the twenty-storied structures of Oberoi Hotel and Express Towers in the upmarket business district of Nariman Point, while on the promontory at the other end stood Raj Bhavan, the official residence of the Governor, at the far end of Malabar Hill. Between the two stretched a row of five- to seven-storied residential buildings, home to old families whose wealth went back two or three generations.

As Pervez stepped out, the full force of the monsoon hit her. It was high tide. The sea was a khaki-olive green. Waves pounded the rocks behind the parapet wall, hurtling foam high into the air to splash over pedestrians in lacy curls. One massive wave-splash followed another so fast that droplets hung in a mist keeping the landscape out of focus. As clouds scudded across the bay, Pervez could see Malabar Hill getting drenched while Marine Drive and Nariman Point remained dry. Within minutes the rain would move to where she stood and in another few minutes blow away again. It was that kind of day.

The time was 6.45 a.m. Traffic was thin but fast at this early hour. She crossed the road, heading for a break in the hedge dividing north- and south-moving traffic. Palm fronds flung anguished limbs in appeal to unhearing gods who drenched them in stinging salt water, regardless. A man in a white dhoti-kurta scattered gram among pigeons in the hope of his ancestors showering him with blessings. The only shower he's certain to get is rain, smiled Pervez, secretly admiring the dozens of devotees who fed birds at the seafront each morning.

Such images were rare in Goa, she thought, despite the inescapable presence of the sea. There, beaches were not barricaded with stone and cement but open with clean, welcoming sands. Like large-hearted Goans. If only Fredrick had not ... She forced the memory away. Once that fire started it would take days to extinguish.

A figure was waving at her. With a start she realised it was Sunday and Naina would be at her parents. Raising her arm, she quickened her step but just as the friends were about to embrace, a huge wave roared into the air above their heads, drenching them.

"One-for-sorrow, two-for-joy! We have to catch the next one!" she laughed, remembering the childhood game that had her and Naina chasing waves as their ayahs tried unsuccessfully to keep them dry.

"The sea was clean then. Look at the junk in it now," replied Naina, plucking a bit of shredded plastic off her head as the sea furiously rejected the garbage dumped into its belly.

"One-for-sorrow, two-for-joy, three-for-a-letter, four-for-a-boy," lisped Pervez in childhood pidgin to coax Naina back in time.

"Five-for-silver, six-for-gold, seven-for-a-secret, never-to-be-told," completed Naina getting into the spirit. "But let's walk closer to the road. Who wants to get drenched in stinking water!"

"If you don't get wet again you'll have sorrow following you all day," said Pervez, continuing the lisp.

"We've grown up now. We can admire the sea without smelling it on ourselves."

"It's still the same sea," she sighed, returning to her adult voice. "The same breakers with the boom-swish sound. From my bedroom it looks and sounds no different from before I went away. And yet so different from Goa."

"Makes you nostalgic?"

"There it made me nostalgic for Bombay, the city with a vital pulse. Here it makes me nostalgic for tranquility ... I guess I'm one of those people who's never satisfied ... How's campus?"

"The usual. Students, classes, inter-departmental politics."

"Campus life is one thing I missed in Goa. I had to graduate by correspondence."

"You can still do post-graduation."

"Darius wants me to start working. He thinks once I'm occupied, I'll get over, what he considers, my depression."

"What do you want?"

"I don't know, Naina … I need time to decide …"

"Take time. But not so much that you become lazy and make excuses for doing nothing …"

They were walking towards the flyover connecting the open expanse of sea and sky with the twisted intestines of the inner city's over-crowded Kalbadevi and Chira Bazaar districts. As a shower started, they ran to the bus stop for shelter. A dozen walkers huddled under this awning, barely successful in their attempt to stay dry, for the wind lashed at them from every side. But, as Pervez predicted, the shower passed and wet strollers resumed their walks with clothes drying in the wind.

"Dhun had another party last night," remarked Pervez.

"Was that the third or fourth?"

"The sixth in eight weeks. I've run out of the clothes Dhun so 'generously' gave me."

"She's really changed Darius. He was never such a socialite before."

"The trouble is not them, Naina. It's me. I've been away so long … I have nothing to say to people … I can't discuss plays I haven't seen … books I haven't read … places I haven't been to … But they … they're smart … sophisticated … they know it all …"

"All spit and polish," retorted Naina. "Take away their fancy clothes and five-star settings and they have less substance than toothpaste. The moment life throws up a challenge, they turn to booze, drug or some other escapism. It's common people like us who confront life head-on."

"You're being too harsh."

"Am I? Look at the people in Darius' circle. Could any of them survive without the paraphernalia money provides? Could they survive on a shoestring for even a week?"

"They don't need to."

"Because they're born with silver spoons.'

"All of them live on what they earn."

"And how are they able to earn it? Because they were born into a certain class, which gave them access to a certain education, which fuels their earning capacity."

"What's wrong with that?" asked Pervez, slowly.

"You have to meet Sidharth. He's the right person to introduce you to Marxist thought. Spend a few days with us at Kalina. We don't live in luxury but we don't live badly either."

They had moved to sit on the cracked parapet wall, stained with a Chalo Ayodhya slogan whose paint had partially washed off in the rain. A vertical white line was topped by a horizontal one followed by a blank. Naina's buttocks obscured the vertical line, while Pervez' legs formed an inverted V in the gap below the horizontal line.

"I'd love to come over," said Pervez, slipping her hand into the crook of Naina's arm. "Often I wonder what your boyfriend is like, envying you and your friends discussing current topics, reciting poetry night after night while I get bored with television. I'm not addicted to luxuries. At Darius' place my life is quite comfortable but so dull."

"Comfort and discomfort are states of mind. I wouldn't change my life with Sidharth for anything in the world."

"That's what they call blind love. I hope your rose-tinted glasses don't shatter as brutally as mine."

"Just because people choose to live differently doesn't make life less satisfying. If you hang around us long enough you'll find Sidhu is an exceptional person. Being his partner is a privilege."

Pervez said nothing.

Pervez stood framed against the entrance of Naina's apartment, barely able to conceal her astonishment. The room before her was almost bare. A small rectangular table with two chairs in one corner, a TV on a trolley with wheels in another, and some seating arrangement fashioned from mattresses, cushions and durries on the floor. An entire wall to her left had books precariously perched on shelves from floor to ceiling. Other walls had patchy paint. Naina had warned her, but this was even more minimal than Goa.

"Sidharth! I've brought Pervez," Naina was announcing, entering an inner room from where the soft strains of folk music could be heard.

Her red VIP suitcase looked incongruous. Light from a square window, muted by long strands of a green and white creeper loosely looped into nails in the wall, touched a corner of the suitcase. The money plant was the only mellowing element in the room. Before she could recover, Sidharth emerged bare-chested, a red and black lungi wrapped around his waist. "I've been looking forward to meeting you, Pervez," he said, smiling into a greying beard.

She tried to smile back but shock made a grimace of her mouth. He was obviously much older than Naina.

"Quite a contrast from my parent's place, isn't it?" laughed Naina, prepared for her consternation. "Don't say I didn't warn you." Naina's laughter broke the ice and Pervez advanced towards Sidharth with an extended hand. He enveloped her in a bear hug, then turned to Naina.

"You didn't tell me she was so thin," he said, gesturing to Pervez to make herself comfortable. "Naina tells me we have a week to bohemianise you?"

"I … I guess so …" she replied uncertainly.

"Let's have tea," interjected Naina. "Want to look around the kitchen so you know what's where when I'm not around?"

Pervez looked at the VIP suitcase standing awkwardly in the middle of the room. Naina moved it to the side along the wall. Pervez opened it and handed a packet to Naina. "I brought you some bebinka from Goa," she said.

"Thanks! I love bebinka. Just let me finish with dinner, then we can chat all night," said Naina, looking fondly into Pervez' eyes. Then almost as an afterthought she asked Sidharth, "Sidhu, did you cook anything over the weekend?"

"Only dahi. Pawan brought batata wadas yesterday. Plus we had leftover dal."

Naina made a face. "Pawan is a photographer. 'Living in sin' like us with Vandana who's desperately trying to become famous."

They'd moved into the kitchen which Pervez was relieved to find well equipped. A broad stone ledge formed the work table at the far end of which stood a mixer-grinder. Shelves were piled with stainless-steel utensils graded from large to small, while a blue Formica cabinet held containers for rice, dals, masalas. A small fridge, tucked into a corner, wore a toaster for a crown and an Aquaguard at the sink ensured safe drinking water.

"How long have you been here?" asked Pervez.

"It'll be three years in October."

"Why don't you do up the place?"

"We have what we need."

"Are you kidding?"

"Sidhu doesn't believe in luxury. I've been trying to de-class myself."

"Why?"

"To identify with the common man in the class struggle."

"This doesn't make sense ..."

"Give me a hand with the veggies. There'll be time for discussion later. Will you chop onions or peel potatoes?"

"Let's have tea first."

"Sure. The chai-patti is here, sugar's in that glass bottle and milk in the fridge. Will you make tea while I tidy up the bedroom? It's always a mess when I return from my parents'."

As Naina slipped into the inner room Pervez welcomed the opportunity to give shape to the chaos in her head. At her parents' place Naina's bedroom overlooked the bay with a rounded cane chair suspended from the ceiling. Her bed was always draped in attractive bedcovers, their earth colours complimenting the Rajasthani pichwai on the wall. She had an assortment of terracotta horses, camels, elephants and tigers in her room. Terracotta was inexpensive. Why was none of it around, wondered Pervez.

She took a small pan, filled it with water and lit the stove with a gas lighter. Five ceramic mugs were hanging from handles on hooks jutting out of a wire dish-holder. She picked three black mugs with geometric designs and spooned sugar into them. In a few minutes, they were steaming with piping hot tea. But there was nothing to carry them out in.

"Tea is ready. Come and get it," she called.

"Bring it here," replied Sidharth.

"I can't find a tray."

"We don't have a tray. Bring it in a thali."

She found a small stainless-steel thali, placed the mugs in it and carried it to the outer room. Her mind refused to call it the drawing room. Placing the thali on the table, she picked up a mug and stood by the window sipping it, her eyes picking out uniform three-storied buildings. Indrani Housing Colony was a complex of twelve identical buildings with identical two-room flats. One flat peeped into another, which peeped into yet another, connecting residents as if they were part of a massive bee-hive with as clearly delineated roles as queen bees and drones. Pervez could see nothing outside the colony.

"Come inside!" came Sidharth's voice from the inner room. She put her half-empty mug on the thali, picked it up and entered the bedroom. A large double mattress on the floor. A steel cupboard. A heap of unwashed clothes. And Naina and Sidharth sprawled across two ends of the mattress, a face-down copy of the *Economic and Political Weekly* between them.

"Where shall I put this?" she asked looking for a table.

"Right here," replied Sidharth, patting the centre of the mattress. Tea mugs on a mattress felt tacky but she said nothing. Handing him the thali she lowered herself to the edge of the mattress near Naina.

"I hear you want to do MA."

"I've been thinking about it."

"In what subject?"

"Probably psychology. That's what I graduated in. Thought I'd bring up kids differently than the way we were brought up."

"Psychology is too inward looking. Go for socio or eco."

"Get focused," cautioned Naina. "The campus is full of guys trying to 'find themselves' for five-six years. They flunk economics, move to sociology, flunk sociology, move to literature and get nowhere at all."

The doorbell rang and Pawan walked in wearing a lungi with a white singlet over his chest. Eyes blazing, he marched into the bedroom demanding a cigarette. Sidharth tossed him Goldflake and a matchbox, watching Pawan's hand tremble as he lit up.

"This is the pits, man! It really is the pits!" said Pawan, forcefully smacking the yellow packet on the mattress.

"We've heard that before," drawled Sidharth, lighting his own cigarette.

"He's had a fight with Vandana," Naina whispered to Pervez.

"If she insists, we're gonna break up this time. Have you heard that also?"

They sat in silence, Pawan morosely blowing smoke rings through the window as if to exhale his problems with the drifting smoke.

Naina had brought out cauliflower, onions and potatoes on a thali, with a knife, potato-peeler and chopping board. "Onions or potatoes?" she asked. Pervez had never chopped vegetables in the bedroom, leave alone on a mattress that served as the bed.

"Potatoes," she replied meekly, starting to loop the brown-grey peel into spirals. "Should we go outside? Maybe he wants to talk to Sidharth privately."

Naina shook her head. "This is routine."

Suddenly Pawan turned to Naina. "Gimme a tenner."

"You already owe me more than four hundred rupees!"

"I'll return it as soon as I get an assignment."

"You can't just come here demanding money any time you feel like it! At least have the decency to ask politely!"

For a minute Pervez thought they were heading for a fight. Then Pawan went down on bended knee holding out an imploring arm to Naina. "My dear Naina, would you please be so good as to forward a short-term loan of ten whole rupees to an impoverished friend without which he might just hang himself from the ceiling fan in your bedroom?" he dramatised, as everyone dissolved into laughter.

"I've been keeping accounts," said Naina. "This tenner makes your debt four hundred and seventy rupees."

"What about the cigarettes he bums off me?" asked Sidharth, still laughing.

"Bhai-bhai, na," said Pawan with a wink that made Pervez distinctly uncomfortable. "Yours is mine and mine is yours."

"You act as if yours is yours and mine is also yours."

"Bhai-bhai, na. What are comrades for?" said Pawan, heading for the door.

"He'll be back for dinner," predicted Naina. "With Vandana in tow."

"And his usual peace offering," added Sidharth, snuffing out his cigarette against the windowsill.

Sure enough by the time Naina had finished cooking subzi and dal and was kneading the atta for chapattis, the doorbell rang again with a sheepish-looking Pawan followed by a sulking Vandana. "We need company," he said buttoning a pale blue shirt over his singlet. "Or we might claw each other's eyes out."

"He brought you flowers," pouted Vandana, handing Naina a posie of six hibiscuses. "I kept two for mehndi in hair."

"You put hibiscus in henna?" asked Pervez, surprised.

"With egg and coffee powder. Flowers give hair better shine than conditioner."

"Whenever there's a fight, Pawan walks to the campus and brings back flowers as peace offerings," Sidharth explained to Pervez. "Now may we know what this fight is all about?"

Pawan and Vandana exchanged glares. "Shall I tell?" he asked between clenched teeth.

"Tell. I'm not scared."

"She wants me to photograph her nude for a calendar. And I refused."

Sleep, that night, was out of the question. Her mind froze stiff as a rock repeatedly ravaged by shock waves. Barely had one wave dissolved before another drowned retreating lace in a fresh attack of salty foam. Pressing her face into the square cushion, Pervez tried to conjure up sea images to relax herself. But instead of the comforting undulating rhythm she felt sharp stabs of fright as she teetered into unfamiliar territory.

So many images swam in her head it was impossible to connect them into thoughts. The packed ladies compartment on the local train with its diaspora of mingled smells—perspiration and perfume, hair oil and fish, fart and talcum powder. Naina's stark flat, now mercifully blanketed by the dark. Pervez could understand Naina going soft on Sidharth. But was she being taken for a ride by his friends as well? Naina was no suffering fool. And she seemed happy. What was Pervez to make of this new-fangled lifestyle?

The mattress was surprisingly comfortable. She didn't mind sleeping on the floor. The round fat bolsters and cushions had been piled near the book rack as Naina straightened the sheet and gave her another to cover herself. She lay with it rolled up to her chin. Though the fan was on full speed her body radiated heat.

A streetlight bouncing off the opposite building softened the darkness. She could trace moneyplant curls along the wall. Each time she changed position the chromium clasp of her suitcase gleamed eerily. She turned on her stomach facing the wall. As her breasts pressed down she felt her nipples harden. Body heat entered the mattress. She reached behind undoing the clasp of her bra.

She had never witnessed such a volatile argument. Sparks flashed off Pawan and Vandana's teeth with Naina and Sidharth good humouredly adding balm and spice. As voices rose with rum, she feared they might come to blows—as Fred had—but just as things seemed to be getting out of hand, Vandana took charge.

Carrying a small mirror from the wall to a corner beside Pawan, she swivelled up her lipstick and began painting a deep red bindi on her forehead. A current of chemistry passed. Pawan's voice trailed as he watched her slowly rub red over her lips, casually flick a tongue over them, keeping her eyes fixed on his reflection.

"Let's go," he said huskily, jumping up and knocking over his glass.

"You've made a puddle on our bed," laughed Naina.

"Make some yourself," grinned Pawan, hand on Vandana's hip.

"Vandy's getting randy," chuckled Sidharth.

"Anger stimulates passion, man," said Pawan halfway to the door, his hand on the skin between Vandana's jeans and shirt.

Then they were gone. Leaving Pervez' imagination full of what they were doing now. What she'd missed for so very long.

2

The first time it happened was bizarre.

She met Fred at Anjali's birthday party. A whacky party that started at midnight and went on. The spacious drawing room with ferns drooping over gleaming brass pots took on a romantic ambience as dozens of old liquor bottles decorated with melted wax became impromptu candlestands with flickering flames reflecting gold dust on tabletops. Pervez in a red miniskirt and black sweater spent much of the evening fast-dancing with Farhad, aware that her flying hair and bouncy breasts were the focus of many male eyes.

A live band comprising a guitarist, a trumpeteer, a drummer and a clarinet player played English and Hindi pop songs. They wore dark pants, pink shirts, dark glasses and sombreros, their theatrical looks setting them apart from party guests. At the last music break, as Farhad headed for the bar, she found herself face to face with Fred.

"The first song after the break is for you. Don't dance to it," he said, looking her straight in the eye. She gaped at his dramatic approach. "I'm from the band. The name's Fred. You dance very well," he continued, brazenly letting his eyes run over her.

"Thank you," she stuttered. "I'm Pervez."

"Hello, Pervez. Can we be friends?"

"Yes," she whispered.

"Don't dance," he repeated, slowly but forcefully. Then he turned abruptly and left.

She positioned herself at the edge of the dance floor. She saw him climb into the drummer's seat and take the mike. The clarinet completed its tune, slow and melodious. The players turned expectantly to Fred. Looking unabashedly at her he began, "Moon river, wider than a mile, I'm crossing you in style some day ... O dream maker you heart breaker, wherever you're going I'm going your way ..."

The deep baritone entered Pervez. Not just through her ears but through eyes, mouth, skin. She could feel it boring into her muscle, filling her body with raw expectation. She could not take her eyes off Fred. When Farhad returned she excused herself and sat at the edge of the dance floor, mesmerised.

Her head remained in the clouds for a week. Then reality asserted itself. It's nothing more than a pleasant memory, she told herself, humming "Moon River". It was then that she started walking on Marine Drive on a night when the moon lay on the water amused by its reflection in the sky. The baritone crooned inside her head. A breeze flicked her shoulder-length hair, curling edges into wisps. "Two drifters off to see the world ..." went the voice in her head as her feet tapped a rhythm on the pavement, oblivious of potholes. She walked with her head in the clouds till her foot slipped into a crack bringing her down to earth with a nasty scratch on her leg.

She had almost put him out of her mind when he showed up at the college canteen three weeks later. Walking straight up to where she was sipping Thums Up with Anjali, he started chatting and within half an hour invited her to a party the next day. From that moment life was never the same.

It happened after only the third party. The first two had him dropping her home, exchanging hurried kisses in the elevator as his friends waited in a cab. The third party was on the rooftop of a bank, a business area deserted at night. On the pretext of buying cigarettes they split with his friends and he suggested walking around the floodlit heritage buildings.

The ornate buildings had arched porticos sheltering them from streetlights. Watchmen on duty were absorbed in a card game. Pavement dwellers huddled asleep in clusters against the wall. Fred's hand slipped from her shoulder to her breast. She drew close, nestling against him. They stumbled along a few steps, his hand rubbing, feeling, squeezing. "Let's go inside," he whispered at the deserted entrance of a building.

Halfway into the foyer his hands were under her clothes. "Someone will come, Fred. Someone will see us," she whispered, even as her body responded to his touch. They climbed to the landing, then the first floor. Then there was no holding back.

They made love at the oddest of places at every opportunity. In a cab, in parks, on rocks facing the sea.

First there was the surprise of discovering pleasure in mounds and crevices. Followed by the delight of learning to give and receive pleasure.

The Four Aces band was popular, with three or four engagements each week. Pervez accompanied them everywhere—to private parties, wedding receptions, even to a christening party at a parish. She would sit at the side, suggesting songs, occasionally dancing. Each evening was filled with fun and ended in passionate embraces.

Her bubbling spirits did not go unnoticed by her parents. "She's out with Farhad almost every night," her mother told her father. "It's time to start preparing wedding bells."

"What's the hurry?" replied her husband absently.

"I was younger than her when we got married."

"Times have changed. Today girls are more independent."

The glow from Pervez' face spread to her mother's. Between arranging fresh flowers on the dining table and sending off the driver to the laundry, she inspected the ceremonial silver, deciding it needed polishing for the auspicious day. She took out her special *ghara* with Chinese embroidery, speculating whether it was good enough to wear for the *adarni* ceremony though, of course, she'd buy a new sari for Pervez' wedding. For Pervez, naturally, the sky was the limit. She could buy as many clothes as she wanted.

The bubble burst when Farhad called while Pervez was out. "Isn't she with you, *dikra*?" asked her surprised mother.

"No. I haven't seen her for weeks."

"But she's out every night ... We thought..."

"Please tell her I called."

She turned to her husband who was engrossed in the latest *Business India*. "She isn't with Farhad," she said, the shock ringing in her voice. "He hasn't seen her for weeks."

"I warned you not to get excited ..."

"But who's she with?"

"She's not the type to do anything rash. Tell her Farhad called. Then casually ask who she was with."

That night Pervez was surprised to find her mother awake when she got home. The party had got over well after midnight and they'd spent an hour cuddling in a cab. She turned her key in the door—hair awry, bra unclasped, mascara staining her cheeks—to find a bright light in the drawing room instead of the dim light normally left on in the passage. When she found her mother dozing in the chesterfield to the tick-tocking of Big Ben, she was alarmed. "Is anything wrong, Mummy?" she asked.

"Where have you been?" Her mother's voice was sharp.

"At a party."

"Whose party?"

"Monica's," she lied, saying the first name that came into her head.

"Who dropped you home?" persisted her mother, taking in her dishevelled appearance.

"A whole bunch of kids."

"Go to bed," said her mother, deciding against a midnight confrontation. "We'll talk in the morning."

Bedlam broke loose at the breakfast table. "Farhad called last night. Said he hasn't seen you for weeks," began her mother, trying to sound nonchalant as she poured steaming tea from a china pot.

"So?"

"Should you be neglecting him like this? Boys like him should be cultivated. Good family. Bright future. What more can you want?"

Pervez stirred her tea, a silent warning going off in her head. "Maybe I want something different," she said after a while.

"Dozens of girls are ready to snatch him up. By the time you regret it'll be too late."

She kept stirring tea morosely, refusing to meet her mother's eye.

"Have you met someone else?" persisted her mother. Pervez was silent. "You have. I can tell from your face. Who is it? Anyone we know?" Pervez said nothing.

"Tell us who you were with last night, Pervez," said her father. "We're naturally worried when you come home late night after night."

"No need to worry. I'm in safe hands."

"Whose?"

"Freddie's," she said at last.

"Freddie? … Faredoon Unwala?"

"Freddie for Fredrick. Not Faredoon. Fredrick Mendonca."

"Koi teewoh chhe!" spat both parents together as she looked from one to the other defiantly.

"We're in love," she announced dramatically.

Her parents froze into statues incapable of sound or movement. Pervez kept looking from mother to father and back again, her eyes flashing. Seconds stretched into minutes. Big Ben alone broke the silence.

"What does he do?" barked her father, recovering his voice. She hesitated. "What does he do?" he demanded more belligerently.

"He's a professional," she said at last.

"Professional what? Doctor?" She shook her head. "Lawyer?" She shook it again. "Is he a chartered accountant or what?"

"A professional musician. He plays in the Four Aces band."

"Bandwala!" Her father dropped the cup he was holding. Hot brown tea stained the table mat under his plate but her mother was too shocked to run for a napkin. Pervez kept looking from one parent to the other, aware her own hand was trembling.

"Only cooks and ayahs come from Goa," gasped her mother.

"*Salo luchcho*! How dare he lay hands on my daughter!" roared her father recovering his voice.

"Freddie is not a rascal, papa. I want him as much as he wants me."

"I forbid you to mention his name in my house! Put an end to this stupidity here and now!"

"But papa—"

"No 'ifs' and 'buts'. My word is final. From now you have to tell your mother who you go out with, where you'll be, what time you'll return."

"You can't start treating me like a twelve-year old … "

"You deserve a spanking like a five year old. No tricks. Okay!"

They eloped because it became impossible to meet. Her parents ensured she was escorted everywhere by their faithful driver Ambalal who could be relied on to report all her movements. Pervez knew it was useless to fight. Her parents could be as tough as nails. She sulked, locking herself into her room, refusing to talk.

But she managed to sneak calls to Fred. Twice he met her at college, but there wasn't a moment's privacy. "Dickey's getting hungry," he said huskily, when no one was near the telephone at the YMCA hostel where he lived.

"Fanny's missing Dickey," she replied, trying to lighten her own impatience.

"Let's go to Goa," he said abruptly.

"Goa? What'll we do in Goa?"

"Live as man and wife."

"Is that a proposal?"

"You could say it is."

"My parents would never agree."

"It's them or me."

By the fourth week nights were impossible. The bedsheets sizzled against her skin as she pressed a pillow between thighs and another over her head. Images of Fred and their lovemaking swam into her dreams. She would curl fingers around her breasts, imagining them to be his.

Two more weeks made up her mind. It would have to be Fred. "But will your parents accept me?" she asked, aware of the momentous step she was taking.

"They won't have a choice, will they?"

"Suppose they throw me out. I'll be neither here nor there."

"They're traditional Goans who'd rather see their son married than living indecently."

"Are you sure?"

"Yes, I am."

"So when do we go?"

"Four Aces have bookings throughout this month, I'll have to give the boys time to find someone."

"Will it be easy to join another band in Goa?

"Goa is teeming with tourists wanting to be entertained. Joining a band is no problem."

Three weeks later Fred had booked two seats on the overnight bus. They spent four days at a beach hotel before going to the village to meet his family. But when she left Bombay it was the last time she saw her own.

His family had been taken aback by their son's sudden reappearance at Villa del Sorrento, a modest four-room house that belied its grandiose name. His announcement of marriage plans set off a flutter that reached the surrounding cashew trees. They kept eyeing her sceptically as they conferred in clusters how to respond to the runaway bride. No one told her Fred himself had run away from home two years earlier.

The simplicity of the villa mildly deflated her. The sprawling *balcao,* the hallmark of Goan homes, had only a sewing machine on which Fred's sister pedalled furiously, tailoring ladies' clothes. Pervez had visualised *balcaos* with sprawling cane furniture and swaying palm fronds. The solitary unit of labour at Villa del Sorrento graphically summed up the future.

After hours of Fred shunting between her and his family group to which the parish priest had been summoned, the verdict was pronounced. She would be accepted provided she got baptised and consented to a church wedding. When Fred assented on her behalf she did not protcst. Though shc kncw that baptism meant giving up the religion of her birth and would seal the nail in her relationship with her parents, she realised she had already burnt her bridges.

She was sitting on the built-in seat along the *balcao* wall when Fred brought her a plate piled with rice and fish curry.

"You forgot the spoon and fork," she called.

"Eat with your hands or they'll think you're stuck-up," he replied.

"I can't eat rice without a fork or spoon!" she exclaimed appalled.

"Why not?"

"I ... I ... I don't know how to."

"You're joking!"

"I'm not. I've never eaten rice with my hands."

"You're not serious."

"I am."

He stared at her incredulously, slowly digesting the fact. "You'll have to learn to do it here," he said at last. "It's not difficult. Just mix it with the tips of your fingers, roll it into a ball and pop it into your mouth."

She stared helplessly at his retreating back. Gingerly she dipped two fingers into the rice, conjuring images of her mother whacking her hand saying "Only servants eat with their hands." The curry-rice mixture felt hot and gooey. She willed her fingers to dip deeper, close around the rice, and, with eyes shut tight, quickly lifted them into her mouth. A trickle spread over her T-shirt leaving an orange stain.

She made a second attempt, raising the plate to chin level to shorten the distance between hand and mouth. Some rice finally entered her mouth. Flavoured by delicious fish curry cooked in coconut milk. Her fingers flaked the fish. This was easier than getting rice into her mouth. She tore at the pomfret relishing its fresh pungency. She tried to knead the curry-rice into balls as Fred was doing. The balls crumbled into grains the moment they left her plate. Her fingers and palms were grubby. And Fred was laughing at her. Luckily they were alone.

The first evening he took her to the beach she squatted on damp ground trying to make sand balls. The sand kept slipping away. Each time she scooped the earth a puddle would form in the hollow. She would shape a sand ball in the cup of her fist and leave her fingerprints on it. But the moment she set it down, it disintegrated into a shapeless heap. Refusing to hold form. Like water. Like recalcitrant rice balls. Refusing to stay connected.

3

She met Prabha on her third trip to Kalina. She was short and plump, her oval face animated by flashing eyes and a wide-lipped mouth. "I've heard so much about you, Pervez," she began. "Naina says your whole personality has changed. That your marriage—I hope you don't mind my mentioning it at our first meeting—set you back by twenty years."

"What do you mean?"

That if you hadn't run off and got married you'd have been ahead of us all. Socially and professionally," said Naina, who was sitting near the bookshelf picking stones from a thali of raw rice grains.

"I don't know ..."

"I hear you want to do MA?"

"I'm thinking about it. But my brother wants me to take up a job."

"Do you need a job?"

"I can just about survive on my inheritance."

"If you can survive without luxuries, do what you want. Once women get saddled with responsibility they never get around to doing what they want."

"The problem is I don't know what I want."

"Post-graduation will legitimise the time you take to find out. Expose you to different people, different situations. You must come to our Feminist Forum meetings on Fridays. We've been discussing the issue of women's bodies, their self-image. I'm planning to bring up Vandana's case."

"Take Vandana to the meeting," suggested Naina, still scanning grains. Her fingers nimbly spread the rice into a thin layer at the centre of the thali, picked out husks and stones, then piled fine white grains into a heap on the opposite side.

"She considers our group beneath her."

"'They're jealous because I'm beautiful,'" mimicked Naina.

"Naina's always bitching about Vandana."

"I thought you were friends."

"She's Pawan's friend and Pawan is our friend."

"It's not that we don't like her ..." said Prabha cautiously. "There is feminist solidarity ... But she's on a different wavelength ... Who'd want to be photographed in the nude, for God's sake!"

"Isn't that too much rice for three people?" asked Pervez to change the subject.

"Sidhu will be back for lunch. Pawan and Vandana will probably drop in at night."

"Do you always cook for everyone?"

Naina looked up sharply. "Don't jump to conclusions. Pawan runs all the errands. If he forgets a single thing I send him back in the sweltering sun, but he goes without complaining. He's a gem." She finished cleaning the rice and smoothed it into the centre, sifting grains through her fingers. "Come on lazy lump. Chop onions for me. You should see her with onions, Prabha. She's a whizz. Chuk-chuk-chuk, chuk-chuk-chuk, chuk-chuk-chuk …"

Pervez laughed. "I learnt from my mother-in-law. We'd use nearly half a kilo every day so I learnt to work fast."

She went to the kitchen returning with three large onions, chopping board and knife. Placing the board on the dining table she deftly peeled away the dry skin, sliced the onion down the centre, placed one half face down, and rhythmically moved the knife in and out of the semi-circle. Shifting the sliced onion ninety degrees, she repeated the chopping movements. Before her was a mound of onion mince.

"See her hands, Prabha! Almost artistic …"

"Almost like a pianist, I'd say."

As Naina predicted, Pawan and Vandana came by in the evening. Pawan came in first, eyes sparkling as he strode past the outer room towards the mattress where the women were chatting with Sidharth.

"I've done it man, I've done it!" he announced dancing around in a circle.

"Done what?"

"Two-in-one. Two-in-one. Soon we're going to see money, man."

"Great! So when do I get back the millions you owe me?"

"Soon man. You'll get all I owe you real soon."

"With interest? Compounded from the date of loan?"

"Don't act like a moneylender!"

"When you borrow money I'm not a moneylender. When it's time to return it I become one."

"Friendship, man, remember? Keep money in perspective. What's mine is yours, what's yours is mine."

"See how his thinking changes once he comes into money," said Prabha. "Now tell us. What's this two-in-one all about?"

"It's like this, man. I went to Creative Unit about the Cadbury assignment. Sorry Vandy, no female models. It's a kid's campaign. Anyway the creative director was impressed by my pix. I'm getting an assignment that'll pay me ten grand!"

"Wow!"

"That's great!"

"Give us a party!"

"That's not all man. Today Lady Luck was really smiling. As I was leaving I ran into Sabina. Remember her? Reporter with the *Independent*? Well Sabina was desperate—"

"Sabina desperate! For you?"

"Next you'll be saying a journalist wants to be a centrespread!"

"Do you guys think cheesecake is all I'm fit for? Huh? You think I'm a male floozie like the babes I shoot? Sorry Vandy, no offence … You know I love you and all that … No man. You are now talking to a news photographer.

Tomorrow my photograph appears in the *Independent*. With Sabina's report. I'm gonna be rich and famous both."

"Great yaar! What did you photograph?"

"A slum demolition."

"A fashion photographer shooting a slum demolition! Too much!"

"Are you sure they'll publish the pix?"

"Hundred percent. Sabina even offered to buy the roll."

"You should stick to what you are good at," said Vandana, examining a fingernail whose polish had chipped. "Fashion photo-graphy. More money in fashion."

"No reason I can't do both."

"Enough horsing around," chided Sidharth, his voice returning to normal as he pulled out the evening paper from his jhola. "Heard the latest on the rath-yatra?"

"Rath-yatra?" asked Pervez. "People were discussing it at Darius' party. Said someone was teaching Muslims a lesson for something ..."

"There's this Hindutva fanatic called Advani who's driving around the country in a Toyota decorated like a fifteenth-century chariot," informed Naina.

"He makes such inflammatory speeches that there are communal riots every place he leaves," added Sidharth. "Gujarat, Maharashtra, Karnataka. The radio just announced that seventeen people including a woman and child were burnt alive in a village near Bidar. Out of the seventeen dead, thirteen are Muslims."

"That man should be flogged, man!"

"If the government wanted they could have stopped him. But Advani's riding a popular wave, and they're worried about their vote bank."

Pervez shrank into herself feeling inadequate and uninformed. Something major was happening. Important enough to disturb people as disparate as Darius and Naina's friends. But she'd lost the newspaper habit during her years in Goa. Resolving to read up on Ayodhya before her next visit to Kalina, she ran her fingers along the tasseled edge of the counterpane covering the mattress. She felt as limp as the threads hanging in the air.

"Did Naina tell you about my big offer?" Vandana asked Prabha, shifting attention to herself.

"Yes she did."

"Don't you think it is big opper-tunity?"

"Opportunity for what? Displaying your body for men to leer at?" Naina's voice was scathing.

"I know you do not like. But Prabha talks of women's independence. Of woman's right to her body. This is opper-tunity to make money. We can buy good flat. Not live in chawl. Shenoy said this is first chance. There will be more offers."

"Look, Vandana," began Prabha tenuously, "the question is not how much money, or what you do with it. The question is what you do to earn it. Do you really like the idea of thousands of eyes staring at your naked body?"

"They will look at photo, not me. Only Pawan will look at me and he has already seen."

"You bet he has! And more than seen ..."

"Shut up, Sidhu!"

"I am not posing with other photo-grapher. But Pawan is Pawan."

"All the same, every time you walk on the road every man who sees the calendar will mentally undress you and—"

"Men who are like that do even without calendar."

"We know lechers exist. But a playboy calendar converts every man into a lecher. In the women's movement we try to bring respect to women whether they are waitresses, scientists or housewives. When women allow themselves to be used as sex objects, when they encourage men to think of them as bodies without brains, without a perspective, they participate in the de-humanisation of all women. A single sleazy photograph undoes all our efforts."

"Money brings respect."

"Sex objects are used, not respected."

"You talk of woman's right to her body."

"That was in a different context. We were talking of sexual freedom. Reproductive control."

"That goes over her head, man," interrupted Pawan disparagingly "All she understands is body language."

"You like too!"

"Of course I do, Vandy. I love it. That's why I want it all to myself!"

"Possessiveness is another face of objectification," Sidharth's voice was a calm contrast to the heated exchange. "Vandana is no more an object for Pawan to possess than Naina is for me to possess. Everyone has the freedom to stay together as long as it is mutually satisfying and move away when it's not."

"Prabha is jealous. If she was not fat she would also want to be in magazine."

"I'd be in a magazine for more worthwhile reasons!" snapped Prabha.

"Have you ever been in magazine?"

"And you?"

"Three times. Twice *Chitralekha.* Once *Woman's Era.* English magazine. Fashion feature."

"That's because of me."

"I know, Pawan. I got a-signment from you. Now you can get a-signment from me."

"Let's discuss this at the forum meeting."

"But it is I who must decide. Not everybody. Like you said it is my body, no?"

"I hope you'll at least take Pawan's views into consideration."

It was through Prabha that Pervez learnt the feminist dimension of the build-up to Advani's campaign. "For years, women's groups have been demanding equality before law for women of different communities," she told Pervez later that evening. "The Women's Conference at Trivandrum was the first to demand a Uniform Civil Code way back in 1984. Now these Hindutva guys have made it into a Hindu versus Muslim campaign to impose their code on Muslims who have been governed by Shariat law ..."

Nineteen eighty-four. Two years after her marriage. The year of Fred's first "fling" as he called it. And the beginning of her slow slide to sloth.

It wasn't the proverbial perfume or lipstick-on-the-collar that did him in. But lack of response.

He had been away with the band at Ootacamund and returned with tea and eucalyptus oil for the family and a black polo-neck sweater for her. "I don't need a sweater in Goa," she had laughed, pleased nonetheless. He'd never brought gifts from trips before. But that night as she snuggled against him his body stayed limp. "Haven't you missed me?" she asked biting his ear, sniffing stale liquor on his breath.

"Tomorrow, baby. I'm all spent," he mumbled half asleep.

"What?"

"I'll make you happy tomorrow." She sat up and switched on the light.

"I wanna sleep," he groaned. "You'll get what you want tomorrow."

"What are you saying, Fred!" she demanded disbelieving.

"Don't you understand you can't get it before tomorrow? Now lemme sleep!"

The implications sank in slowly congealing into shock. She started pumelling his chest. He grabbed her wrists, twisting her arms till he had immobilised her, her back against his chest. "Lemme sleep!" he sneered in the nastiest voice she had heard. "Or you won't get it tomorrow either."

She sat huddled on the floor hugging her knees all night. Too shocked to cry or sleep. The foremost emotion indignation. Then the pain of betrayal.

She was out of the room before he woke up. And avoided him all day. By afternoon he was trying to mollify her, bringing out the koala bear she'd brought from Bombay. "Mummy's angry with daddy, baby bear," he cajoled, stroking his cheek with the bear's soft paw. "Tell mummy to make up … Tell mummy, daddy ver-ry sorry …"

It didn't take long to crack her armour. She capitulated, sobbing into his arms as he licked away her tears. As hysteria abated they made passionate love, Fred promising to never stray again. A common promise, made only to be broken.

Every few months would see a replay of that scene, Pervez' self-respect ebbing as her body hungered for what her mind began to abhor. Scars of each episode drew a wall between them. A wall whose cement hardened with each shower. Wrestling away memory she forced her mind back to what Prabha was saying.

"Did you read about the celebrated Shahbanu case?" Pervez shook her head. "Shahbanu was a seventy-five-year-old woman who went to court when her husband refused to pay maintenance after divorcing her. The court upheld her appeal but Muslim fundas were up in arms because according to the Shariat a man is not obliged to pay maintenance after the three-month idaat period. They kicked up a huge campaign till Rajiv Gandhi caved in and enacted the Muslim Women's Bill accepting Muslims' right to be governed by Shariat law."

"This sounds bizarre. How's a seventy-five-year-old woman expected to fend for herself!"

"It is bizarre. Rajiv Gandhi's decision got Hindu fundas worked up accusing him of bending over backwards to appease Muslims. So he made an even bigger blunder. He gave in to their long-standing demand for opening the gates of Babri Masjid which had been sealed from 1947 ..."

"I feel such a moron, Prabha ... I've been out of touch so long!"

She should have left Goa earlier, not let herself stagnate. But she had no qualifications and too much pride to return to her parents. After Fred's fifth indiscretion she registered for graduation by correspondence. To complete one chapter and lay the ground for the next.

But the next never happened. Studies that kept her from brooding also trapped her in routine. She became listless, spending hours wandering among cashew trees, carrying books to the top of the hill behind the house. A tiny notepad accompanied her to the beach where she'd walk for hours at the water's edge shrivelling up in the sun.

"The sea abandons shoals of shells," began one poem. "Into one, out of another, Out of one, into another, Does a wheel, ever stop to feel?" she wrote the day Fred left for an engagement in Madras. "Salt remains, when sea water flies to the sun," wept a poem, the day after a major brawl. Within weeks she needed another notepad.

Her poems were short. She didn't bother about technical finesse. For her pen and paper provided space for catharsis. She needed nothing more.

The couplings with Fred became fewer, less satisfying. Each time they made love she loved him less and hated herself afterwards. Each time she resolved to refuse, only to find refusal stuck in her throat.

Only Darius knew. She had no idea whether he told her parents, whether they sympathised or said "Serves her right". When a month after their accident he sent a cheque for her airfare, she followed instructions like a zombie. And returned to the city of her birth with the freedom and comfort it provided.

Pervez began to relax into Kalina's open atmosphere as she sipped rum for the first time in Bombay. Sprawled across the mattress she swilled the golden liquid around her mouth, savouring its zing before swallowing it. A warm glow spread within her.

Around eight o'clock the doorbell rang and cries of "Hi dost! Kya haal hai!" rent the air. "That's Vishal and Saeed," Naina told Pervez. "They've come after months."

As the newcomers entered, Pervez was in for another shock. They were distinctly working class. The taller one, whom she learnt was Vishal, was square-faced and broad-shouldered, a shock of curly hair falling over his chocolate-brown brow. Though he wore a sparkling white kurta pyjama, paan-stained teeth, black lining the edge of his nails and grey-black cracked soles gave away his class. Saeed wore a cream terylene shirt with brown pants and was accompanied by a younger man. As soon as they entered, conversation switched to Hindi and Pervez had to pay close attention to catch the vernacular.

Sebastian looks smarter than them, she thought, unconsciously comparing the newcomers to Dhun's cook, surprised at the warmth with which they were received. She had been brought up to treat servants courteously but keep a distance. Naina's taking this de-classing business too far, she thought.

Introductions were done with the third person being introduced as Saeed's younger brother Munawar. Naina went into the kitchen, and Pawan made a beeline for the door to replenish drinks before shops shut. Vishal helped himself to rum but Saeed and Munawar did not drink. They had come to see Sidharth.

"Many things happening in Dharavi are not good," began Vishal.

"Because of this rath yatra?"

"What else? Kiranawala Bashir Ahmed's brother was killed at Gonda. He was a rickshaw puller supporting three children. Now Bashir has vowed revenge. He is instigating Muslim boys to learn self-defence. You know what that means."

"Are people listening to him?"

"People are frightened. They are also angry. They will listen to anyone who talks of self-defence. Nobody trusts anyone. Not in fifty years have I seen tension like this. We brought Munawar to tell you what he's seen."

"Bol Munawar. What's alarmed you?"

Munawar hesitated, looking from Saeed to Vishal. "I'm in twelfth standard, sa'ab. I go for tuition at six in morning," he began, pulling out a small comb from the back pocket of his trousers and running it through his well-oiled hair.

"Don't call me sa'ab."

Munawar looked confused. "Dada bol," said Saeed reassuringly.

"To reach station I pass three water tap," continued Munawar, warming to his narrative. "Every morning fight is happening. Because water is coming less and everybody wants. From childhood I am seeing water-fight. Two-three everyday must happen. But after two-three hours women gossiping again. About vegetable price, mother-in-law, daughter-in-law. Now women not talking after fighting. They are staying inside and goos-goosing. Bad feeling not going away. So much tension there is. I think if I light bidi whole Dharavi will catch fire."

"Have there been any specific incidents?"

"Small-small things. Hindu boys teasing Muslim girl. Yesterday one boy pull Khatija's chaddar from face. Now Muslim boys also teasing Hindu girls. And Hindu boys getting angry. Big-big trouble will come soon."

"You must defuse the situation."

"How?"

"Do you know the boys who are eve-teasing?"

"I know one Muslim leader. Two Hindu boys in my tuition class."

"You must talk to them. Tell them you're ashamed of the behaviour of Muslim brothers. No, wait. Talk to the Muslim leader first. Tell him it's in everyone's interest to put an end to eve-teasing. It doesn't matter who started. Muslims are outnumbered. If things become worse they'll suffer the most. He must persuade others to stop eve-teasing. Then tell the Hindu boys what he says. Convince them to talk to their leaders."

"You think that will work?"

"No one knows what will or won't work. We can only try."

As Pervez glimpsed the clear thinking and the quiet strength that made Sidharth a natural leader she began to understand Naina's dedication. Abruptly becoming aware that she was the only woman in the room she got up. The four men continued talking in low voices till Naina called them for dinner.

4

The first thing she did on returning from Kalina was to have a long hot shower. Not that she minded bucket baths, she told herself, but it was more relaxing to have water wash away dirt without having to pour it over the body mug by mug. Pervez turned her face into the hissing steam, enjoying a feeling of abundance as she ran her hands luxuriantly over her body.

Much as she enjoyed the Kalina experience it was good to be back. She stepped into her room appreciating its comforts as she had on her return from Goa. Recalling her own words "I'm not addicted to luxury," she told herself addiction was one thing, enjoyment another. While it was important to know one could do without things, it was also good to have them.

As she pressed a piano switch the naked bulb came on. She resolved to buy a lamp shade the very next day. Doubting she'd find one to match the other, she decided to buy a pair of modern shades and put the antique away.

“Is it necessary? If not, do without,” came Sidharth’s voice into her head. I have not opted for the de-class binge, she told herself. I like Naina’s friends but they’ll have to accept me as I am. Pulling the chesterfield towards the window she sank into its springy softness, feet dangling over armrest, head curled against backrest. Big Ben chimed the quarter hour.

Her eyes took in the twinkling lights of Malabar Hill, the black bay separating her from them. Neither seagulls nor pigeons were visible. The steady hum of crisscrossing cars periodically punctuated by the roar of a bike was reassuring. She breathed in the familiar and relaxed.

A cockroach on the window pane caught her attention. It was running towards her. She jumped up, grabbing a chappal to swat it but it took off into the air. Relieved, for she hated the gooey mess of dead cockroaches, she settled back into the chesterfield.

The reflection of Malabar Hill in the window panes merged with the lights at the edge of the bay to ensconce her in a twinkling semicircle. An unexpected fusion of reality and illusion. If she shifted her head the semicircle was broken by a black bar. The abyss is never far from illusion, she told herself as more areas of darkness swam into view. She had to juggle her head to return to the position where the incandescence seemed complete. But since the thrill of spontaneity had passed it became only a pretty picture. The kind you saw on postcards for tourists.

Her immediate dilemma was filtering information for Darius. What he didn’t know he couldn’t worry about. Or stop her from doing. Describing Naina’s flat or her relationship with Sidharth was out of the question. As were Vishal, Saeed and Munawar. Or Pawan and Vandana.

So she talked of the campus canteen with large windows opening onto a lawn shaded by umbrella trees from which bell-shaped yellow flowers glided to the ground. She spoke about attending a women's meeting with Prabha. She mentioned meeting Vandana, an aspiring model Dhun could try in a fashion show. Constrained to black out the colourful, her narrative sounded pedestrian and neither Darius nor Dhun seemed interested.

"Advani's been arrested in Lucknow to prevent him from reaching Ayodhya," commented Darius from behind the *Times of India*.

"But now there are riots protesting his arrest," said Pervez, peering into the paper from behind.

"I don't understand why you're getting so worked up about this Ayodhya business," said Dhun, buttering a toast for her husband.

"That man stirs up trouble wherever he goes. First he defies the government to arrest him, then he says the courts have no jurisdiction in the mandir-masjid issue. He has no respect for law."

"Mandir or masjid. How does it concern us? I can understand Chawla getting worked up. After all he is a Hindu. What are Advani's followers saying? That India is for Hindus. Nobody can deny eighty percent of our population is Hindu. In a democracy you have to go with the majority."

"Even if the majority is misled?"

"We Parsis are such a tiny minority we can't afford to interfere. If ten Parsis are killed we'll become extinct.

Even UNESCO says so. Besides, why risk upsetting an important client?"

"Chawla keeps talking about the hotel at Vashi but I wonder how serious he is. I doubt the majority of Hindus back Advani. He's a rabble rouser."

"Naina and her friends are dead against him."

"See? Hinduism has so many faces. There's the Hinduism of mythology where heroes like Ram represent the triumph of good over evil. There's the Hinduism of philosophy incorporated in the Vedas, the Bhagvad Gita. There's the Hinduism practised in yoga, representing union of body, mind and spirit. There's the Hinduism of superstition and blind faith. The Hindutva Advani espouses is the lowest form of political aggrandisement."

"Good thing we belong to a religion whose tenets are simple," sighed Dhun, helping herself to scrambled eggs from a china bowl. "'Good thoughts, good words, good deeds' sums up Zarathustra's teachings. Sweet and simple."

"But is it so easy to practise?" asked Pervez. "Can we stop feeling angry, jealous, vindictive? Papa used to emphasise doing a good deed every day but I can't remember the last time I did one."

"Doing good deeds alone is a simplistic way of looking at it," said Darius slowly. "Unless an action is done in the right spirit it's not worth doing. Like building a temple may be good, but if it involves bloodshed it loses goodness."

"The more I think about it, the more I feel 'good words' is the most important tenet of Zarthost's teaching," he continued. "Words bring intelligence to life, as breath brings life to matter. Words give shape to thoughts, create understanding, make communication possible. Good words enable us to build on ideas, appreciate diverse points of view … lead on to good actions …"

"Why do you always make things complex, Darius?" chided Dhun. "I'm talking of the simplicity of our religion and you bring in all this philosophy. I just don't want you rubbing up Chawla the wrong way. Why risk an important client because there are communal riots in some godforsaken village?"

Pervez longed to mention the tension in Dharavi that Vishal and Munawar had spoken about but was reluctant to open a Pandora's box before she'd worked out an alibi for knowing what she knew. Wanting to open an interface with her brother and the new world she was entering she asked, "What do you think should be a feminist's response to women posing topless?"

"Is that what that model wants to do?"

"Of course not!" she lied. "It was one of the questions discussed at the women's meeting."

"Feminists should not support cheap women," said Darius.

"Feminists support all women. Including devdasis."

"Never heard of them," sniffed Dhun disparagingly.

"Devdasis are temple dancers. Girls given to temples at a young age to spend their lives in service of the gods."

"Like nuns?"

"No, silly!" said Pervez, enjoying the bemused expression on her brother's face as she brandished new knowledge. "Devdasis are also expected to gratify priests. It's a common practice in the South."

"My father always said there's something primitive about Hinduism," sniffed Dhun. "So many gods, goddesses you can't even remember their names. He says idol worship is idle worship—your prayers don't go beyond stone."

"I hope you're considering Chawla's offer," said Darius, gulping down his tea.

Pervez looked doubtful. "What does he do?" she asked.

"He owns a chain of hotels. Three star. Everything but the swimming pool. He could fix you up at the reception. Or at one of the boutiques. You could progress into marketing conference rooms, banquet halls ... You'd meet lots of nice people."

"Let's see," said Pervez noncommittally. Something told her her perception of nice people might be different from Darius'.

A middle-aged man was doing push-ups, resting both palms against the parapet wall. Fifty feet further, a younger man jumped astride-together, astride-together, rhythmically raising arms. Pervez could see a good-looking man walk his Alsatian through a cluster of pigeons that fluttered, circled and re-settled, resuming their pecking on the concrete pavement.

She had walked past the buildings towards the open expanse fringed by cricket fields where she could feel the fury of the wind. As pounding waves sprayed foam, Pervez shaped her dupatta into a hood encasing her head and sat on the wall where a narrow strip of sand held off the waves. Drawing knees to her chin she faced the horizon letting thoughts scatter into fragments like sea-spray, emerge, disperse, re-group at random. Like grains of sand in each wave.

Were Sidharth and Pawan both taking advantage of Naina, she worried. Could Sidharth help avert violence in a slum? What was Vandana all about? What was de-classing all about? What if Naina wanted to re-class? Would she be able to?

Clouds scudded faster than the rising sun. Pervez could see waves curling and dissipating far out at sea. A white plastic bag sailed on air currents in front of her face. She stretched a hand to grab it but it rose over her head, handles spread out like seagulls' wings. Seagulls kept away in the monsoons, she mused, afraid of being smashed against rocks. Only pigeons remained. Pampered on bagsful of grain. Pervez hated pigeons. They made her balcony a stinking mess.

She had encountered strange smells at Kalina. Henna, for one. One day she found Vandana whipping henna, coffee, egg and crushed hibiscus into a batter-like paste. She had offered to apply some on Pervez' hair. Pervez couldn't stand the acrid smell of henna. She declined to experiment with an unknown beauty aid.

All walls in the third-floor apartment were plastered with Vandana's photographs. Blown up and unrecognisably glamorous. Vandana in a traditional saree, pallu draped over her arm. Vandana in denims, short shirt knotted at the waist. Vandana in shorts with an over-sized ball on the beach. And portraits of her face—smiling, pouting, looking cheeky, insolent, angry. Her entire portfolio found space along the walls.

"Pawan's a good photographer," she remarked, immediately aware of her gaffe. But the irony was lost on Vandana who pointed to the photograph in the saree.

"This one came in *Woman's Era,*" said Vandana. "Saree cost eight hundred rupees. After modelling they gave me only."

She really is a narcissist, thought Pervez, straightening the dupatta that had blown off in the breeze. She had seen Vandana involved in nothing but body care. Exercising, creaming her face, hands, legs, endlessly changing nail polish. All meals were at Naina's and though Pawan fetched, carried and helped chop vegetables, Vandana would arrive just in timc to eat.

Yet she intrigued Pervez. It was bold to want to pose in the nude. Pervez was not prudish about nudity. Fred would sometimes bring home a *Playboy* or *Penthouse* and, after they spent an evening flipping through one, nights would be ecstatic. She found herself wondering if one day Fred might see a pin-up of Vandana's and get turned on. The thought was neither pleasant nor unpleasant.

A screech of skidding tyres compelled her to turn. A motorist had swerved to avoid three giggly girls crossing the road with a Walkman shared by two. Traffic flowed fast along both lanes of Marine Drive. Darius would have left for the office, thought Pervez, retracing her steps back home.

At Sagar Mahal a dumpy figure was waiting for the elevator. The clumsy saree worn Parsi style over the right shoulder rode above the ankles, gnarled toes sticking out of misshapen sandals. Spectacles sat on a wrinkled face.

The woman squinted at Pervez then hesitatingly asked, "Aren't you Par-veej?"

"Tehmie masi!" exclaimed Pervez, barely recognizing her aunt. "What are you doing here?"

"I've come to see Darius."

"He must have left."

"Never mind. He leaves envelope for me."

"Envelope?"

"Help. He gives help every month. Leaves envelope with *mistaree*. Name is Sebastioun, no?"

This was an unknown side of Darius. Pervez felt good discovering it. She had not met any relatives after returning from Goa and was shocked to find her mother's cousin in an obvious state of poverty. Impulsively she invited the old lady in.

"You look in bad shape, Tehmie masi," she began after instructing Sebastian to bring tea.

"That lousy husband. Brought home a *ganga* and threw me out."

"What are you saying!"

"It is true. He started sleeping with that *ganga* and threw me out of my own house."

"With a servant!"

"All *sakubais* are *gangas*, no? This one works in office. Now he's become ve-ge-tarian. Such nice chicken-meat-fish we used to have. Gave it all up. Eats grass. Like cow."

"You've had a rough time ..."

"I am living on charity. Everyone knows my case. Wadia Trust gave me room. But where? Jogeshwari. Malcolm Baug ... I, Tehmina Bulsara, who would make big fuss to go to Dadar ... now I am living in Jogeshwari!

Go up and down, up and down on train. *Parvardegaar*! What have I done to deserve this in my old age ..."

Sebastian wheeled in the tea trolley. As Pervez stirred the teapot to coax colour into the tea, Tehmie masi's eyes lit up at the sight of the biscuits. "Cream biscuit?" she asked. Pervez nodded. "Chocolate cream?" She nodded again. Tehmie masi bit into a biscuit gingerly, then crunching it fast she swallowed it with a gulp. Blowing on the tea, she slurped noisily, then reached for another biscuit. She was about to stretch for a third, then changed her mind. "Can I ... take home ... two biscuits?" she asked.

"Of course!" replied Pervez, taken aback.

"If I eat all together I get gas. *Atkaar-atkaar*, whole day. At my age only one-two, one-two I can eat."

Pervez fetched a paper bag, emptied the biscuits into it, folded and stapled the edge and handed it to Tehmie masi.

"Living on charity is terrible," the elderly woman was saying. "One day go to Parsi Panchayat. One day to Petit Trust, this trust, that trust ... Two hundred rupees from here, three hundred from there ... so much *dhakka-khavana* ..."

"What would you do without Parsi trusts?" wondered Pervez.

"Live in a *jhopadpatti* like the *ghatis*. What else!"

She looked around the room with the cup poised halfway to her mouth. "That clock ... was your *bapawa*'s ... Every Sunday a clock winder used to come to wind it. Your *bapawa* never let him leave without rose sharbat in his stomach and five rupees in his hand. Those days five rupees was like fifty rupees ..."

Pervez had almost forgotten the old clock winder who kept coming even after her grandfather died. As memories rekindled, a bony face with a long aquiline nose that curved like a parrot's beak emerged in her mind's eye. "Parsi nose on a non-Parsi face," she and Darius would chortle behind curtains when the clock winder came.

Luckily they'd escaped having the Parsi trademark on their own faces.

"You also had bad husband, no?" Tehmie masi's question cut short her nostalgia. "He didn't let you come for parent's funeral."

"We didn't have a phone. Darius' telegram reached late ..."

"You didn't come for *uthamnu, dusmu, masiso* ..."

"If you can't be at the funeral what's the use of attending ceremonies?"

"Terrible accident that was ... whole car falling into valley... Your father was such a cautious driver..."

Pervez' eyes brimmed. She had not cried on receiving the news. Not even after returning to the familiar surroundings of the house she grew up in. But her mother's cousin was about to crack the dam she had so assidously built. What must her parents have felt as the car tumbled into the valley? Did they die instantly or struggle with flames? Was there a fleeting thought for her in either of their minds?

"Stop putting fingers in your plate!"

Pervez continued breaking a piece of chapatti with the index finger of her right hand, swivelling it around a small portion of minced meat and putting it into her mouth. She was prepared for her sister-in-law's reprimand. "You can't eat a chapatti with a fork, can you?" she said, trying to sound nonchalant. "At Kalina everyone eats with their hands."

"Kalina is Kalina. I expect table manners in my house."

"Even when there are no guests?"

"What do guests have to do with etiquette? Only servants eat with their hands."

"Vasant Chawla eats with his hands."

"Vasant Chawla is a boor."

"Then why do you chat him up?"

"I'd chat up anyone if there's a deal to be struck. Chawla's building a posh hotel. A plum contract for Darius."

"If Darius' client can eat with his hands what's wrong with his sister doing the same?"

"I have no objection to people eating with their hands as long as they're not sloppy about it," intervened Darius, balancing mince at the edge of his fork. "But some people, especially South Indians, make a mess with rice, curd, rasam—"

"Soon your sister will be like that," grimaced Dhun.

"As I was saying, I have no objection to people eating decently with their hands but it's just not done in our kind of homes."

"What's special about 'our kind of homes'?" asked Pervez.

"Cultured homes. Dad wouldn't even let us come to the dining table in pyjamas, remember?"

"I remember how you used to fight with him about that ..."

"Kids always want things informal."

"I still like things informal. Especially at home."

"Frankly, so do I."

"Can I come to the table in my nightie tomorrow?"

"If brother and sister are going to lower standards in my house, I'll start having my meals in the bedroom," said Dhun, thoroughly peeved.

"Stop getting so worked up, Dhun," Darius' voice was unusually sharp. "As I was saying, Pervez, certain kinds of behaviour are alright for other people, not us. What you do outside is your business but at Sagar Mahal we expect table decorum." He strode off into the bedroom to pre-empt further argument. Dhun followed.

Pervez continued sitting at the table defiantly, relishing the crunch of onions and corriander between her teeth, as she dipped chapatti into *kachumber* before popping it into her mouth. She had not dared to eat with her hands when she returned from Goa, feeling as much an outsider in her brother's house as she had on her first day at Fred's. But some confrontations were necessary to assert her identity.

She was some distance away when Pervez first saw her. A buxom woman in white, snowy hair pulled into a bun, a jhumka of keys jangling at her waist ... And incongruous Adidas shoes!

The sports shoes made a mockery of her gracious appearance. They were shoes for the young and she was old. They were shoes for jogging and she could barely walk. But age provides the insouciance to dress as you please and look cute for it. Pervez attempted a smile as they passed each other but the older woman ignored her.

Darius laughed at her description of the "gujju granny". "See all the things an open economy makes possible," he chuckled. "In a few years you'll be able to buy everything in India—shoes, jeans, perfumes, cosmetics. The days of going to Singapore for shopping are numbered."

"I bought two nonstick cooking pans from Akbarally's last week," said Dhun. "Quite sleek. You wouldn't dream they were made in India."

"I used the smaller one for frying omelettes with hardly any oil," said Pervez, placing a mushroom omlette in front of Darius. She enjoyed messing around the Sagar Mahal kitchen, well stocked as it was with an array of sauces, nuts and other exotic ingredients.

"Put it away after you're through with it," cautioned Dhun. "I don't want Sebastian ruining my nonsticks."

"Then why did you buy them?" asked Pervez.

"Because they're new. Everyone's buying them."

"So it's settled," Darius was saying as Pervez walked down the Bombay Gymkhana verandah with cushioned cane sofas and tables with tiny bells to summon waiters. "We sign the contract on Wednesday and construction begins next month."

"When do I get possession?" asked Dilip.

"Twelve to fifteen months."

"Can I plan a Diwali party?"

Darius hesitated. "That may be cutting it fine. Why not New Year's Eve?"

"Done. But if you deliver by Diwali there'll be a bonus."

"What's the incentive?"

"Free medical consultation for the family ..."

"We get that anyway!"

The men laughed as Pervez sank into the armchair beside Dilip. "Your brother's building a bungalow for me at Khandala, my dear," he told her beaming. "I commissioned designs from three architects but Darius' was the best. The bay window he's designed to take in the view of the valley is superb. Just superb."

Pride swelled in Pervez' heart. Her brother was developing a reputation as a leading architect. A couple of weeks ago a magazine had carried his photograph with excerpts of a lecture he'd given on the conservation of heritage buildings. Till then no one had expressed concern about preserving elegant old buildings that were falling apart due to apathy and neglect. Darius' eye-opener won him respect.

"Can I consult you about a health problem, Dr Kanitkar?" asked Pervez.

"Of course. But if I'm Dr Kanitkar you'll have to pay my consultation fee of two thousand rupees per minute," he smiled, eyes twinkling. "Call me Dilip."

"I can't call an older person by the first name," she said shyly.

"Stop making me old! What's the problem?"

"I've been getting this rash behind my knees. It itches violently for a few weeks, disappears and comes back."

Dhun and Shweta were walking towards their husbands together. Pervez marvelled at her sister-in-law's impeccable appearance. Her navy blue pantsuit was offset with coral earrings and bracelet, red shoes and handbag to match, with lips and nails painted the perfect shade of red.

"We've closed the deal," announced Dilip to his wife. "Make sure my schedule allows weekends in Khandala to oversee construction."

"I wish Vasant took decisions as quickly," sighed Dhun. "He's been making Darius dance a jig for the Vashi hotel."

"A hotel's a bigger project, my dear. So many people are involved in decision making."

"They've made Darius change the design four times already. Imagine the waste of time. Is Vasant coming today?"

"He always says he's busy but he shows up without fail."

Just then Chawla walked in with a young boy swinging a squash racquet. "I had to cancel two meetings because my grandson wanted to play squash," he said, his eyes following the lithe young figure striding away.

"You'll live a hundred years, Mr Chawla," simpered Dhun, her voice taking on a cajoling tone. "We were just talking about you."

"Not gossiping, no?"

"Do you imagine I'd allow anyone to gossip about you?" she pouted.

His eyes ran over her appreciatively. "So what were you saying?"

"Dr Kanitkar has just signed up Darius for his Khandala bungalow. Took a decision in two weeks. Your Vashi hotel project's been hanging fire for months ..."

"Business," he said dismissively as Iqbal Rahimtoola passed their table ignoring him. "Saturday, no business." He looked around spotting Pervez. "So, lady from Goa? When are you coming to me for job?"

Pervez hesitated. "I don't think I want to work in a hotel," she said, aware of Darius' disapproving glare.

"Why not?" snapped Chawla.

"It's ... it's not my scene ... I'm thinking of going back to studying ..."

"Studying what?"

"MA."

"I am offering you job without yem-a fem-a and you are refusing?"

"She's going to think about it, Mr Chawla," intervened Dhun soothingly. "Let me pour you some beer." Tilting the glass till froth touched the brim she handed it to Chawla. "As I was saying your Vashi project—"

"No business on weekend."

"I thought you cancelled two meetings," said Darius drily.

"Meetings not for business."

"Don't tell us you had to cancel some naughty-naughty meeting," flirted Dhun as Pervez looked away. Her sister-in-law's ingratiating manner disgusted her, especially when she knew what Dhun really thought of Chawla.

"Meeting was for Ram temple at Ayodhya," he announced. "Building fund meeting postponed to tomorrow."

"What building fund!" retorted Darius. "The court hasn't cleared the site."

"Court or no court, temple will come."

"Will you take the law into your own hands?"

"Religion comes before law. Law is only hundred years old. Hinduism goes back thousands of years."

"Nothing in Hinduism would justify breaking one place of worship to build another," said Dilip quietly. " Babri Masjid is hundreds of years old. Why not build a Ram temple next to it?"

"Masjid was built by barbarian Babar. He broke temple to build mosque. Now we will break mosque and build temple again."

"That was in a different age," reasoned Dilip. "Conquerers destroyed temples to get the gold stored in them."

"So he is 'lootera Babar'. And Babri Masjid is standing in place Ram was born."

"Bosh!" retorted Dilip. "Till today it's not certain whether Ram was a historical figure or a mythological hero. We respect him for the moral values he stands for—regardless of whether he lived or was created by an artist writing an epic. How can anyone talk of his birthplace when we don't even know whether he actually lived?"

"Whether Ram lived or not is not important. If Hindus believe this is where he was born then that piece of land becomes sacred to them. And they must have Ram temple."

"That's brainwashing. Repeat a lie often enough so people believe it."

Chawla gave Darius a withering look. "You Parsis are outsiders. Too Western. You don't know what it is to experience Partition-like bloodshed. I lost one brother in Lahore. Killed by the son of the Muslim dai who breastfed him."

No one spoke for a while. Then Pervez entered the discussion. "I read that Advani wants a 'reverential relocation' of Babri Masjid," she said tentatively. "He wants Muslims to voluntarily give it up after which Hindus will help them build another grand masjid in Ayodhya."

"That's the biggest fake-pious hypocrisy I've ever heard!" exploded Darius, surprising them with his vehemence. "Like saying fall at my feet and I'll give you a pat on the back."

As Chawla turned purple Dhun intervened. "Stop getting so worked up, Darius," she said grimacing. "Forgive him for my sake, Mr Chawla. I don't know why he's in such a sour mood today. I must have forgotten to put sugar in his tea this morning. Let's decide what we're having for lunch ..." She took over the conversation, not giving the men a chance to get into an argument. But the black look remained on Chawla's face. He left without lunch.

5

Pervez' handbag slipped off her shoulder as she held up one corner of a banner proclaiming Sati Is Murder. She felt awkward entering Dharavi for the first time in her life with a band of street-theatre activists. Behind her a drummer belted out a rhythm on a dholak. The troupe of actors followed.

"Naa-tak! Naa-tak! Naa-tak!" whooped children, running out in droves. The group moved towards an open space where a handful of chairs had been placed behind a sea of Hessian sacks on the ground. Kids ran to grab front space. Older boys climbed onto tin roofs of huts, younger ones onto fathers' shoulders, the more agile scaling the branches of a solitary withered tree that managed to support seven or eight youngsters.

The performers started clapping and the audience joined in. Within seconds the crowd had cohesed into a mass of clapping humanity. Prabha, dupatta draped theatrically at a diagonal, stepped forward raising her hand. Immediately there was silence. The effect was electric.

The street theatre group had entered Asia's largest slum from Koliwada, its most colourful sector. Pervez was surprised to pass not just fruit and vegetable vendors but chemists, saree shops, shops with blue, red and orange buckets, general merchants' shops, shops with long floral venis for the hair and even a whole row of gold jewellery shops. Oil sizzling in pans on handcarts fried onion-batter into crisp bhajias whose aromas tempted her palate. Piled on another cart were succulent gulabjamuns.

Three years had passed since Roop Kanwar was immolated on her husband's funeral pyre at Deorala. The ancient Rajput custom, practised by women to escape being gangraped by invaders in medieval times, had been glorified to fuel Hindu revivalism in 1987, with Hindutva proponents projecting Roop Kanwar as a contemporary goddess. Prabha's group was enacting a street play to put sati into perspective.

An actor prostrated himself on the floor feigning death. Prabha draped a white dupatta over her head like a widow and crouched in a corner opposite him. Other actors marched around chanting "Ram naam satya hai" till one of them spotted her.

"Eh? What are you doing? Your place is beside your husband," called a woman activist, enacting the role of the village headman.

"Yes, yes, her place is beside her husband. Where else should she be?" the actors chorused. The widow shrank into herself, weeping.

"Go to your husband," ordered the headman. Her sobs became louder. "What kind of wife is this? So young and refusing to be at her husband's bedside! Today's women even have to be taught their marital duties … Listen, woman! If you don't go to your husband on your own you'll be dragged there hand and foot!"

Pervez felt a tremor run through the crowd. People's attention was riveted. Even kids had their eyes glued to the tableau.

"I … I … I don't want to die," wailed the woman. "I don't want to die before I have lived …"

"Eh? What is this blasphemy?" snarled the headman. "You want to live a good life after your husband has died? What is the world coming to?" Turning to the others, he gestured dramatically, "What are you waiting for? Take her where she belongs!"

The widow's wailing became louder as the actors dragged her towards the corpse. She struggled as they tried to place his head in her lap till one actor pushed her and she fell with a thud. A ripple went through the audience.

"What's going on?" came a loud voice as an activist with a red bandana around his waist strode from the audience onto stage space. "Arre didi, what are they doing to you?"

"Bhau! Bhau!" screamed the woman, flinging herself at the newcomer's feet. "Mujhe bachao! There is no one to save me but you."

"Don't worry, didi. I am here now. Tell me what happened. Who are all these people?" He saw the corpse. "Hey Ram! What's happened to your husband!"

"He is dead," said the village headman grimly.

"How did he die?"

"Snakebite."

"They want to burn me with him," sobbed the young widow. "I don't want to die ... I am afraid of fire ... It will be so painful ..."

"No one will touch a single hair of your head as long as I'm alive, didi. You have nothing to fear now that Bhimsingh is back."

The actors gathered at a corner of the impromptu stage as the widow was comforted by her brother. After a while one of them beckoned him. "You have returned to our village after a long time, Bhimsingh."

"After two years, Charanbhai."

"Long enough to forget our customs. Our ancient culture is dying because youngsters go to big-big cities and forget customs."

"No Rasulbhai, can anyone escape their roots? I go to the city to carn a living but I was born here and will come back here to die."

"Hmm . .. what brings you back now?"

"Mother is ill.. . then there's the drought... I got a message that three of our buffaloes have died..."

"He is a good son ..."

"He has come to look after his mother ..."

"Poor mother ... No food ..."

"Now she has one more to feed ..."

"One more?"

"Who's going to feed the widow? Not her in-laws ..."

"Poor family. Bechara ... Besahara ..." The troupe took up the chant as Bhimsingh stood forlorn at the centre. Pervez could hear people clucking tongues in sympathy. Then the headman took Bhimsingh aside and put an arm around him conspiratorially.

"Don't misunderstand me, brother, but I can make one suggestion that will end your problems for always."

"Ours as well ..." remarked a voice to be silenced by a loud "Shh ... shh ... shh ..."

"What is your suggestion?"

"Come, sit near me. These are personal matters ... We don't want the whole village hearing, do we?" They mimed a conversation, Bhimsingh's expression changing from horror to resignation to anticipated greed.

"The village will build a temple in my sister's name?" he asked aloud.

"Of course."

"My sister will become a goddess? A sati mata?"

"Definitely."

"You promise half the money from temple offerings will come to our family?"

"Didn't I say so?"

"Will you give us space for a puja shop next to the temple?"

"We'll give you that also ..."

"Then how can I stand in the way of my sister becoming immortalised!"

The widow's shrieks were drowned by shouts of sati mata ki jai! Sati mata ki jai!" as she and the corpse were carried away to the beat of the dholak.

As the crowd applauded, Prabha returned without the white dupatta that had given her the widow's personna. "Is killing a widow something to applaud?" she asked. The audience looked shamefaced.

"It is an ancient practice," muttered an elderly man.

"Why bring it up in this day?" asked a young girl in a green salwaar kameez.

"Even today women commit sati if they love their husbands. Look at Roop Kanwar."

"Why don't husbands commit sati?" demanded the spirited girl. "Don't they love their wives?"

"Did the woman in the play look like she was committing sati out of love? Or was she being forced into it?" asked Prabha.

"She was forced."

"That panchayat was comprised of swines."

"Of course that woman was forced." Voices arose from different sides.

"And who gained from her death?" asked Prabha.

"Her brother."

"The headman."

"The whole village," clarified Prabha. "Once a sati takes place a temple will come up, people will come from all over the place, make offerings to the sati-mata, give donations to the temple. They will need places to stay, food to eat."

"You are right ..."

"Right ..."

"Of course she's right."

A woman with a child suckling her breast stood up. "Roop Kanwar was very pure. I saw a photo of her being struck by a single ray of light and taken straight to heaven. While her body was burning many miracles happened. Blind people started seeing. People with leprosy were healed ..."

"Who told you this?"

"The pundit."

"How did he know?"

"Pundits know such things."

"Suppose he's lying?"

"Of course he's lying!" said the spirited girl in green. "Isn't he the same pundit who forced everyone to pay hundred-hundred rupees for his satyanarayan puja?"

As the discussion grew animated, Pervez glanced around Koli Maidan, an open plot that served as a dumping ground for all kinds of throwaways. To her left, tin trunks piled higher than her head beyond which a cluster of broken table fans rusted on the ground. Three tyres hung on ropes from the withered tree, and Pervez could see a small girl swinging on one, oblivious of the babble of adult voices.

A drawing of a car on the wall behind caught her attention. A child had given it five wheels instead of four. To its right, Arun Loves Shika was embedded into a heart and an arrow in the universal language of love, below which was the ubiquitous slogan of Hindu pride, Gaurav Se Kaho Hum Hindu Hain. Further up, cracks in the plaster revealed bricks beneath peeling paint. Pervez was startled by the aggressive graffitti. Kutte Ka Chamcha, Kutte Ki Maut Marega. She wondered whether it had been written by a child or an adult, whether it was a threat or merely an expletive, whether the person addressed had seen it ...

Letting her eyes wander with more curiosity, she found a brick-red silhouette of a boy holding a cricket bat with Sunil scrawled across his T-shirt. Further up, a face resembled Amitabh Bachchan, with a parrot on a pointed finger. As she neared the edge of the wall she found the black dirt scratched into English letters. Don't Halt Me read the misspelt words underscoring the pathos. Was this written by a child rejected by his family, she wondered. Or was he the victim of some prejudice? Communal? Caste? Any other? Pervez' heart went out to the unknown writer.

Persuading Darius to let her move to Kalina had not been easy. She did not rush it, spending occasional weeks with Naina getting to know the campus and its environs. Darius must have seen it coming, but when she finally told him she'd decided to rent a small flat near Naina he was sceptical.

"MA in psychology means nothing in the job market. Not at age thirty. Think twice before rejecting Chawla."

"I don't like that man. I don't want to work for him."

Darius shrugged. "Why do you want to live at the back of beyond? Are you unhappy with us?"

"Not at all. Dhun has been very generous. With clothes, perfumes ... But I've grown away from this kind of life ..."

He kept looking at her quizzically. "You really have," he said at last. "You don't even make an effort to fit in."

"I have to move in my own direction."

"Okay. But if things don't work this is still your home."

She rented a flat at Indrani colony, three buildings away from Naina's. It was an identical two-room kitchen apartment but Pervez decided on doing hers up. She could do without Darius and Dhun's luxurious lifestyle, but eight years of surviving on simplicity whetted her appetite for congenial surroundings.

The flat came with a sofa-cum-bed, dining table and three chairs in the drawing room and a bed and cupboard in the bedroom. Pervez painted all a gleaming, washable white. She hung the antique lampshade from her Sagar Mahal bedroom over the dining table, covered the floor with cane matting and bought a few brass and ceramic knick-knacks.

She was particularly pleased at being able to shift the old chesterfield to Kalina. She placed it next to the window where the light was right for reading. And on the windowsill she placed shells from beaches in Goa.

Pervez liked carrying away bits of places as she moved. And leaving bits of herself behind. Small significant bits. When she left Bombay, she'd taken the koala bear that her parents had brought from a trip to Australia when she was only five. She'd slept with the bear throughout her childhood and selected him alone to accompany her into her new life.

Fred used to tease her about the koala. Calling her a baby with a toy. She started calling him hairy bear and mock-flirting with the koala. Koala became part of their love games. But she left him behind in Goa. He was too suffused with memories to live with any longer.

Instead she brought back a boxful of shells of different shapes and colours. Small, round, pink and brown snail-shaped shells. Large crustaceans fanning out like natural sculptures. Shells that curled into themselves. Shells with mother-of-pearl surfaces. Shells flat as a plate to serve some delicacy in. She arranged them on windowsills placing pots of miniature cacti between them. She would have liked to bring the brass pot with ferns from her bedroom balcony but sensing Sidharth's disapproval of its ornate carving she decided to leave it at Sagar Máhal.

"I am not de-classing," she had told him firmly. "Experimenting. Because I respond to your rhythm. But I don't go along with your class-conflict theories."

"Our rhythm comes from the work we do. Without it we'd be as deadpan as everyone else," he replied. "What we do in cities is nothing. Meera and Kuldip are actually living with coal miners in Chinchwada in Madhya Pradesh. Praful and Shilpa are organising Warlis in the Dahanu belt. Ranbir is helping tribals fight for their rights in the Sunderbans. Hundreds have given up the comfort of living in a house with running water and electricity to become catalysts in people's struggles."

"I appreciate all that but can only support your work selectively."

"That's sitting on the fence."

"Better than jumping in on one side to find you sympathise with the other. I honestly can't buy your line about the upper classes. My brother is upper class. He's not a bad guy. When my parents died he need not have let me know I was entitled to half their estate but he did."

"You have an unusual brother."

"You're so stuck on this class-enemy idea you don't even see upper-class people as human beings."

Sidharth looked at her pensively. "You have grown, Pervez," he said at last. "Six months ago you wouldn't open your mouth. Now you're debating ideology."

"I'm not suggesting I know better than you, Sidharth. You have years of experience while I'm only a novice. But my background is different. My life has been different. I can't be honest with myself and go along with you at the same time. We have to live with our differences. Dialogue them—"

Sidharth's face broke into a wry smile. "Dialogue? Where does dialogue get anyone these days ..."

The week-old conversation surfaced in her mind as she tried to digest the experience of being in Dharavi. There was something totally honest about people's response to street theatre. No veneer of sophistication to trip the spontaneous. Instinctively she knew the pulsating energy of the performers came from a shared vision, shared convictions and the desire to pass them on. Could she draw on that energy without sharing the vision?

"Thanks," she said as Pawan thrust an ice-cold Limca into her hand. He was also in Dharavi for the first time. The slum demolition photograph won him compliments and enthused him so he had begun accompanying Sabina on other assignments, taking his own pix.

"I'd imagined Dharavi to be full of dirt, squalor and huts, man," he said. "Who'd have thought there'd be a Meenakari jewellery shop here of all places!"

"The gold workmanship is quite good," said Prabha.

"And STD/ISD booths! Video parlours where you can see films for just one rupee! I was talking to someone who has a business supplying leather handbags to a boutique at the Oberoi. You bet he's raking in the lolly!"

"Everyone here works. It's bunkum that Dharavi is full of pickpockets and thieves. There are taxi drivers, electricians, school teachers … Only the unemployed take to crime like anywhere in the world."

"Did you see the addas, man? Beer bars. Country-liquor bars. Foreign-liquor bars."

"Pawan's tongue is tingling," laughed Pervez.

"No drinking in Dharavi. You'll give us a bad name," chided Prabha.

"I know how to behave, man."

"Please get a chair for Prabha. She's been standing for ages," said Pervez who'd been sitting on a folding tin chair against the graffiti wall. Pawan looked around, spotted a rickety chair and brought it for Prabha. "Thanks," said Pervez.

"Quit this politeness, man. 'Please', 'thank you' for every thing. Talk straight."

"Parsis are too polite," chuckled Prabha. "You should see my neighbours. Two Parsi sisters. Unmarried. So refined you never hear them raising their voice. *Dikra* this, *mailou* that…"

"Too polite for passion, man! Teach them some swear words."

"They'd never use them. I knew a Parsi boy in college. He would never swear! B-dash for bloody, d-dash for damn… So funny these Parsis can be!"

Pervez was taken aback. "We can get as angry as anyone else!" she retorted. "Have you heard Parsis fight over money? Whenever there's a death in a rich Parsi family they end up in court."

"You're right!" chortled Prabha. "The only time I heard Khushroo get angry—this guy in college—was when his stereo was stolen. We came out of a film and he found his car open. So he caught a street kid, and for the first time we heard him shouting 'Sala sooer, behnchod'. Came close to beating him up ... I hope you don't mind us talking like this, Pervez?"

Pervez didn't mind the jibing about Parsis as much as she resented being put on the mat for a positive aspect of her upbringing.

"Where's Vandana today?" she asked to change the subject.

"Can you imagine madam in a place like this! You gotta be outa your mind, man. She's probably painting her lovely long nails."

"All the better to scratch you with," mocked Prabha. "Have you sorted out this calendar photography business yet?"

"Nah!" he spat, striding away.

She was contrasting the placidity of the family-planning hoarding with its visual of two smiling adults and two smiling kids with the spontaneous sketches she'd seen on the wall when a voice blared "hullo" into the mike. Pervez strode eagerly towards the stage where Vishal was raising the mike to his height. Sheila, the municipal schoolteacher who had invited the street theatre group to Dharavi, had just finished a speech and Vishal was getting ready for songs.

He had sung at a small dinner she hosted on her first weekend in her new apartment. Saeed had arranged for biryani and raita from a Moghlai caterer which she supplemented with American potato and dill salad. The odd blend of Eastern and Western cuisine went down well with the uninitiated, especially with Vishal who'd never tasted potato salad before. It felt strange, watching tangy mayonnaise licked off fingers as they ate. But she felt satisfied seeing her guests enjoy her cooking.

Vishal had brought along his harmonium, and as rum warmed spirits they settled down to film songs, twisting lyrics to lampoon filmstars and politicians. Ignoring the furniture Vishal sat cross-legged on the floor under the window, white kurta gleaming, examining a conical shell with a mother-of-pearl surface, turning it over and over in his hands.

Pervez and Naina huddled together on the chesterfield. Pawan, Vandana and Sidharth shared the sofa while Prabha, Saeed and Munawar pulled dining chairs into a semicircle.

It was past eleven when Sidharth asked Vishal to sing solo. A hush fell over the room as the horsing around stopped. Pervez got up and switched off the overhead light leaving on a small ceramic lamp. Warmth spilt over its shade connecting them in its intimate glow.

"Chale chalo dilon mein ghaav," began Vishal his rich baritone belying the simplicity of his dress. "Le ke bhi chale chalo ... Chalo lahu luhan paon ... le ke bhi chale chalo ..."

"This is a beautiful song written by Brijmohan," whispered Naina to Pervez. "Loosely translated it says 'Carrying grief in your heart keep walking, despite bleeding feet keep walking.'"

"Chalo ki aaj sath-sath ... chalne ki zarooratein ..." the voice rose not from the throat but deeper within Vishal's being. "Chalo ki khatma ho na jayen ... zindagi ki hasratein ..."

"We need to walk together to prevent our dreams from being crushed to ashes," whispered Naina but Pervez had shut her eyes. She was tuned in to Vishal's cadence. It seeped into her being as Fred's first rendering of "Moon River" but with deeper pain. The pain of a people humiliated over centuries, regarded untouchable, oppressed in the name of social stratification. A stratification sanctified by Hinduism.

"Zameen, khwaab, zindagi... yakeen sab ko baant kar ..." The voice rose in timbre and decibel. "Woh chahte hain bei basi mein ... aadmi jhukaye sar ..."

Naina's eyes glazed as the mesmeric music took over. She gave up the effort to translate.

"Woh chahte hain zindagi ho ... ho roshni se be- khabar ... woh ek ek kar ke sab jala rahe hain har shahar..."

The crescendo rose from deep within his body, to reverberate into the cosmos. An oppressed people's cry of perennial pain.

"Jale hue gharon ke khwaab ... le ke bhi chale chalo ... chalo lahu luhan paon ... le ke bhi chale chalo ..."

As he returned to the refrain Vishal looked up to find Sidharth misty-eyed, Prabha ecstatic, and Naina and Pervez in frozen stupor. Only Vandana had fallen asleep.

"You should record this, man!" said Pawan after a while, his voice strangely hoarse.

"I have made two cassettes. I can give you."

"I mean commercially. For big record companies. You need money, man. That voice is one in a million. If I were to play this tape to a music company …"

"No way!" snapped Sidharth.

"Okay boss. I'm just saying if I did, our friend would be in gravy. He'd be raking in the lolly faster than he could spend it."

"Do you want to make a lot of money?" Pervez asked Vishal.

"Tell me who does not need money? Such a person does not exist. Even big-big sahebs living on twenty-first, twenty-second floors need money. They need for three-three four-four cars. I need for three children."

"Zameen aasmaan ka farq," commented Saeed.

"Would you like to make a cassette that brings you a lot of money?" persisted Pervez.

"Friendship is more important than money. Sidharth helped in many difficulties. How can I make him angry!"

"Forget me. Aren't you opposed to capitalist strategies?"

"Capitalists exploit workers. Thousands have lost their jobs in the textile strike. People who were standing on their own feet have come into clutches of moneylenders … If your child falls sick medicines have to be bought … There is no escape. You have to go to moneylender even if he sucks your blood."

"Making cassettes commercially could free you from moneylenders," said Pervez.

"What about the thousands who don't have Vishal's voice?" interjected Sidharth, sharply. "The individual should not break class solidarity."

"Let's hear Vishal ..." Pervez urged him on.

"I will tell you true-life experience. Six-seven years ago I was like mill workers. Only one step away from moneylender. How far can peon's salary go! To make extra money I was singing. At wedding, Ramleela. At one wedding one film director heard me. He sent a man afterwards. Offered ten thousand rupees for one song. Immediately I said yes. Ten thousand rupees is lot of money. After two-three days he called me to studio. Badiya mast... Air conditioned. Big-big speakers. Red lights. Green lights ... badiya mast studio ... In three hours they recorded song, gave me ten thousand rupees and sent me home in a taxi. Like a sa'ab. I was very happy.

"After some months film was released. My song became superhit. I was hearing my voice on TV, in bustee, everywhere ... So I went back to studio. Told one lady that my song is super-hit, I should get more money. She told me to wait but never came back. After some time chowkidar threw me out."

Pervez was shocked. "Didn't you sign a contract?" she asked.

"I just saw ten thousand rupees coming in one day and agreed. Like I was saying big money does not come to people like me. Friends like Sidharth more important. When my father died he gave money for funeral."

Images of that night came back as Pervez stood at the edge of the audience. Three women and five men crowded the stage behind Vishal. He was considerably taller than them. The mike was adjusted to an in-between height. "Hindu-Muslim-Sikh-Isai ..." boomed Vishal, his voice reverberating off tin roofs in the descending darkness.

"Mehnat karte bhai bhai," responded his troupe.

They repeated the slogan three times before switching to "Khamosh ho!"

"Hum ek hain!"

This was also repeated three times. Then a man in a red shirt pelted out a beat on the dholak. Vishal's fingers ran over the harmonium keyboard. "Mandir masjid gurdware mein baant liya bhagwan ko, dharti baanti sagar baanta mat banto insaan ko ..." they began.

Halfway through the song a man in a black shirt abruptly strode on stage grabbing the mike. "Laandyas! Have you come for women's meeting or to make trouble!" he barked, his eyes blazing. "Go home everyone! If these dogs try to create trouble they'll be beaten to pulp."

"No one was making trouble ..." murmured Pervez to no one in particular.

"Manohar is from the shakha," muttered a woman standing beside her with a purple Maharashtrian-style saree tucked between her legs. "We have to listen to him."

"But there's no trouble," replied Pervez.

"If we don't do what he says they'll make trouble."

"This is blackmail!"

"Matlab?"

Pervez didn't know the Hindi word for blackmail. But the woman was in a hurry to get away, calling to a child in the crowd. The black-shirted man held on to the mike till people dispersed. Vishal made no attempt to retrieve it. The square cleared faster than it had filled. But a few curious men hovered in the shadows.

"How dare you disrupt our meeting!" demanded Prabha, stepping forward.

The beefy man looked her up and down. "Trouble-making outsiders. Say you're having women's meeting then start political propaganda. Keep away from Koliwada if you know what's good for you."

"Dharavi doesn't belong to you!"

"It belongs to my grandfather, you slut! Do you know who you're speaking to?"

Saeed drew Prabha away, speaking to her in a low voice. Pervez could see alarm on his face. "Eh batmeez! Where's that randy brother of yours?" sneered Manohar spotting Saeed. "Running after Hindu girls as usual? Tell him if he comes near my sister again we'll castrate him and feed his thingee to the dogs."

"Preeti is not your sister!" Munawar's voice rose shrilly from the dark.

"All Hindu girls are my sisters, behnchod. Preeti, Neeti, Sweety. No difference. Girl is girl. Hindu is Hindu. And you maderchod Mussalmaans should be castrated before you overpopulate India with snakes from your seed."

Words were flying fast. Prabha was looking stunned at the sudden turn of events. No one challenged Manohar. He looked around satisfied at the effect he was having, spat on the ground, threw the mike at Vishal and strode off.

Pervez got off the bus one stop before the campus. She desperately needed to clear her head before locking herself between four walls. The muddy edge of the road was a poor substitute for Marine Drive. But it would have to suffice.

She walked briskly, the dark enveloping her in an eerie embrace. The station clock had said 9.35. She had not expected streets to be so deserted. Her fluttering dupatta and the clip-clop of her footsteps were the only signs of life.

She was not unnerved at being alone. Not even when approaching headlights picked out her solitary silhouette. The car sped past reversing her shadow at top speed. The approaching streetlights reversed it again at a slower pace.

She tried not to think as she walked, purging her head of all images and sound except the clip-clop of walking feet. Only when known thoughts are out can fresh ones enter the head. But thoughts in the vacuum seemed grey and dismal. Kalina had no sea breeze to blow them away.

In ten minutes she had reached Indrani colony. Naina's lights were off. She entered her own building and climbed to the second floor surprised by a slit of light under her door. Cautiously she turned the key to find her friend waiting.

"Vishal called. Told us what happened," said Naina. "Sidharth's gone to Dharavi. I used your spare key to let myself in."

"Thanks. But first I need a bath."

She went into the bathroom, opening the tap to fill the red bucket under it. Stripping, she heaped her sweaty-dusty clothes in a corner and began flinging mugsful of cold water over her head and shoulders. The first mug stung her skin but as she continued flinging mug after mug her body cooled. Only then did she sit on the tiny wooden stool and rub soap over her body and shampoo into her hair. As dirt washed away so did tension. Shutting off the tap over a half-full bucket she sprinkled in a handful of detergent whipping it into a foamy lather. Starting with underwear she soaked her clothes. Then she rubbed herself dry, slipped into a kaftan and opened the door with a towel turbaned around her head.

Naina had set the table for dinner. "I cooked the bhindi I found in your fridge. Also dal and chapattis," she said.

"Thanks. There's mango pickle somewhere."

They ate quietly, washed up and settled into their favourite positions—Pervez on the chesterfield, legs swinging over arm-rest, Naina sprawled across the sofa.

"You've had a nasty first exposure to slums," began Naina.

"The street theatre was fun. I wasn't prepared for the rest."

"Nor was anyone else. Koliwada is a Shiv Sena stronghold. Prabha should have anticipated trouble."

"I shouldn't have abandoned everyone and run away."

"Anyone would panic in your place."

"I was terrified. I've never heard such foul language, such viciousness. Will they really harm Munawar?"

"No one can say."

"But he's only a kid!"

"He should've told us he's involved with a Hindu girl. Damn foolish."

"We don't make choices in love, Naina. You know that. There's nothing wrong with him being in love with a Hindu girl. If anyone should object it's their families. Not some gunda who proclaims every Hindu girl is his sister! Can you imagine a bunch of Parsi boys stopping me from marrying Fred!"

"Parsis aren't militant."

"We must protect Munawar. The young couple should have a chance to make their lives together."

"What if their life ends up a mess? Like yours ..."

"My life isn't a mess. I had an eight-year marriage-partly good, partly bad. Even marriages that last are partly good, partly bad. Ending it hasn't been such a disaster. If I'd married Farhad I'd never have got out of it. Been bored to tears for ever and ever, amen."

They laughed. "Let's drink to your escape!" said Naina, cheerily.

"Let's," agreed Pervez, who'd begun to unwind. "I have something special."

"What's that?"

"Cointreau."

"Where on earth did you get Cointreau!"

"Darius got two bottles on his birthday and gave me one to 're-develop' my taste for the good life."

"Sidhu will consider it decadent... But what the hell! Let's have it anyway."

Pervez took out the square brown bottle from her cupboard where she'd hidden it behind a pile of clothes. She went to the kitchen in search of glasses but nothing seemed appropriate. She didn't even have wine glasses, leave aside tiny liqueur glasses. And tumblers seemed ridiculously large.

"Shall we have Cointreau in coffee mugs or glasses?" she called as Naina guffawed.

"I have a more absurd idea," she chortled. "Let's have it in the vatis we use for dal … Even Sidhu might approve—making Cointreau into a working-class drink!"

"That's sacrilege!"

"They're closer to the right size."

"I am NOT serving Cointreau …"

"Okay, okay. Let's have it in glasses then."

Pervez poured half a finger-span of the transparent liquid into two glasses and handed one to Naina. "Cheers!" she said settling back into the chesterfield. "Is Pawan back?" she asked, running her tongue along the run of the glass. "He was looking almost as terrified as me." Naina shook her head. "What's happening with Vandana?"

"That's a bad scene. I think he came to Dharavi to get away. Prabha tried to get her involved in the movement, get her to take adult literacy classes, teach beauty culture like waxing and make-up. She's not interested in anything but herself. She wouldn't have anything to do with Pawan if he didn't make a pin-up goddess of her. She wants money, fame, success. Pawan is her means for achieving these. But he comes from a conservative North Indian family …"

"For all his conservatism he doesn't mind sleeping with her," said Pervez sarcastically, taking another sip of Cointreau. "Tell me about the Shiv Sena."

"The Sena was born in the sixties under the leadership of Bal Thackeray, a cartoonist-cum-journalist who's an ardent admirer of Hitler—"

"Admirer of Hitler!"

"That's right. He doesn't believe in democracy but openly advocates dictatorship. Calls it 'benevolent dictatorship' meaning benevolent to himself, family and followers ... His party shot into the limelight attacking South Indians who they claimed were depriving local Maharashtrians of jobs. Now they've turned against Muslims. Ten years later they could turn against Christians, Parsis, Jews—whatever suits their convenience ... They're so parochial they even want to introduce a permit system for non-Maharashtrians working in Bombay to stop the influx of 'outsiders' into a city that's bursting at the seams."

"But you've got to admit that Bombay is overcrowded."

"Of course it is. But you can't make Indians feel like aliens in their own country. The way to stop people migrating to cities is to develop the interiors. If living conditions were better in villages why would people come to cities to live in slums?"

"That'll take years."

"Why do Indians go to the Middle East to work? Why do they migrate to the US, Canada, Australia, England? If locals are to be prioritised in Maharashtra, what's to stop those governments from doing the same?"

Pervez stared thoughtfully into her glass, sloshing the liquid around. Noticing a black fleck bobbing, she dipped in her little finger, dragged it to the rim and casually flicked it away.

"That militant guy was from the shakha. What's a shakha?" she asked.

"A shakha is the local centre. Shiv Sena has a network all over Maharashtra. Initially they claimed that eighty percent of them did social work but now they're primarily a political party. Several of their leaders have criminal records."

From what Pervez had seen of Manohar she had no reason to doubt Naina.

"Two wada sambhar, two puri bhaji, one masala dosa, one sada dosa, one aaloo chaat, three coffees and four teas," said Sidharth as Dhondu memorised the order.

"I'll have a dosa instead of puri bhaji," said Pervez.

"One puri bhaji, two masala dosas," instructed Sidharth.

"And I'll have coffee, not tea."

"Four coffees, three teas."

"Final?" enquired Dhondu.

"Final. Repeat the order."

"Two wada sambhar, one puri bhaji, two masala dosas, one sada dosa..."

"Aren't you also having sada dosa?" Prabha asked Pervez.

"Didn't I say so?"

"I thought you wanted masala dosa."

"I meant sada."

"Okay. So one masala and two sada dosas. Repeat the order, Dhondu."

Dhondu went through the ritual again. As the oldest waiter in the canteen he often had seven, ten, twelve students ordering food simultaneously, changing their minds, yet expecting him to deliver faultlessly which he did most of the time. Pervez marvelled at his memory. In six months she had only known him to goof up once.

The mood at their table was sombre. Sidharth had called Saeed, Munawar and Vishal to the campus and with each face gloomier than the next, their table was a contrast to the chattering students crowding others.

"We should have told you about Preeti earlier ..." began Saeed hesitantly.

"Do you think ... they'll harm Munawar?" asked Pervez anxiously.

"Who can tell? Those hotheads are capable of anything."

"But how can anyone get away with—"

"Stop being naïve, Pervez," Sidharth abruptly cut her off. "This is a world where might is right. People operate out of a system of checks and balances. We must let those goons know Munawar has support. Not just in Dharavi but also among middle-class people like us."

"Once it's known he's involved with a Hindu girl Muslims will turn against him," pointed out Prabha.

"Right. He'll be completely isolated."

Pervez stared out of the glass windows at the peaked Ashoka trees lining the path. Another tree sprouted yellow bell-shaped flowers around which bumble-bees buzzed. Students chatted on a stone bench underneath waiting for the bus to take them to Santa Cruz station. They seemed as aloof from Dharavi as Darius and his friends.

"How long have you known Preeti?" Sidharth asked Munawar.

"Three years … But her parents don't know," he said timidly.

"I thought as much. Do yours?"

He shook his head. "Only Saeed knows."

"Anyone else?"

"Her sister has stopped talking to her."

Dhondu arrived with an over-laden tray slapping down plate after plate at Sidharth's end of the table. Sidharth passed them around till everyone had what they'd ordered. Dhondu was going back for the tea and coffee when Prabha called, "Get me a Thums Up instead of tea." Dhondu returned with the Thums Up but an extra mug of tea sat at the centre of the table waiting for anyone who wanted a second.

"No one can predict what might happen," Sidharth told Munawar, irritating Pervez by lighting a Goldflake, inches away from her nose. "I can't see things improving till this mandir-masjid issue is settled."

"At some video parlours they are showing cassettes of Ayodhya. Also speeches by Sadhvi Rithambara, Uma Bharati," said Vishal. "The speeches really excite people …"

"Muslims are getting fed up," said Saeed. "In the train all I hear is people talking against us. That we are dirty, we have too many children, we love Pakistan more than India … As if there is nothing else to talk about."

"The majority of Hindus are not against Muslims," countered Sidharth. "Some people may have got carried away by Hindutva rhetoric but most of us haven't."

"There is also caste politics," said Vishal. "Upper castes don't like lower castes coming up. After Mandal agitation they are getting scared of OBCs."

"The Mandal agitation is about reserving seats in educational institutions for untouchables, right?" asked Pervez tentatively.

"We don't use the word 'untouchables' any more," corrected Sidharth. "'Dalit,' 'harijan' or 'SC/ST', meaning Scheduled Caste or Scheduled Tribe, are the politically correct terms."

"Why should they have special privileges? In this day and age everyone should be considered equal."

"Equality is a myth if you're a Dalit," retorted Sidharth.

"It's nearly fifty years since my community, Mahar, converted to Buddhism," Vishal informed Pervez without sounding condescending. "Before that our work was to skin dead animals, collect firewood and carry messages of death from one village to another for which we were not paid but given a tiny share of the harvest. Fifty years after Independence only two percent of our community has managed to qualify for professional jobs. Even that has been possible only because of reservations."

"When the Constitution was drafted some seats in educational institutions were reserved for Dalits," said Sidharth, looking disdainful at Pervez' ignorance as he exhaled smoke at her. "The Mandal agitation is about other backward castes demanding similar reservations."

"I've been reading about students immolating themselves when they have a better percentage than an untou … er, than a Dalit, yet can't get admission to medical colleges because seats are reserved," said Pervez, relieved at being able to respond to Sidharth. "If less competent students get into medical college, won't patients' lives be in the hands of third-rate doctors?"

"Reservation is only at the admission level. To qualify as a doctor you have to pass the same exam."

"I can't believe caste still matters in cities like Bombay!"

"Stop being in fantasy land Pervez! Reality is tough."

Pervez bit her lip and jabbed a spoon into her dosa resolving not to make further comments. But Vishal took Sidharth on. "Many people think like her, dada. They think that since we sit together on buses and trains, since we work in the same factory, eat in the same canteen, caste is not a problem in cities. But when we apply for a job, the minute you give your name they know that you're a mahar or chamar. So we never get the job of a cook in a hotel or with caterer. In hospitals we get the dirtiest jobs in the sanitation department or cold room—jobs no one wants. They have to give us some jobs so their records show they are employing Dalits."

"The private milk trade in Bombay is controlled by bhaiyas from UP," he continued. "That community has tentacles into the village. If a chamar tries to set up a milk booth his relatives will be harassed in the village. They may be beaten up, their houses burnt. So they plead with their city-based relatives to stay in line."

Pervez could no longer stomach the food in her plate. Till this moment "untouchable", "harijan", "Dalit" were only words. Polite words hiding the horror of lived experience. Speaking in his low voice Vishal had made that experience come alive for her.

"You Parsis with your fancy Marine Drive houses know nothing about the grassroots," sneered Sidharth. Turning to Munawar he added, "The only thing I can say is that you're not alone any more. You have my phone number. If there's a problem, just call me."

Pervez pushed back her chair and got up. "Today's treat is on me," she said, heading for the counter.

"Don't take trouble," said Vishal, reaching into his trouser pocket. "We always share bill."

But Sidharth stopped him. "Let her pay. She's got two-two houses. She doesn't work for a living. She can afford it."

Pervez walked away without a word.

6

Wonder whether the gull will grab a fish, she mused, watching a white seagull circling a patch below which a shoal must certainly be in disarray. The tide was out leaving crescent-shaped sandbars. Wave followed wave carrying away sand only to deposit fresh grains with its next attack. Sandbars kept changing shape.

A breeze tousled her short hair. Her checked shirt billowed behind her. A vendor deftly lobbing off chips to shape coconuts into pointed heads, stared at her exposed midriff. She remained oblivious of him.

The sea was letting her mind drift back to the familiar. The unchanging. Was anything unchanging? Sometimes the mysterious moods of the sea appeared monotonous for weeks despite waves imperceptibly changing the shape and combination of sandgrains. Nothing is permanent but change, Fred had said on her last day in Goa, gazing at her hair which she'd cut short just that morning. But Kalina had shaken so many notions that instinctively she realised she was heading for a seminal change. Like ripples widening from the epicentre of a dropped stone, change would cover larger and larger areas of her before merging into the horizon.

Behind her cars whizzed, tyres hissing against asphalt. Two lanes for cars chasing in opposite directions. Beyond the boulevard were the cricket fields bordered by community gymkhanas. Parsi gymkhana. Islam gymkhana. Hindu gymkhana. Catholic gymkhana. She remembered her father talking of pentangular matches when the gymkhanas of each community played cricket against the other in a spirit of camaraderie. Was that spirit under threat nearly fifty years after the British departed from Indian soil? How could it be re-kindled? Be made to percolate where it was needed?

After the Dharavi adventure she felt strangely protected as she sat in the cusp of the bay despite her back being exposed to traffic. South Bombay would always be more inured against violence than Dharavi or Kalina. That was the unwritten privilege of class.

De-class. Strange concept. Imbued with egalitarian idealism. But, as with most ideals, unrealistically Utopian. Was a classless society possible, however desirable it might be?

Could class be shed by simple living and high thinking? What about years of conditioning that made up the psyche? Was it possible to re-condition one's childhood to fit in with an alien class? What about education, the mental development that would always set one apart from those not exposed to the same privilege?

Yet belief in a classless society, combined with the conviction that a people's revolution would achieve it, had fuelled the passions of Sidharth, Prabha and others, kept them working selflessly for years. Their idealism certainly made the world better for the underprivileged.

However fired Pervez was by their enthusiasm she could not share their convictions. She had argued with Sidharth that waiting for the red revolution was like *Waiting for Godot* which she'd recently seen with Farhad and Anaita. They had bought tickets because it starred Naseeruddin Shah and had been surprised to find it had no storyline but featured two tramps amusing themselves with intelligent sparring waiting for someone who never shows up, something that never happens. Like the permanently imminent revolution.

The revolution was an idea that had charged generations around the world, Sidharth had argued. So had the idea of the kingdom of heaven promised by Christianity to those who followed its tenets, countered Pervez.

Sidharth was outraged by the comparison, calling religion the opiate of the masses whereas the revolution would liberate masses. "Throughout history the worst crimes against humanity have been committed in the name of religion," he had raged. "Better be a good atheist than a fake fundamentalist." Pervez kept quiet. She was not ready to challenge him.

Her musings were interrupted by distant singing. It was the third time she was encountering the Ram bhakt immersed in morning ragas, face suffused in spiritual ecstasy. He was in his early sixties, blanketing out the material world as he poured out his heart to an Unseen Being. As the voice approached she turned to see him walk with eyes raised to the sky without bumping into a person, pole or tree, without tripping into the potholed pavement. She admired his faith, knowing herself incapable of it. Instinctively she knew Sidharth would have an opposite perception of this man.

Her eye turned to a pigeon waddling on the parapet, not far from where she sat. He was half grey, half white, pecking into a grove at his feet. Peering closer, she spied a silver ring around the pigeon's foot and laughed aloud. Could he be a carrier pigeon at the dawn of the telecom age?

Stretching her legs she stood up sensing he'd fly off. But he fluttered into the air, only to settle a few yards away. Again he began pecking the ground but now she noticed he was pecking at his own foot, trying to get the ring off. Perhaps it was itching him. Perhaps it had grown too tight for him. Perhaps he didn't realise that it didn't trap him, that he could fly carrying it.

Being born into a privileged class was a bit like that, she reflected walking towards Sagar Mahal. It need not trap you into a narrow spectrum unless you let it.

"Pliss queue to left side only," boomed a voice over the microphone as Pervez and Darius became two grains of sand among the flotsam that thronged Chowpatty Beach. "Pliss queue to left side only," repeated the voice. "Right enclosure for VIP only. Peaceful march starting four o'clock. Pliss queue to left side only ..."

Chowpatty Beach wore its festive face. Barricades had been erected for a public meeting as ice cream and coconut vendors did brisk business replenishing the energies of peace marchers streaming sweat even before the march began. White kurta pyjamas, the ubiquitous uniform for politicians, rippled in the afternoon sun. A maroon and cream patch represented a bunch of girls from a public school, hair neatly tied in red ribbons. A navy blue patch indicated kids from municipal schools. Perspiration softened the stiff collars of gentlemen in Western suits standing beside chiffon-clad ladies with their indispensable strands of pearls. Here and there groups of factory workers, clerical staff, fisherfolk, domestic servants.

Darius had not been averse to joining the Governor's peace march. The Governor, an old-time Gandhian and convenor of the Sarva Dharma Maitri Pratishthan, was initiating measures to counter the slow process of communalisation creeping into society. A few months earlier he had organised an inter-religious prayer meeting at his residence and was following it up with a peace march in which citizens of all communities were to participate.

Sidharth had scoffed at the march, calling it an exercise in public relations. "It only makes the elite feel they're doing something useful when it's nothing more than band-aid on cancer," he said.

"At least the governor has a finger on the pulse," countered Pervez.

"So instead of controlling hardliners he's holding a march of people who wouldn't lift a stone anyway. How gratifying!" His sarcasm left Pervez uncomfortable.

Realising no one from Kalina would join the march she had approached Darius.

Initially he was circumspect. "I agree with your Kalina friends that the people on the march are unlikely to become violent, but that doesn't mean the upper classes are immune to the communal virus," he said. Then he went on to tell her about two Muslim draughtsmen in his office who were increasingly being isolated. "At lunch time no one talks to them. And when Bhatia's daughter got married they were the only two not invited."

"How would a peace march help?"

"It lets people know that leaders of every community, of every profession, believe in religious tolerance. Read the list of participants," he said, pointing to the news report she had handed him. "J.R.D. Tata, Rajmohan Gandhi, Sunil Dutt, Justice Bakhtawar Lentin, Usha Mehta, Rafiq Zakaria. Also religious heads like the Shankaracharya, Swami Agnivesh, Cardinal Pimenta, Maulana Wajiduddin Khan, Jain munis, even our Parsi Dastur Jamaspasa. It would be an honour to walk shoulder to shoulder with someone like J.R.D. Tata."

Farhad had pooh-poohed the march refusing to forfeit his weekend siesta for what he called a "merry-go-round". "All people vying to see and be seen upholding the 'right cause' but if things come to the crunch they'll be the first to run with the hares and hunt with the hounds," he mocked.

At 3.45 p.m. the governor drove up in a white limousine. Policemen waved batons to part the crowd as he made his way to the podium where dignitaries sat under a shamiana protecting them from the October sun. Darius was peering into the enclosure when Vasant Chawla tapped him on the shoulder.

"Good you have come for peace march," he began thumping Darius like an approving schoolmaster. "But where is beautiful wife?"

"She had an appointment with a foreign client," replied Darius, wincing.

"Good you brought sister. Young people must take interest in nation ... Have you seen Chandrakant Desai?" Darius shook his head. There was a pause as Chawla craned over the sea of heads but he was unable to spot his friend. "I have looked at your design again," he said to Darius. "Good they are. Just one-two small alterations. Can you come to office on Monday?"

Pervez sensed the groan in Darius' throat. "I'm afraid I'm tied up Monday and Tuesday," she heard her brother saying. "Can we make it Wednesday?"

The mike crackled. The governor spoke words of encouragement, urging people to march over the charted course and congregate at August Kranti Maidan to take a pledge for communal harmony. Red-robed Buddhist lamas took up position at the front, their necks straddled with huge drums. A slow boom-boom-boom sounded and the procession snaked forward. It was to be a silent march. No slogans. No songs.

A group of serious-faced, simply dressed men and women marched behind a banner announcing Gandhi Smarak Nidhi. Pervez examined them, recalling her father's admiration for Gandhian nonviolence. These people appeared too gentle to counter the Manohars of the world, she thought. Yet they had dedicated their lives to toiling with peasants and harijans. Could they rise to the new challenge of today?

Pervez was impressed by the never-ending waves of people flooding the street. Factory workers, middle-class citizens, the upper crust, class boundaries dissolved for a day. She wished Sidharth was there to experience it. Seeing her brother marching alongside a man who might well be a chanawala or a chaprasi she felt convinced that the battle against communal hatred transcended class. And demanded coordination between classes. What role could she play in that process?

She had set her alarm for six but woke to the chimes of Big Ben earlier. She showered and dressed quickly. Ever since moving to Kalina she had spent weekends at Sagar Mahal. Often she joined Farhad and Anaita at the theatre, cinema or for coffee at Sea Lounge but today they had invited her to go sailing to Mandwa where Anaita's family had a weekend shack.

She slipped into the denim shorts she had not worn since Goa. Frayed edges indicated they were remnants of jeans. But it was fashionable for shorts to end in a fringe of raw ends and she had spent much of the previous night making the edges even and neat. She liked the idea of wearing Goa shorts for going out to sea.

A tingle ran down her spine as she saw Farhad's eyes run appreciatively over her legs. Anaita unlocked the back of the car. "Save your colourful Kalina stories till we're in the boat," she laughed as Pervez got in.

Pervez settled into the back seat. "Where's Kareena?" she asked, disappointed at not seeing their six-year-old.

"She has ballet class. Then she's seeing a film with her friends," replied Anaita.

"We have to leave early because the wind drops by ten," said Farhad. "A couple of times we've got stuck in the harbour for hours. Do you enjoy sailing, Pervez?"

"I've never been sailing."

"All those years in Goa and you've never sailed!"

"Sailing is for tourists. Locals rarely do what tourists do."

"Surely that blighter could have given you a good time once in a while."

"I'm sure he did, Farhad!" admonished his wife. "That's no way to talk about Pervez' husband."

"Ex-husband."

"Anyway I've never been sailing so I'm looking forward to it."

"I hope it doesn't make you queasy. We're carrying ham sandwiches and chips."

"And lots of beer. If you're sick on the boat you can have it at Mandwa."

They parked the car at the Yacht Club and walked to the pier at the Gateway of India. Pigeons from the minarets swarmed to the pavement where a sleepy-eyed child with sun-bleached hair was struggling to fold bedraggled bedding into a bundle. An orange glow reflected off the glass panes of the Taj Mahal Hotel but the sun was not yet visible.

The picnickers walked down the sloping stone jetty, two crows swooping over their heads. A *tindel* was waiting with a rowing boat. Pervez walked gingerly, carrying the food. Farhad carried a mini ice-box with Kingfisher snuggled against ice. Waves licked stone leaving it slippery. The row-boat rocked as each got in. The *tindel* held it steady. Casting off, he rowed energetically till they drew alongside a navy blue boat, *Dabchick*.

Soon they were clambering on, undoing ropes, dropping the rudder into water, fixing the wooden tiller, fastening sail to mast and setting out to meet the rising sun.

"This is beautiful!" exclaimed Pervez taking the full force of the wind on her face. "Can I move up front and dip my feet into water?"

"Only if you can swim ..."

"Don't worry."

Leaving her shoes at the bottom of the boat Pervez climbed onto the seat holding the rope over her head. Raising her foot onto the navy-blue ledge she felt fine spray wetting her toes. Holding the rope tighter she raised her second foot and moved forward to perch on the bobbing bow. Settling at the edge she lowered her feet, kicking them up and down. Froth splashed her cheeks.

Dabchick cut foaming curls on a fluted glass plane, the wake behind them expanding in an ever-widening V. They passed the carcass of a rotting steel mammoth, rust corroding its innards as it squatted sullenly on water. Gliding past the deserted lighthouse was a graceful dhow, tall masts and curved hull resembling a Viking ship as it ferried vegetables and dates between the Middle East and India.

"The water is filthy," she called as a garland of wilting flowers stuck on her foot.

"It'll clean up once we're out of the harbour," replied Farhad one hand on the rudder, the other holding a rope from the sail.

Reluctantly, Pervez pulled her feet away and moved into the belly of the boat. Anaita had put on sunglasses and was lying with her face to the sky. "That gull just swallowed a fish," she said and Pervez noticed two gulls overhead, orange feet tucked into horizontal parallels.

"Great way of spending a day," sighed Pervez, biting into a sandwich. "Just what I needed after Dharavi."

"Dharavi!" sputtered Farhad and Anaita in unision.

"Last Thursday I went to Dharavi."

"What on earth made you go to Dharavi?"

For two days she had debated whether or not to share her Dharavi experiences with her friends. She needed a sounding board to voice confusions and doubts but she knew they'd disapprove. Finally she'd tossed a coin. Heads she'd tell, tails she wouldn't. When the coin fell to the Ashoka emblem she decided to chisel out an edited version.

"I went with our women's group which was performing a street play."

"Like those monkeywalas at Gateway of India?"

"Not quite," said Pervez. "Street plays communicate political ideas to the illiterate. You should have seen the response. People climbing trees, roofs … kids sitting attentive though the message went over their heads …"

"You shouldn't be going to places like Dharavi. They're full of hoodlums," reprimanded Farhad. "Didn't you get put off by the filth?"

"There is filth, but not where we performed."

"Does Darius know you went to Dharavi?"

"Darius is my brother, not my keeper."

"It's one thing to leave home and go off 'in search of yourself'—whatever that means. It's quite another to get yourself mixed up with dubious characters."

"Which dubious characters?"

"Whoever is making you do things no girl from a decent family would do."

"No one is pushing me. I went because I'd never seen a street play. Nor had I been into a slum. So I was curious."

"Curious? About a slum? You see them all over the place. Walk down any road and they're there. Take a train any morning and you can't miss slumdwellers defecating on the tracks. Drive in from the airport and there they are—kids running across the highway as if drivers have nothing better to do but save their lives. What did you see in Dharavi that you haven't seen before?"

Pervez waited till his storm passed before she answered. "You don't see people as human beings when you whiz past in a car or tram," she said, carefully choosing her words. "A slum is something you pass cursing its nuisance value. Only when you go there do you feel the presence of so many faces. So many people with thoughts, feelings, hopes. And few means to actualise them. I'd never thought about Dharavi till I went there, Farhad. Then the people came alive. Because our eyes met, we shared smiles. Tiny gestures speaking a language without words. It's been as important as going off to Goa."

"I don't understand you, Pervez. You suffered in Goa. Your marriage was rotten. You left at the first opportunity. Yet you call it important?"

"If I hadn't done it I'd never have gained my independence. I feel life is just beginning. And I'm hungry for experience."

"You seem to enjoy taking hard decisions regardless of consequences. But why should life be tough? It's short enough. Why not enjoy it?"

"I have to find where I belong."

"Why? Only because you married that low-class blighter?" A tinge of bitterness crept into Farhad's voice.

"Not 'because' I married him but to find out how that experience has shaken me out of taking things for granted."

Silence hung between them refusing to blow away in the breeze. Anaita had fallen asleep. As so many times before Pervez became acutely aware of Farhad's physical presence. His light-brown eyes examining her. The hairy torso erupting from an unbuttoned shirt. The bare legs forming an inverted V at the crotch ... It was such a long time since ...

"The water seems cleaner. I'm dipping my feet in again," she said standing up impulsively to hit her head against the boom. "Ouch!"

"All part of the experience of sailing," laughed Farhad.

She stuck out her tongue at him, put her thumb on her nose and waggled five fingers in a playful gesture. Turning her back she lowered her feet into the water, dragging them over curling foam, as the sun gleamed off the pink flesh of her wet thighs. The city had receded into indistinguishable silhouettes. No gulls followed their boat. And ships were far between.

She sat with her feet trailing the water all the way to Mandwa, closing her eyes, savouring the steady sound of lapping water, the sensation of wind over arms, cheeks, hair, the taste of salt on lips.

This is as close to being a seagull as I'll ever get, she mused, visualising herself skimming through the air, diving down, grabbing fish invisible to human eyes and soaring skyward again. Wonder what the view from the sky is like, she mused, seeing boat-specks on water as her mind's eye carried her into flaky clouds. Ships became miniscule, with the sailboat just a white dot. Closing eyes she hunched shoulders to slice the air like a gull, fluffy clouds caressing her skin. The rope-holding hand alone tethered her to earth. Her spirit was far away.

"Good thing I have an appointment at the beauty parlour tomorrow," Anaita was saying, rolling her long auburn hair into a top knot. "Salt air plays havoc with the hair."

"Luckily my hair is short. I go to the parlour only for a monthly trim. Even that raises eyebrows at Kalina. When Naina had her hair done for her parents' anniversary she washed it off before returning to Kalina. Sidharth would have turned blue if she'd arrived with some fancy hair-do."

"Just for going to the beauty parlour!" exclaimed Anaita. "Pervez, it's time you found a new set of friends."

"This Sidharth seems terribly dogmatic," commented Farhad. "Didn't let that poor singer make cassettes! Doesn't let Naina go to the beauty parlour! Who does he think he is?"

"That's a man-woman thing between them, Farhad. I've told you they have this unusual relationship."

"All these bunkum socialist ideas standing in the way of progress. If it weren't for Sidharth your singer friend might have been a star."

"Sidhu wants justice for all. Not just his friends."

"Is that possible? Has it ever happened in history? Socialists talk about dividing the cake equally between capitalists and workers but I say make a bigger cake so there's more to go round. So what if some have more and others less. In a free-market economy even those who have less will get more than they did under socialism. Look at America. Even factory workers drive to work in their own cars."

They were sitting on the patio of the tiny two-room shack overlooking the sea. Tall coconut palms shaded fruit trees laden with cheekoo, banana and lime. The pride of the garden was a multi-coloured champa to the left of the patio. Anaita had planted two saplings—one with white flowers, the other with red—in the same pit, intertwining branches till both trees grew tall. Five years later the champa looked like a single tree sprouting red and white blossoms in clumps.

"Pervez, there's a really nice guy working in our factory," began Anita cautiously. "He's Farhad's right-hand man. His name is Percy and he wants to settle down. Would you like to meet him?"

"I don't want to settle down."

"You're too young to get embittered by one bad experience, Pervez. This is the right time to find a life partner."

"Marriage isn't on my agenda!"

"Pervez and Percy sound such a sweet pair ..."

Pervez burst into laughter. "As good a reason for getting together as any, but sorry to disappoint you!"

The cat was an aberration on the promenade. Pigeons, seagulls, dogs belonged and sometimes she'd see rats nosing at debris dumped by the sea. But a cat?

Pervez observed the grey-striped creature whose colour merged with the rocks. Back arched, tail tip waving, it glared down a crack between rocks just below where she sat. Had a crab stung it, she wondered. Or was it trying to grab fish? As a wave swept up to wet its nose the furry feline leapt way. Backing off it jumped to the tallest rock. With the returning tide it would claw its way up the parapet and home—wherever that was.

A light tap on her shoulder startled her. She swung around to a smiling face. "Vishal! What are you doing at Marine Drive early in the morning!" she exclaimed.

"Some days I come to sea and sun to write," he replied.

"Write what?"

"Kavita. Songs."

"You write poetry?" asked Pervez. Naina had introduced Vishal as a poet but it hadn't quite registered.

Vishal nodded, sitting on the parapet beside her. "Dalit poetry is angry, painful, sometimes even violent."

"What do you write about?" she asked.

"Life," he replied with a shrug. "In the city, in village, everywhere the same problem. Some people treat others like kuchra. Some people work and work but their stomachs remain empty and their eyes full of tears."

Pervez said nothing. She just watched water swell to a crest before breaking into swirls of frothing foam. After a long pause, during which Vishal seemed to have retreated into himself, she asked, "Does writing make you feel better?"

He shrugged. "Writing is writing. And life is life. Only revolution can make life better."

"You sound like Sidharth."

"But isn't it true? Only when people who laugh too much learn to cry also, will life become better." He said it matter of factly, without bitterness.

"Rich people also cry, Vishal," she chided as a shadow crossed his face.

The man with the Alsatian strolled past looking at them quizzically. Pervez realised she cut an odd figure chatting familiarly with Vishal. Momentarily self-conscious she shifted position looking up to find him abstractedly poking at the cement parapet with a small stick. "I also write poetry," she blurted out without planning to. No one knows but I have four booksful."

He scanned her face with new interest. "What do you write about?"

She hesitated. She had not even mentioned her poems to Naina. Should she discuss them with someone as different as Vishal? But he had opened the topic and now there was no escape.

"Also of pain," she began tentatively. "Another kind of pain, you know. When someone you love lets you down again and again ..." her voice trailed off. She looked away, towards rocks where seagulls stood lost in contemplation, oblivious of waves washing webbed feet.

"That kind of pain is like dying," nodded Vishal understandingly. "If pain makes you angry you can fight things. But to cry for pain is sad."

"I finished my crying before I came to Bombay, Vishal," said Pervez, touched by his response.

An unusual current flowed through them as if the universality of sea and sun neutralised distances. They sat with the horizon behind, the boulevard in front, indifferent to pedestrians or speeding cars. Each lost in themselves, yet connected. "Are you writing in Bombay?" asked Vishal, as breeze carried sounds of the cat's moaning towards them.

"Hardly."

"Keep writing," he advised. "Writing is important. Now sing me your poem."

"I'm not you! I can't sing!" exclaimed Pervez.

"Alright. Speak it then."

She became self-conscious. Pouring pain on paper was one thing, reciting it another. "I ... I can't remember any," she said, spotting the cat silhouetted against a flapping newspaper.

"Try to remember," urged Vishal gently. "Have you written about the sea?"

She nodded.

"The sky?"

She nodded again.

"So tell me a poem about the sky."

She remained silent.

"Look at the sky and think of your poem," persisted Vishal.

Obediently she turned her face skyward where a cloud reflected pink from the rising sun. "I don't know if this is a poem," she said hesitantly. "It's just a thought that came into my head so I wrote it down."

"Say it."

She shut her eyes for a minute, then gave voice to words. "'When the sky dives into a coffin, what colour does the void take?'"

It sounded mawkish to her ears but Vishal's eyebrows rose approvingly. "'Sky diving into coffin' is like Kharat's poem. You know Prakash Kharat?"

She shook her head.

"Famous Dalit poet. Wrote one poem about sky wrapped in white shroud. You also think of cloud as shroud?"

"Not really, but it's an interesting comparison," said Pervez relaxing. "Now let's hear one of your poems," she said.

"In Marathi?"

"Oh ..." she groaned. "Wish I could understand Marathi. Can't you translate?"

"My English is not so good."

"Please try."

"I will say it in Marathi, then give you the meaning in English."

His recitation was theatrical, the language guttural, provocative. Though Pervez didn't follow the words she sensed the passion. Curious eyes observed them as he gesticulated dramatically but she didn't care. As he came to the end she sheepishly said, "I feel it is good but I don't know why."

He smiled. "It is about spitting at the sun which is so far away that the spit only flies back on your face."

"Helpless anger?" Hearing the Alsatian bark furiously, she saw the cat streak across the road barely escaping speeding wheels.

"Dalit anger isn't helpless any more. First Ambedkar, then Panthers, now Bahujan. The Dalit Panther Party was started by poet-writer Namdeo Dhasal. Named after the Black Panther movement by black people in America."

Pervez groaned inwardly. She wanted the encounter to continue but not to switch from poetry to politics early in the morning. Stretching her back she stood up watching seagulls bobbing in clusters like fragmented islands. "Do you come to Marine Drive often?" she asked, slapping dust off her backside.

"On some holidays."

"Phone me at Kalina when you're coming," she said, walking towards Sagar Mahal. "I'd invite you up for tea but my brother's house is being painted."

His eyes told her he knew she was lying but somehow understood.

7

Munawar started frequenting the campus. Under instruction from Sidharth, he volunteered at the Social Service Centre where students worked in slums, attaching himself to a balwadi at Dharavi. As Dharavi residents saw him teaching slum children alongside university students he assumed stature in their eyes. Sidharth's design of developing him into a leader began taking shape.

Pervez had registered for a master's degree in psychology. Late one afternoon she bumped into Munawar near the hexagonal lecture-room complex shaded by towering rain trees and invited him over for tea. Then remembering she had to pick up milk and other provisions she took him along to the market.

She enjoyed the short walk from Indrani colony, past the cluster of timber merchants with wood spilling onto the road and the rambling old bungalows of Sundar Nagari into the market road lined with confectioners, laundries, stationery and crockery shops, with vendors displaying colourful fruits and vegetables on handcarts along the road.

The municipal market was a large shed with a divider of stalls running through the centre. At the entrance women sold fish—pomfret, shrimp, bhangda, rawas, hilsa, shingara and crabs. Beyond the fisherwomen sat chicken and mutton vendors while at the far end were counters for inexpensive pork and beef favoured by the predominantly Catholic population of Kalina.

Turning the bend at the end of the shed you encountered grain and spice merchants, dry red chillies, garlic, coriander and cumin seeds spilling out of sacks on one side, while the other was piled with white—rice, salt, sugar—and a variety of yellow and red dais. Hanging on hooks from the roof were bunches of bananas—yellow, red and green. More species than she'd ever seen under one roof.

On days when Munawar accompanied her they'd stop for fresh sugarcane juice at Anand juice stall. Sitting on a long, rickety bench they'd watch a twelve-year-old boy shove sugarcane stalks between rollers, pull them out on the opposite side, fold them in two and squeeze them through the rollers again and again till they were grass dry. A bowl below the rollers collected juice. Munawar would urge the vendor to add a piece of ginger between cane stalks so their juice had a tangy edge. Two large glasses cost Pervez just one rupee.

Back at the apartment she'd rustle up a sandwich, omelette or sometimes serve sponge cake picked up in the market. Gradually she learnt that Munawar's family came from a village near Allahabad, that his grandfather had migrated to Bombay more than fifty years ago, that he had started life handcrafting shoes for the affluent residents of Malabar Hill and Colaba. Munawar's father had studied till eighth standard. Saeed was the first to go to college.

"How did you meet Preeti?" asked Pervez on his fourth visit to her home.

"For long time I look without talking," he replied, fingering a shell that curled into itself like a cunt, running his thumb over its lipped edge. "We would take same bus to school. My school two stops after hers. She was always with girls. Sometimes I touch her when bus crowded, sometimes I find seat near her. I not speak her. Then I came to ten standard. Soon school would finish and bus rides end. I have to do something ..."

"When SSC results came I bought Cadbury chocolate. I force myself in bus next to her, told her I pass exam and gave chocolate. Her smile took my heart to sky ... whole day I was singing like mad clown ... Everyone thought I was happy with result. Only I knew it was for Preeti ..."

He paused, looking pleased as punch as he took out the comb he normally carried in his hip pocket, twanged a finger through its teeth before running it through his hair. "After few days I gave her note to meet me for fillum at Capitol cinema far from Dharavi. I buy two tickets for balcony but I don't know if she coming. When I see her I want to sing in cinema ..."

"That was one-two years ago," he continued, picking up a brown and white shell from which arms fanned out like antlers, rubbing their pointed tips on the back of his palm. "We not talk in Dharavi. On road I don't know her.

In one-two months we meet for fillum. Nobody knows. Sala Manohar found out because he was in theatre. Gave dhamki then and there. Want to take Preeti with him. She was so frighten. Start crying. I never seen crying. I had pen-knife in pocket. I took out, they ran holding tails between legs. Afterward I have to tell Saeed ..."

"Do you realise how dangerous a Hindu-Muslim love affair is these days?" asked Pervez, touched by the apparent innocence of the romance.

Munawar nodded. "We decide if we can't live together we will take Tik-20 and die together."

"Don't do anything stupid, Munawar!" cried Pervez, alarmed. "Problems are part of life. Look at me. I married a Christian, ran away from my family ... still things didn't work out. I didn't go kill myself. I picked up the threads of my life and moved on."

"It's alright for people with money. If you can't do this, can do that. Like going to market. One day buy fish, one day chicken. Without money only can buy vegetable."

"Money has nothing to do with your problem, Munawar ..."

"It is everything. If we lived in a twenty-floor building they wouldn't say they kill us. If we had money we could buy house in Kerala ..."

If they'd been sitting anywhere except in her flat he might have spat on the floor. But his frustration was apparent in the abrupt way he banged the shell on the windowsill, chipping two of its seven tips. As he lit a bidi from his upper shirt pocket a cheap stench filled the room. Pervez felt a rough tickling in her throat. She got up indicating the visit was over. But she invited Munawar to join her for lunch the following Thursday.

"The first person we met in Ayodhya was Balram Chandra Vohra who told us he was forced to sign a document handing over his land as daan to the Ram mandir complex," said Sidharth, pressing five fingertips together as he sat on the cane armchair Pervez had given Naina on her thirtieth birthday.

"We also met Chhaganlal Sinha who's been promised a shop in the new complex in exchange for his land and Yeshwantrao Patwari who's received compensation of eleven thousand rupees," he continued. "But none of them are happy. Patwari is so upset about losing his ancestral property that he wants to leave Ayodhya. The thought of his kutiya being razed before his eyes is too terrible to bear."

He had just returned from Ayodhya, where he had gone to make an on-the-spot evaluation of the mandir-masjid controversy following rumours about local residents being bullied out of their homes by temple enthusiasts. Just weeks earlier the Allahabad High Court had permitted the state government to start acquiring land for the proposed temple.

"Ironically, bhoomi-pujan for the Ram mandir started after demolishing two small Hindu shrines including a Hanuman temple," continued Sidharth. "Many Hindus are upset, pointing out that Hanuman was Ram's most trusted devotee, that Ram would disapprove of a Hanuman temple being razed to make space for his own.

They want a grand Ram temple at Ayodhya but not at the expense of destroying older ones."

"They don't want temples touched but have no compunctions about destroying a four-hundred-year-old mosque!" commented Pervez, better informed on current affairs after almost a year at Kalina. Ever since the cane armchair came into the flat, the outer room—she still refused to call it the drawing room—had replaced the inner as the focus of activity, with Sidharth predictably perched on it. Naina only used it when he was out.

"What's Ayodhya like as a city?" Naina wanted to know.

"Holy, man ... Real holy!" said Pawan, rolling his eyes heavenward. He had accompanied Sidharth as photographer and sat subdued on a durrie between Naina and Prabha. "Temples here, dargahs there ... Mosques here, ashrams there ... So holy that any direction you pee you're bound to hit something holy!"

As everyone laughed Naina put an affectionate arm around Pawan. "Your humour will get you into trouble one of these days," she said, gently chafing his arm.

"We also met the eighty-four-year-old Imam who'd been conducting namaaz at Babri Masjid till the gates were sealed in 1949," said Sidharth, resuming his narrative. "He told us Babri Masjid had been in the exclusive posession of Muslims since it was constructed in 1528, and that Muslims have documentary evidence including records of court cases favouring Muslims from 1885 onwards. He also told us that he himself had conducted namaaz on the evening of 22 December 1949—to be woken by a sweeper telling him that some idols had mysteriously appeared inside next morning."

"After that we went to a shastriji who admitted placing the Ram Lalla idol in the mosque. His reason? A dream in which a boy of four or five kept urging him to do that. Several people in Ayodhya reported having identical dreams that night, which they took as a sign of Lord Ram indicating his birthplace."

"Tell them about the fake priest," guffawed Pawan.

"Laldas is not a fake!"

"Ever heard of a commie pundit?" said Pawan, turning to Naina. "One who refuses to perform rituals? That's Laldas."

"Laldas is with CPI but he's also head priest of the Ram temple," said Sidharth, visibly irritated by Pawan. "To him Ram rajya, where Ram's subjects live in peace and prosperity, is the same as a classless society. He calls VHP leaders opportunists who only perform pujas before cameras and says they are creating insecurity among Hindus only to fill the BJP vote bank. Don't forget, after they raked up the Ramjanmabhoomi issue, BJP's strength has gone up from two to eighty-five seats in the last election."

It irritated Pervez that ever since she'd given Naina the armchair Sidharth always occupied it while everyone sat on the mattress and durries looking up at him. She had wanted to introduce a touch of comfort into Naina's environment but had not anticipated him appropriating it without a murmur from Naina.

"Did you uncover any clues about Babri Masjid being built at Ram's birthplace?" she asked.

"We were told there are ten thousand temples in Ayodhya, many of them dedicated to Lord Ram. At least fifty percent are old," said Sidharth. "But the Ram cult gained popularity only in the sixteenth century after Tulsidas wrote *Ram Charita Manas* in Ayodhya around the same time that Babri Masjid was built. Later, Ram temples were built there. As Pawan said, the whole city is sacred."

"Even a non-believer like me senses something in the atmosphere. Advani and his cohorts could build a Ram temple anywhere in Ayodhya but their aim is not devotional. It is to establish Hindu dominion over Muslims. That's their reason for insisting 'Mandir wahim banayenge'."

He fell silent taking long drags on a cigarette while drumming fingertips against rounded cane. Pervez swallowed her irritation at the wafting smoke, noticing that the money-plant was no longer looped around a nail but had been neatly attached with roots gripping the wall and that it had been joined by a cactus in a smaller pot. Naina's fingers abstractedly traced the weave of the durrie she sat on.

"The people in the villages were wonderful, man," said Pawan. "Both Hindus and Muslims told us they've been celebrating each others' festivals, attending each others' weddings, helping each other through sickness and death ... They're determined not to let outsiders disrupt their lives."

"That's the real India," said Prabha quietly. "Simple but wise."

"On that note I think we need some tea," said Sidharth, and Naina obediently went into the kitchen ... Like a traditional wife, thought Pervez irritably, observing that being submissive to Sidharth came naturally to Naina. She would have liked to ask about the river, fields and trees around Ayodhya but knew that would risk a scornful remark. Abruptly she got up and went to the window switching off the drone of voices within.

Sucking fresh air into her lungs she eased her mind onto a dragon-shaped cloud. As it moved closer its contours changed, and in a few minutes the dragon had metamorphosed into a deer, antlers looming long till they metamorphosed again into rabbits' ears. If only the Babri Masjid controversy would, like the cloud, give up its malevolent shape ...

"You want pink colour or orange?"

"Do you have something brownish?"

"I am too brown for brown. I have red. Maroon red."

"Definitely not red. I'm too white for red."

Pervez and Vandana laughed into each other's eyes as they sat in front of Vandana's dressing table, surveying her range of nail polishes. She had got into the habit of dropping in on Vandana and applying nail polish before returning to Sagar Mahal for the weekend. Vandana never seemed to mind.

She ran a finger over the blunted tops of nail polish bottles, tilting one after another, to examine the colours. She picked out a pale-pink polish.

"I have frosted in same colour. You like frosted?"

"Can I see it?"

Vandana went over the tray, selected one and handed it to Pervez. "Try on one-one finger, then decide," she said.

Pervez decided on the frosted pink and stretched out her right hand to Vandana who placed it against her knee and began applying nail polish, rubbing a finger along the edge when it smudged. As she came to the index finger she paused and looked into Pervez' face. "I have something to tell. Promise you won't tell Pawan?"

"What's up?"

"I have another offer."

"For modelling?"

"No. Acting. Lots of money in acting."

"You really want to act in silly Hindi films?" Running around trees, singing like a jackass?"

"Always I wanted to be actress. You didn't know? At one party—with Pawan only—I met Mukesh. He is agent for many filmwalas. Pawan was talking about Ayodhya and Mukesh was talking to me. He can fix me up with big-big directors. But first I must learn dancing. He has given me address of dancing class ..."

"These agents are sharks, Vandy."

"What is wrong in joining dancing class?"

"Nothing. But be careful. Why don't you want to tell Pawan?"

"He will not let me do. And he will tell Sidharth, and Naina and Prabha and all will give combined lecture."

"They mean well, Vandana."

"They don't like what I do. And I don't like what they do."

"You don't respect their work?"

"Why go to dirty-filthy place like Dharavi? What for to do? They talk one thing, do another. Talk of freedom but do they give me freedom? Freedom is only to do what they want. I can't keep them happy all the time."

"Not even Pawan?"

The fine-edged brush slipped off Pervez' nail as Vandana looked up sharply. Polish smudged onto the blue cotton skirt covering her knee. Unsuccessfully she rubbed the blob with a small wad of cotton but the stain remained.

"Don't you want to keep Pawan happy?" repeated Pervez slowly.

Vandana took a fresh dip into the polish bottle and applied it on three nails before replying. "Two bulls make bullock cart run," she said at last. "If one wants to go north and the other south, can bullock cart run? The stronger will pull the other for some time but both will be tired and unhappy. Better to leave cart, no?"

"Are you thinking of leaving Pawan?"

"I do not like this life."

"But he takes you to so many parties ..."

"Where I meet people. Beautiful people. Wearing nice clothes and all. But coming home Pawan says, 'This is all sham, Sidharth would call waste of money.' Sidharth this, Sidharth that ... So all fun spoilt. Sometimes I hate Sidharth. Why he is so anti-fun? Why Pawan becoming like him?"

"You're seriously thinking of splitting up?"

Vandana shrugged. "If it is necessary ..."

The sparrow's weight made the gulmohur twig bob up and down but the bird held on, chirruping to the swinging rhythm. Before the swaying stopped it hopped onto another twig making both twigs bounce simultaneously. Between running an iron over a dupatta and folding clothes, Pervez watched flame-flowered boughs become enlivened by the bird. She was happy that her apartment overlooked the only gulmohur tree at Indrani colony.

To her left was a neat pile of folded clothes and to her right another waiting for the iron. She squatted on a stool between them, ironing on the mattress of her bed. Each Monday she ironed clothes for the week, folding them into predictable creases before stacking them in the cupboard that had no hanging space. In Goa she had learnt that ironing once a week cuts costs on electricity. That lesson came handy at Kalina.

She looked up to find the gulmohur branches still. The sparrow had flown away. Barely a few sprays of leaves remained on the blossom-laden tree that defied drying up in summer with joyful abandon. For a full month her room would be infused by red light. But green would return as monsoon set in and flowers fell to be crushed by passing feet.

Time to rush, she thought, glancing at her wrist watch. Putting the tall pile into the cupboard, she selected a maroon salwaar kameez. She had ironed two dupattas for Naina, planning to drop them off on her way to the library. But when Saeed opened the door with a grim face she was alarmed. He would not have come so early unless something was wrong.

Sidharth and Naina's doleful expressions confirmed her fear. Ash grew along the length of Sidharth's cigarette like a hibernating caterpillar as he gazed at the ceiling lost in thought. Naina poked at earth around the cactus with a small stick.

"A temple has suddenly sprouted outside Saeed's house," said Naina morosely.

"How can a temple sprout overnight?"

"Not a real temple, didi," replied Saeed. "A Ram idol has been placed at the side of the road and a bell hung over it. No one is allowed to touch them. Soon devotees will bring offerings ..." his voice trailed off as Pervez tried to digest the import of this strange development.

"Haven't they broken some law by doing this? Don't they need BMC permission or something?" asked Naina.

"They've done it. With or without permission. Our question is how to undo what they've done without causing trouble."

"Nahin ho sakta, dada. If any Muslim touches those idols there'll be a riot. Shiv Sena boys are watching every minute."

"Do you think they deliberately ..."

"No, Pervez! They were sleepwalking carrying the idols in their arms and accidently forgot them outside Saeed's house, which incidentally is also Munawar's house, remember?" Sidharth's sarcasm cut to the core. She felt as tiny as an ant wishing she had no voice so she couldn't say anything foolish.

"Did anyone ask why idols were suddenly brought into a Muslim locality?" Sidharth asked Saeed.

"Who to ask?"

"It's a bait, Saeed. They're provoking Munawar into a fight. You must restrain him."

"I'm trying dada. But my brother has a hot head. Other Muslims are also getting angry. Saying if idols can come in Socialnagar we can make dargah at Koliwada."

"Let's go," said Sidharth, abruptly getting up and reaching for the jhola hanging from a hook on the wall.

"Where are you going?" asked Naina, alarmed.

"Dharavi."

"What're you going to do in Dharavi?"

"Muslims can't shift the idols. That's clear. Let's see if a Hindu can."

"Be careful ..." called Naina after his retreating back.

"Can I have bath?"

Pervez was taken aback. She had never had such a request from a visitor. And hated the thought of Munawar messing around her bathroom.

"The water has gone. It won't come till six o'clock," she replied shortly.

"You have two buckets. I use one. You can fill when water comes."

The boy is getting brazen, she thought but couldn't think up an excuse. Making her displeasure obvious she went into the kitchen. Ever since the Thursday lunches became regular Munawar was getting over-familiar. Two weeks ago he had borrowed fifty rupees she knew she'd never see again. Before that he had asked for a shirt to wear at a picnic with the balwadi teachers. While she didn't mind giving him Darius' old shirt she definitely objected to sharing her bathroom with a Dharavi resident.

She felt irritation rise as she heard him splash noisily while she added tadka to the dal. The boy has to be checked, she thought. Deciding to confront him the minute he stepped out, she took in the sight of his youth, water dripping from curly hair onto the collar of his shirt. Then she firmly said, "This is the last time you're having a bath here. Don't ask again."

"Why?" he asked, slicking down wet hair with his narrow comb and preening before the mirror.

"Because … because … I don't like it," she said, nonplussed for an excuse.

"Why?" he asked again.

"I'm … I'm … possessive about my bathroom … I don't like anyone using it."

"You should live at Dharavi," he said disdainfully, rubbing his hair with a towel he'd found in the bathroom. "Two-two hundred people for one-one tap."

"Stop exaggerating."

He shrugged. "Not believing, ask students. They only did survey."

Pervez bristled. He had no right to slam her after enjoying her hospitality. "Maybe I don't live at Dharavi but I've tasted the rough edge of life in other ways," she said, her tone aimed at silencing him.

"Dharavi people taste danda in all ways," he sneered.

She let his mood pass but decided against bringing out the first mango of the season she'd bought that morning. The first mango of the season was special. Suddenly she didn't feel like sharing it with Munawar.

"I wouldn't worry too much about Pawan," Sidharth was saying, comfortably slouched into the chesterfield. "He can take care of himself."

"How long have they been together?"

"A couple of years."

"Not too short," sighed Pervez, sinking into the sofa opposite him. "Won't he be cut up when she leaves?"

"He'll get over it faster than you think. Some men are led by their balls, not brains."

"That's a mean thing to say about a friend!"

"If he had brains would he have got together with a woman like Vandy? The kind of woman a man connects with tells you what kind of person he is."

"You're too supercilious about your friends, Sidharth. First me, now Pawan."

"When was I supercilious with you"

"All the time. Blowing smoke in my face. Calling me naïve. Disparaging what you call my class ..."

"You can't deny you're politically naïve. All Parsis are. It's not your fault, it's your background."

"I'm not denying anything. I respect the work you're doing. But I'd like to be treated with respect as well."

"Gawd! Don't go bandying that word! Respect women, respect Dalits, respect this, respect that! Respect isn't something you give like a bunch of flowers. Respect is earned for something you do. Or resist doing. Some people expect respect simply because they're born into a certain class."

"That's completely unfair! You bring everything down to class which isn't the only yardstick of existence!

If I expected respect on the basis of my family connection I wouldn't be here."

"So you want to be respected for being with us? How patronising!"

"You're driving me up a wall! You know damn well that's not true! But I do feel put upon when I'm expected to foot bills and be treated disparagingly as well."

"Why do you volunteer to pay?"

"I don't resent it but at times I'm also tight.

"You! Financially tight! Don't make me laugh . All you have to do is run to brother dear."

"I'm living off my inheritance, not my brother."

"How many people have the luxury of 'living off their inheritance' as you call it?"

"No more than men who live off women! You have a pretty good thing going. Naina footing your bills, cooking, cleaning, hostessing your friends ..."

"So you think I live off Naina!"

"That's obvious."

"For your information we have a joint bank account into which we put all our earnings and from which we draw for our needs."

"Which means she deposits and you draw."

"Not entirely. She does earn more than me but I get paid for articles. Besides she respects our work. It's her way of supporting it."

"I also respect your work. But I want to be treated decently as well."

"Aren't you?"

"I ... I guess I am ... But sometimes I feel I don't belong any more than Vandy. It was the same in Goa. I was always an outsider. Fred's family were kind to me … Too kind … My mother-in-law lost her temper with everyone except me … as if… as if I were made of glass … At times I'd deliberately do things that made her angry, like plucking a cashew-fruit before it was ripe. If Fred or Sandra did that she'd yell but not at me. Why?"

"See how imperceptibly class rules us," said Sidharth, sagely shaking his head. "Mothers-in-law are historically at loggerheads with daughters-in-law. More in a mixed marriage. But when the class factor comes in the whole dynamic changes."

"You and your class analysis. I don't think it was anything to do with class. They'd never met my family or seen our Bombay house …"

"You want us to treat you with kid gloves like your mother-in-law?"

"I want to be treated normally. You're the extended family I want to be part of."

"We are a family," said Sidharth quietly. "Connected by ideological not blood links. And you are part of it. Just do your bit so you feel it."

"What do you want me to do?"

She saw Sidharth sizing her up thoughtfully. "Something you believe in," he said slowly. "Never support anything you don't believe … But Munawar and Preeti…" He paused, taking in her expectant expression. "You believe they should have an opportunity to be together?" She nodded. "He's been coming to see you. Keep an eye on him. Get him to talk about Dharavi. Win his confidence …"

That seemed easy. "Anything else?"

Sidharth looked hesitant. "Do you want to be part of something big?"

"What's that?"

"Sahmat is organising an Artists Against Communalism week in Bombay. They've been taking this exhibition all over the country and are coming to Bombay next month. They need volunteers."

"Who's Sahmat?"

"O-fo!" moaned Sidharth banging his fist against his forehead. "Talk about being naïve Sahmat is the organisation founded in memory of Safdar Hashmi who was killed in the middle of a street-theatre performance on New Year's Day 1989."

"Killed!"

Sidharth laughed as he saw fear in her eyes. "Don't worry. Nothing like that is going to happen in Bombay. Leading artists from the fine arts, music, dance, theatre, cinema are coming to Bombay under the Sahmat banner for a cultural programme. They need volunteers."

"What would I have to do?"

"I don't know. But it won't be anything dangerous ..."

It was one of those days when Pervez was feeling good about little things. A squirrel had appeared on the gulmohur tree. Like the sparrow it bounced from branch to branch, its bushy tail in an asymmetrical rhythm to green leaves. Squirrels are not common in Bombay. She felt privileged to have spotted one.

At the market that morning she'd picked up a dozen succulent bhangdas after haggling over the price. From the fish counter she walked over to the spice merchants and bought Bedekar's tandoori masala. Rubbing it into the diagonal slits of the fish she put eight into the fridge and fried four for lunch. The beatific expression on Munawar's face as he flaked fresh fish with his fingers heightened her satisfaction.

"Grandfather telling one time Dharavi supplying fish to whole Bombay," said Munawar, tucking into the bhangda with relish. "Dharavi Koliwada is old fishing village. Big-big crabs one time getting. Now all gone. Because kerosene coming inside water. Times changed. Now-days even frying fish making big-big fight."

"How can frying fish cause a fight?"

"Last Friday Pereira and Choudhury had big fight about fish fry. Pereira is Catholic. On Fridays Catholic eat fish only. But his neighbour Choudhury is vegetarian. Not liking fish smell. Long time punga happening but now-days Hindus getting too much blood into heads. Two-three weeks Choudhury ordered Pereira to stop fry fish. Who he is to order? So Pereira said, 'What goes of my father! Dharavi does not belong to your father or grandfather. I fried fish whole life and will fry till I die!' So Choudhury caught Pereira's daughter on road and gave her dhamki. Poor girl, so scared she was. Went crying home. Now mother is also scared. But you know Goanese. How they can to live without fish ..."

"Small things become so volatile!"

"These are bad times, didi. Something bad will happen soon. I can smell like I smell fry fish. When apna Sidharth moved murtis, sala gundas kept quiet. But now small-small temples coming up everywhere. And that Thackeray!

He is saying removing murti will hurt Hindu sentiment. So they are left sitting there only. Illegal but sitting. No policewalas do anything. Congress government is sitting in gaddi but Shiv Sena is giving orders. Mussalmaan have to make own bandobast."

"Stay out of this Munawar," she said. "Be a peacemaker and you have a bright future."

He had finished lunch and was examining his reflection in the bathroom mirror after washing his hands. Narrowing eyes, he changed posture imitating Govinda's swagger, pulling out a pocket comb with two missing teeth and running it through his hair. "Who listens to peacemaker when fire is raging?" he said, sticking out his tongue as he concentrated on matching the filmstar's puff. Heavy with oil his hair kept falling flat.

"You must see no fires start. Don't people respect you as a balwadi teacher?" replied Pervez, amused at his antics. She had kept the towel he used after his bath exclusively for him. Each Thursday morning she ensured her own was safely put away.

"For small-small things they come. But when something big happens nobody will listen to anybody."

"If you want to create a future for yourself with Preeti you must make them listen."

That evening Pervez fried the remaining bhangda, put them into an insulated casserole and took them to Naina's. "They're fresh," she said, placing the casserole on the table, neatly covered with a paisley patterned cloth.

"One of those fancy dishes that have hit the market, man," said Pawan, eyeing the casserole admiringly.

"From her brother's house, I bet."

Pervez grimaced but let Sidharth's remark pass. "I bought it to keep chapattis warm but also use it for fried stuff," she said shortly, then proceeded to tell Sidharth about the quarrels between Pereira and Choudhury.

"Go to Dharavi again, man," said Pawan, jocularly. "Repeat what you did with the murtis and we'll crown you king of the secular brigade."

"Kings are ornamental. This requires people of action," responded Sidharth. "Let's see if Prabha has any ideas ..."

They called Prabha, fixed up to meet at Sion station next evening and worked out the dynamics for contacting Pereira and Choudhury. As they walked down the station slope Pervez instinctively felt she was about to participate in something momentous.

At the foot of the bridge they turned left into a winding area called Socialnagar at Dharavi's eastern end. Vendors with orange papayas and red pomegranates split open like flowers lined the roadside. One-storied houses had single two-square-foot windows sealed with an iron grill at the upper level. They passed a barber shaving his client in the street, cages of chickens awaiting butcher's knives, women covered in black from head to toe, a rundown taxi with all its tyres deflated, a tethered goat munching a newspaper.

Reaching the Urdu-medium municipal school they turned into a narrow lane overflowing with gutter water. Bare-chested men lounged on charpoys, immune to the stench. Shielding her nose with her dupatta Pervez stepped gingerly on the uneven ground, trying to prevent water from entering her chappals. As a fat rat scooted past she clutched Sidharth's elbow. He turned to her jocularly, "They say there are five rats to every person in Dharavi. Do you want to do a head count?"

A shiver ran down her spine but Shramik Vidyapeeth was ahead and she stepped onto its dry floors with relief. Soon she was being introduced to Shantabai, a round-faced woman with a large nath in her left nostril, a social worker at the balwadi Munawar had joined. They set off through lanes narrower than the one they had passed. Angular iron steps led to lofts with grilled windows under which every square inch was put to use. A dhobi running an iron over bedsheets that remained miraculously clean amidst street squalor. A tailor pedalling a foot-operated sewing machine. An unattended cauldron hissing over a brazier. A woman washing utensils next to an open gutter that would carry greasy water away.

Emerging behind the police station at the Ninety Foot Road they turned towards Khumbharwada, the potter's colony with an attractive display of brick-coloured earthernware pots. Each potter's family had display space along the road while they shared kilns behind and between houses. Pervez wanted to buy a small terracotta bowl for Naina but Sidharth's impatient stride inhibited her from asking him to stop.

Choudhury's residence was a brick and cement structure whose tin roof trapped heat indoors. It was a ten-square-foot room, with steel utensils piled on shelves in one corner, an almirah with a full-length mirror, a table fan whirring on the floor, and a low khatia on which an elderly woman was wheezing. Above her a pink kite hung against the wall beside a calendar depicting Shiva as Natraj. As they pushed aside a flimsy curtain she made a feeble attempt to get up, to be waved down by Shantabai.

"Don't get up, maaji," said Shantabai. "We've come to see your husband."

"He ... he's not home ..." she said, breaking into a spasm of coughing.

"Can I get you some water?" asked Shantabai. The old lady pointed to an earthenware pot over which sat an inverted steel glass. Shantabai filled half the glass and held it to Choudhury-ma's lips. The frail woman took a few sips, then sank back to the mattress, wheezing but not as heavily as before.

"What do you want with him?" she asked, her eyes clouding.

"Relax, maaji. Nothing to get worried about."

"Has that Pereira been complaining?"

"We heard there's been some tension," said Sidharth.

"Neighbours. Twenty years we have been neighbours. Now when it's time to leave my body, trouble comes," she said.

Speaking a full sentence had a long bout of coughing rack her bony body. She raised a trembling hand for a brown-stained cloth beside her pillow and brought it to her mouth. A fresh red stain spread. Pervez looked away.

Expurgating phlegm seemed to bring relief. She began speaking in a low voice. "You can see my state ... and understand ... Here I am ... on my deathbed ... coughing-coughing ... whole day, whole night... Those people ... everything they cook smells ... We have to tolerate, we tolerate ... Only for fish he told them ... don't fry fish ...

Will they listen? No … I told him jaane do … Everyone has to die … one-two months early-late what difference? But he is man, no? He has pride, no? He cannot hear coughing-coughing day after day, night after night … If he does not threaten what he will do?"

The long speech exhausted her and she sank back onto her pillow, wispy hair falling apart to expose a brown scalp, shrivelled breasts rising and falling as a whistling sound escaped her lips. Shantabai wiped perspiration off the old lady's forehead, crouching beside the khatia to rub her chest. As her breathing steadied she caught Shanta's wrist. "He … he … didn't mean it," she pleaded into her eyes. "He … he won't harm the child … People say things when they are angry … He is a good man …"

"Don't worry, maaji. Where is Choudhury sa'ab?"

"Gone to … shakha … Dr Nimbalkar gives medicine …"

There was no point tormenting the sick lady further. Ensuring she was comfortable Shantabai got up, rinsed her hands in the open drain outside and prepared to leave.

A few moments later they stood in front of Pereira's house. He had seen them emerging from Choudhury's and was suspicious. "What you want?" barked the portly balding man in khaki half-pants before they could speak.

"We heard there's some problem between you and your neighbour," began Sidharth.

"What problem? No problem. Khali peeli outsiders interfering. There's no problem. Go."

"Who you are talking to?" called a voice from inside.

"Some interfering fellows. Poking nose here, there …"

An overweight woman with black-rimmed glasses over flashing eyes came to the door. "What you want, eh?" she demanded, her tone matching her husband's.

"You have a problem with the Choudhurys?"

"We? Yes. Yes we have problem. Why we should hide? That man … Threaten to molest my child! Sixty-five-year-old man threatening fifteen-year-old girl! No shame! Twenty years we have to been neighbours. My daughter born in front of him. Grown up under his nose. And he threatens to molest her! Shameless! I tell you shameless!"

"So there is a problem …"

"What you will to do? Protect my child? Take her to school? Bring her home? You are her father, what?"

"Please calm down. If we talk calmly maybe we can think of a solution." Pervez was surprised to hear herself speak.

"Eh … eh … calm down, she says. Who she think she is!" mocked the fat woman, arms aggressively across hips. "Would you be calm if your child is threaten?" As her eyes blazed over Pervez her expression changed and suddenly her jaw dropped. "You? … Mother Mary pray for me!" Absent-mindedly she made the sign of the cross, blinked and looked at Pervez again. "You? Aren't you … Clara's … daughter-in-law?"

"Maggie aunty!" Pervez' face contorted in recognition of Freddie's aunt.

"Mother Mary pray for me," repeated the astonished woman touching both cheeks with her fingers in a gesture of contrition. "Why you have come here?"

"Meet my friends Prabha, Sidharth, Shanta," said Pervez, struggling to recover.

“What you are to doing in Dharavi? Freddie told us you went to rich-rich brother.”

“My brother is at Marine Drive but I live at Kalina.”

“Kalina? My niece is at Kalina ... Belinda ... you remember?”

“Can we come inside?”

“Yes-yes. Joachim take out chair. What you will to having? Tea? Coffee? Col-drink?”

“Nothing, thanks.”

“Mus-have. Jus-now Violette will come from tuition. Sit-sit, no? Why you are standing like lam-post!”

“Bringing you along was a fluke masterstroke,” murmured Sidharth as he took a tin chair from Joachim, unfolded it and sat down.

The house was different from the Choudhury’s. It was larger with an inner room behind the first. A red refrigerator occupied a niche in a wall behind which iron steps led to a low loft. A large portrait of Jesus Christ exposing a heart surrounded by thorns hung on the wall, below which a shelf held two candlesticks in front of a photograph of a young woman. A television sat diagonally across a corner, making the screen visible from every part of the room.

Maggie aunty bustled around, bringing out bowls of Goa cashewnuts, patting Pervez on the head as if she were her own prodigal child. As her inner turmoil settled, Pervez learnt that Fred’s sister Sandra had given birth to a second son, that her father-in-law had undergone surgery for a kidney stone, that Fred was travelling with a new band.

“House standing on khari-land,” Maggie aunty told them, beaming as she divided two Thums Up into four glasses with Queen of Hearts along their sides and passed them around in a plastic tray. "Twenty years before, you put down one leg can't pick up. So chikkad it was. From far-far we had to carrying mud. Mother-in-law, father-in-law, brother-in-law… all carrying. Live in Transit Camp, carry mud to fill plot. So black-black gutters had to passing. Even snakes there was inside."

"I was new-new married from Goa. Crying-crying why I come to Bombay. After many months water stopping from ground. Then only can build pucca house. One room built first. Two-three years six-six people in one room only. Then water come again from ground. Walls getting cracks. Breaking. So again carrying mud. Again building house. All money going into house only. Still I am thanking Jesus our house breaking only once. Other house breaking two-two, three-three times. Surya begum's four times, Jamilabai's three times, Gajrabai's two times. Government no help. Not one stone giving. Only piece paper saying take chikkad-land …"

"How did you get water and electricity?" asked Prabha.

"All together wrote BEST. Need light, no? Eight-ten years light came. Water came … three-four years … One day come two hours, one day not come …"

"The important thing is for people to cooperate," said Prabha. "Whether it's for big things like water and electricity connections or for accomodating neighbours."

"It is not that we don't want to cor-perate," responded Maggie aunty catching her import. "We are very cor-perating people. We know frying fish making smell. But twenty years you have not had smell, what? You are not used to, what? Making trouble after twenty-twenty years. Only because that Thackeray fellow put dum into their stomachs ..."

"Choudhury's wife is sick, Maggie aunty, " said Pervez. "She could barely speak without coughing."

"Arre she is always sick. One day cough, one day fever, one day back problem, one day head problem . .. Twenty years I am seeing her like that only ..."

"She's coughing blood."

"We have been ver-rry understanding," interjected Joachim, slapping the side of his thigh where a mosquito had bitten him. "First we was having fish daily. Then Choudhury coming, making me request, I told missus we will have only two-three times in week. After two-three months again Choudhury coming. Again saying wife is coughing-coughing. Again I am telling missus we will have fish on Sunday only. And missus saying Friday mus-have, no? Because Friday can't eat meat. So what we mus-do? Starve?"

"Why not have vegetables?" asked Prabha.

"Why mus-not eat own food? Fish is life-blood to Goanese. Everyday mus-have. We cor-perate with Choudhury five-six times week. One-two days he can't cor-perate us!"

We've reached an impasse, thought Pervez, dolefully reaching for cashewnuts with husks still on, recalling the umpteen times she'd munched them freshly roasted in Goa. Cashewnut grew wild on the hill behind their house. Often she'd wander over the hill where the bell-shaped fruit grew to the size of an apple, the kidney-shaped nut hanging below. Once she had bitten into the fruit to find it unbearably bitter. The bitterness would be distilled into a potent brew kajoo feni. Somehow she had never developed a taste for Goa's most famous drink.

"Can I see where you cook?" she heard Sidharth ask Maggie aunty.

"Come-come," said Maggie aunty, waddling inside. They crowded into a tiny dark room whose ceiling was only inches above their heads. Maggie aunty switched on a tubelight hanging on chains from a wooden beam. One wall was stacked with utensils. A stone slab under a square window held two gas rings. A red cylinder nestled in the corner. That is Choudhury's house," said Maggie aunty, pointing to a window with yellow flowers hanging from a discoloured Dalda tin.

"So close! You could almost shake hands!" exclaimed Prabha.

"Till few months we been good-good neighbours, sighed Maggie aunty. "Borrow-return from window only. Jus-now only change coming. After Suresh going to shakha."

"That Thackeray fellow no-good," added her husband. "Putting too much dum into people's khopdis."

"People have to get on with their lives despite politicians," said Prabha.

"Is this stone platform fixed?" asked Sidharth.

"Anytime can fix," said Maggie aunty. "Have own shop, no? Not see board outside? 'Pereira Welding Works.'"

"Mr Pereira makes grills?"

"Yes-yes. Joachim, tell them you making round design, flower design."

Her husband remained where he was. "Any design you wanting I making in one week," he said proudly. "Pereira Welding reputation to deliver on time. So much orders coming. Big-big contractors from Bandra, Maiad, Byculla. Also making stool." And he pointed to a high stool on which sat a huge drum of water.

"The workmanship is good," said Sidharth, examining it. Casually he let his eyes wander around the kitchen running a finger along the wall to squash a larger black ant and returned to the sink to rinse his hand. Picking up a red checked duster he smiled at Maggie aunty and asked, "Would you think about closing the window when you'rc cooking?"

"Too hot becoming."

Stepping out of the tiny kitchen he looked directly into her eyes and pressed on, "Suppose you close the window ... Not all the time ... But only when frying fish ..." he said measuring his words slowly. "Less smell would reach the Choudhurys."

"Huh?"

"Can't do," said Joachim in a tone of finality. "Latch is broken."

"Shuttup men! So much welding you are to be doing. Can't fit one latch, what ... Yes-yes. We will get new latch tomorrow only. Problem will getting solved ... But you tell that Choudhury he mus-not touch my child. So young innocent girl. Even in Dharavi she is like flower. Unspoilt. You tell him we will shut window. Never mind if we smell one-two hours. But he mus-not frighten child. Or we will open window again."

Pervez looked at Sidharth incredulously. A simple solution for what a few minutes ago had seemed an insurmountable problem. For all his dogmatism Sidharth was exceptional, she realised, recalling how, a few months ago, he had handled the equally tangled problem of the idols outside Munawar's house.

That day he had left the house armed with little more than determination to defuse the situation. All he knew was that the murtis had to be removed and that they could not be removed without the cooperation of Shiv Sena.

He had gone to the local shakha pramukh, a small-built man with a tikka on his forehead and a handlebar moustache reaching his earlobes. Five hours later the pramukh ordered his men to shift the idols to an open space near the English medium municipal school.

When Naina and Pervez questioned how he had achieved mission impossible he told them he'd begun by quoting shlokas from the Bhagwad Gita.

"I didn't know you studied the Gita!" Naina had said, incredulously.

"My grandmother made me memorise verses when I was too young to understand or protest," he replied with a wry smile. "I never thought the Gita could be used in activist work but it was probably the only approach that could have worked in that situation."

"What did you quote?"

"A shloka from the fourth chapter. It says: '*Kim karma, kim akarma, itt kavyo py'atre mohitat; tat te karma pravakshyami, yaj jnatva mokshya asubhat.*' Roughly translated it means 'Even wise men are confounded to know what is right action, what is inaction and what is wrong action. I will teach you action that will free you from repeated cycles of wrong action."

"Somehow this shloka came to mind as I was on my way to Dharavi. I quoted it to the shakha pramukh questioning the validity of using Ram's idols in a provocative manner, asking him to think about what is right action, that provoking aggression could never be right, that even Arjun went into battle at Kurukshetra reluctantly.

"At first he was belligerent, refusing to listen. Then he became defensive, saying his boys had placed the murtis out of devotion, that he could not hurt his boys' sentiments—"

"What about Muslims' sentiments?" Naina interjected.

"If I'd said that he'd never have relented. Instead I questioned his authority. Not directly, but again through the scriptures, bringing in the concept of 'sva-dharma', being true to yourself. I asked him to consider his duty as a leader, whether or not a leader had a duty to distinguish right from wrong, to guide followers along the right path, what was the use of leadership if followers couldn't be made to obey ... However unreasonable a person is, if you argue with him from his own perspective—in this case the Hindu perspective—he has to become reasonable."

Pervez had been impressed by Sidharth then and was more impressed witnessing him in action now. As they left Dharavi, she walked subdued through dark stretches punctuated by the infrequent orange glow of streetlights, around which millions of mosquitoes buzzed. Between lampposts, she had to watch her step to avoid stepping into squelch, but blue fluorescent light spilling out of doors with curtains hanging limply from strings, helped. As they reached Dharavi Main Road she split with her friends and took a cab. She desperately needed the seafront to organize the chaos in her head.

First there was elation at the outcome of what they'd started. For once Pervez felt satisfied by her role in a positive action.

The encounter with Maggie aunty had been a jolt. The surprise being nostalgia at news from Goa. She'd been particularly touched when, as they were leaving, Maggie aunty thrust a small plastic bag into her hand. "Home-made Goa sausage," said the plump woman, smiling through thick glasses.

Pervez took the packet, her tongue tingling at the memory of the spicy sausage. Her mind flashed to the drama of pig slaughtering in the backyard of their Goa home. In eight years she had not once participated in it. But she could not escape the sounds of the dying pig as a red-hot rod was shoved up its rectum and twisted till the poor animal died. She would put on music at full volume, stay away from the backyard till silence was restored. But she couldn't escape the sight of the trussed animal and had to help wash blood off the floor.

All families in Raia bred pigs. Pigs were needed for sewage disposal since the village had no drainage system. Nor did villagers have septic tanks. On her first day, Pervez had the fright of her life when a pig came nosing below as she used the outdoor toilet. She had quickly pulled up her panty and fled down the four steps of the raised toilet. Fred laughed as she clung to him close to tears. For weeks she made him stand guard outside the door. By the time things soured she'd got used to the existence of pigs.

Yet she enjoyed pork. *Sorpotel,* combining liver and blood with succulent flesh, *vindaloo,* made with tangy spices, and the Goa sausage. Each time a pig was slaughtered its intestines would be squeezed clean, washed and dried in the sun hanging from trees like shiny Christmas streamers. Then the fatty flesh, chopped into tiny pieces and marinated in vinegar and spices would be stuffed into intestine skins crudely tied at four-inch intervals. These could be preserved for months. Strings of such sausages hung from hooks in Goan bazaars as bananas hung at Kalina. Holding the sausage-filled bag in her hand Pervez felt connected to both worlds.

The family house in Goa had been spacious though sparsely furnished. The front door opened to doors of inner rooms so that from the *balcao* you could look past four rooms straight into the kitchen and beyond into the courtyard with a square well and an area demarcated for wood-fires. Well water, wood-fire and clay cooking pots gave the cuisine a special flavour. She realised this only when Sebastian's *vindaloo* tasted different despite using the same spices as her mother-in-law.

A sudden gust tugged at her dupatta. Inhaling salt air into her lungs Pervez waited for the pedestrian light to turn green. The inky sea seemed asleep with not a single white wave rearing its head. Lights of ghost ships dotted the horizon. Malabar Hill stretched a twitching arm to Nariman Point as cars flashed orange-yellow lights like fireflies.

There was no space to sit along the parapet wall. Pervez walked past chattering groups, past peanut and gram vendors, past lovers with arms entwined, recalling her early days with Fred. That memory stabbed from heart to crotch. Vicariously she let her eyes rove over a man caressing a girl's thigh, shifted them to a girl throwing her head back in laughter and again to the silhouette of two glued heads facing the horizon, aware of hands fumbling in the dark. A warmth spread between her thighs. She forced her gaze away.

She had known her father-in-law had been a garage mechanic. But the rambling family house surrounded by lush land veiled the reality of class. Meeting Maggie Aunty at Dharavi slapped home that reality. The sting would smart a while.

In eight years she had never accompanied Fred to Bombay—ostensibly to avoid facing her family. Now she asked herself whether it was also to avoid confronting his.

Would illusions have shattered earlier had reality asserted itself? How empty were her musings on de-classing. She had inadvertently de-classed and remained unaware of it. Her father had tried to impress awareness and finally written her off. Today she empathised with his humiliation.

Vaguely she became aware that footsteps were keeping pace beside her and that a man was observing her. A giggle rose in her throat but she checked it. Turning away from the seafront she headed for a gap in the hedge as cars flew fast on both sides. Lights blazed on the third floor of Sagar Mahal. A party was on. But it was too late to return to Kalina. She entered the building like a mouse searching for its hole.

Darius opened the door. "Hi! What a surprise! How come you're here on a Thursday?" he asked, taking in her dishevelled appearance.

"I ... I had a problem. Came for fresh air and lost track of time ..."

"Anything serious?"

She gazed at her brother's face a long time before answering. "I ran into Freddie's aunt," she said at last. "Can I turn in? I'm dog tired." She escaped into her room, throwing herself on the bed without bathing or changing. Through the darkness she heard Big Ben's chimes.

8

"Pervez! It's seven. I've been banging your door for ages!" Darius' voice chased her dreams away. She sat up, clutching a pillow to her chest, staring into the corners of the semi-dark room.

"Coming!" she called, reaching for the bedside switch. As light flooded the room the knocking stopped.

"Okay. We leave in ten minutes," said Darius. Hearing footsteps scrape back to his room, she jumped out of bed blinking sleep away. Soon they were striding along the Bombay Gymkhana verandah, towards the tennis courts where men in white shorts slammed yellow balls chased by khaki-clad kids.

"That's Sunil Gavaskar," said Darius, pointing to the cricket star who cut an attractive picture on the court. For a while they stood watching balls fly between racquets.

At the pool, Pervez quickly changed into her swimsuit and was testing the water with her toes by the time Darius emerged. She stepped in and out of the foot-bath letting coolness enter her body from below. Then she descended the steps on the shallow side of the pool.

The water reached her knees, thighs, crotch. She took a few steps feeling it on her waist, breasts. Slowly she slipped into horizontal position, kicking legs behind her, letting arms cut through the water till they touched the wall at the other end of the pool. Shaking her head gasping, she bobbed up and down clutching a niche along the wall.

Losing body gravity to water felt good. Her legs frog-legged below her. Slipping horizontal, face up, she lay on her back seeing pink-tinted clouds as toes steered her to the centre of the pool. She let them drop into the water, turning, holding her face down till she reached the wall again. She had swum two breadths and was halfway down the length, from where she could no longer touch the bottom.

"You're doing pretty good," said Darius, swimming up beside her. "But you'll be stiff tomorrow."

"Let tomorrow take care of itself ..."

Brother and sister swam side by side till they reached the deep end, turned and swam back. Pervez felt tautness return to forgotten muscles. After two lengths she felt exhausted and pulled herself out, dripping puddles on her way to the white beach chair under a red and white umbrella. Darius joined her, furiously towelling his hair as he dropped into a chair and rang for the waiter in the same movement.

A child had climbed to the diving board. Inflatable floats sat on his arms as he jumped into the water feet first. Pervez had never learnt to dive. She recalled standing at the same board, with her father in the water urging her to jump. Time after time she'd climb down, afraid of the height. Had her father been disappointed?

"We'll have mushroom on toast, waffles with honey and french fries," ordered Darius.

"Can I have a club sandwich?" asked Pervez.

"Why didn't you say so?"

"You didn't ask!"

"Okay, okay. What would you like?"

"A club sandwich and watermelon juice."

They stretched out on beach chairs unconcerned whether the droplets drying off their bodies were sweat or chlorinated water. The sun had shortened shadows. Their legs stuck out from the umbrella's shade. Two tables away, the kid from the diving board munched a hamburger. His mother was persuading him to have a milk-shake but the child had his eye on a Cola.

"Do you want to talk about Fredrick's aunt?" asked Darius.

Pervez shut her eyes. "There's nothing to tell," she said at last. She had spent the previous day speculating about the possible situations where she could have claimed to have met Maggie aunty and decided on the most innocuous. "I ran into her at Kalina market," she lied.

"Why did it upset you?"

"Memories. And news from home. My father-in-law's been ill, I have a new nephew and don't even know his name ... Suddenly it hit me that I'm excluded from the family."

They were quiet as a uniformed waiter brought glasses filled with deep red watermelon juice. Pervez saw the kid pointing and heard the bell tinkle as his mother summoned the waiter. As he moved out of earshot Darius spoke again.

"What about Fredrick?"

"He's on tour again."

"With the band?"

She nodded. "If a woman's with him the family will be the last to know."

"Why did you put up with it for so long?"

She looked up sharply. "Did I have a choice?" She bit her tongue as she saw her brother wince.

His face became vulnerable, his lower lip sagged and a defensive expression clouded his eyes. Pervez felt wretched as she recalled his visit to Goa when he had left his friends at Aguada Beach resort to visit her in the village. Her marriage was already under strain but she had managed to put up a façade till Fred came in, rancid smell on breath, and saw the perfume and silk kaftan Darius had brought.

"You can take these back. My wife doesn't need your fancy things," he said, examining Darius peremptorily.

"It's sweet of my brother to bring them," she snapped. "You've started your evening drink early today!"

"Take them back," he snarled, ignoring her. "Comes visiting after five years with presents. Did he get me a wedding gift? Haah?"

"Shut up, Fred!"

"Of course I have something for you," responded Darius, taking out another gift-wrapped packet from is haversack.

Fred examined the package, turning it over and over, raising it to his face as if he expected it to bite him.

"Smells like a dead rat," he said disdainfully, holding it at arm's length.

"Dead … rat …" Pervez and Darius' eyes widened simultaneously. Suddenly they dropped their formal positions and fell onto each other, slapping palms, hugging, laughing. Fred looked from one to the other perplexed.

"Dead rat!" gasped Pervez, clutching Darius' sleeve as the image of being chased around the garden by her ten-year-old brother swinging a rat from its tail flashed into memory.

"And the mali … Remember the mali you hugged …"

"I did not!"

"You did! Grabbed his legs so the poor man was frozen with embarrassment …"

"Mom gave you a nice whack for that!"

"And I lost my beautiful rat because of a silly sister …"

Fred was ignoring them, intent on unwrapping his gift. As the last bit of scotch tape gave way he pulled out a grey and red silk tie in a red travelling case. Squinting he tossed it on the sofa disdainfully. "Who wears ties in Goa?"

Pervez sobered at once. "At least say thank you!"

"Bah … Can I wear it on the beach?"

"You must be going to good restaurants sometimes," said Darius genially. "I'm sure Pervez would like you to dress up once in a while."

"So it's to please her, not me." His voice ensured that rancour was not mistaken for bantering. Mortified, Pervez returned to her formal posture but Darius had seen through the chink in her mask to know things were very wrong in her marriage.

"What do you want to do now?" he asked, oblivious of her train of thought.

"Nothing."

"I hope you're not thinking of going back ..."

Before she could answer, Iqbal Rahimtoola was standing in front of them dripping water from turquoise-blue trunks. "Mind if I join you?" he asked, flopping into the chair beside Darius. As they remained silent he looked confused. "Am I interrupting something?"

"Not really," said Pervez quickly.

"My whole blasted day's fucked up," grumbled Iqbal, rolling the towel into a bundle and swishing it over his stomach. "I was to take my son to the first cricket match of his life and those wretched Shiv Sainiks go and ruin it. Pouring tar on the pitch just hours before the start—it's too much!"

"Take the kid to Esselworld instead," suggested Darius. "He'll soon forget the match." The waiter brought breakfast, shooing away a gaggle of crows. They chatted inanities—about camping in the Himalayas, a BMW being up for sale, the price of ACC shares nearing two thousand, Darius' face remaining uncharacteristically pensive. "Isn't it time someone put these Sainiks in their place?" he said, unexpectedly.

"Muslim fundamentalists can be equally bad," retorted Iqbal, noisily slurping coffee. "I don't blame Thackeray for saying we shouldn't have sporting ties with Pakistan as long as they keep training terrorists. But the Sena uses such crude methods."

The contours of Darius' face softened as he looked towards the poolside clock. It was ten o'clock, time for his weekly badminton game with Dilip. He got up, telling Pervez to join him at the clubhouse when she was through with swimming. Watching him stride away she turned to Iqbal, the grey in his goatee giving away his age though his hair was dyed black.

"I'm surprised you agree with Bal Thackeray," she said. "I thought Muslims were against him."

"What's 'Muslims against this', 'Hindus for that'! People should do their own thinking, not follow the herd. Muslim fundas can be worse than Hindus. Do you know that in Kerala the Jamaat ordered a woman to be publicly lashed a hundred and one times for adultery."

"How barbaric!" cried Pervez, shocked.

"Where were the secular protests then? My feminist sister tells me because the minority is under attack, we can't protest. And I say, rubbish! Speak up! Wrong is wrong regardless of who does it. Silence is dangerous because it appears to condone."

Pervez regretted her question. She had come for a swim to wash away the week, not to get into political discussions. Excusing herself she walked to the deep end of the pool, mounting five steps to the springboard. The water was a clear blue. She raised fingers to cover her nose, shut her eyes, lifted her chin skywards, took a deep breath and plunged in, feeling her body sink. Kicking reversed the momentum. She felt her body rise till it broke through the water's surface. Sharp chlorine tingled her nostrils. She swam to the edge of the pool and clambered onto the springboard again.

The kid was sipping red juice. Crows pecked french fries at an abandoned table. As her right hand closed over nostrils, she glimpsed Iqbal covering the food at their table with an inverted plate. For the moment she was content to slip into the leisure of a poolside Saturday but she needed to think about what he'd said. She plunged into the water regardless of the kid's insolent stare.

She swam and lazed through the morning, putting Dharavi, Kalina, Goa, all out of her mind. Lush grass surrounded the tables. She rubbed her soles over it, toes tugging, hearing a crunch as grass blades emerged at toe tips. By the time the clock behind the counter said eleven-thirty, only saucer-sized shade remained under umbrellas with only a pot-bellied foreigner roasting red in the sun remaining at the poolside. She got up, took a fresh towel and went in for a shower.

A bright blue banner fluttered against the Marine Drive skyline. Artists Against Communalism, it announced as motorists slowed down in curiosity. A tent-like enclosure had been erected and the broad pavement was spread with paintings mounted on jute and bamboo stands. The mood was upbeat.

A taxi drove up to the tent. Its driver, a bearded Sikh, got off, proudly pointing to the slogan painted on his rear windscreen. Hindu-Muslim-Sikh-Isaee, Taxi Driver Sab Ka Bhai, it said in Hindi. Below it an English translation read Taxi Driver, Brother Of All Community.

Pervez sat at a small table, a long ledger book in front of her. She wrote down the slogan and taxi number before asking for the driver's name. "Kartar Singh," beamed the elderly man whose tightly tied beard had streaks of grey.

"Good to have competition putting friendship slogan on taxi. Everybody sees taxi. In one day I go Goregaon to Nariman Point, Byculla to Andheri. I put in Hindi also, English also. So everybody can read."

"So you believe in secularism?" said Madhu, a volunteer from Delhi.

"To taxi driver everybody is passenger. All hospital passengers I take free. That is my service to society." Pervez warmed to this garrulous man. "Why don't you include Parsis when you make slogans about Hindus, Muslims, Christians and Sikhs?" she asked.

He looked perplexed. "Never thought of it," he said at last. "You must be Parsi. Bura mat mano. I like Parsis. Such good housing colonies they have. Colaba, Dadar, Byculla …"

Another taxi had driven up, its driver waiting. He gave his name as Yunus Mohammed Sheikh. His slogan read, Anekta Mein Ekta, Unity In Diversity. A cliché, thought Pervez, dutifully jotting it down. "Why are you participating in this competition?" asked Madhu.

"For months I was waiting for opportunity to do some good work. If even ten people listen to messages it will make a difference in society."

He moved away, examining the jute panels that had to be spread flat for the wind kept knocking down the stands. Each panel held nine works of art—paintings, photographs, hand-written poems on the theme of secularism. Yunus scanned them so long Pervez worried about him losing clientele. But he seemed unperturbed.

Half an hour passed before the next cab arrived, the slogan almost covering its rear windscreen. Na Mazaa

Nare Mein, Na Rajnaitik Ishare Mein; Mazaa Ho To Shanti, Ekta Aur Bhaichare Mein, read scarlet letters carefully outlined with white. The driver gave his name as Gulabrao Patil, a resident of Sangharsh Nagar, Malad, then sauntered off.

The next taxi's slogan was poetic. I Love A Tree Where All Kinds Of Birds Can Nest, it said as the driver gave his name as Victor Sequiera. He's Goan, she thought, smiling as she asked how long he'd been in Bombay. "I grew up here," he said shortly, eyes shielded by wire-rimmed dark glasses. "Taxi drivers get stoned for any problem in city," he said, replying to Madhu's question. "If there is bandh or morcha first stone will be thrown at taxi only. Three times my glass smashed. What for."

By late afternoon almost a hundred taxis had registered. As strollers came out for evening walks they crowded around the paintings. The good-looking man with the Alsatian saw Pervez and asked what the display was all about. She told him that more than three hundred artists from all over the country had sent works for an exhibition called Images And Ideas, that it had travelled to thirty cities before coming to Bombay. She told him about Sahmat's anti-communalism campaign. He seemed impressed.

"Can I contribute to the organisation?" he volunteered. She took him to Madhu.

"I don't have a receipt book. But why don't you come to the art auction at Jehangir Art Gallery on Friday?"

The man nodded and left. Pervez resolved to tell Darius about the auction. As an art collector with secular ideals he should not miss it.

Vandana's jaw dropped as she took in the crystal, porcelain and silverware of the Sagar Mahal drawing room. "This ... is ... your brother's house ... So-o beauti-ful! Why you want to live in chawl in Kalina?"

Pervez was prepared for this reaction. "Beautiful objects don't make beautiful lives," she replied, trying to steer Vandana into her room. With thick make-up Vandana looked so gawky that Pervez felt she'd blundered in inviting her over.

But Vandana was in no hurry to leave. She slowly moved around the elegant room, running fingers over a sculpture, caressing a porcelaine figurine, lifting a crystal ashtray to admire its delicate grooves.

"Your brother is also good man, no?" she asked, gazing up at the chandelier with seven tulip-shaped bulbs. "That he is," conceded Pervez.

"And you have own room, no?"

"Yes, I do."

"Then why you not stay in so beautiful house?"

"Look at it this way, Vandana. I have the best of both worlds. When I want to be at Kalina I can be there. When I want to be here I can be here."

"What there is to be at Kalina? Everyone wants to make money and become rich. You are rich and live like poor ... No sense ... Why?"

Pervez was at a loss for words. Vandana's limited worldview made it impossible for her to comprehend class conflict, de-classing or personal choice. Not that Pervez subscribed to Left ideology. But an existing ideology did provide an excuse for doing what she wanted.

"Dhun will be here any minute," she said. "Come to my room fast. We have to get this make-up off your face."

"Why?" said Vandana alarmed. "She wants model, no? Models use make-up, no?"

"Not loads of it."

"First time must impress, no? I bought special ... imported ..."

"Come and wash it off or there's no chance of your modelling for Dhun," said Pervez firmly.

Reluctantly Vandana followed Pervez grumbling. "There listen to Pawan, Prabha, here listen to you. And all talk of independence ..."

Pervez closed the door behind Vandana. Since she had no make-up remover she pulled out a roll of cottonwool, dipped wads into a jar of cold cream and began wiping Vandana's face. Then she washed her face with cold water till every trace was off.

"There. That's better," she said, examining Vandana. "You make me look like ghost,' said Vandana dolefully. "What about hair? You want me to tie?"

"No, Vandy, leave it open. Now let's go meet Dhun."

At her suggestion Vandana had worn a pale green salwaar kameez with silver earrings and bangles. Not only was green Dhun's favourite colour, it went well with the leather décor making the seated Vandana an instantly attractive picture. As Dhun entered in a red pantsuit edged in white, she stood up respectfully, but the older woman waved her back to the chair.

"I hear you want to do modelling, Vandana?" began Dhun.

"Yes, madam," gaped Vandana, taking in Dhun's coiffeured, manicured appearance. "But you are beautiful! Also your house ..."

"Why, thank you!" said Dhun, pleasantly taken aback by the flattery.

"Yes madam, I will be happy to model for you."

"Have you done any assignments before?"

"Yes madam. I have brought photo and portfolio," said Vandana, handing Dhun a large envelope with clippings from *Chitralekha* and *Woman's Era* and a few other photographs.

"Not bad," said Dhun passing them to Pervez. "Who's the photographer?"

"Pawan Sinha. But he is not inter-ested in model photo-graphy any more," said Vandana, sending pleading eye signals to Pervez.

"This one's particularly good," said Dhun, comparing reality with image. "As Pervez might have told you, I run an exclusive boutique. The most fashion-conscious ladies come to me. Filmstars, models, society women ... Next month we're hosting a fashion show at President Hotel and ..."

Vandana was lapping up every word. Her guileless flattery had won Dhun over. But when Dhun invited Vandana to join them for lunch Pervez became apprehensive. Would her table manners pass muster? But Vandana had socialised often enough to be as competent with cutlery as with conversation.

"Tell me about yourself," Dhun asked Vandana. "You are not from Bombay?"

"I am from North, madam. Kanpur side."

"And what does your father do?"

"We have land. Not very big but not very small also. Grandfather big zamindar. More than hundred acres he had. But seven sons. Also had to give daughter's dowry. And government taking away land for making road. So father got only ten acres."

"I see. And what do you grow?"

"Mainly sunflowers. For making oil."

"Does that give a good return?"

"Not so much. I got three brothers, one sister. After eighth standard father want to get me married. I not want to spend life in village. So I ran away. To Bombay."

"That was spunky. Where are you staying?"

"With my uncle," she lied.

"And your parents have accepted your decision?"

Vandana shrugged.

Pervez wondered whether Vandana's grandfather really had a hundred acres of land or whether she was making it up to impress Dhun. The girl isn't as dumb as Naina and Prabha believe, she thought, impressed by Vandana's aplomb. "Am I to believe you haven't completed school?" she heard her sister-in-law asking.

"Oh no-no-no," lied Vandana again, visualising her dream of walking the ramp crumbling before it took off. "Uncle force me to study. He said, 'If you not marry, must study.' So I did S.S.C. Hindi medium."

"That explains your strange syntax."

"Sorry?"

"Your way of speaking. You speak English in a way someone educated in the language wouldn't. But if you are to model for me your English will have to improve.

Because the modelling world is very sophisticated ... Suppose I pay the fees would you attend an English class?"

Pervez found Vandana looking at Dhun with an adoring expression. Dhun and Vandana made a strange combination but they were going to hit it off. Realising that Vandana was taking off on a new path she felt guilty at the thought of Pawan. But as Vandy said they were moving in opposite directions. Sooner or later a split was inevitable.

Barely had Vandana left when the doorbell rang again. It was Tehmie Masi, looking more bedraggled than before. She was thinner, the lines on her face had deepened and the stained georgette saree hitched above her ankles revealed grubby feet. *"Kent chhe,* Par-veej," she said from outside the door.

"*Sari-kaani.* How are you?" enquired Pervez politely.

"Not good at all ... this last year has been just terrible ..."

"Why don't you come in?"

"Darius' wife doesn't like it..."

"Don't worry."

As Tehmie masi shuffled in carrying a Babubhai Jagjivandas plastic bag, Pervez became aware of the fetid smell of unwashed underwear. "Can you ... give me chocolate biscuit? Like last time?" pleaded the old woman expectantly.

"Of course," she said. At the dining table dishes waited to be cleared. "We've just finished lunch. Would you like some prawn curry rice?"

"Ha-varee ... Oh yes, yes."

Pervez went to the kitchen and brought out a plate, spoon and fork, serving curry, rice and a mince pancake into it. Tehmie masi's hands shook as she ate, eyes never leaving the plate. Pervez watched with pity. Hers was not the hunger of a starving person. It was different. The hunger of one who has known good times and lost them. Hunger for a revival that would never be.

Her dentures wiggled inside her cheeks. Nonchalantly she took out the lower denture, put it in her plate, drank water and put it on again. Pervez squirmed, glad Dhun was not around. Escaping into the kitchen she selected three varieties of biscuits, put them into a paper bag and took them to Tehmie masi.

"Thank you, *dikra,*" said Tehmie masi, taking the bag. "I am eating prawns after months ... So well I used to make *kolmi-no-patio* ... That *luchho* husband of mine used to lick his plate clean ... Now he's become a *ghas-khao* ..."

"Are you still getting money from the trusts?"

"Yes-yes. But they are not giving on doorstep, no? I have to come all the way from Jogeshwari. I am old ... Diabetes ... Varicose veins ... Heart problem ... Blood pressure ... Life has become so tiring ..."

Her plate was empty but her fork and spoon still apart. "Would you like some more?" asked Pervez.

The old lady hesitated. "If there are one or two prawns ..." Pervez slopped the spoon into the curry bowl and cradled four prawns to the edge. Draining away the curry she put them in Tehmie masi's plate.

"That's all?"

Pervez fished in the curry bowl agam but there were no more prawns. The old lady sighed and sat back in her chair. You are a good girl," she said, patting Pervez' hand.

"Just like your *bapawa.* Tell me about that husband of yours. Has he begun to appreciate you yet?"

"I've had no news since I came to Bombay."

"Good you have a brother like Darius. Otherwise you would be like me. Waiting for kindness from house to house. These days in short supply. Ve-rry short supply. Soon kindness will become as expensive as gold."

"You can't put a price tag on kindness, masi."

"Without price there will be no kindness. Only business."

"How can you say that when you are dependent on charity!"

"Arre, charity has become big business. Even trustees take commission. To get hundred rupees I have to give twenty-five back. I told accountant, *'Dikra,* you are young man with job. Why you are taking money from old woman?' And he said, 'All is not for me, I have to give half to trustee.' I was shocked. I said, 'You are lying' and he said, 'You want money, sign for hundred rupees, take seventy-five and go. Otherwise I can give seventy-five to someone else …'"

"You should report him!"

"To whom? Train travel so difficult … Last month I fell on platform. My knee was black for days … Kept rubbing haldi-milk … Slowly the swelling came down."

"Would you like Darius to send you money orders to save you a trip into town?"

"You are kind, like your *bapawa.* But I like coming to this house … remembering old days … Afterwards I get good dreams … er … *Sahebji* Dhun-*mai…*"

Dhun was standing behind Pervez, an incredulous expression on her face. "Who let her in?" she hissed, ignoring the greeting.

"I did," said Pervez.

"Can't you smell her filthy clothes?"

Pervez pretended she had not heard. Picking up Tehmie masi's plate she escorted her aunt to the elevator, handing her Darius' envelope. "She's just leaving. I'll clear up," she said cheerily as if nothing was wrong.

"Ghulam Sheikh, Sabavala, Krishen Khanna, Padamsee … the leading artists of the country are here," murmured Darius, examining the panels at Jehangir Art Gallery where artists, activists, buyers chatted in animated groups. Pervez was pleased at his approving tone. The interface between her brother's world and hers was beginning.

Through the week Images And Words had been exhibited at railway stations, slums, colleges, workers' colonies, accompanied by street plays and songs, with artists adding colour with their presence.

"Is this Malayalam or Telugu?" asked Darius, pointing to a square of writing between a painting of dancing tribal figures and a hideous mask cracking with the word "communalism" spilling out.

"I wouldn't know," replied Pervez. "Poems and proverbs have come in sixteen languages from forty cities." She spotted Sidharth talking to someone in a khadi kurta.

"Come and meet Sidharth," she urged her brother. "He's Naina's special friend but… he may be a bit difficult…"

As they approached, Sidharth looked Darius up and down imperiously. "So you're the one who gives her a good life?" he said.

"I beg your pardon!"

"You're the brother who pampers Pervez so she doesn't need to work?"

"I keep telling Sidhu I'm not living off you but he doesn't believe me," exclaimed Pervez exasperated.

"You don't know my sister," said Darius recovering. "She's proud as a peacock when it comes to money. She won't even take an outfit from my wife without paying for it."

Sidharth looked sceptical. "What do you think of the exhibition?" he asked.

"Lots of big names. Some good works, some not so good."

"The concept?"

"I support it heartily. Art opens the mind, communalism narrows it. Artists can't be anything except against communalism."

Sidharth's eyes narrowed. "Are you going to buy?"

"If I get a good work at the right price."

"Pucca businessman," spat Sidharth, stalking off.

"Why does he carry such a chip on his shoulder?" exclaimed Darius, unruffled by the churlishness. But Pervez was angry. She didn't think Sidharth would act out his class-enemy fixation so crudely.

"Look there's Shekhar Kapoor!" They turned to see Naseeruddin Shah and Shekhar Kapoor climbing to the podium from where the auction would be conducted.

Both wore striking black, with none of the aura of stardom about them. As Naseer picked up the auctioneer's hammer a hush descended. Madhu brought forward a panel with nine paintings, the first lot to be auctioned.

Darius' paddle had the number thirteen. He raised it for a panel with a Tyeb Mehta painting and kept it raised till the bidding reached forty thousand. It sold for sixty-five. Another panel with a Hussain also escaped him. As did one with a Padamsee.

"Why don't you raise bids beyond thirty-forty thousand?" asked Pervez, vexed at her brother's parsimony. "The Sabavala you bought last month cost more."

"I'm sceptical of art with a cause," he replied. "Causes limit art. Art should be sublime. I'd happily pay a lakh for Sabavala's pure vision. But when artists are limited to a nine-inch square what can you expect."

"You should buy to support the cause," persisted Pervez.

"I can give a donation."

"That's not the same. Sidharth will have plenty to say about 'moneybags' and their donations," said Pervez, disappointed in her brother.

The finale of the anti-communalism week was an all-night music, dance and poetry event at Shivaji Park, the Shiv Sena heartland. Leading classical musicians—Alla Rakha, Shiv Kumar Sharma, Hariprasad Chaurasia as well as poets like Kaifi Azmi, Ali Sardar Jaffery, Javed Akhtar were to perform and recite specially composed works against the backdrop of a huge Tyeb Mehta painting.

The grounds spilled over with as many common people as celebrities. Pervez, Prabha and Pawan arrived to find every inch of the vast maidan covered with people sprawled over chatais, sheets, newspapers and sleeping bags. But everyone was ready to huddle into closer knots to make space for more. As they spread their durrie between students and a family group, Pervez spotted Kartar Singh, the taxi driver, folding his hands in greeting. Barely had he introduced his wife when Amjad Ali Khan climbed on stage and a ripple went through the crowd.

"India is a bouquet comprising flowers of different colours and fragrances. Creative people have a responsibility in ensuring no flower withers, no fragrance dies," the sarod maestro said to thundering applause. "Music is concerned with purity of sound, not the identity of the performer," he continued. "Music creates oneness of spirit regardless of community, caste, class ..."

Pervez lay on her back drifting with the music and its elevating sentiments. A full moon dimmed starlight, but when she looked in a different direction the three stars of Orion's belt were clearly visible. She kept looking from the moon to Orion, reflecting on distances, on the time required to traverse them, on the limited span of human life.

Suddenly she felt Prabha prodding her arm. "You're snoring. People are turning," she whispered. Pervez rubbed her eyes guiltily and sat up. Surely at 4 a.m. she could be excused for giving in to sleep.

9

Dead streets. A ghoul perched on an antenna. Midday sun caking dog shit crisp. The smell of wood ash smouldering. And swarming flies.

Flies were the only sign of life in the ghostly street. Their haphazard movements and the clip-clop, clip-clop, clip-clop of leather hitting asphalt. Bluebottles buzzed over garbage, undisturbed. A pink plastic bag floated on air currents eerily.

Her feet walked, her eyes blind to the locked doors of deserted homes, her hand clutching a notepad and a pen. She was aware of eyeballs peering from cracks in doors. Palpably aware that the slightest wrong move might cost her her life.

The man walked at a brisk clip. "Look straight", "Keep notepad visible", he'd caution every now and again. Pervez held them so awkwardly she felt sure anyone could see that she was no journalist. But she followed orders like a robot programmed to look neither left nor right.

Suddenly he bent to pick up something. A small bottle, rag tied around its mouth like a used condom. He held it to his nose sniffing. "Kerosene," he muttered under his breath. "Not enough in ration shops but used for burning." Slipping the bottle into his pocket he walked on.

A shrill shriek pierced the gloom. The crow burst into a frenzy of cawing. She could hear feet running as screams grew louder. Curfew that kept people off the main streets of Dharavi was ignored in the narrow lanes where looting and rioting continued unabated.

"Keep walking!" commanded the man as a chill ran down her spine. Guiltily ignoring the voices that had risen to a cacophony she walked on. "My beat ends at Mahim Cross Road. From there you have to walk to the station alone. It's just ten minutes ..."

Pervez turned her frightened face to the policeman who had been her sole source of confidence. Together they'd passed the debris of thousands of clay pots at Khumbharwada, the litter of looted shoes at Dharavi Main Road, the charred ruins of what, till a few hours earlier, must have been homes.

"Look in front!" he snapped, and she obediently returned her gaze to the asphalt. "Walking alone might be safer than walking with me," he said somewhat contritely after a while. "Half the ruffians in these lanes would bump you off targetting me."

They walked without speaking, Pervez concentrating on footsteps to calm her mind. The crow kept pace, prancing from rooftop to signboard to garbage like a comic escort. Clip-clop, clip-clop, clip-clop ... but fear remained the silent melody meshing into the rhythm of her feet.

At the crossroad Inspector Ahire stopped. "Walk straight till you see the railway bridge, then turn left. The ticket counter will be at your right, Mahim station up ahead. Get into a general compartment, not the ladies. Very few ladies would be so foolish as to venture out at times like this. Who do you think you are? Rani of Jhansi?"

With his words ringing in her ears Pervez marched ahead forgetting to thank him or ask him to keep watch till she reached the end of the road. The crow dropped away, examining the entrails of a squashed rat. The silence became more eerie. Not even a dog nosed the gutters. No echo returned the sound of footsteps. Her footfalls were lighter than Ahire's boots had been.

She sensed before she saw movement up ahead. A man in a white shirt came into view, two crows swooping low over his head. He was followed by another and yet another. Fear froze Pervez' mind but she had to keep moving. Towards the men that soon became five, seven, ten. Then a brown and yellow caterpillar lumbered past and she heaved a sigh of relief. They had spilled out of a local train and were on their way home. She saw her fear mirrored on their faces. Danger awaited them as they entered the curfew-bound Dharavi as it receded from her as she left.

Only a handful of people were in the compartment. All wore dazed expressions. An elderly man chattered to himself gesticulating aimlessly. A woman with a basket of vegetables looked relieved as Pervez entered. A man with a bandaged foot had an arm protectively around a child apparently asleep on his shoulder. But when the child jerked up whimpering, Pervez noticed a bloody gash across his right thigh.

At Santa Cruz, a 313 was at the bus stop and took off the minute Pervez got in. She noticed vermilion tikas on several men's heads. Assuming them to be Shiv Sainiks she took the single seat near the driver. Later it struck her that they might be identifying themselves as Hindus only to protect themselves.

Barely had she turned her key in the lock when the phone rang. She stepped out of her chappals before walking across to answer it.

"Where have you been?"

"I've just walked in, Darius. I'm alright."

"You'vc been missing for two days ... Have you been going to places like Dharavi?"

"Oh Gawd ... Not now!"

"Have you?"

"Yes. Now leave me alone!" She hung up.

As usual she went straight into the bathroom, missing the Sagar Mahal shower. But feeling sweat and grime leave her body felt good anyway. She shampooed her hair four times, soaped her body twice and emerged in a kaftan with the towel turbaned around her head. The phone was ringing again.

"Are you out of your mind going to Dharavi when half of Bombay is under curfew!" yelled Farhad without bothering to say hello.

"I'm not stupid, Farhad. I didn't go after riots started. I was there and happened to get stuck."

"Everyone's worried. When are you coming home?"

"In a couple of days. I need to unwind."

"We'll take you sailing to unwind."

"Nothing's further from my mind than sailing ..."

She was more tired than hungry. But there was no food in the house. The palak and bhindi in the fridge looked pathetically dry and even the milk had turned sour. She found a packet of Coconut Crunchies in a jar and munched through half the pack, downing it with black tea. Then she lay on her bed and was lost to the world for the next ten hours.

When she awoke it was dark. She could sense the dark through her lids though her eyes were shut. She lay in foetal position, breathing reassurance from the familiar whirr of the fan. Slowly she stretched one leg, let the ankle drop over the edge of the mattress, curling her toes to hear knuckles crack. After repeating the movement with the other foot she reached for the alarm clock. Its luminous dial said 10.25. Stretching her arms upwards, she yawned loudly. Breaking the silence energised her. Abruptly she sat up welcoming the familiarity of her room.

Swinging her legs over the bed, she went to the window barefoot. Only a handful of flats had lights. One was Naina's. She dialled her number. "I'm starving. Do you have something to eat?" she asked in a deadpan voice.

"Today I'd give you champagne, if I had it!" came Naina's voice.

"Bread and butter will be fine."

As she skipped down her stairs and up Naina's, Dharavi images swam in her head. Maggie aunty's face spitting defiance. The rescued child's marble. And frantic crowds.

"What on earth made you go to Dharavi on 6 December of all days!" demanded Naina, placing a fluffy omelette, bread and cheese in front of her friend.

"I forgot that that was the day karsevaks were gathering at Ayodhya. I just went to give Maggie aunty some Parsi pickle. I used to talk about *gharap-nu-achar* and *lagan-nu-achar* in Goa so when Maggie aunty gave me sausages I thought it would be nice to reciprocate."

"No one dreamt Babri Masjid would be destroyed," sighed Naina. "No one expected trouble in Bombay. Not on this scale."

Maggie aunty had been surprised to see Pervez. She fussed over her, plying her with cake and biscuits when Choudhury came to use her phone. The small-built man with wire-rimmed glasses and grey moustache was agitated because he needed to reach a doctor fast. Maggie had gone next door, returning within minutes to say the old lady had passed away.

Pervez got up to leave when there was a commotion in the street. Men on cycles and motorbikes carrying saffron flags were shouting "Shiv Sena zindabad", "Bal Thackeray zindabad" while dozens marched beside them. As more and more marchers came into view the motorcyclists revved up engines and their chant changed to "Kasam Ram ki khate hain, mandir wahin banayenge." Suddenly it dawned on Pervez that something must have happened at Ayodhya.

From the entrance of Pereira Welding, she saw clusters of people staring at the processionists. A man with a saffron band around his forehead held up his hand and the marchers fell quiet on cue. "Hath mein lungi moonh mein paan," he yelled at the top of his voice. "Bhago laandiya Pakistan," roared the crowd behind him. "Hath mein lungi moohn mein paan," he repeated. A white-capped boy with blazing eyes grabbed the handlebar of a bicycle. The cyclist gave him a resounding slap. Another boy picked up a stone to be restrained by an older man catching his hand.

Gradually word trickled in. A bearded man with tears streaming down his cheeks told a knot of people that he had seen trishul-wielding karsevaks hacking the dome of Babri Masjid which had just caved in. Disbelief gave way to shock.

Pervez picked up her handbag but Maggie aunty restrained her. "Can't go alone," she said. "I will reach you to station."

Choudhury's jaw dropped. "Missus body not cold yet," he croaked in a trembling voice. "And all Mussalmaan angry on road ..."

Torn between the two, Maggie aunty implored Pervez to wait. Soon Joachim would bring Violette home from school, then he would reach her to the station. Pervez agreed. She was not keen to step into the tense street. Settling into the folding chair she listened to Choudhury calling his sons, telling them to contact the shakha. She heard him say that if anyone could get them to their mother's deathbed at such a time it would be the Shiv Sena.

Snatches of street voices floated in. People spoke of organising raasta roko, Bombay bandh, Bharat bandh ...

Some boys piled crates of bottles at street corners. Others brought choppers and rods. As it started getting dark with no sign of Joachim uncle she began getting restless. Suddenly a voice rose above the babble calling Choudhury by his name.

The elderly man shrank into himself petrified. The voice called again. Pervez saw a tall man with a black straggly beard and angry eyes surrounded by twenty others. "We know you contacted Shiv Sena," he barked. "Come out before we drag you out!"

The wrinkles on Choudhury's grief-stricken face deepened. He stepped outside gingerly mumbling, "My wife has just died, come and see her body."

The young men ignored him. "Why did you call Shiv Sena?" asked their leader.

Choudhury had no reply.

"Why did you call Shiv Sena?" repeated another voice. Choudhury remained silent.

"We're going to kill you," said their leader between clenched teeth. "Then you and your wife can go to hell together."

This was too much for Maggie aunty. She rolled up the shutters of Pereira Welding. "With Jesus Christ as my witness I swear you will not touch my neighbour as long as I am alive!" she shouted, stepping into the crowded street. "What are you children up to? Where are your parents? Haven't they put sense in your heads? How can you harass a man when he's just lost his wife!"

"Keep out of this, fisherwoman!" yelled a hothead. "We can kill two as easily as one."

"Did your parents bring you up to be murderers?"

A middle-aged man with the boys intervened. "Look maaji, I'm a father. I understand you. But these boys are not angry for nothing. First they break our mosque, then they call us eunuchs, ask us to go to Pakistan ... Why should we take all their bullshit? Have you seen television? How they climbed on Babri Masjid and broke it stone by stone!"

"Babri Masjid is in Ayodhya. We are in Bombay where we've lived in peace for years. An old man has just lost his life partner. Decency demands we leave him to mourn in peace."

"Will you take responsibility for our safety if Shiv Sena comes?"

"With Jesus Christ beside me, I will," replied the spirited woman and an uneasy calm descended. Everyone knew a single woman was helpless against the Sena but Maggie aunty was invincible in her defiance, and the crowd melted away. After this Pervez felt impelled to wait till Joachim uncle returned.

Mosquitoes froze into tight clusters around street-lamps as darkness descended on the street. Skull-capped boys greeted each other with Allah-o-Akbar. A hill of bricks appeared beside the soft drinks crates and it dawned on Pervez that they were to be used as missiles. Her watch crawled slower than a hibernating bear. She regretted not leaving Dharavi before it was abandoned by the sun.

It was 8.25 before Joachim uncle called. Anticipating trouble at the news about Babri Masjid, he had taken Violette to the safety of relatives at—of all places—Kalina. He promised to return within the hour.

That would make it 9.30 at the earliest. The streets were full of hotheads. Pervez quaked at the thought of encountering them alone. Hesitantly, Maggie aunty asked whether she'd like to spend the night in their humble home. Reluctantly Pervez agreed.

"I never dreamt I'd spend a night in Dharavi, of all places," she told Naina, shuddering. "But aunty-uncle were really kind. They took me up to the loft, gave me a mattress, pillow, clean sheets and a small table fan on the floor … Yet I couldn't sleep … You know how terrified I am of rats …"

"Rats?"

"Sidharth said there are five rats to every person in Dharavi."

"In the middle of a riot you were thinking of rats!"

"I swear, Naina, that night I was more scared of the rustles inside the house than of all the noise outside."

Pervez must have dropped off, for the next thing she remembered was waking to a loud blast, followed by another. The tin roof over her head chattered as if it were being pelted with stones. Instinctively she dug into the coverlet.

As the roof settled into silence she peeped out. Crawling to the small square grill over the window she saw people on rooftops, flinging stones, bottles and ducking as similar missiles were hurled at them. Some had rods and knives in hand, others looked bewildered. The street was strewn with broken glass. A man in a purple lungi was gesticulating wildly. Pervez couldn't hear a word above the din.

Suddenly she spotted a child below the window observing the scene as if it were a film on screen. She clapped to catch his attention. He couldn't hear her. She clapped again. He looked up but didn't move. A solitary policeman observed the scene without moving from his rickety stool.

Clutching a knotted rope to balance on perpendicular steps she climbed down the loft backwards. Pereira Welding was dark and deserted. Only a pair of feet were visible behind the shutters. Pervez knocked on the metal rollers, raising them waist high. Joachim uncle pushed them down. She pushed them up again, telling him about the child under the window. He disappeared. Seconds later he was bundling the boy into Pervez' arms and rolling down the shutter. Strangely the child was not crying.

"Daamar Company on fire," said Joachim uncle. "Blast was tar drums bursting. You stay inside only."

"Where is aunty?" she asked.

"With Choudhury. He is very frighten."

"Have his sons come?"

"No chance. Missus arranging funeral. Talking to police. Police station on our road only."

Pervez took the child up to the loft where it was brighter. He looked barely three or four. Taking out a blue marble from his pocket he placed it against the index finger of his right hand aiming at a cigarette packet thrown in a corner. She returned to the window.

A man clutching a bleeding arm staggered into view, the right side of his shirt and trousers stained red. Blood drops trailed on the road behind him. As he leaned on the wall below she could hear his laboured breathing. She sat paralysed till he moved away.

Maggie aunty returned to clasp the child to her bosom giving him biscuits from a box. Pervez was also hungry. No one had eaten the previous night. She offered to cook lunch. Maggie aunty handed her rice, dal and a coconut, pointing to spices on a shelf. Leaving the boy in Pervez' custody she went back to Choudhury's.

Despite being a Catholic, Maggie aunty knew all about Hindu funeral rites and had contacted the pundit, the men who made biers for carrying the body, the crematorium … She'd even called a Muslim youth leader whose barbershop was across the road and a Hindu boy from the shakha asking them to let the funeral pass peacefully. Pervez was impressed.

She had finished grating half the coconut when sudden screams rent the air. Pereira Welding's shutters were down. Wiping hands on a washcloth she grabbed the rough rope and climbed to the loft. Men, women and children ran for their lives as black smoke billowed behind them. "Ghar jal gaya … Satyanash!" came an anguished voice.

"Pani lao! Jaldi pani lao!" screamed a bearded man in a lungi. A young girl helped her grandmother hobble as fast as she could.

"Bacche ko nikaal!" sobbed a hysterical woman pushing a man towards the fire. "Mere munne ko aag se bacha de …"

The lanes were too narrow for a fire brigade. Houses shared walls so fire that engulfed one also swallowed the other. One by one homes were reduced to rubble as feeble buckets of water hissed into steam. An overpowering smell had eyes streaming, throats coughing.

Not only on the street but also in the loft where Pervez coughed into her dupatta as she sat watching as if from the balcony of a theatre. An unfamilar acrid smoke. Not the musky smoke from burning dry leaves in Goa. Not the smoke of wood-fire in the kitchen courtyard. Not the odourless smoke of burning paper with handwritten poems. But unimaginable pain. Worse than any she'd known.

She first burnt a poem the day after Fred first slapped her. In an argument late at night. She couldn't remember what the fight was about but she would never forget the sting of that slap. Humiliation more intense than pain.

Again, she'd spent the night huddled on the floor. Refusing to touch his bed. The next day she burnt an old poem called "Ode to My Man", a silly sentimental poem, written in a weak moment. Watching the paper curl, crumble and scatter into fragments she felt a weight dropping off her chest.

Pervez didn't cry as the poems burnt. Watched dry eyed as she let emotion go. Sometimes she'd hold a burning poem watching fire eat words, hearing the crackle, adding paper to leaves watching flames leap as she sniffed musky smells.

One by one her poems became ash, weightless as the hollow within her. But each burnt bunch fuelled her angst, giving birth to new poems. The fodder was limitless. Like the people in the street.

She watched helplessly as the man with the hysterical woman went back into the lane from where smoke was billowing. His wife trailed behind. Suddenly she was knocked down by a man in a black shirt running wildly, a TV set clasped in his arms. She dragged herself to the side to escape trampling feet, looking terrified. Someone helped her up, urging her to move. Reluctantly she accompanied her saviour, forlornly scanning faces in the crowd.

The man in the black shirt appeared again, carrying another TV, pushing people out of his way. "He's looting," gasped Pervez, hand covering her mouth. "The swine's got the cheek to loot when people are running for their lives!"

Clasping the rope she ran down to tell Joachim uncle.

"What we will to do with our TV?" he worried, scratching the side of his neck.

"Your shutters are down. It's safe here, isn't it?"

"Can't say. Everybody knows Joe Pereira has TV, fridge. All come to see *Mahabharata* serial."

Maggie aunty was also worried. "Mus-put TV away," she said, looking around the room. There was no place to hide it. "Come, we take upstairs," she told her husband. He nodded, unplugging the television from its socket. But getting it up perpendicular steps was not easy. They struggled. Pervez lent a hand. At last it was up, Maggie aunty panting as she surveyed it on the floor of the loft. Dragging it to a corner, she covered it with three thin mattresses and a sheet. Still panting, she went down again.

But there was no way to hide the fridge. So she made just one move. Removing the portrait of Jesus from the

Frank Kürschner-Pelkmann

Entdeckungsreise in die Welt der Hamburger Originale

Rediroma-Verlag

Bibliografische Information der Deutschen Nationalbibliothek:
Die Deutsche Nationalbibliothek verzeichnet diese Publikation in der Deutschen Nationalbibliografie; detaillierte bibliografische Daten sind im Internet über http://portal.dnb.de abrufbar.

ISBN 978-3-98885-248-9
Copyright (2024) Rediroma-Verlag
Foto: michael_hamburg69
Alle Rechte beim Autor
www.rediroma-verlag.de
15,95 Euro (D)

Inhalt

Einleitung

Dieses Buch lädt dazu ein, die Geschichte Hamburgs durch Porträts von Hamburger Originalen kennenzulernen. Oft erscheinen Hamburgs Originale lediglich als komische Figuren oder als Staffage für eine verklärte Präsentation des Alten Hamburg. Aber viele Hamburger Originale waren weder komisch, noch führten sie ein fröhliches Leben. Es gab Ausnahmen wie den „vergneugten" Vetter Kirchhoff. Aber mehr Originale fristeten ein tristes Leben, verspottet von ihren Mitmenschen und wirtschaftlich verelendet. In einem Wikipedia-Beitrag über Originale steht: „Einige Schicksale lokaler Personen wurden zudem in Gedichten, Geschichten und Theaterstücken thematisiert. Dabei werden mitunter die tragischen Züge wie Armut, Alkoholismus oder sonstige Krankheiten ausgeblendet und die Lebensgeschichte eher verklärend wiedergegeben."

Dieses Buch ist trotzdem nicht voller trauriger Lebensbeschreibungen. Viele Originale waren humorvolle Menschen und zögerten nicht, sich selbst und ihre Mitmenschen mit ihren originellen Seiten darzustellen. Gern verspotteten sie die Arroganz und Selbstgerechtigkeit der Reichen und Mächtigen der Stadt. Manche historischen Gedichte und Anekdoten kann man auch heute noch schmunzelnd lesen und sich fragen, was sich eigentlich seither geändert hat. Und so ganz nebenbei lernt man durch die Porträts der Originale auch viel über das alltägliche Leben in der „guten alten Zeit" in Hamburg kennen, die so gut oft gar nicht war.

Was ist ein Original? Lesen wir nach im *Brockhaus Conversations-Lexikon* aus dem Jahr 1839, aus einer Zeit, als es viele Originale in Hamburg gab: „Auch Menschen werden Originale genannt, wenn sie sich durch Originalität ihrer Denkungsart oder ihres Benehmens auf eigenthümliche und auffallende Weise vom Gewöhnlichen entfernen; dies kann jedoch ebenso gut durch Seltsamkeit und Thorheit, wie durch edle und vortreffliche Eigenschaften geschehen."

Mehr als dreißig Hamburgerinnen und Hamburger werden in diesem Buch porträtiert. Es sind bei weitem nicht alle Originale der Stadt. Über viele Originale konnten ich nicht ausreichend Informationen zusammengetragen, um ein Porträt zu schreiben. Auch sollte erwähnt werden, dass lebende Originale nicht in dieses Buch aufgenommen worden sind. Dass über die einzelnen Hamburger Originale sehr unterschiedlich viel zu erfahren ist, bildet den wichtigsten Grund dafür, dass die Porträts unterschiedlich ausführlich sind. Auch nehmen manche Porträts mehr Raum ein, um den besonders komplexen Persönlichkeiten gerecht zu werden, zum Beispiel Hans Albers. Bei allen Porträts habe ich mich bemüht, auf der Grundlage intensiver Beschäftigung mit diesen Menschen und ihrer Zeit ein realistisches Bild zu zeichnen. Deshalb wird auch keine „Heldenverehrung" betrieben, sondern die Originale werden auch mit ihren Fehlern und Schwächen dargestellt. Aber stets werden die vorgestellten Originale mit einer großen Portion Sympathie präsentiert. Das haben sie schon deshalb verdient, weil sie zu Lebzeiten von ihren Mitmenschen häufig vergeblich auf Anerkennung oder auch nur Tolerierung hofften.

Die in diesem Buch vorgestellten Hamburger Originale sind wegen ihres von den gesellschaftlichen Normen und Vorstellungen abweichenden Auftretens und/oder ihres Humors in Erinnerung geblieben. Alle sind mit oft beeindruckender Hartnäckigkeit ihren Weg gegangen. Sie sind in Erinnerung geblieben als Menschen, die sich durch das Getuschel oder die Angriffe ihrer Mitmenschen nicht von diesem Weg abbringen ließen. Das gilt zum Beispiel für Vogeljette.

Sie unterschieden sich stark in dem, was sie zum Original machte. Da gab es die berühmten volkstümlichen Sänger und Schauspieler wie Hein Köllisch und Henry Vahl. Ebenso Menschen, die wegen ihres Verhaltens verspottet und ausgegrenzt wurden wie Hummel und Zitronenjette. Einige Originale besaßen eine beeindruckende Bildung wie der Theologe Johann Balthasar Schupp. Andere haben nur eine geringe Schulbildung genossen oder waren geistig zurückgeblieben. Einige Originale nutzten ihre Redegewandtheit und ihren Humor, um ihre Waren an die Frau und den Mann zu bringen wie Aalweber und Oskar vom Pferdemarkt. Andere hatten große Mühe, finanziell zu überleben, und verarmten.

Die meisten historischen Originale, von denen wir heute noch wissen, waren Männer. Sie genossen weit größere Freiheiten als Frauen, sich abweichend von den herrschenden Normen und Gewohnheiten zu äußern und zu verhalten. Frauen, die durch Spott und Originalität auffielen, landeten rasch im Zuchthaus oder in der Irrenanstalt. Über andere Frauenoriginale schüttelten die gutbürgerlichen Hamburger den Kopf, ignorierten sie und dachten gar nicht daran, deren Sprüche oder Späße der

Nachwelt zu überliefern. Immerhin gab es auch Wirtinnen wie die Marianne und später Hermine, die ihre Lokale mit Erfolg geführt haben.

Viele Originale wurden wie früher die Hofnarren so lange geschätzt, wie sie ihre Verse schmiedeten, ihre Späße machten und ihre Mitbürger zum Narren hielten. Aber ein altes, gebrechliches und müde gewordenes Original, ignorierten die Mitmenschen rasch.

Für die wenigsten Originale sind Denkmäler errichtet worden. Dieses Buch soll dazu beitragen, dass Hamburgs Originale trotzdem nicht in Vergessenheit geraten. Das wäre nicht nur wegen der vielen Gedichte und Anekdoten schade, sondern auch, weil die Lebensgeschichten der Originale den heutigen Menschen Mut machen können, entschlossen und selbstbewusst den eigenen Weg zu gehen. Und das auch dann, wenn er oder sie den herrschenden Normen und Erwartungen nicht entsprachen. Der berühmte Schlagertitel von Frank Sinatra „I did it my way" bringt eine Einstellung zum Leben zum Ausdruck, die das Leben vieler Hamburger Originale bestimmt hat.

Zum Schluss ein Hinweis für alle, die mein Buch „Entdeckungsreise durch die Hamburger Geschichte – 240 Porträts aus 12 Jahrhunderten" gelesen haben. Einige der dort Porträtierten haben auch in diesem Buch einen Platz gefunden. Aber diese Porträts habe ich gründlich bearbeitet und erweitert mit dem Ziel, die Originalität der Porträtierten sichtbar werden zu lassen.

Noch zu erwähnen ist: Auf dem Buchumschlag ist die Bronzestatue von Heidi Kabel zu sehen, ein Werk von Inka Uzoma, aufgestellt auf dem Heidi-Kabel-Platz.

Aalweber

Mein lüttje Madamm, Ihr Kaufen ehrt mich sehr,
woll'n Sie nich noch'n büschen mehr?

Mit solchen Sprüchen kurbelte Johann Jürgen Weber seinen Absatz als Straßenhändler an. Der um 1780 in Bremerlehe geborene Weber hatte das Bürstenbinder-Handwerk erlernt. Vormittags war er in Hamburg mit einer Karre unterwegs und verkaufte Bürsten, nachmittags und abends Aale. Er trat als eleganter Herr mit weißer Hose, roter Weste, heller Jacke und hellem Zylinder auf. Wenn er mit zwei Körben voller Aale durch die Straßen zog, rief er unüberhörbar „Smuttool! Smuttool!" („Räucheraal! Räucheraal!"). Die Fische soll er gelegentlich im Fischladen der Familie Hagenbeck in St. Pauli gekauft haben.

Aussuchen konnte man sich seine Aale nicht. Die Kunden sagten, wieviel sie ausgeben wollten und der Händler entschied dann, wie viele Aale von welcher Qualität er ihnen für dieses Geld übereignen wollte. Seiner Kundschaft machte er unmissverständlich klar, dass es sein großes Entgegenkommen war, die Aale zu verkaufen. Johannes Sass hat in seinem Buch „Hamburger Originale und originelle Hamburger" überliefert, dass Weber von der Kundschaft mit einer gewissen Vorsicht zu behandeln war: „Fragen, ob die Aale auch frisch geräuchert seien, nahm er als persönliche Beleidigung. Sie brachten die Gefahr mit sich, dass man überhaupt keine Aale bekam. Er war eben nicht irgendwer, er war der Herr J. J. Weber, von dem bedient zu werden, ein Entgegenkommen bedeutete. So empfindlich war er auch, wenn er gerade Schluss gemacht hatte und dann noch jemand etwas kaufen wollte. Dann konnte er wohl eine Kundin anfahren: ‚Kannst nich to rechte Tiet kamen? Bün ick dien Hansnarr?' Man musste schon gut bei ihm angeschrieben sein, um dann noch bedient zu werden."

Dank der flotten Sprüche, Witze und Gedichte des Aalverkäufers versammelte sich stets eine Menschenmenge um seine Karre. Besonders erfolgreich war Aalweber an Markttagen, wo er mit dem Verkaufen kaum hinterherkam. An solchen Tagen beteiligte sich seine Frau am Verkauf. Aalweber nutzte auch die Märkte in Altona und Wandsbek, um seinen Absatz zu steigern. Hier ein weiterer seiner Verse:

Allerhand Waar – von de Kaar!
Kaufen Sie ein klein'n Reinmacherstock
für ihren neuen Winterrock!
Glanzbürsten und Wichsbürsten! Mamsell von'n Saal.
Kommen Sie doch schnell mal hendal!
Was hat der Mann zu Kauf?
Bürsten hat der Mann zu Kauf!
Nehmen Sie eine mit rauf
oder 'n Schwanz von die kleine arabische Pferd,
ist unter Brüdern 4 Schillinge wert.

Carl Hagenbecks Erinnerungen an den Aalverkäufer

Carl Hagenbeck hat als Kind Aalweber erlebt und anerkennend in seinen Lebenserinnerungen geschrieben: „Ich sehe ihn noch vor mir mit seiner hellen Jacke, seiner roten Weste und auf dem Kopf den hohen weißen Filzhut. Am Arm trug er stets den von einer Serviette bedeckten Korb mit leckeren Räucheraalen. Es gab in Hamburg keinen Menschen, der nicht einmal am Lämmermarkt oder in der Waisengrünanlage von Aalwebers Bude in der Kirchenallee zu St. Georg ... erschienen oder sonst zu dem Genuß Aalweberscher Aale gekommen wäre. Wohl niemals hat sich irgendein Straßenverkäufer, der es verstand, in einem unendlichen Singsang von originellen Knüppelversen seine Ware anzupreisen, größerer Popularität erfreut."

Seine Gedichte sollen Aalweber jeweils spontan eingefallen sein. Beim Bürstenverkauf sang er zum Beispiel mit lauter Stimme:

Der Weber ist da! Der Weber ist da!
Kommt nun alle her von fern und nah!
Die Bürsten sind alle patente Ware
Und halten an die hundert Jahre.

„So vergeht aller Glanz der Welt"

Aalweber war in Hamburg so bekannt, dass in dem Stück „Gustav oder der Maskenball" ein Schauspieler in der Rolle Webers als origineller Straßenhändler zu sehen war. Das Stück kam bereits im ersten Jahr mehr als 150 Mal zur Aufführung. Der geschäftstüchtige Aalweber stellte dem *Steinstraßen-Theater* seinen Original-Verkaufskarren zur Verfügung. Später führte man das Stück auch in anderen Hamburger Theatern mit Erfolg auf.

Wie so manches Hamburger Original geriet auch Aalweber im Alter in Vergessenheit. Seine Frau Catharina Maria war bereits 1830 verstorben, und er hatte seine zweite

Frau Elisabeth Margaretha 1835 geheiratet. Es lässt sich nicht mehr herausfinden, wie der erfolgreiche Straßenverkäufer verarmte und warum seine Familie ihn nicht unterstützte. Er lebte im Alter im Werk- und Armenhaus der Stadt und war so bettelarm, dass frühere Kunden eine Sammlung veranstalteten, um ihm einen Vorrat seines geliebten Tabaks zu kaufen. Weber starb 1854, übrigens ein Jahr nach Hans Hummel. Später erinnerte sich kaum noch jemand an das einst berühmte Original. In einem Buch von 1912 über Hamburger Originale und lustige Geschichten lautet der letzte Satz über Aalweber. „So vergeht aller Glanz der Welt!"

In Erinnerung gerufen hat Hamburg das Original Aalweber 1922 ausgerechnet auf „Notgeld", das in der Wirtschaftskrise von der Stadt ausgegeben wurde, um den Mangel an Kleingeld zu beheben. Es ist dem Architekten Dieter Grohs zu verdanken, dass seit 2011 vor dem Haus Spadenteich 1 in St. Georg ein koloriertes Stahlrelief an Aalweber erinnert. Grohs sagte anerkennend bei der Denkmalseinweihung: „Der Aalweber wusste genau, wie man verkauft. Er kleidete sich auffällig und präsentierte sein Angebot in Form von gereimten Versen ... Seine Verkaufsmethode hatte Unterhaltungswert, so wie es heute noch der Aale-Dieter vom Fischmarkt hat." Auch auf Wikipedia gibt es mittlerweile einen kurzen Beitrag über Aalweber. Der *Original Hamburger Hummel-Club von 1902* ruft Aalweber wie andere Originalen bei Auftritten ehrenamtlicher Schauspielerinnen und Schauspieler in historischen Kostümen in Erinnerung.

Aale-Aale

„Aale-Aale" hieß mit bürgerlichem Namen Karl Wilhelm Schreiber. Er kam 1892 in Dresden zur Welt und arbeitete zunächst auf einem Elbschiff, ließ sich dann aber in Hamburg nieder. Das kam so: Sein Schiffer schickte ihn in Hamburg zum Aalkauf los. Schreiber kaufte nicht nur die Fische, sondern erkannte auch, welches Potenzial im Aalgeschäft lag. Er gab seinen bisherigen Beruf auf und verkaufte von 1919 an geräucherte Aale in Hamburg, sonntags auf dem Fischmarkt und in der Woche an anderen Stellen in der Stadt. Mit seinem umgebauten Kinderwagen, seiner Melone mit Blumen und seiner besonders hohen Stimme, mit der er „Aale, Aale!" rief, gehörte er rasch zu den bekanntesten Hamburger Straßenverkäufern. Oft stand er mit seinem Wagen vor Karstadt in Eppendorf oder vor Woolworth in der Innenstadt.

Bereits 1952 wurde Aale-Aale in der Presse irrtümlich für tot erklärt. Damals starb der Fischhändler Hermann Münch, der sich in der Gerichtsmedizin als Frau erwies. Da eine Ähnlichkeit mit Aale-Aale bestand, kam es zu einer Verwechslung. In den Morgenzeitungen war zu lesen: „Aale-Aale eine Frau". Der Irrtum klärte sich rasch auf und die Presse hatte am nächsten Tag erneut eine absatzfördernde Schlagzeile: „Hei lewet noch! Aale-Aale lebt!" Es war nun geklärt, dass der Fischverkäufer Aale-Aale nicht gestorben war. Auch sprach sich rasch herum, dass er verheiratet war und zwei Kinder hatte, also keine Frau war. Die Falschmeldung erwies sich als sehr vorteilhaft für das Original Aale-Aale, der sich über Zeitungsinterviews und viel Publicity freuen konnte.

Es gab noch einmal eine Falschmeldung, weil Aale-Aale mit Aalweber verwechselt wurde. Die Leser des *Hamburger Abendblatts* lasen 16. Januar 1965: „Originale sterben aus. Der Aalweber ist eines der letzten in Hamburg. Wer kennt nicht das kleine Männchen mit dem Blumenstrauß am verbeultem schwarzen Hut, in einem Kinderwagen die selbstgeräucherten Aale durch die Straße schiebend und sie anpreisend: ‚Aale, Aale, Aale …'" Da war Aalweber schon mehr als ein Jahrhundert tot, Aale-Aale aus der Seilerstraße aber noch quicklebendig. Auch diese Falschmeldung musste den Aalverkäufer nicht ärgern, denn Publicity war schon damals verkaufsfördernd.

Nicht zuletzt aufgrund der Falschmeldungen verkaufte das Hamburger Original noch jahrelang mit großem Erfolg seine Räucheraale, etwa 200 Stück am Tag. Er selbst aß übrigens keinen Aal, sondern bevorzugte Karpfen, aber das behielt er wohlweislich für sich. „Aale-Aale" starb am 30. Oktober 1970 in einem Heim in Farmsen. Das *Hamburger Abendblatt* nahm das zum Anlass für einen ausführlichen Beitrag, der mit dem Satz endete: „Jetzt ist Hamburg wirklich um ein Original ärmer geworden."

Hans Albers

Auf der Reeperbahn nachts um halb eins,
ob Du'n Mädel hast oder auch keins,
amüsierst Du Dich, denn das findet sich,
auf der Reeperbahn nachts um halb eins.

Dieses Lied von der Reeperbahn ist bis heute das bekannteste Lied, das mit Hans Albers in Verbindung gebracht wird. Er sang es im Film „Große Freiheit Nr. 7". Als Hamburg 1943 schon in Trümmern lag, spielte Hans Albers einen alternden Seemann in einem Film ohne Trümmer und auch ohne Hakenkreuze. Albers, der auf einem Schiff nie weiter als bis nach Helgoland gekommen war, wurde mit dem Film zum bekanntesten Seemann der deutschen Filmgeschichte.

Matthias Wegner schrieb in seiner Albers-Biografie über „Große Freiheit Nr. 7": „Von den mehr als hundertfünfzig Filmen mit Hans Albers sollte dieser sein wohl berühmtester, manche sagen: sein bester, werden. Das verdankt er vor allem dem Regisseur Helmut Käutner, dem es gelang, in dem ewigen Sieger und Herzensbrecher die melancholischen, sanftmütigen und resignativen Saiten anzuschlagen. Der Film ist ebenso eine Hommage auf die Seefahrt wie auf Hamburg, genauer St. Pauli."

Der ehemalige Seemann Hannes Krüger muss sich im Film in Hamburg als Sänger und Musiker im Hippodrom durchschlagen, wo Besucher versuchen, sich mehrere Runden auf bockigen Pferden zu halten. Das Lokal auf St. Pauli hat es tatsächlich gegeben. Kurt Tucholsky hat dieses *Hippodrom* besucht, und seine Eindrücke unterscheiden sich deutlich von der launigen Darstellung im Film: „Die Pferde hatten müde, traurige Augen, weil sie nachts hier unten, ein paar Kellerstufen unter dem Trottoirpegel, herumlaufen mussten, ohne jemals ans Ziel zu kommen.“ Das *Hippodrom* an der Großen Freiheit hatte nicht die Hausnummer 7, sondern 10-12. Aber die Hausnummer verdankte der Filmtitel ohnehin nicht dem Lokal, sondern den staatlichen Zensoren des Naziregimes. Die fanden den ursprünglich geplanten Titel „Große Freiheit“ zu „missverständlich“. Man hätte ja denken können, es ginge in dem Film tatsächlich um die Freiheit, dazu noch die große Freiheit. Also mussten der Titel um „Nr. 7“ erweitert werden. Auch bestand Goebbels darauf, dass die Hauptfigur nicht Johnny Kröger heißen durfte, das klinge zu Englisch. Man verständigte sich auf Hannes.

Der berühmteste St. Pauli-Film wurde vor allem in Babelsberg und Prag gedreht

Das waren kleine Entgegenkommen des Regisseurs, wenn man bedenkt, dass der ursprüngliche Auftrag gelautet hatte, einen Durchhaltefilm über die deutsche U-Boot-Flotte zu drehen. Käutner konnte Goebbels überzeugen, stattdessen einen Film über deutsche Seeleute zu produzieren, einen Unterhaltungsfilm, der den Menschen in schweren Zeiten einige Stunden Frohsinn bieten sollte. Und für einen solchen Film war Hans Albers die Idealbesetzung eines alternden Seemanns. Weder Käutner noch Albers hätten sich für einen plumpen Durchhaltefilm zur Verfügung gestellt, zumal Mitte 1943 nicht mehr zu übersehen war, dass die Naziherrschaft ihrem Ende entgegenging.

Goebbels war in dieser Zeit neben den Durchhaltefilmen auch an Unterhaltungsfilmen interessiert, denn nach der Niederlage in Stalingrad und angesichts der immer heftigeren alliierten Bombenangriffe auf deutsche Städte notierte der Propagandaminister in seinem Tagebuch: „Der breiten Massen hat sich eine gewisse Skepsis, um nicht zu sagen Hoffnungslosigkeit bemächtigt." Schon im Jahr zuvor hatte er in seinem Tagebuch notiert: „Auch die Unterhaltung ist heute staatspolitisch wichtig, wenn nicht sogar kriegsentscheidend." Die Kombination des Regisseurs Helmut Käutner, der gerade den erfolgreichen Komödienfilm „Wir machen Musik" fertiggestellt hatte, mit dem populären Draufgänger Hans Albers schien eine gute Unterhaltung zu garantieren.

Gedreht hat man die Innenaufnahmen nicht im *Hippodrom* auf St. Pauli, sondern in einem aufwendig hergestellten Kulissen-Hippodrom. Während das reale St. Pauli und große Teile Hamburgs im Bombenhagel zerstört wurden, drehte man in Babelsberg bei Berlin den vielleicht berühmtesten St.-Pauli-Film.

Das Zentrum des Film-Hippodroms bildete eine Pferdemanege, die von Sitzplätzen umgeben war. Der frühere Seemann Hannes Kröger tritt hier als Sänger und Musiker auf und soll maritime Stimmung verbreiten. Er singt auch das berühmte Lied „La Paloma" in der Textfassung von Helmut Käutner:

Seemannsbraut ist die See
Und nur ihr kann er treu sein.
Wenn der Sturmwind sein Lied singt,
Dann winkt mir der Großen Freiheit Glück!

Kröger verliebt sich in das junge Mädchen Gisa und ist bereit, für sie einen seriösen Beruf zu ergreifen und mit einer Barkasse Hafenrundfahrten anzubieten. Aber Gisa zieht einen jüngeren Mann vor und Hannes Kröger heuert auf dem Segelschiff *Padua* an, um sich auf die Reise nach Australien zu begeben. Er fährt nicht für „Volk und Vaterland" auf einem U-Boot in den Krieg, sondern wegen seines gebrochenen Herzens unter vollen Segeln in die Ferne. Weiter konnte sich der Film nicht von den ursprünglichen Erwartungen der Marineführung entfernen.

Ein „wehrkraftzersetzender" Film

Die Produktion des Films war mit großen Schwierigkeiten verbunden. Mitte 1943 hatten die Bombenangriffe auf Berlin ein solches Ausmaß angenommen, dass das Filmteam nach Prag umziehen musste, wo die Kulissen neu gebaut wurden. Ganz ohne Außenaufnahmen in Hamburg ließ sich der maritime Film allerdings nicht produzieren. Es gelangt Regisseur und Kameramännern, in St. Pauli und im Hafen so zu drehen, dass keine zerstörten Häuser, keine Nazifahnen und keine Kriegsschiffe zu sehen waren. Im Hafen war dies nur möglich, indem man viel künstlichen Nebel erzeugte.

Und mittendrin Hans Albers. Er spielte nicht nur einen alternden angetrunkenen Mann, sondern er war es auch. Die Nächte verbrachte er im *Atlantic Hotel*, und wenn mal wieder Bombenalarm war, erwies es sich als sehr günstig, dass sich der Schutzraum im Keller des Hotels in der Nähe des Weinkellers befand. Auch die melancholische Grundstimmung, die Käutner dem Film gab, entsprach der Stimmung des Hauptdarstellers, der noch einsamer dastand als früher schon. Er hatte nie viele enge Freunde gehabt, nun war er so vereinsamt wie Kapitän Kröger am Ende des Films.

Zudem machte sich Albers wahrscheinlich auch keine Illusionen darüber, dass die Fröhlichkeit im Hippodrom einen krassen Gegensatz zu der realen Katastrophe um ihn herum darstellte. Der Film hat Hans Albers zum Original, zu *dem* Hamburger Seemann gemacht. Aber es gab die Seefahrerromantik und die Verklärung von St. Pauli mit Schifferklavier, fröhlichen Liedern und leicht bekleideten Mädchen nur noch in den Studios in Prag.

Gezeigt werden durfte der Streifen zunächst nicht, das verhinderte Großadmiral Dönitz. Ein Seemann, der sich ständig betrinkt, melancholisch wirkt und in zweifelhaften Kreisen verkehrt, war nicht der Held, den Deutschland im „Endkampf" brauchte. Der Film wäre „wehrkraftzersetzend", erklärte der Großadmiral. Propagandaminister Goebbels störte sich an der schwermütigen Grundstimmung des Films sowie an Sätze wie „Einmal wird alles vorbei sein" in dem Lied „La Paloma". Zwar fand eine Uraufführung in Prag statt, aber im Deutschen Reich durfte der Film nicht gezeigt werden. Die ursprünglich geplante große Premiere in Hamburg fiel aus, zumal der Hamburger Reichsstatthalter Kaufmann zu den vehementesten Gegnern des Films gehörte.

Erst nach Kriegsende, am 19. Oktober 1945, war der Film im *Waterloo-Kino* in der Dammtorstraße zu sehen. Die Warteschlange reichte damals bis zum Gänsemarkt. Zur Premiere kamen die am Film beteiligten Stars Ilse

Werner, Gustav Knuth und Hans Söhnker. Wer fehlte, war Hans Albers. Dabei hatte er seiner Schwester geschrieben: „Die Große Freiheit ist einer der schönsten und wertvollsten Filme geworden, die ich je gemacht habe."

Einzelne negative Beurteilungen des Films gab es auch nach dem Ende der Naziherrschaft. Die Kirchen beklagten sich über das unmoralische Treiben, vor allem „die Hingabe vor der Ehe". Von den Filmkritikern wurde der Film aber überwiegend sehr positiv bewertet und der Hauptdarsteller Albers konnte sich über viele lobende Kommentare freuen. „Große Freiheit Nr. 7" war übrigens einer der ersten erfolgreichen Farbfilme in Deutschland.

Ein schlagkräftiger Schüler

Geboren wurde Hans Albers an 22. September 1891 in der Langen Reihe 71 in St. Georg als jüngstes von sechs Kindern einer Schlachterfamilie. Der wohlhabende Vater, eine stattliche Gestalt mit großem Backenbart, liebte das Theater und war mit Schauspielerinnen und Schauspielern befreundet – was ihn später nicht daran hinderte, den Theaterplänen seines Sohnes völlig ablehnend gegenüberzustehen.

Hans war schlagkräftig, wie es auch sein Zeichenlehrer erleben musste. Der Lehrer ging, nachdem er den Jungen mit einem Lineal geschlagen hatte, beim Gegenangriff mit verletztem Knöchel zu Boden. K.O. hieße das beim Boxen, aber im schulischen Leben war alles anders: Hans Albers flog von der Schule. Schlachter wie sein Vater wollte er trotzdem nicht werden: „Die ganze Wursterei hat mich nie interessiert."

Seit er als Kind im *Deutschen Schauspielhaus* „Wilhelm Tell" gesehen hatte, war er fasziniert vom Theater. Er schlich sich abends aus dem Haus, um von einem Stehplatz im Zweiten Rang in die Welt der Illusionen und der großen Gefühle einzutauchen. Im *Hansa-Theater* bewunderte er die Artisten und konnte natürlich nicht ahnen, dass er einmal mit artistischen Leistungen als Schauspieler viel Anerkennung finden sollte. Wenn er nach einem Theaterbesuch spätabends heimkehrte oder tagsüber zu lange auf der Alster gerudert hatte, setzte es Schläge vom Vater. Der Sohn musste häufiger vom benachbarten Korbmacher den passenden Stock holen, mit dem ihn der Vater dann verprügelte.

Aus dem Junge sollte etwas „Ordentliches werden" – und wurde trotzdem ein Schauspieler

Hans Albers wechselte die Schule, blieb aber ein Schulversager. Nach dem Abbruch der Schulbildung ordnete sein Vater an: „Du kommst in die Lehre. Aus dir soll mal was Ordentliches werden." Deshalb begann Hans Albers erst einmal eine Lehre in einer Farbenhandlung, aber er gab die Hoffnung nicht auf, Schauspieler zu werden. Er sprach hoffnungsvoll im *Deutschen Schauspielhaus* vor, aber dort war man der Auffassung, dass sein Talent nicht ausreichte. Der Oberspielleiter des *Deutschen Schauspielhauses* attestierte ihm: „Junger Mann, Sie haben nicht die Spur von Talent, geben Sie die Hoffnung auf."

Hans Albers gab trotzdem die Bemühungen nicht auf, Schauspieler zu werden. Es kam deshalb nicht überraschend, dass er seine Lehre in der Farbenhandlung ohne einen Abschluss abbrach. Auf Geheiß des Vaters begann er nun eine Ausbildung in einem Seidenhaus in Frankfurt am Main. Das hatte für den jungen Mann den Vorteil, dass er sich durch den Ortswechsel der Kontrolle durch seinen Vater entziehen konnte. In Frankfurt nahm er Schauspielunterricht und sprach in einem Theater vor, wo er den Rat erhielt, es erst einmal auf einer Bühne in der Provinz zu versuchen.

Hans Albers schrieb sich die Finger wund, um ein Engagement zu bekommen. Es klappte 1911 in Schandau in der Nähe von Dresden und anschließend im mecklenburgische Güstrow. Hier musste Albers sich nicht nur als „junger Liebhaber", sondern in den Umbaupausen auch als Bühnenarbeiter bewähren. In Güstrow und bei vielen Gastspielen in der Provinz lernte Albers kennen und schätzen, was gemeinhin als „Schmierentheater" bezeichnet wird: „Nun werden Sie lächeln, wenn ich Ihnen sage, dass die ‚Schmiere' ein Paradies war. Ein Paradies der Groschen – sofern wir überhaupt die Gage sahen -, aber ein Paradies. Sie müssen sich vorstellen, man kam als blutjunger Dachs auf die Bretter, man konnte spielen, spielen, spielen. Heute den Romeo, morgen den Tell, übermorgen den Trafft, überübermorgen den Hamlet. Das war Literatur am laufenden Band. Aber man spielte mit einer Begeisterung, die es nirgends auf der Welt gibt. Über Hunger, über tausend Kalamitäten hinweg."

Der mühsame Weg zum bekannten Schauspieler

Aber die „Schmiere" hatte auch ihre Schattenseiten. Als Albers in einem Provinznest in einer „Faust"-Aufführung gerade den Theatertod starb, ging der gastronomische Betrieb im Saal munter weiter. Was dann geschah, hat

Albers so beschrieben: „In der Sterbeszene Valentins erklangen die prosaischen Worte: ‚Zwei Bockwurst, drei Helle'. Da packte mich der heilige Zorn. Eigentlich hatte ich schon ‚tot' zu sein. Aber ich richtete mich auf und rief ganz ungoethisch in den Saal: ‚Mir auch!' Die Mecklenburger nahmen mir das sehr übel. Ich durfte mich in diesem Städtchen nie wieder auf der Bühne zeigen."

Albers spielte auch kleine Rollen mit großer Sorgfalt. Von negativer Kritik ließ er sich nicht beirren, etwa von dieser Bemerkung eines Theaterkritikers in Güstrow: „Derartige Darstellungen, die alles zu wünschen übrig lassen, sind wir Gott sei Dank an unserem Theater nicht gewohnt." Trotzdem war Albers bald darauf auf der Bühne des *Neuen Theaters* in Frankfurt zu sehen und danach in Köln.

1913 engagierte man Albers für die Sommersaison im Kurtheater der Insel Helgoland. Anschließend schaffte er es endlich, auf Hamburger Bühnen zu spielen. Öfter waren dies Nebenrollen, aber das focht ihn nicht an: „Kein Mensch startet mit einem Zwölf-Zylinder-Motor ins Glück." (Später fuhr er mit umso größerer Begeisterung einen Zwölf-Zylinder-Cadillac.) Größere Rollen durfte er im Altonaer *Schillertheater* spielen, hier sah ihn auch endlich sein Vater und erkannte ihn prompt nicht hinter der Maske. 1914 hatte sich Albers ans *Thalia Theater* hochgearbeitet, spielte den Helden in einem patriotischen Stück und wurde bejubelt.

Vom Theaterhelden zum Soldaten

Aber es herrschte Krieg, und der Schauspieler wurde vom Theaterhelden zum Soldaten. Nach einer schweren Kriegsverletzung konnte er nur mit großer Mühe verhindern, dass die Ärzte ein Bein amputierten. Er brauchte Monate, um zu gesunden. Anschließend stand er in Wiesbaden auf der Bühne. Besonders Lustspiele und Operetten waren gefragt, um sich von dem tristen Kriegsalltag abzulenken.

Nach Kriegsende wagte Albers den Sprung nach Berlin. Vor allem in Revuen trat Hans Albers mit Komik, Schlagfertigkeit und akrobatischen Fähigkeiten in Erscheinung. Unvergessen, wie er an einem Kronleuchter hing, mit einem eleganten Kopfsprung in einem kleinen Wasserbassin landete und in kürzester Zeit wieder trocken in Frack und Zylinder auf der Bühne stand. Oder jene turbulente Tanznummer, an deren Ende er scheinbar zufällig ausrutschte und im Souffleusenkasten verschwand. Während Albers nun fast jeden Abend auf der Bühne stand, verbrachte er die Tage als Schauspieler in meist billig gemachten Stummfilmen, von denen viele mittlerweile verschollen sind.

Der Durchbruch am „Deutschen Theater"

Der große Fleiß von Hans Albers zahlte sich aus, nicht nur finanziell (er wohnte nun als Dauergast im *Hotel Adlon*), sondern auch auf dem Weg zum erfolgreichen Schauspieler. 1928 engagierte ihn der berühmte Max Reinhardt für das *Deutsche Theater* in Berlin, weil ein anderer Schauspieler ausgefallen war. Hans Albers nutzte die Chance, und endlich gelang mit dem Stück „Die Verbrecher" der Durchbruch: „Ich musste 20 Jahre warten und schuften, bis meine große Chance kam." Er stand nun mit Schauspielern wie Gustaf Gründgens auf der Bühne und spielte den Mackie Messer in Brechts „Dreigroschenoper". Hinzu kamen zahlreiche Filmrollen. Im Gegensatz zu vielen anderen Schauspielern gelang es Albers, den Sprung vom Stumm- zum Tonfilm zu schaffen.

Er wirkte insgesamt an etwa 150 Stumm- und Tonfilmen mit. Der „blonde Hans" mit den blauen Augen machte als Held und Draufgänger Karriere. An der Seite von Marlene Dietrich glänzte er im Film „Der blaue Engel". Mit Heinz Rühmann drehte er den Film „Bomben auf Monte Carlo".

Inzwischen waren der Mensch Hans Albers und der berühmte Schauspieler kaum mehr zu unterscheiden. Biograf Matthias Wegner schreibt dazu: „Man wusste jetzt nicht mehr, ob er eine Rolle spielte oder er selbst war. Er lebte auf großem Fuß und schien ständig zu sagen: ‚Seid umschlungen, Millionen!' Er schien von sich selbst restlos überzeugt – oder war das nur eine Pose?" Albers spielte in Theater und Film nicht nur eine Rolle, sondern er überzeugte dadurch, dass er die dargestellte Person war. Und im Alltag spielte er ebenso überzeugend seine Rolle als trinkfester, fröhlicher, eleganter Herr, der sich durch nichts erschüttern ließ.

Hans Albers verliebte sich in die Schauspielerin Hansi Burg. Sie war nur mäßig erfolgreich, und nachdem die beiden ein Paar geworden waren, gab sie ihre eigene künstlerische Arbeit auf und konzentriere sich ganz darauf, ihren Lebenspartner dabei zu unterstützen, gute Rollen in Theater und Film zu erhalten – und das zu lukrativen finanziellen Bedingungen. Auch sorgte sie dafür, dass Albers das Zocken aufgab. Aber von seiner Alkoholabhängigkeit konnte sie ihn nicht befreien und auch nicht von seinen vielen „Frauengeschichten".

Große Erfolge eines vielseitigen Schauspielers

Hans Albers beeindruckte nun sowohl als Revueschauspieler als auch als Mime in ernsten Stücken. Immer wieder sang er in den Filmen, obwohl seine Kritiker behaupteten, er könnte gar nicht singen – und Schifferklavier spielen schon gar nicht. Schlager wie „Komm auf die Schaukel Luise", „Flieger, grüß mir die Sonne", „Hoppla, jetzt komm ich" und „La Paloma" machten ihn trotzdem berühmt. Enge Freunde hatte er nicht, wirkte distanziert. Der Kabarettist Sammy Drechsel sagte später über die Freunde des volkstümlichen Schauspielers: „Keinen einzigen, mit dem er durch dick und dünn gehen konnte!" Der Regisseur Helmut Käutner erlebte Albers als einen „Mann voll unerfüllter Träume, einen einsamen Menschen".

Der „blonde Hans" war ein Star, aber keiner, der abhob. Immer wieder unterhielt er sich kumpelhaft mit Leuten in einer Kneipe oder beim Sechstagerennen. Hemdsärmelich ließ er eine Distanz zwischen dem berühmten Schauspieler und den einfachen Leuten aus dem Volk gar nicht erst aufkommen. Und wenn ihn Arbeiter im Hamburger Hafen um ein Autogramm baten, soll er manchmal zu Tränen gerührt gewesen sein. So jemand konnte zum geliebten Hamburger Original werden, zumal wenn er die Heimatstadt und ihren Hafen liebte und besang. Er sagte einem Freund bei einem Hafenbesuch: „Hier am Hafen schlägt das Herz von Hamburg, meiner Heimatstadt."

Als Schauspieler blieb er sich treu: Hans Albers spielte immer Hans Albers. Und er spielte so, wie er es intuitiv für richtig hielt. Da ließ er sich von Filmregisseuren nicht viel sagen. War er mit einer Szene zufrieden, verkündete er, die Sache wäre „Otto-Otto", was bedeutete, sie sei in Ordnung und damit war die Sache für ihn erledigt.

„Er kümmerte sich nur um seine eigene Karriere"

Seine größte Theaterrolle wurde der „Liliom". Fast l.900 Mal spielte er von 1930 an den Rummelplatzausrufer, einen kleinen Gauner mit rüden Methoden und weichem Herzen. Auch im *Thalia Theater* kam er in dieser Rolle 1931 groß heraus. Autor Molnár war begeistert: „Jetzt sehe ich meinen Liliom erst richtig. Sie haben mir mein Stück erst gezeigt, wie es wirklich ist."

Während die Weimarer Republik im Chaos versank, genoss Hans Albers, dass er endlich große Erfolge in Theater und Film feiern konnte. Matthias Wegner schreibt in seiner Albers-Biografie über diese Jahre, der Schauspieler „interessiert sich nicht im Geringsten für Politik. Er kümmert sich mit überschäumender Lebenslust und kühl-strategischer Professionalität nur um seine eigene Karriere, der alles andere untergeordnet wird." Albers „liefert gute Laune für einige Stunden und fördert die Zuversicht seiner Anhänger, was viel bedeutet in diesen bedrückenden Zeiten".

Er tat dies mit großem Selbstbewusstsein und sang:

> *Hoppla, jetzt komm ich!*
> *Alle Türen auf, alle Fenster auf,*
> *Hoppla, jetzt komm ich*
> *Und wer mit mir geht,*
> *der kommt eins rauf!*

Allein 1932 wirkte er an fünf Filmen mit und das neben seinen Theaterengagements. Er arbeitete hart für seinen Erfolg – und er trank immer mehr. In einem Lokal schrieb er unter ein Albers-Foto, das dort aufgehängt worden war: „Was ich in Berlin getrunken habe – darauf könnte ein Panzerkreuzer schwimmen."

In Hamburg entstand der Film „Der Draufgänger", in dem Albers die Rolle des Hafenpolizisten übernahm. Obwohl er nur noch als Gast in seine Geburtsstadt kam, erwarb er sich durch seine Film- und Theaterrollen allmählich den Ruf als Hamburger Jung und später vor allem als Seemann. Er war vielleicht das einzige Hamburger Original, das sich diesen Ruf erwarb, als er schon gar nicht mehr in der Stadt lebte. Er blieb, wie Bürgermeister Max Brauer verkündete, ein „großartiger Hamburger Jung".

Ein ambivalentes Verhältnis zu den Naziherrschern

Beim Machtantritt der Nazis verließen viele Schauspielerinnen, Schauspieler und Dramaturgen Deutschland, auch manche von denen, mit denen Hans Albers jahrelang gut zusammengearbeitet hatte. Darunter war Franz Molnár, der Verfasser des Stückes „Liliom", mit dem Hans Albers so große Erfolge gefeiert hatte. Albers blieb und wanderte wohl auch deshalb nicht aus, weil sein Englisch sehr mangelhaft war. In Deutschland war er ein Star, im Ausland hingegen fast unbekannt und hätte dort seine Karriere als Schauspieler nur unter großen Mühen fortsetzen können.

Hans Albers spielte weiter in der Heimat, musste allerdings stärker als früher um die Höhe seiner Gagen feilschen, denn die UFA taxierte, dass der Marktwert des unangepassten Schauspielers unter den neuen politischen Verhältnissen gesunken war. Goebbels forderte, dass die Gagen dieses Schauspielers sinken müssten. Aber als blonder und blauäugiger Mann mit stechendem Blick entsprach er so ganz dem Bild der Nazis von einem deutschen Mann und durfte mit hohen Gagen weiterspielen. Vor allem im Krieg sollte er gute Laune in trüben Zeiten verbreiten. Er selbst war noch einsamer geworden, nachdem seine Eltern in Hamburg gestorben waren. Er ertränkte seine Sorgen mit großen Mengen Alkohol, blieb dabei aber ein zuverlässiger Schauspieler, der pünktlich zu den Filmaufnahmen erschien.

Zwar musste er sich mit den neuen Machthabern arrangieren, aber er blieb rebellisch, ja manchmal anarchisch, im Leben und im Film. Im Gegensatz zu anderen dagebliebenen Schauspielern vermied er es konsequent, sich an der Seite von Nazigrößen ablichten zu lassen und hatte ein distanziertes Verhältnis zu Goebbels.

„Ich spiele Helden. Aber ich bin keiner."

Die Nazis brauchten den populären Schauspieler umso mehr, je größer die Zahl derer war, die ins Exil gingen oder als „Nichtarier" nicht mehr spielen durften. Albers spielte in diesen Jahren in zwanzig Filmen Hauptrollen und war ein Publikumsliebling. Berühmt wurde er unter anderem durch den Film „Münchhausen".

Er war finanziell so erfolgreich, dass er sich ein Landhaus mit einem großen Grundstück direkt am Starnberger See leisten konnte. Er blieb mit Hansi Burg liiert, der „halbjüdischen" Schauspielerin, wie sie in den Kategorien der Nazis nun bezeichnet wurde. Goebbels höchstpersönlich forderte Albers auf, die Verbindung zu lösen. Albers tat das 1935 schließlich formal, aber lebte weiterhin mit Hansi Burg zusammen im Haus am Starnberger See. Im Dezember 1938, nach der Reichspogromnacht, floh sie in die Schweiz und von dort aus nach England. Dass Hans Albers sie im Exil finanziell unterstützt haben soll, gehört in das Reich der Legenden. Sie war zunächst auf die Unterstützung einer Wohltätigkeitsorganisation angewiesen und arbeitete später in einer Textilfabrik.

Albers spielte weiter, auch in Propagandafilmen. Und er setzte sich nicht für bedrohte Kolleginnen und Kollegen ein. Später bekannte er: „Ich spiele Helden. Aber ich bin keiner.“ Vielleicht war gerade das der große Bruch zwischen dem Hans Albers im Film und dem Hans Albers im Alltag. Erschrecken muss diese Diagnose des Albers-Biografen Matthias Wegner: „Er hat weder offen noch versteckt Widerstand geleistet, dafür war er nicht politisch und nicht altruistisch genug. Er interessierte sich nur für sich selbst.“

Erfolge und Vereinsamung in der Nachkriegszeit

Dass Albers eine gewisse Distanz zu den Naziherrschern gewahrt hatte, zahlte sich nach Kriegsende aus. Er konnte mühelos den Entnazifizisierungsprozess durchlaufen und weiterhin als Schauspieler arbeiten. Dass der Film „Große Freiheit Nr. 7“ in der letzten Phase der Naziherrschaft verboten worden war, erwies sich für eine Karriere im Nachkriegsdeutschland als vorteilhaft. Der Film von der Großen Freiheit gehörte zu den ersten Filmen, die in den Kinos gezeigt werden durften. Vom April 1946 an spielte Hans Albers erneut die Hauptrolle in seinem geliebten Stück „Liliom". Es war wegen des jüdischen Verfassers in der Nazizeit verboten gewesen, nun feierte Albers mit dem Stück erneut große Erfolge.

1946 kehrte Hansi Burg nach Deutschland und zu Hans Albers zurück. Das Paar lebte - weiterhin unverheiratet – in der Villa am Starnberger See. Hans Albers konnte nun nicht mehr den jungen Draufgänger verkörpern, sondern spielte häufiger ernste Rollen, so einen gealterten Zirkusdirektor in Zuckmayers Stück „Katharina Knie" und in dem Film „Der letzte Mann" den Oberkellner, der auf den untersten Posten im Hotel versetzt wird, eine Rolle, für die Albers bedeutende Auszeichnungen erhielt.

Er arbeitete weiterhin viel – und trank viel. Und wie sein Publikum wollte er die letzten zwölf Jahre rasch vergessen und zu neuen Ufern aufbrechen. Als Fernfahrer in dem Film „Nachts auf den Straßen" mit dem Regisseur Helmut Käutner konnte Albers noch einmal sein ganzes Können zeigen. Das „Lexikon des internationalen Films" lobt den Film und seinen Hauptdarsteller so: „Der zeitnahe und zeitkritische Film ist realistisch, kunstlos und gradlinig inszeniert. Hans Albers nutzt die Gelegenheit, die besten Seiten seiner Persönlichkeit und seines Naturtalents zu zeigen." 1953 wurde die Produktion mit dem Deutschen Filmpreis ausgezeichnet.

In nicht einmal drei Monaten drehte Helmut Käutner mit seinem Star Hans Albers im letzten Quartal 1952 den Film „Käpt'n Bay-Bay". In dieser Zeit war das Produktionsteam für Dreharbeiten zwischen Hamburg-Blankenese, Wiesbaden, Ischia und Neapel unterwegs. Bereits Ende Januar 1953 kam der Streifen in die Kinos. Ein solches Tempo schaffen heutzutage nur Vorabend-Fernsehserien. Die Handlung des Films lässt sich so zusammenfassen: Kapitän Christian Droste, genannt Käpt'n Bay-Bay, hat bereits drei Mal versucht, die gleiche Frau zu heiraten, aber immer kam kurz vor der Trauung etwas dazwischen. Aber beim vierten Versuch klappt es endlich und der Kapitän, gespielt von Hans Albers, kann seine Frau zum Traualtar führen. Käutner und Albers bemühten sich, mit diesem Film an ihren Erfolg mit dem Film „Große Freiheit Nr. 7" anzuknüpfen. Aber dieses Mal scheiterte der Versuch. Im erwähnten „Lexikon des internationalen Films" heißt es über diese Produktion: „Langatmige musikalische Komödie, die Versatzstücke aus Revue, Abenteuer und Love-Story vereint."

„Auf der Reeperbahn nachts um halb eins"

1954 unternahm der Regisseur Wolfgang Liebeneiner einen erneuten Versuch, den Erfolg von „Große Freiheit Nr. 7" zu wiederholen. Neben Hans Albers spielten bekannte Schauspieler wie Heinz Rühmann und Gustav Knuth in dem Film „Auf der Reeperbahn nachts um halb eins" mit. Die Hauptperson, ein in die Heimat zurückkehrender Seemann, gespielt von Hans Albers, trug den Namen Hannes Wedderkamp. Das war eine unübersehbare Anknüpfung an den Namen Hannes Kröger im Film „Große Freiheit Nr. 7". Dass das Lokal in St. Pauli, das der Heimkehrer vor dem Konkurs rettete, den Namen „Galopp-Diele" trug, war ebenfalls kein Zufall, sondern weckte Erinnerungen an das Hippodrom im Vorgängerfilm.

Hannes Wedderkamp verliebt sich im Film in die Tochter seines Geschäftspartners. Sie heiratet nach einigen Verwirrungen einen jüngeren Mann und Hannes Wedderkamp segelt dieses Mal nicht nach Australien, kehrt aber in den Hafen zurück. Wie im Film „Große Freiheit Nr. 7" spielt Hans Albers alle Mitspielerinnen und Mitspieler an die Wand und bereichert den Film mit etlichen bekannten Liedern wie „Komm auf die Schaukel, Luise", „Kleine Möwe, flieg nach Helgoland" und selbstverständlich „Auf der Reeperbahn nachts um halb eins". Ein Filmkritiker bescheinigte der Produktion eine „Mischung aus Film-St. Pauli und etwas Wirklichkeit". Ein anderer Kritiker sprach von einem „Abklatsch eines einstigen Erfolges". Das Original des Seemanns Hannes aus „Große Freiheit Nr. 7" hatte sich verselbständigt, und nun spielte Hans Albers erneut diesen Seemann. Er hat sich damit keinen Gefallen getan.

„Das Herz von St. Pauli"

Noch einmal trat Albers 1957 in dem Hamburg-Film „Das Herz von St. Pauli" als Seemann auf. Er tat dies mit Begeisterung und schrieb damals: „Zum ersten Mal in einem Hamburger Studio. Das ist eine große Freude für mich! Der Herzschlag von St. Pauli, das ist auch mein Herzschlag. Ich bin ja wie's im Lied heißt ‚In Hamburg zu Haus'." Der Schauspieler, der weniger als ein Viertel seines Lebens in Hamburg verbracht hat, bekannte: „Mein Herz ist hiergeblieben an Elbe und Alster, auch wenn mein Haus am Starnberger See steht."

Hans Albers spielt in dem Film einen ehemaligen Kapitän, der eine Bar betreibt. Aber dieses Lokal mit dem Namen „Das Herz von St. Pauli" läuft schlecht, und als sich die Schulden beim Finanzamt auf 6.000 Mark summiert haben, steht der Lokalbesitzer vor der Zahlungsunfähigkeit. Er nimmt einen Geschäftspartner auf, der die Bar aber in einen Nachtclub verwandelt und außerdem die Beute von Raubzügen in Rumfässern im Keller versteckt. Kapitän Jensen muss widerstrebend als „letzter Volkssänger von St. Pauli“ auftreten, um dem Lokal einen Rest maritimen Charakters zu verleihen. Die Polizei kommt den Verbrechern auf die Spur, und der frühere Kapitän kann froh sein, nicht mit verhaftet zu werden. Die Handlung wird mit einer Reihe von Liedern von Hans Albers angereichert.

Als Teil der Filmaufnahmen fuhr Hans Albers in der Rolle des Kapitäns auf der „Wapen von Hamburg“ nach Helgoland. Vierunddreißig Jahre vorher war er als junger Schauspieler nach Helgoland gereist, um dort im Kurtheater zu spielen. Nun unternahm er, der so überzeugend Seeleute gespielt hatte, seine zweite und auch schon letzte Hochseereise. Die Überfahrt nach Helgoland war stürmisch, ebenso die Rückreise, gut für die Filmaufnahmen, aber auch das konnte diesen Film nicht retten.

Manchen erschien Hans Albers in diesem Film als die Verkörperung der eigenen Legende, allerdings von Rheuma und Alkoholproblemen geplagt. Der „Filmdienst“ urteilte: „Ein mit einer simplen Kriminalhandlung gestreckter Unterhaltungsfilm, der allenfalls durch einige stimmungsvolle Außenaufnahmen auffällt. Ansonsten der recht plumpe Versuch, mit Albers‘ Star-Image und Anleihen an Käutners Film ‚Große Freiheit Nr. 7‘ auf Publikumsfang zu gehen.“

Die Sehnsucht nach Hamburg am Starnberger See

Der Film wurde zu einem Flop, wie manche Albers-Filme in den 1950er Jahren. Die Seefahrt-Filme festigten das öffentliche Bild von Hans Albers als Kapitän, und es reduzierte damit die Wahrnehmung seines eigentlich vielfältigen Schaffens auf diese Rolle. Und auch der reale Hans Albers ähnelte im Alter immer mehr den alternden Seebären, die er im Film dargestellt hatte.

Das Tuten der Nebelhörner, das Hämmern der Werftarbeiter und das Schreien der Möwen schallten über den Starnberger See. Von seiner Heimatstadt träumend lauschte Hans Albers auf dem Bootssteg mit Hamburger Wappen den Schellackplatten, und rechts und links leuchteten die Positionslampen. Dazu trank er Grog oder Cognac und rauchte eine Zigarre. Am Ende seines Lebenswegs blieb ihm, was durch das Lied „La Paloma“ unvergessen ist: die Sehnsucht nach einer fernen Heimat, nach einer anderen, besseren Welt. Seine Verbindung zur Seefahrt bestand nun nur noch darin, dass er gelegentlich Buddelschiffe baute.

„Das Herz von St. Pauli, das ist meine Heimat, in Hamburg, da bin ich zu Haus“, hatte er gesungen, aber er fuhr nun nur noch zu Besuch dorthin. Einem Hamburger Besucher gestand er im März 1957: „Ich würde gern eine kleine Wohnung an der Alster haben. Damit ich richtig zu Hause bin, wenn ich Hamburger Luft atmen möchte.“ Auch bat Albers den Hamburger Senatssprecher Erich Lüth, sich nach einem Haus mit Garten für ihn umzusehen. Aber diese Pläne hat Albers nicht mehr verwirklicht.

Die Schauspielerin Ilse Werner, mit der er eine Reihe Filme drehte und die ihn auch persönlich gut kannte, hat geäußert, dass man nicht nur im Film, sondern auch im privaten Leben von ihm „die abenteuerlichsten Eskapaden" erwartete. Er habe diese Erwartungen erfüllen wollen, „immer und überall. In diese Hauptrolle seines Lebens hatte er sich so hineingesteigert, dass er sie nicht nur in seinen rund hundertfünfzig Filmen spielte, sondern auch in der Wirklichkeit."

Seinen Fahrer in Berlin soll er ermahnt haben: „Fahr langsam, Junge, wir wollen gesehen werden." So muss es ihn tief getroffen, dass er als Schauspieler nicht mehr gefragt war. Er übernahm nun auch Nebenrollen in zweitklassigen Filmen. Sein letzter Satz im letzten Film lautete: „Das ist das Ende." Weiterhin nahm er Theaterengagements an, die aber über seine Kräfte gingen. Er brauchte das Rampenlicht ebenso wie den Cognac und nutzte jede Gelegenheit, auf einer Bühne zu stehen. Michaela Krützen hat in ihrer Dissertation diagnostiziert, dass sich Albers am Lebensende „auf dem Tiefpunkt seiner Karriere" befand.

„La Paloma adé"

Anfang März 1960 brach Hans Albers auf der Bühne eines Wiener Theaters mit schweren inneren Blutungen zusammen. Seine letzten Lebenswochen verbrachte er in Kliniken am Starnberger See. Er, der im Film keine Furcht gezeigt hatte, fürchtete sich vor dem Tod: „Ein großes schwarzes Loch – dann das Vergessen." Er starb am 24. Juli 1960. Beigesetzt wurde Albers auf dem *Ohlsdorfer Friedhof* in Hamburg. Er hatte Hansi Burg gesagt: „Bayern ist ein wunderschönes Land und der Starnberger See ist ein romantischer Flecken. Ich bin glücklich hier. Aber wenn ich mal sterbe, möchte ich nicht in Tutzing auf dem Friedhof liegen. Dann soll es Hamburg sein, in meiner Vaterstadt." Mehr als 10.000 Trauernde folgten dem Sarg und lauschten dem Lied, das Albers berühmt gemacht hatte: „Einmal wird alles vorbei sein ... La Paloma adé!"

Hansi Burg musste das Erbe von Hans Albers erst erstreiten, weil die beiden nicht verheiratet gewesen waren. Dann meldete sich das Finanzamt und verlangte 48 Prozent Erbschaftssteuer, weil die Erbin nicht die Ehefrau des Verstorbenen war. Hansi Burg lebte bis zu ihrem Tod am 14. März 1975 in der Villa am Starnberger See. Wie eng sie sich mit Hans Albers verbunden fühlte, kann man auf dem Friedhof in Tutzing feststellen. Obwohl die beiden nie geheiratet hatten, steht auf ihren Wunsch hin auf dem Grabstein der Name „Hansi Burg-Albers". Sie starb einsam. Eine langjährige Freundin war bei ihrer Beisetzung der einzige Trauergast.

Hamburg hat 1964 einen Platz mitten in St. Pauli nach Hans Albers benannt. Der bekannte Künstler Jörg Immendorff hat 1986 für den Platz eine Bronzestatue des Schauspielers mit Schifferklavier geschaffen. Das Geburtshaus von Hans Albers in der Langen Reihe 71 ist erhalten geblieben. Eine Tafel neben dem Hauseingang informiert darüber, dass er hier das Licht der Welt erblickt hat.

Clara Benthien

„Die Hauptfigur selbst, um die herum sich eine kulturell prototypische Gruppierung der Zeit versammelte, war von bescheidenem Charakter, kümmerte sich nicht um ihre ‚publicity', sondern lebte für die, die sich ihr anvertrauten, ihre Freunde und ihre Familie. Sie hielt es niemals für wichtig, etwas von ihrer persönlichen Geschichte für die Nachwelt aufzuzeichnen. Lediglich die von ihr geretteten Objekte überlebten in Woll- oder Wachstuchdecken gewickelt auf Dachböden. Der Künstlerkeller, seine Gäste, der Moritatengesang, der Kunsthandel und mit ihnen alles, was in den vorderen und den hinteren Räumen am Brandsende 13 / Ecke Raboisen geschah, wurden nach und nach vergessen."

Es ist Nele Lipp zu verdanken, dass Clara Benthien und ihre Hamburger Künstlerkneipe inzwischen dem Vergessen entrissen worden ist. Die Künstlerin Nele Lipp ist eine Enkelin der Frau, die als „Hamburgs Sphinx" in die Kulturgeschichte eingegangen ist. Clara Benthien steht zu Recht im Ruf, eine der vielseitigsten Originale im Hamburg der 1920er und 1930er Jahre gewesen zu sein. Nele Lipp hat 2013 eine Ausstellung in der *Staats- und Universitätsbibliothek Hamburg* über ihre Großmutter verantwortet und nur auf der Grundlage des Katalogs der Ausstellung wurde dieses Porträt möglich.

Von der Hutmacherin zur Wirtin

Zur Welt kam Clara Benthien am 27. September 1887 in Düsseldorf. Sie hat keine Lebenserinnerungen hinterlassen und auch aus anderen Quellen ist wenig über ihre

Kindheit und Jugend zu erfahren. Ihr Vater war Architekt. Ihre Mutter starb früh und der Vater heiratete erneut. Die künstlerische Begabung der Tochter wurde rasch erkannt und gefördert. Damit sie Kunst und Broterwerb verbinden konnte, erlernte sie den Beruf einer Hutmacherin. Die junge Frau lernte bei einem Ostseeurlaub den Dekorationsmaler und Künstler Hans Benthien kennen. Obwohl er ein großes Talent als Zeichner und Maler besaß, hatte er zunächst das Anstreicherhandwerk erlernt. Das Paar heiratete 1912 in Hamburg. Ein Jahr später kam die Tochter Henni zur Welt.

Hans Benthien machte sich mit einem Malerbetrieb selbstständig und beschäftigte bald mehrere Maler. Er hatte als Dekorateur der Eingangsbereiche und Treppenhäuser von Villen großen Erfolg. Benthien fand daneben Zeit für eigene künstlerische Arbeiten und unterhielt freundschaftliche Beziehungen zu vielen Hamburger Künstlerinnen und Künstlern. Im Ersten Weltkrieg musste Hans Benthien als Soldat an die Ostfront. Seine Frau sicherte sich und der Tochter mit einem kleinen Modeladen mühsam das Überleben. Als ihr Mann 1918 nach Hamburg zurückkehrte, musste er feststellen, dass mehrere seiner Beschäftigten gefallen waren und dass es in den wirtschaftlich schlechten Zeiten kein Auskommen für einen Dekorationsmaler gab.

Er entschloss sich deshalb, den Beruf zu wechseln und einen Weinhandel aufzubauen. In einem unterirdischen Gewölbe an der Straße Hahntrapp richtete er eine Weinprobierstube ein, die rasch zu einem Treffpunkt der Hamburger Künstlerszene wurde, zu der der Maler Benthien enge Kontakte pflegte. Die Weinprobierstube war so erfolgreich, dass sie 1932 in größere Kellerräume an der Ecke Brandsende/Raboisen umzog.

Benthiens Weinprobierstuben war günstig gelegen zwischen kulturellen Zentren der Stadt wie der *Kunsthalle* und dem *Thalia-Theater*. Sie war so gut besucht, dass Clara Benthien es übernahm, sich um das gastronomische Angebot zu kümmern. Sie begann bescheiden mit belegten Broten und weitete das Angebot rasch aus. Sie servierte neben Wein auch Getränke wie Sekt und Bier.

Während Hans Benthien sich auf den Weinhandel konzentrierte, erwies sich seine Frau Clara als begnadete Gastgeberin. In der Künstlerkneipe *Tante Clara,* wie die Weinstube bald hieß, fühlte sich die Hamburger Bohème ebenso wohl wie Seeleute und Touristen aus aller Welt. Ein Seemann hinterließ im Gästebuch die Eintragung: „So eine gute Frau habe ich noch nicht früher gesehen. Unsere Mutter. Ich fühle mich wohl in Tante Claras Lokal."

Clara Benthien kümmerte sich besonders fürsorglich um Künstlerinnen und Künstler. Wenn einer von ihnen seine Zeche nicht bezahlen konnte, nahm sie eines seiner Bilder in Zahlung und verkaufte es in ihrem Lokal. Anderen Künstlern ermöglichte sie es, ihre Bilder, Skulpturen und kunstgewerbliche Arbeiten in der Kneipe auszustellen, und verkaufte auch diese. Hier ein Beleg dafür, wie beliebt die Wirtin und ihr Lokal in Schauspieler- und Künstlerkreisen war:

Hier trifft man Hamburger Geistes-Crème
Devise ist: Bohème, Bohème!
Hier folgt ein Jeder seinem Spleen –
drum: Jeder einmal bei Benthien!

Die „Hamburger Sphinx" als Seele des Lokals

Bekannte Persönlichkeiten wie der Dichter Joachim Ringelnatz, der Verleger Ernst Rowohlt und der kommunistische Schriftsteller Johannes R. Becher zählten zu den Gästen des Lokals. Auch der Philosoph Oswald Spengler besuchte öfter *Tante Clara,* und es hieß über ihn, dass er in dieser Umgebung den von ihm postulierten „Untergang des Abendlandes" vorübergehend vergessen hätte.

Der Erfolg des Lokals war zweifellos in der Ausstrahlung der Wirtin begründet, die nicht nur humorvoll, sondern auch intellektuell auf der Höhe ihrer Zeit war, sich an gebildeten Gesprächen beteiligte und sich mit ihrer magischen Ausstrahlung den Ruf als „Hamburger Sphinx" erwarb.

Zu den Attraktionen des Lokals gehörte es zweifellos, dass die Wirtin abends humorvolle Moritaten vortrug. Dazu hat Nele Lipp geschrieben: „In den dreißiger Jahren wurden Moritatentafeln gemalt, zu denen ‚Tante Clara' – ebenfalls humorvoll von Künstler-Gästen verfasste – Bänkellieder ... in ihrem leicht rheinisch eingefärbten Sprechgesang kommentierte. Die Bilder waren auf Rollos gemalt, die an der Decke befestigt waren und nach Bedarf herunter gelassen wurden. Wenn die Wirtin keine Moritat vortrug, konnte man das an der Wand dahinter angebrachte Porträt der ‚Tante Clara' von Otto Wild sehen." Die Moritaten-Rollos haben Gäste des Lokals für diesen Zweck gestaltet. Auch Wandgemälde trugen zur einmaligen Atmosphäre des Künstlerlokals bei.

Mutiges Engagement in der Nazizeit

Nach der Machtübernahme der Nazis gestaltete sich der Betrieb der Künstlerkneipe schwierig. Vielen Künstlern, die hier verkehrten, warfen die neuen Herrn des Landes „entartete Kunst“ vor. Hinzu kam, dass Hans Benthien Freimaurer war und diese Vereinigungen von den Nazis verfolgt wurden. Das Lokal *Tante Clara* entwickelte sich rasch zu einem Treffpunkt der Verfemten und Verfolgten. Nun erwies es sich als günstig, dass das Kellerlokal einige hintere Räumlichkeiten besaß, in denen man sich unbeobachtet treffen und offen miteinander reden konnte. Hier planten Clara und Hans Benthien auch, wie sie politisch Verfolgten und Juden bei ihrer Flucht helfen konnten. Unter denen, die mit Unterstützung der Benthiens das Land verlassen konnten, war der bekannte jüdische Pädagoge Ernst Loewenberg, der in Hamburg eine Reformschule geleitet hatte.

Nele Lipp hat über die Verdienste ihrer Großmutter in den schwierigen Zeiten herausgefunden: „… ‚Tante Clara‘ (konnte) mit ihrem Humor und ihrem nicht alltäglichen Mut, mit dem sie und ihr im Hintergrund mit seinen Freimaurerfreunden … wirkenden Mann Hans Benthien vielen Menschen das Durchhalten und in einigen Fällen auch das Überleben ermöglichen“.

Es blieb nicht aus, dass sich gelegentlich Nazis in braunen Uniformen in das Lokal verirrten. Um alle anderen Gäste vor deren Betreten der Künstlerkneipe zu warnen, hatte Clara Benthien einige Türsteher engagiert, die bei drohender Gefahr eine verabredete Melodie pfiffen. Von da an führten die Stammgäste nur noch unverfängliche

Gespräche. Wie gut die Tarnung funktionierte, zeigte sich 1936, als ein sehr positiver Beitrag über das Lokal und seine Wirtin unbeanstandet von der Zensur in einer Tageszeitung erscheinen konnte:

„Eine schmale Treppe geht in den ausgedehnten weiten Keller. Tante Klara wird die liebenswürdige Wirtin genannt, die hier die Maler und Schauspieler bemuttert. Sie sitzen Bank an Bank hinter hölzernen Tischen, trinken wenig oder viel, wie sie es gerade können, und sind unbändig vergnügt dabei. Die Bilder, die sie hier verkaufen, sind gar nicht erst aufgehängt, sie stehen fertig und unfertig, gerahmt und ungerahmt an den Wänden, in den Ecken und legen Zeugnis dafür ab, wie der Geist dieser arbeitsamen und begabten Stadt auch den Malern nicht fremd blieb. Tante Klara ist eine Künstlermutter, wie sie sein muss, sie sorgt für ihre Gäste, hat ein freigiebiges Herz, rheinischen Humor, einen klugen Kopf und ein scharfes Urteil."

Ergänzend sei hier erwähnt, dass Clara Benthien im Krieg für verarmte und ausgebombte Besucher stets eine kostenlose warme Mahlzeit bereit hielt. Im Gespräch mit „Hinz und Kunzt" sagte Nele Lipp über diese Zeit: „Außerdem hatte meine Oma ein großes Herz, sie hat viele durchgefüttert. Sie selbst war bescheiden und hatte immer nur zwei Paar Schuhe."

Der vergebliche Versuch eines Neuanfangs

Im Juni 1944 trafen Bomben das Gebäude, in dem sich das Lokal *Tante Clara* im Keller befand. Es war noch möglich, Kunstwerke aus den Trümmern zu bergen, aber die Einrichtung, die Deckengemälde und die Moritatenrollos gingen unwiederbringlich verloren. Ein Weiterbetrieb des Lokals war nicht möglich.

Nach dem Krieg eröffnete Clara Benthien ein neues Lokal in der Warburgstraße, aber der Versuch einer Neubelebung ihres traditionsreichen Künstlerlokals scheiterte. Clara Benthien starb am 16. November 1962, ihr Mann war bereit 1947 gestorben. Im *Garten der Frauen* in Ohlsdorf erinnert eine Stele an Clara Benthien.

Matthias Claudius

Der Mond ist aufgegangen,
die goldnen Sternlein prangen
am Himmel hell und klar;
der Wald steht schwarz und schweiget,
und aus den Wiesen steiget
der weiße Nebel wunderbar.

Ohne sein Gedicht vom Mond wäre Matthias Claudius wohl längst in Vergessenheit geraten. Dieses Gedicht bringt anrührend die Liebe des Dichters zur Natur und seinen tiefen Glauben zum Ausdruck. Es enthält auch eine Gegenposition zu den Gedanken der Aufklärung, denen Claudius ratlos und ablehnend gegenüberstand. Er misstraute allen Versuchen, die Welt wissenschaftlich zu durchdringen und Abschied von einem naiven christlichen Glauben zu nehmen. Das hat er in diesen Versen seines Gedichtes vom Mond zum Ausdruck gebracht:

Seht ihr den Mond dort stehen?
Er ist nur halb zu sehen
und ist doch rund und schön.
So sind wohl manche Sachen,
die wir getrost belachen,
weil unsre Augen sie nicht sehn.
Wir stolzen Menschenkinder
sind eitel arme Sünder
und wissen gar nicht viel;
wir spinnen Luftgespinste
und suchen viele Künste
und kommen weiter von dem Ziel.

Claudius galt vielen Zeitgenossen als kauziges Original. Überliefert ist, wie der Gelehrte Wilhelm von Humboldt den Dichter 1796 beschrieb: „Brav, gutmütig, herzlich, gesellig, und in der Gesellschaft witzig und launig in sehr hohem Grade. Doch soll er von dieser seiner Originalität viel verloren haben. In religiösen Ideen soll er schwärmerisch und mystisch seyn. Ausser einiger Lektüre und seinen wenigen Geschäften, lebt er ganz in und für seine Familie. Sein Aeussres ist nicht eben angenehm, obgleich offen und natürlich."

Matthias Claudius soll, so ein anderer Beobachter, auf abendlichen Spaziergängen unfrisiert und ungepudert durch Wandsbek gegangen sein. Aber die Vernachlässigung des Äußeren hatte gelegentlich auch Vorteile. Immer mehr Menschen pilgerten in das dörfliche Wandsbek, um den Verfasser der schönen Gedichte zu sehen und vielleicht auch zu sprechen. Claudius, der häufig bis spät in den Tag hinein eine Nachtmütze trug, spielte dann den Hausdiener, trat aus der Tür und verkündete den Besuchern, der Herr Dichter sei leider gerade nicht zu Hause.

Wer war dieses Wandsbeker Original? Matthias Claudius wurde am 15. August 1740 im holsteinischen Reinfeld geboren. Sein Vater war Pastor des Ortes. Matthias wuchs in einer großen Geschwisterschar auf. Er und sein älterer Bruder Josias sollten Theologen werden, entschieden die Eltern. Dafür besuchten beide vier Jahre lang die Lateinschule in Plön und begannen 1759 gemeinsam mit dem Studium in Jena. Während der Bruder zielstrebig Theologie studierte, besuchte Matthias Claudius zahlreiche Vorlesungen unterschiedlicher Fakultäten. Das eröffnete ihm einen Zugang zu viel Wissen und zu vielen Einsichten – nur nicht zu einem Studienabschluss. Nach drei Jahren gab er das Studium auf und kehrte in das Pfarrhaus nach Reinfeld zurück.

Der Traum von dem ganz anderen Leben auf Tahiti

Der besorgte Vater musste alle Hoffnung aufgeben, dass sein Sohn Pastor werden könnte, aber wenigstens eine bezahlte Anstellung sollte er annehmen. Verschiedene phantastisch klingende Pläne des gescheiterten Studenten werden die Eltern beunruhigt haben, so einige Jahre später die Idee, mit anderen Schriftstellern eine Dichterkolonie auf Tahiti in der Südsee zu gründen. In der zweiten Hälfte des 18. Jahrhunderts brach in intellektuellen Kreisen und besonders in Schriftstellerkreisen in Europa eine Tahiti-Begeisterung aus.

1767 und 1768 hatten mit Wallis, Bougainville und Cook gleich drei Kapitäne das pazifische Tahiti besucht. Ihre Beschreibungen glichen einander stark und weckten die Hoffnung, hier am anderen Ende der Welt ein Paradies entdeckt zu haben. Die Reiseberichte von Georg Forster aus dem Jahr 1773 festigten in Deutschland das Bild von einem paradiesischen Leben von kindlich-unschuldigen Menschen inmitten einer üppigen Natur. Das anscheinend freie sexuelle Leben erhöhte noch das Interesse an diesen Naturkindern und ihrem so ganz anderen Leben ohne die Zwänge der Zivilisation.

Die Vorstellungen Rousseaus von einem Leben in der Natur verschmolzen hier mit den Paradiesvorstellungen früherer Zeiten. Dichter wie Johann Heinrich Voß und eben auch der mit ihm befreundete Matthias Claudius träumten von einer Dichterkolonie auf Tahiti. Der Schriftsteller Christian Adolf Overbeck schrieb 1777 an Voß: „Horchen Sie, Voss! – Gerstenberg und ich, wir sind uns einig geworden, unsere besten Freunde allesamt aufzubieten, mit uns die falsche Europäische Welt zu verlassen und den glücklichen Gefilden eines Zweyten Paradieses entgegenzueilen.“

Matthias Claudius und die befreundeten Dichter sind nie in Tahiti angekommen. Aber der fröhlich ungezwungene Umgang mit den Kindern, das in den Tag Hineinleben und die später oft beschriebene Idylle des Familienlebens im Hause Claudius inmitten einer sich rasch verändernden Welt können auch als Nachklang der Sehnsucht nach paradiesischen Verhältnissen verstanden werden. Und mochte die Welt auch nicht paradiesisch sein, so blieb Claudius doch immerhin der feste Glaube an ein himmlisches Paradies.

Das Leben in den Großstädten Kopenhagen und Hamburg

Erst einmal rückte das Paradies in weite Ferne, denn Claudius nahm 1764 die Stelle eines Sekretärs des Grafen Ulrich Adolph von Holstein in Kopenhagen an. Die laute Großstadt und die Arroganz seines Arbeitgebers veranlassten ihn rasch, nach Reinfeld zurückzukehren. Drei Jahre blieb er bei seinen Eltern, und wir wissen aus dieser Zeit vor allem, dass er Orgel spielte und in der Welt der Musik ein Zuhause fand.

1768 bekam Matthias Claudius in Hamburg eine Stelle als Redakteur der Wirtschaftszeitung *Adreß-Comptoir-Nachrichten*. Die Bezahlung war bescheiden und die Arbeit öde, denn der neue Redakteur musste vor allem die Schiffsankünfte im Hamburger Hafen und Wechselkurse vermelden. Viel wichtiger wurde ihm der geistige Austausch mit Klopstock, Lessing und Herder. Deshalb war es für Matthias Claudius wohl eher eine Erleichterung, als ihm der Verleger 1770 kündigte. Anlass war ein „Wiegenlied, bei Mondschein zu singen", das der dichtende Redakteur zwischen die Angaben über Wechselkurse eingefügt hatte.

Der Redakteur des „Wandsbecker Bothen"

Claudius zog danach in das noch ländliche Wandsbek. Auf der Suche nach einer Bleibe kam er in Kontakt mit dem Zimmermeister Behn, genauer gesagt zuerst mit dessen 16-jähriger Tochter Rebecca, denn die öffnete dem Fremden die Tür. Sie wusste, dass ihr abwesender Vater den Schlüssel für das kleine Haus, für das der Redakteur und Schriftsteller sich interessierte, in ein Kästchen gelegt hatte. Das war allerdings verschlossen, aber Rebecca holte beherzt passendes Werkzeug und öffnete es. Aus diesem „Schlüsselerlebnis" entwickelte sich eine lebenslange Verbindung. Claudius bekannte später in einem Brief an Gottfried Herder, „mir glühen oft die Fußsohlen für Liebe". Wer Rebecca Claudius kennenlernte, war tief beeindruckt von ihrer Herzlichkeit und Gewandtheit. Wilhelm von Humboldt äußerte nach einem Besuch: „Sie hat etwas überaus Edles, Sanftes und Feines in ihrer Bildung, ist sicherlich eine höhere Natur, als der Mann."

Matthias Claudius nannte seine Ehefrau zeitlebens liebevoll „mein Bauernmädchen". Er meinte damit, dass sie eine Frau aus dem Volke war. Claudius fand eine

Anstellung als Redakteur der neu gegründeten kleinformatigen Zeitung *Wandsbecker Bothe* von vier Seiten Umfang, die vier Mal in der Woche erschien. Die Initiative für dieses Zeitungsprojekt ging von Heinrich Carl Schimmelmann aus, dem dänischen Schatzmeister und Schlossherrn des Ortes. Er war überzeugt, dass eine gute Zeitung dem aufstrebenden Wandsbek mit damals 500 bis 600 Einwohnern gut anstehen würde.

Der Redakteur Claudius gewann viele berühmte Schriftsteller als Autoren für sein kleines Blatt, für das er einen Bildungsanspruch hatte: „Man muss den Menschen nur vernünftig ansprechen, und man wird sich wundern, wie er‘s begreift." Aber mochte die literarische Qualität der Zeitung in gebildeten Kreisen auch anerkannt werden, im kleinen Ort Wandsbek fand sie kaum Leser und entwickelte sich wirtschaftlich zu einem Desaster. Die Bewohner Wandsbeks schätzten die Skandalblätter aus Hamburg und nicht die geistigen Höhenflüge der Dichter der Klassik. Nach nicht einmal fünf Jahren musste die Zeitung, von der nie mehr als 400 Exemplare verkauft wurden, eingestellt werden.

Claudius war inzwischen selbst zum *Wandsbecker Bothen* geworden, zum Dichter und Übersetzer, der von seinem bescheidenen Häuschen am Rande von Hamburg aus die Welt betrachtete und Gedichte, kurze Geschichten und Artikel zu Fragen der Zeit verfasste. Dabei bewies er immer wieder, dass er bedingungslos am traditionellen Wahrheitsanspruch der Bibel festhielt, aber gleichzeitig überzeugt war, dass zum Beispiel in den asiatischen Religionen die göttliche Botschaft zu erkennen wäre: „Alle sind übermenschlichen Ursprungs und durch ein himmlisches Wesen geoffenbaret und mitgeteilt worden."

Dass Claudius auch dem katholischen Glauben gegenüber Toleranz zeigte, war im damaligen Hamburg keine Selbstverständlichkeit, denn evangelische Prediger sahen in der Stadt ein „lutherisches Zion". Sie verhinderten den Bau katholischer Gotteshäuser entschlossen. Matthias Claudius schrieb einem zum Katholizismus konvertierten Freund, „wir haben einen Herrn Christus und wollen gegenseitig uns auffordern, wer ihn von uns beiden am meisten lieben wird".

Ein einfaches, aber zufriedenes Leben

Nach der Einstellung der Zeitung fand Claudius mehr Muße zum Dichten und für das Familienleben. Zu diesem einfachen, gottesfürchtigen Leben gehörte es für den Dichter, seine Kinder zu unterrichten und mit ihnen zu musizieren und zu spielen. Wenn er mit seinen Kindern im Garten herumtollte, löste das bei nicht wenigen Wandsbekern ein Stirnrunzeln aus. Konnte ein gesetzter Mann, dazu noch eine Berühmtheit, so mit seinen Kindern im Garten Bockspringen? Dass Claudius ein häufiger Gast beim Kegeln auf der Anlage seiner Schwiegereltern war, bot hingegen keinen Anlass zur Kritik, frönten doch viele Wandsbeker diesem Sport, auch der Pastor.

Rebecca und Matthias Claudius lebten in dem kleinen Häuschen und bald krabbelte eine Kinderschar durch die winzigen Zimmer. Die Möbel hatte der Vater Rebeccas gezimmert, und die Briefe des Ehemanns an Freunde, sie möchten ihn unterstützen, brachten etwas Geld in die Kasse. In der Familie mit schließlich zehn Kindern ging es meistens fröhlich zu, auch wenn es immer wieder Sorgen um das tägliche Auskommen gab. Claudius schrieb in einem Brief: „Ich lebe sehr vergnügt und glücklich, und wenn ich jährlich hundert Taler mehr hätte, würde ich mich um nichts umsehen."

Claudius nahm gern Ereignisse in seiner Familie zum Anlass, Gedichte zu verfassen, zum Beispiel den ersten Zahn eines der Kinder:

Victoria! Victoria!
Der kleine weiße Zahn ist da.
Du Mutter! komm, und Groß und Klein
Im Hause! kommt und kuckt hinein,
Und seht den hellen weißen Schein.

Die Enkelin Agnes Perthes erinnerte sich gern an die Besuche im Hause Claudius: „Mein Großpapa stand sehr früh auf und frühstückte allein; war das Wetter schlecht, in seiner gelben Stube. Wir Enkel schliefen in der Nebenstube bei seinen Töchtern und dann brachte er uns teelöffelweise seinen süßen Kaffee ins Bett und war unbeschreiblich freundlich. Bei gutem Wetter trank er vor dem Hause, ging in der langen Lindenallee mit der weißen Tonpfeife und der weißen Nachtmütze auf und ab ... Nach dem Frühstück ging Großpapa in seine Stube, in früherer Zeit gab er seinen Kindern Unterricht ... Um 1 Uhr wurde gegessen, vor Tische machte Großpapa einen Spaziergang in den sogenannten englischen Garten, wozu er den Schlüssel vom Grafen Schimmelmann bekommen hatte. Er nahm uns Kinder und seinen treuen Hund Phylax meist mit. Wenn wir nach Hause kamen, wurde gegessen. Vor und nach Tische wurde gebetet. Ich sehe den lieben ehrfürchtigen Mann noch lebendig vor mir stehen, die Nachtmütze in den gefalteten Händen. Bei Tische legte der Hund seine beiden Pfoten auf beide Achseln seines Herrn und bekam mit der Gabel manchen guten Brocken ... Gegen Abend spielte Großpapa gerne eine Partie Schach mit seiner Tochter Rebecca oder mit Pastor Schröder. Nach 9 Uhr ging er ins Bett und trank noch ein Glas Grog gegen seinen langjährigen Husten. Die Schlafkammertüren waren weit geöffnet und seine Söhne und Töchter musizierten."

Die große Gastfreundschaft der Familie Claudius

Der Dichter Johann Heinrich Voß, der mit seiner Frau einige Jahre in Wandsbek lebte, hat seine erste Begegnung mit Matthias Claudius im Jahr 1775 so beschrieben: „Auf dem Rückweg nach dem Wirtshaus gingen wir bei Claudius, der den *Wandbecker Bothen* schreibt, vorbei. Er war hinten in seinem kleinen Gärtchen. Ich hatte den Mann schon vorher, aus dem wenigen, was ich in seiner Zeitung von ihm gelesen ... liebgewonnen; aber die halbe Stunde, die ich jetzt bei ihm zubrachte, machte mir sein Andenken ewig unvergesslich und heilig. Man glaubt, wenn er spricht, die Wahrheit und Liebe selbst zu hören. Herzlichkeit, Zutraulichkeit und Güte begleiten alle seine Reden. Man muss ihn lieben ... alle Zurückhaltung fällt weg, wie er selbst keine zeigt; es ist einem so wohl um ihn, wie in den goldenen Zeiten der Unschuld."

Nicht alle Zeitgenossen haben den Dichter so positiv beschrieben. Der Hamburger Schriftsteller Johann Hermann Stoever schrieb 1789 über Besuche in Wandsbek: „Die reisenden schönen Geister und Belletristen sprechen hier auch unausbleiblich vor, um nachher sagen zu können, den sonderbaren Claudius ... von Angesicht zu Angesicht gesehen zu haben. Dieser Dichter gehört ohnstreitig unter die bizarresten und launischsten gelehrten Menschenköpfe, und es scheint, als wenn Hans Jakob Rousseau ihm zu seinem ganzen Wesen und Betragen das Original lieferte. Wovon er gern eine Copie machen möchte ... Ihm behagte es lieber, seine Kartoffeln zu pflanzen, und wieder auszuwühlen, seine Kuh zu hüten, und sich und seine Familie von ihrer Milch und dem Korn seines Bodens und der Frucht seines Gartens zu ernähren, statt sich eine Wampe von Gnadengeldern anzufressen."

Tatsächlich hat Claudius mehrfach „Gnadengelder" erbeten und erhalten, aber daneben waren seine Frau und er darauf angewiesen, von den Früchten ihrer kleinen Landwirtschaft zu leben. Claudius war nicht so abgehoben, dass er keine Freude daran empfand, selbst zu pflanzen und zu ernten, statt ausschließlich in einem Studierzimmer zu sitzen – das er in seinem kleinen Haus nicht einmal besaß.

Matthias und Rebecca Claudius waren trotz ihrer Armut für ihre Freunde sehr herzliche Gastgeber und holten alles hervor, was ihre Küche und Speisekammer boten. Viel war es nicht. Ein Besucher schrieb über die Gastfreundschaft der Familie Claudius: „Die Wohnstube des Claudius wimmelte gewöhnlich von Köpfen, und gab es keine Stühle und Schemel zum Niederlassen für die Anwesenden mehr, so rückte das heitere Wirthspaar unbefangen eine Commode fort oder man nahm in dem Hause der Patriarchen da Platz, wo man ihn gerade finden konnte.

Was Küche und Keller boten, Milch, Obst, Brot u.s.w. wurden vorgesetzt und nur Eins, Heiterkeit und Frohsinn, dafür verlangt."

Zu der Gastlichkeit im Hause Claudius trug Rebecca entscheidend bei. Einer der Besucher der Dichterfamilie, der Regierungsrat Anton Matthias Sprickmann, schrieb 1776: „Seine Frau – oder Engel! – empfing uns mit der offenherzigen Freundschaft, die sogleich ankettet. Ich hätte sie meine Schwester nennen mögen ... Dazu ihr offenes, heiteres Wesen!"

Das Weihnachtsfest mit einer großen Überraschung

Die Berichte über die Weihnachtsfeier 1796 geben einen Einblick In das Leben der Familie Claudius. Angesichts der ärmlichen Verhältnisse zu Hause genossen die Kinder den Heiligabend im Schloss besonders, das die Grafenfamilie Schimmelmann der Dichterfamilie ermöglicht hatte.

Es waren auch gute Freunde gekommen, allen voran der greise Dichter Friedrich Klopstock, der an diesem Abend aus seinem „Messias" vorlas, seinem berühmten Gedicht vom Leben und Sterben des Heilands. Dass an diesem Abend der Geburt und des Todes Jesu gedacht wurde, mag für manche heutige Christinnen und Christen seltsam klingen, aber für Matthias Claudius gehörten der Anfang und das Ende des Lebens aufs Engste zusammen.

Leben und Sterben, Leid und Glück waren bei dem Weihnachtsfest im Wandsbeker Schloss präsent. Man gedachte der toten Tochter Christiane – und es bahnte sich ein neuer Lebensabschnitt für eine ihrer Schwestern an.

Einer der Gäste war der junge Buchhändler und Verleger Friedrich Perthes, der später zu den führenden Köpfen des Hamburger Kulturlebens zählen sollte. Aber noch war er unbekannt und finanziell klamm. Friedrich Perthes hatte sich in die Tochter Caroline verliebt, und vermutlich schweiften seine Gedanken ab, während die Weihnachtsgesellschaft „Es ist ein Ros' entsprungen" sang und Matthias Claudius wie jedes Jahr die Weihnachtsgeschichte vorlas.

Danach war die Zeit gekommen, die Geschenke auszutauschen, aber der arme Buchhändler konnte „seiner" Caroline kein großes Geschenk machen. Allerdings, ist uns überliefert worden, wusste er sich zu helfen. Umständlich rückte er einen Sessel an den Weihnachtsbaum, stieg hinauf und holte den schönsten vergoldeten Apfel von der Spitze des Baums herunter. Damit ging er auf die überraschte Caroline zu und überreichte ihn ihr feierlich.

Sie war so sprachlos, dass sie sich nicht bedanken konnte. Auch die übrige Runde war vollkommen verwirrt. Vater Claudius räusperte sich, wusste aber nichts zu sagen. Eine der kleinen Claudius-Töchter rettete die Situation, indem sie vorschlug, ihr Bruder möchte doch das schöne Gedicht des Vaters „Der Winter ist ein rechter Mann" aufsagen. Es hat acht Verse, genug Zeit für die Erwachsenen, die Verlegenheit zu überwinden und anschließend umso fröhlicher zu feiern. Beim nächsten Weihnachtsfest standen Caroline und Friedrich schon als Buchhändlerehepaar Perthes unter dem Weihnachtsbaum.

Weder Macht noch Reichtum angestrebt

Dank der Übersetzungshonorare, der Autorentantiemen, der Unterstützung durch Freunde und Gönner und nicht zuletzt der sparsamen Haushaltsführung Rebeccas konnte die Familie 1781 ein bescheidenes Haus erwerben. Ein kleiner Gemüse- und Obstgarten bereicherten die Mahlzeiten. Hoch geschätzt wurde auch die Kuh auf der Weide. Von einem Leben im Wohlstand waren Rebecca und Matthias Claudius weit entfernt, hatten aber endlich doch ihr Auskommen:

Gott gebe mir nur jeden Tag,
Soviel ich darf zum Leben.
Er gibt's dem Sperling auf dem Dach;
Wie sollt er's mir nicht geben!

Auch andere Schriftsteller, selbst die berühmten unter ihnen, konnten damals von ihren Autorenhonoraren nicht leben. Sie mussten zusätzlich Einnahmen erzielen, zum Beispiel Lessing als Bibliothekar, oder brauchten großzügige Gönner wie Klopstock. Claudius war viel weniger ehrgeizig und viel weniger fleißig als viele andere Dichter seiner Zeit. Binnen mehrerer Jahrzehnte schrieb er eine durchaus überschaubare Zahl von Gedichten und Prosatexten.

Das Leben war ihm wichtiger als das Schreiben. In dem Gedicht „Täglich zu singen“ brachte er seine Einstellung zu Macht und Reichtum zum Ausdruck, hier vier Verse des Gedichts:

Ich danke Gott mit Saitenspiel,
Daß ich kein König worden;

Ich wär geschmeichelt worden viel,
Und wär vielleicht verdorben.

Auch bet' ich ihn von Herzen an,
Daß ich auf dieser Erde
Nicht bin ein großer reicher Mann,
Und auch wohl keiner werde.

Denn Ehr' und Reichtum treibt und bläht,
Hat mancherlei Gefahren,
Und vielen hat's das Herz verdreht,
Die weiland wacker waren.

Und all das Geld und all das Gut
Gewährt zwar viele Sachen;
Gesundheit, Schlaf und guten Mut
Kann's aber doch nicht machen.

Freud und Leid der Familie Claudius

Wie ruhig und angenehm das Leben mit der Familie Claudius trotz fehlenden Wohlstands sein konnte, hat der Dichter Johann Heinrich Voß beschrieben: „Wir sind den ganzen Tag bei Bruder Claudius und liegen gewöhnlich bei seiner Gartenlaube auf einem Rasenstück im Garten und hören den Kuckuck und die Nachtigall. Seine Frau liegt mit ihrer kleinen Tochter im Arm neben uns ... So trinken wir Kaffee oder Thee, rauchen ein Pfeifchen dabei, und schwatzen oder dichten ...“

Allerdings, dass Matthias Claudius so sorglos in den Tag hinein leben konnte, verdankte er ganz wesentlich der harten Arbeit seiner Frau. Sie kümmerte sich nicht nur um den Haushalt und die wachsende Kinderschar, sondern sorgte auch für die Beköstigung und Betreuung der Jungen aus wohlhabenden Familien.

Matthias Claudius nahm sie gegen Bezahlung in sein Haus auf und unterrichtete sie in einigen Fächern, während sie daneben am Unterricht der Dorfschule teilnahmen. Dass der Hausherr die Jungen auch in den Fächern Latein, Englisch und Italienisch unterrichten konnte, zeugte von seiner vielfältigen Bildung. Unter den Hamburger Originalen, die in diesem Buch vorgestellt werden, war Claudius einer derjenigen mit einer beeindruckenden Bildung.

Ungetrübt war das Leben der Familie Claudius nicht. Als 1796 die zwanzigjährige Tochter Christiane an Typhus starb, brachte der Vater seine Verzweiflung in dem Gedicht „Christiane" zum Ausdruck, das mit diesen Zeilen begann:

Es stand ein Sternlein am Himmel,
Ein Sternlein guter Art;
Das tät so lieblich scheinen,
So lieblich und so zart!

Das Gedicht schloss mit diesem Vers:

Das Sternlein ist verschwunden;
Ich suche hin und her,
Wo ich es sonst gefunden,
Und find es nun nicht mehr.

Die Not der Mitmenschen zur Sprache bringen

Der Dichter blieb wach für die Not anderer Menschen, selbst für die Not der Sklaven in der Karibik, von deren Situation er vermutlich von einem „Kammermohren" des Wandsbeker Gutsherrn Schimmelmann erfahren hatte. Der Reichtum der Familie Schimmelmann beruhte ganz wesentlich auf den Profiten aus dem Sklavenhandel und der Ausbeutung der Sklaven auf ihren karibischen Plantagen. Matthias Claudius schrieb 1773 das wahrscheinlich erste deutsche Gedichte gegen die Sklaverei:

Weit von meinem Vaterlande
Muß ich hier verschmachten und vergehn,
Ohne Trost, in Müh' und Schande;
Ohhh die weißen Männer!! klug und schön!

Und ich hab' den Männern ohn' Erbarmen
Nichts getan.
Du im Himmel! hilf mir armen
Schwarzen Mann!

Claudius war zugleich sensibel für die Not in seiner Umgebung. In einem Gedicht brachte er das Elend und die Mühen der Bauern zur Sprache. Hier einige Verse dieses Gedichtes zum Neujahr:

Zuerst dem lieben Bauernstande;
Ich bin von Bauern her,
Und weiß, wie nötig auf dem Lande
Ein fröhlich Neujahr wär.

Gehn viele da gebückt, und welken
In Elend und in Müh,
Und andre zerren dran und melken;
Wie an dem lieben Vieh.

Und ist doch nicht zu defendieren,
Und gar ein böser Brauch;
Die Bauern gehn ja nicht auf vieren,
Es sind doch Menschen auch.

Claudius war von einer tiefen Friedensliebe beseelt. Das zeigte sich auch 1778, als er angesichts eines Krieges zwischen Preußen und Österreich sein berühmtes Friedensgedicht verfasste, das mit diesem Vers beginnt:

's Krieg!, 's Krieg!
o Gottes Engel wehre,
und rede Du darein!
's leider Krieg – und ich begehre,
nicht schuld daran zu sein!

Aber so sehr er politische und wirtschaftliche Missstände beklagte, so setzte er sich doch keineswegs für grundlegende politische Veränderungen ein, sondern appellierte an die Herrschenden, nach Gottes Geboten zu handeln. Er forderte dazu auf, angesichts des nahe herbeigekommenen Reiches Gottes am Bau dieses Reiches mitzuwirken:

„Zuerst und vor allem können die Fürsten und Vorgesetzten der Völker dazu beitragen. Ihren Händen ist die Sorge für andre Menschen von Gott anvertraut ... Der geringste ihrer Untertanen und Untergebenen ist ein Mensch wie sie und wird geachtet vor Gott."

Den Gedanken der Aufklärung stand Claudius wie erwähnt ablehnend gegenüber. Besonders stark war seine Ablehnung der Französischen Revolution. Der Dichter verteidigte die feudale Ständeordnung, obwohl viele seiner Zeitgenossen erkannt hatten, dass es eben diese verkrusteten Strukturen waren, die so viel Unrecht und Gewalt verursachten. Claudius zog sich in den unruhigen politischen Verhältnissen noch weiter auf das Leben mit seiner geliebten Rebecca und seinen Kindern zurück. Und je älter er wurde, desto mehr richtete er seine ganze Hoffnung auf das himmlische Paradies. Das wird besonders deutlich in seinem Gedicht „An Frau Rebecca" zur Silbernen Hochzeit im Jahre 1797, das mit diesen Zeilen beginnt:

Ich habe Dich geliebet und ich will Dich lieben,
Solang' Du goldner Engel bist;
In diesem wüsten Lande hier, und drüben
Im Lande wo es besser ist.

Matthias und Rebecca Claudius auf der Flucht

1814 musste der über siebzigjährige Claudius mit seiner Frau vor dem Krieg zwischen den französischen Besatzungstruppen und den heranrückenden europäischen Armeen fliehen. Sie fanden Zuflucht bei befreundeten Familien in Holstein und kehrten nach der Niederlage der Franzosen nach Wandsbek zurück. Aber wegen ihrer sich verschlechternden Gesundheit zogen sie zu ihrer Tochter Caroline und deren Mann Friedrich Perthes nach Hamburg.

Die Enkeltochter Agnes Perthes hat das letzte Weihnachtsfest des Dichters im Jahr 1814 so überliefert:

„... Weihnachten kam, und Groß und Klein berieten, welche Freude wir unserm kranken Großpapa machen könnten. Mama kaufte einen kleinen Weihnachtsbaum, welcher in einen großen, hübschen Blumentopf gesetzt ward, in unserer runden Stube wurden unter vielen Tränen Äpfel und Nüsse vergoldet. Mama sagte uns, es sei der letzte Weihnachtsbaum, welchen Großpapa auf der Erde sehen werde, ein ander Jahr wäre er beim Jesuskind selbst ... Am Heiligen Abend zogen wir alle in das Krankenzimmer, Großpapa lag im Bette, unser Papa voran mit dem Baume. Großpapa wurde sehr bewegt und ergoß sich in Dank gegen Gott und Menschen."

Der Dichter starb am 21. Januar 1815. Er hatte in seinem berühmten Gedicht vom Mond auch den Tod zum Thema gemacht, der für ihn untrennbar zu einem gottesfürchtigen Leben gehörte:

Wollst endlich sonder Grämen
Aus dieser Welt uns nehmen
Durch einen sanften Tod,
Und wenn du uns genommen,
Laß uns in Himmel kommen,
Du lieber treuer frommer Gott!

Friedrich Eduard Dannenberg

„Schön war der berühmte Mann gerade nicht, denn sein von einem schwarzen Backenbart umrahmtes Gesicht wurde durch eine eingesunkene Nase entstellt. In den Ohren trug er kleine Ringe, wie man es heute noch bei Seeleuten sieht. Dem unschönen Äußeren stand aber ein um so anständigeres Inneres gegenüber. Es gab keine Arbeit, die dieser Mann, der eigentlich von Beruf Schauspieler war, nicht für Geld und gute Worte angegriffen hätte. Wenn ein Kind oder ein Hund sich verlaufen hatte, wenn irgendwo frisch eingetroffene Eßwaren angekommen waren, wenn etwas versteigert wurde: Dannenberg kündigte alles an. Gab es nichts auszurufen, dann sah man den Tätigen Holz zerkleinern, beim Umzug helfen oder allerhand andere Verrichtungen besorgen."

Wir verdanken Carl Hagenbeck, dem Gründer des gleichnamigen Tierparks, diese Beschreibung des Theaterdirektors Friedrich Eduard Dannenberg, denn als Kind wohnte er mit seiner Familie im gleichen Haus in der Großen Peterstraße (später Lincolnstraße 33). Die Bemühungen, dieses Haus vor dem Abriss zu retten, scheiterten Anfang unseres Jahrhunderts. Auch eine Stellungnahme des Denkmalschutzamtes für die Erhaltung des Gebäudes änderte daran nichts. Heute erinnert die *Patriotischen Gesellschaft* mit einer Tafel an einem Neubau an der Ecke Lincolnstraße/Trommelstraße an das frühere Wohnhaus der Familie Hagenbeck. Daran, dass hier auch der Theaterdirektor Dannenberg mit seiner Familie wohnte, wird nicht erinnert.

Zurück zum historischen Dannenberg. Zu den vielen Aufgaben, die er vormittags übernahm, gehörte es, die Hagenbeck-Kinder zu beaufsichtigen. Auch bot er auf der Straße Fische an, die er im Fischgeschäft der Familie Hagenbeck erworben hatte. Dann zog er in Manchesterhose und blauem Hemd durch die Straßen von St. Pauli, läutete seine große Glocke und verkündete lautstark „Schulln, Schulln, Schellfisch un Stenbütt!“. Auch als Ausrufer für die Angebote des Fischladens betätigte er sich: „Hört, Lüd! Frisch gerökerte warme Neesen! Bi Hogenbeck in de Peterstroot giwt dat acht dicke, fette warme Neesen för eenen Schilling!“

Dannenberg arbeitete sich vom Marktausrufer über den Heldendarsteller zum Theaterdirektor hoch. Hoch her ging es oft in seinem *Elysium-Theater*, eine Mitte des 19. Jahrhunderts weit über Hamburg hinaus bekannte Bühne am Spielbudenplatz. Vormittags betätigte sich Dannenberg weiterhin als Ausrufer und Gelegenheitsarbeiter.

Aber nachmittags legte er seine Ritterrüstung an und lockte die vorübergehenden Seeleute in sein Theater: „Man rin in de Bood, Smuttje, wenn du dien Geld noch nich all versopen hest!“ Jede Aufführung dauerte nur eine dreiviertel Stunde. Das war genug fürs Eintrittsgeld, fand Dannenberg, und bearbeitete auch Klassiker wie „Wilhelm Tell“ und „Hamlet“ eigenhändig. Diese Stücke pries er als „verkürzt und verbessert“ an. Manche Aufführungen nahmen als Folge der Interventionen des Publikums einen überraschenden Fortgang.

Als Faust und Gretchen heiraten musste

„Wat heet hier Goethe! Datt sünd nur Utreden! Heiroden sall he se! Heiroden!" Theaterdirektor Dannenberg war machtlos. Schon flogen Äpfel, Kartoffeln und Zigarettenstummel. Anständig zugehen sollte es am Spielbudenplatz, fand das Publikum, und deshalb hatte Doktor Faust gefälligst Gretchen zu heiraten, egal was dieser Goethe sich ausgedacht hatte. Bevor das Theater kurz und klein gehauen wurde, lenkte der Direktor ein. Die „Faust"-Aufführung bekam einen neuen Schluss, und unter dem Jubel des Publikums heiratete Faust sein Gretchen.

Noch einmal ging eine Faust-Aufführung in die Annalen der Hamburger Theatergeschichte ein, jedenfalls in die humorvollen Annalen. Der Chronist des lustigen Hamburg, Albert Borcherdt, hat diese Aufführung miterlebt: „Der Direktor, noch ganz erhitzt von der Aufregung, die es ihn gekostet hatte, um noch nachträglich einiges Publikum zum Eintritt in sein Theater zu bewegen, hatte glücklich wieder das Podium erreicht, um sich als Hamlet dem Geist seines Vaters gegenüberzusehen. Tiefe Stille herrschte im ganzen Hause, mit einem geheimen Grauen sah man das fürchterliche Gespenst daherkommen. Der dumpfe Druck, der auf den Zuschauern lastete, löste sich aber plötzlich in eine wohltuende Heiterkeit auf ..."

Die Heiterkeit war nicht in Dannenbergs Regieplan vorgesehen, aber es war eben auch nicht vorgesehen, dass das Gespenst merkwürdig hin- und hertaumelte. Hamlet, also Dannenberg, durchschaute den Grund für das Taumeln und schrie das Gespenst an: „Minsch, Du büst ja all wedder besopen!"

Erschrocken versuchte das Gespenst, Haltung zu bewahren, genauer gesagt, wieder Halt zu finden. Es lehnte sich an das Rosengebüsch, das in vielen Stücken des *Elysium-Theaters* zum Einsatz kam und deshalb zu den wertvollsten Requisiten gehörte. Es war allerdings im Laufe der Zeit morsch geworden und zerbrach nun unter der Last des keineswegs schwebenden Gespenstes.

Das machte selbst den eloquenten Dannenberg für eine Weile sprachlos, aber dann stürzte er sich auf das Gespenst und schüttelte es so heftig, dass es sein Bettlaken verlor. Hamlet schrie, so hat es Borcherdt überliefert, mit wuterstickter Stimme: „Dat sast Du mi betaalen!" Wie Gespenst und Hamlet es geschafft haben, nicht länger aus der Rolle zu fallen und zur Handlung des Stückes zurückzukehren, ist leider nicht überliefert.

Auch der Mord an Präsident Lincoln und die Hinrichtung von Kaiser Maximilian in Mexiko wurden verkürzt, aber in ihrer ganzen Schauerlichkeit auf die Bühne gebracht. Ein Erfolgsstück stand in drei Wochen 80 Mal auf dem Programm. Wenn das Theater einmal nicht ausreichend gefüllt war, mussten die Zuschauer so lange auf den Beginn eines Stückes warten, bis der Direktor genügend zusätzliche Personen angelockt hatte.

Als drei Jungen zum Eintrittspreis für ein Kind ins Theater kamen

Gelegentlich ließ der Direktor auch über die Höhe des Eintrittsgeldes mit sich verhandeln. Bei einer Nachmittagsaufführung, zu der immer viele Kinder kamen, stellten sich auch drei Brüder an. Der älteste von ihnen bezahlte sein Eintrittsgeld von einem Dreiling, die anderen beiden versuchten, sich ins Theater zu schleichen. Aber das entging Dannenberg nicht und er stellte den Jungen, der bezahlt hatte, zur Rede: „Wo hest du dat Geld för de beiden annern?"

Der Junge antwortete schlagfertig: „Ik heff man enen Dreeling mitkregen und sall op miene Bröder oppassen. Un wenn we dree för den Dreeling nich rinkoomt, denn süllt wi wedder no Huus gohn und dat Geld wedder mitbringen." Vor die Wahl gestellt, den gerade eingenommenen Dreiling wieder herauszurücken oder die drei Bengel ins Theater hineinzulassen, entschied Dannenberg sich für den Dreiling.

Der Direktor warb nicht nur das Publikum an, er spielte anschließend auch gleichzeitig mehrere Hauptrollen, um Gagen zu sparen. Das erforderte gewisse Eingriffe in Goethes und Schillers Werke, denn selbstverständlich konnten nie zwei von Dannenberg gespielte Helden gleichzeitig auf der Bühne auftreten. Nicht genug damit: Zwischendurch erschien der vielbeschäftigte Direktor immer mal wieder vor dem Theater, um lautstark neues Publikum anzulocken.

Bevor ein Stück begann, hatte eine Musikerin ihren großen Auftritt, den Albert Borchardt beschrieben hat. Sie „hämmerte unermüdlich auf ein über alle Maßen verstimmtes Klavier los und ließ sich weder durch den ihre Musik begleitenden Gesang des Publikums, noch durch den über sie ausschüttenden Kartoffelregen beirren."

Das Publikum beteiligte sich am Programm

Der größte Reiz des *Elysium-Theaters* bestand darin, wie Schauspieler und Publikum miteinander agierten. Johannes Sass hat in seinem Buch „Hamburger Originale und originelle Hamburger" beschrieben, was passierte, wenn statt der Klavierspielerin eine kleine Kapelle zur Verfügung stand: „Ehe die Vorstellung begann, trat der Kapellmeister des Hauses an ein ziemlich abgespieltes Klavier und fragte die Anwesenden: ‚Wat sall ik för enen opspeeln?' Anregungen kamen meistens von der Galerie, wo man alsdann mitzusingen pflegte ... Dieses gemütliche Miteinander bestand auch während der Vorstellung. Das Publikum spielte mit, wenn es von der Handlung gepackt wurde, oder es unterhielt sich, wenn es sich langweilte. Wurde diese Unterhaltung zu laut geführt, so trat Dannenberg, seine Rolle unterbrechend, an die Rampe und rief: ‚Wenn ji nicht ruhig sien wüllt, denn holll ik eenfach op to speeln!'" Dann kehrte Ruhe ein, denn alle wussten, dass die Drohung ernst gemeint war.

In einem Stück traten vier Kinder als Sprösslinge der gleichen Familie auf. Die vier Jungen waren aber gleich groß und offenbar auch gleich alt. Aus dem Publikum kam mitten im Stück der Ruf: „De Kinner hebbt woll all den sülbigern Dag Geburtsdag?" Dannenberg wurde zornig, unterbrach das Stück und rief dem Zwischenrufer zu: „Jo, du Dööskopp, dat sünd all veer Dwilllings ... Teuf man noch twee Minuten, ik koom glieks no di röber!" Der Direktor kam nicht zu dem Zwischenrufer herunter, und mehr als einmal blieb unklar, ob Zorn und Drohungen gespielt oder echt waren.

Die Schauspieler engagierte Dannenberg von der Straße weg, und neben der mäßigen Gage winkte ihnen bei Zufriedenheit des Publikums ein Bier, welches ihnen der Direktor auf offener Bühne reichte. Gelegentlich warf jemand aus dem Publikum den Akteuren auch schon mal eine Mettwurst auf die Bühne. Im Publikum strickten derweil die Damen und tranken Kaffee, während die Männer dem Grog zusprachen. Wenn die kleine Kapelle volkstümliche Weisen spielte, sangen alle mit.

Wenn das Visier herunterklappte

Durch bunte Phantasiekostüme glich Dannenberg sein Manko der fehlenden Schönheit aus. Er ließ sich durch nichts irritieren. Wenn das Visier seiner Ritterrüstung wieder einmal zu unpassender Zeit herunterklappte und ihn zur Gaudi des Publikums mitten im Satz unterbrach, klappte er es seelenruhig wieder hoch und setzte den Satz dort fort, wo das Missgeschick ihn unterbrochen hatte.

Der kleine Carl Hagenbeck hatte immer freien Eintritt im *Elysium-Theater* und erinnerte sich später: „Mehr als einmal habe ich als Galeriebesucher den Aufführungen beigewohnt und die heitersten Szenen miterlebt. Mitten in die hochtrabendsten Ritterdialoge sausten zuweilen vom hohen Olymp *(der Galerie, der Autor)* herab faule Äpfel und Eier auf die Bühne. Während die Vorstellung unterbrochen wurde, stürmten im Laufschritt die Schauspieler zur Galerie, um den Übeltäter an die Luft zu setzen."

Als die Glocke am Millerntor läutete

Zum Textlernen war beim häufigen Programmwechsel kaum Zeit, zumal es häufig keine Textbücher gab, also musste improvisiert werden. Dann kam es vor, dass die Handlung erst auf Umwegen dem vorgesehenen Ende entgegengespielt werden konnte. So auch an einem Abend, an dem ein Stück mit dramatischem Königsmord auf dem Programm stand. Nun gab es zu dieser Zeit noch eine Torsperre am Millerntor, und wer zu spät kam, musste eine Strafe zahlen, um noch in die Stadt gelassen zu werden. Das Stück zog sich hin, Publikum und Direktor wurden unruhig. Nachdem es schon zwei Mal vom Millerntor her geläutet hatte, rief Dannenberg aus dem Zuschauerraum: „Mookt to, mookt to! Dat hett al tweemol lüüdt!“ Auf die Antwort, der König sei noch immer nicht tot, brüllte er zurück „Denn pett em in'n Moors!“

Unvergessen auch diese Szene, die Albert Borcherdt überliefert hat: „Einmal hatte der Ritter Albrecht von Waldsee, indem er ... den Bären weidlich mit seinem Schwert bearbeitete, zu sagen: ‚Hierher Genossen, das Untier ist gleich erlegt! Ein kräftiger Lanzenstoß noch!‘, worauf der erzürnte Bär seine Maske abwarf und schrie: ‚Du verdreite Schinner! Meenst Du, dat ik mi för veer Schilling den ganzen Dag dat Lief mit din olen Bratspeer tweipeeken laten will?‘“

Das unerwünschte Lob einer Zeitung

Die Presse ignorierte das Erfolgstheater am Spielbudenplatz. Nur einmal wurde es lobend erwähnt, und schon tauchte Direktor Dannenberg wutschnaubend in der Redaktion auf: Das dürfe nicht wieder vorkommen! Die

Schauspieler seines als „Kunstinstitut“ bezeichneten Theaters hätten daraufhin eine Erhöhung der Gagen gefordert: „De Bande hett dat lesen un will nu Tolag hebben!“ Dabei war der Direktor ohnehin immer knapp bei Kasse, und ohne den morgendlichen Fischverkauf war sein Theater nicht zu erhalten.

Selbstbewusst war Dannenberg aber trotz aller Schwierigkeiten und sah sich offenbar auf einer Ebene mit den etablierten Theatern der Stadt. Als eines Tages fünf Schauspieler des *Thalia-Theaters* am *Elysium-Theater* vorbeikamen, wollten sie sich dort auch einmal ein Stück ansehen. Sie hatten bereits ihre Geldbörsen gezückt, als Dannenberg zu ihrer Überraschung auf eine Bezahlung verzichtete: „Kollegen haben bei mir stets freien Eintritt!“

Als Dannenberg vor der wachsenden Konkurrenz kapitulieren musste

Wer unzufrieden war, erhielt sein Eintrittsgeld zurück - es soll aber nicht oft vorgekommen sein. Seeleute und Hafenarbeiter, Straßen- und Dienstmädchen genossen die Aufführungen Dannenbergs. Viel Geld war bei diesem Publikum nicht zu verdienen. Die Zeiten für das Privattheater wurden noch schwieriger, als Hamburg 1860 die Torsperre aufhob. Denn nun eröffneten binnen kurzer Zeit rund um den Spielbudenplatz viele neue Varietés, Revuetheater und volkstümliche Bühnen ihre Pforten. Sie profitierten davon, dass die Hamburger auch abends ungehindert nach St. Pauli kommen konnten, ohne bei der Rückkehr an den Stadttoren eine Strafe zahlen zu müssen.

Dieser Konkurrenz war Dannenberg mit seinem Theater nicht gewachsen. Anlässlich seines 25-jährigen Bühnenjubiläums lud er zu einer großen Tafelrunde ein und hielt eine Rede. Er ahnte bereits das nahende Ende seines Theaters und sagte: „Von düsse Tieden is nich veel mehr to hoffen. Ich heff gor keen Lust mehr to den Krom, denn de Lüüd wöllt nix Klassisches mehr sehn!“

Im Mai 1868 fand die letzte Aufführung statt. Das Stück hieß „Tim Tode, ein Hamburger Raubmörder“, und nun war also auch der Tod des Volkstheaters gekommen. Immerhin, einige Hamburger Zeitungen, die Dannenbergs Bühne so hartnäckig ignoriert hatten, veröffentlichten nun ehrende Nachrufe für ein Theater, das längst ein Teil des Hamburger Volkslebens geworden war. Dannenberg musste sein Geld nun wieder als Ausrufer verdienen.

Noch nicht ganz vergessen

Ein Stück des *Elysium-Theaters* hat auf Initiative von Michael Leinert 1978 eine Wiederaufführung in der Hamburger *Opera stabile* erlebt. Der Dramaturg an der *Hamburgischen Staatsoper* hatte ein altes von Dannenberg verfasstes Textbuch des Stücks entdeckt. Der Theaterdirektor hatte die Opernparodie „Der Hamburger Freischütz – de Bruutschuss“ auf die Bühne gebracht, gegenüber dem Original von Carl Maria von Weber verkürzt, aber um ein bengalisches Feuerwerk bereichert.

Liebhaber von Webers „Freischütz“ mussten sich auch bei der Neuaufführung auf bedeutende Änderungen einstellen. Der Hamburger „Freischütz“ spielt in Poppenbüttel und nicht in Böhmen. Das hat Konsequenzen. In dem berühmten Lied „Wir winden dir den Jungfernkranz“

wird aus „Lavendel, Myrt und Thymian“ nun „allerlei Kökenkruut“. Und die Dialoge sind durchaus volkstümlicher als bei Carl Maria von Weber. So wirft Kaspar seinem Mitspieler Max an den Kopf: „Wat gröölst du hier rum? Tüffelachtein!“

Beim Höhepunkt des volkstümlichen Stücks, dem Brautschuss auf eine Taube, hatte sich Dannenberg eine für heutige Tierschutzfreunde durchaus akzeptable Lösung ausgedacht. Ein Schauspieler trat nämlich kurz vor dem geplanten Schuss auf die Bühne und verkündete dem Publikum, der Schuss auf die Taube müsse ausfallen: „De Duv hätt de swarte Kater opfreten.“ So konnte das *Elysium-Theater* Abend für Abend auf eine echte Taube verzichten.

Erinnerungen an ein Volkstheater

Zu ihrem 80. Geburtstag hat das *Hamburger Abendblatt* im September 1957 Johanna Denker besucht, die jüngste Tochter Dannenbergs. Sie erinnerte sich an die Zeiten, als ihre Mutter abends müde aus dem Souffleurkasten stieg und die Kasse zählte. Oft reichte das Geld nicht aus, um die siebenköpfige Familie zu ernähren.

Es kam 1883 noch schlimmer: „Die große Not zog aber bei uns ein, als mein lieber Vater starb. Wir beiden jüngsten Mädchen kamen ins Waisenhaus.“ Dort litt sie unter Heimweh und schlechter Behandlung. Das Leben nahm dann doch noch eine positive Wendung für das Dienstmädchen Johanna: „Auf dem Werftarbeiterball von Blohm & Voss lernte ich einen jungen Mann kennen. Liebe auf dem ersten Blick! Er heiratete mich, und dann begann die schönste Zeit, 54 Jahre einer glücklichen Ehe, aus der Kinder, Enkel und Urenkel hervorgingen." Ein Schluss, der auch dem Publikum des *Elysium-Theaters* gefallen hätte!

Johann Matthias Dreyer

Als ein Zweifler, doch nicht als Gottloser habe ich gelebt,
Voller Ungewißheit sterb' ich, doch keineswegs unruhig.
Unwissenheit und Irrtum sind des Menschen Los,
Wesen aller Wesen, erbarme Dich meiner!

Das sollte auf dem Grabstein von Johann Matthias Dreyer stehen. Das war sein Wunsch, aber der wurde ihm nicht erfüllt. Der Verstorbene gehörte zu den bekanntesten Spöttern im Hamburg des 18. Jahrhunderts und war gleichzeitig Diplomat. Er zählte zu den Anhängern der Aufklärung, stritt sich mit der kirchlichen Obrigkeit und blieb doch ein frommer Mensch. Er hat viel veröffentlicht und geriet trotzdem schon zu Lebzeiten allmählich in Vergessenheit. In all seiner scheinbaren Widersprüchlichkeit war Dreyer auf jeden Fall eines, ein Hamburger Original mit einem tragischen Lebensweg.

Johann Matthias Dreyer kam am 16. Februar 1717 zur Welt. Seine Eltern gehörten zu den wohlhabenden Kaufmannsfamilien der Stadt. Das Leben von Johann Matthias wurde von Anfang an dadurch überschattet, dass er kleinwüchsig, schmächtig und – wie man es damals nannte – „verwachsen" war. Wahrscheinlich ist er als Schüler der Gelehrtenschule Johanneum von seinen Mitschülern verspottet worden. Der Historiker Alfred Dreyer, der 1934 eine ausführliche Biografie über Johann Matthias Dreyer veröffentlichte, schrieb zu den Reaktionen des Jungen auf den Spott:

„Früh gewohnt, beiseite zu stehen, lernte er die Menschen beobachten und ihnen mißtrauen. So erkannte er leichter und zeitiger als viele Andere die Schwächen und Fehler seiner Mitmenschen, und lernte diese behandeln und verspotten. Neben einer auffallend entwickelten Neigung zu Spott und Hohn in der Brust des ‚von so Manchem Ausgestoßenen', wie er sich selbst einmal wehmütig charakterisiert, ein heißer Drang nach Lebensgenuß und -freude, ferner der aufstachelnde Wunsch, etwas zu gelten und sich beachtet zu sehen. Und als dieser Wunsch wenigstens in seinen jüngeren Jahren nicht oder doch nur unvollkommen in Erfüllung ging, da wurde aus ihm jener unverbesserliche und gefürchtete Spötter und Verächter, dem nichts heilig blieb, der alles mit ätzendem Hohn übergießend die Menschen, ihre Leidenschaften und Schwächen, durchschaute und sich über sie lustig machte."

Der folgenschwere Abbruch des Jurastudiums

Nach dem Abschluss der Schule studierte Dreyer gemäß dem Wunsch seines Vaters in Leipzig Jura. Aber der vielseitig interessierte Student fühlte sich in der Welt der Paragraphen nicht wohl. Er trat der *Deutschübenden Poetischen Gesellschaft* bei und beschäftigte sich von nun an vor allem mit Poesie und Theater. Das Jurastudium gab er auf. Das hat das ohnehin schwieriges Verhältnis zu seinem Vater weiter getrübt. In all seinen Schriften erwähnte er seinen Vater kein einziges Mal, seine früh verstorbene Mutter übrigens auch nicht.

Für die damals berühmte Theaterprinzipalin Neuberin übersetzte Dreyer eine Oper aus dem Italienischen und hat offenbar auch andere Arbeiten als Theaterautor übernommen. Einzelheiten sind heute nicht mehr bekannt. Nach drei Jahren kehrte er 1740 nach Hamburg zurück. Dass er sein Jurastudium nicht beendet hatte, verbaute ihm viele berufliche Möglichkeiten. Er bemühte sich, ein Auskommen als Schriftsteller zu finden, damals ein fast aussichtsloser Versuch, mit dem auch bekanntere Dichter scheiterten. Einnahmen erzielte Dreyer vor allem als Gelegenheitsdichter, der gereimte Verse für Hochzeiten, Trauerfeiern und andere feierliche Anlässe lieferte. Viel mehr interessierte ihn die Theaterstücke, die er übersetzte oder veröffentlichte sowie Vorreden und Vorspiele für Theateraufführungen. So verfasste er zum Beispiel für die Neuberin das Vorspiel „Hamburgs Vorzüge", das das lokale Publikum ansprechen und positiv auf das dann folgende Schauspiel einstimmen sollte. Einige Zeilen aus dem gereimten Vorspiel lassen die Absicht des Verfassers gut erkennen:

In dieser reizenden,
in dieser freien Stadt,
wo man Gesetz und Mut,
statt Zwang und Herrschaft hat ...

Solche schmeichelnden Verse werden ihre Wirkung nicht verfehlt haben, aber viel Geld war nicht mit ihnen zu verdienen, arbeitete die Theatertruppe der Neuberin doch häufig am Rande des finanziellen Ruins. Zudem reichten Dreyers Verse nicht aus, das Hamburger Publikum für die Neuberin und ihre ernsthafte Theaterkunst einzunehmen, waren die Theaterbesucher doch vor allem an seichten Unterhaltungsstücken interessiert. Nachdem die Neuberin die Hamburger 1740 durch eine Publikumsbeschimpfung endgültig gegen sich aufgebracht hatte, durfte sie in der Stadt nicht mehr auftreten. Damit verlor

Dreyer eine wichtige Auftraggeberin. Immerhin konnte er ein von der Neuberin aufgeführtes Trauerspiel als Buch herausbringen und so der Nachwelt erhalten. Der Hamburger Kaufmann und Dichter Georg Behrmann, der das Stück verfasst hatte, nutzte es für ein flammendes Plädoyer für die Freiheit. Zwei Zeilen mögen dies belegen:

Die Freiheit ist gewiß der Bürger größter Schatz.
Ist sie einmal dahin, so ist sie stets verloren.

Dreyer teilte dieses Engagement für die Freiheit. Deshalb entschloss er sich 1741, nach Berlin überzusiedeln, die Residenzstadt des jungen preußischen Königs Friedrich II. In ihn setzten viele Anhänger von Aufklärung und Freiheit in ganz Deutschland große Hoffnungen.

Die Suche nach einer gut bezahlten Stelle

Dreyer hoffte vergeblich, durch die Vermittlung von Freunden in Berlin eine Anstellung in preußischen Diensten zu erhalten und damit endlich finanziell abgesichert zu leben. Stattdessen musste er sich mit einer schlecht bezahlten Stelle als Autor und Redakteur der Zeitschrift „Weltbürger" begnügen. Der Tod eines Förderers, aber auch das Verfassen von bissigen Spottversen über Berliner Zeitgenossen ließen alle Hoffnungen auf eine angemessen bezahlte Stelle schwinden.

Enttäuscht kehrte Dreyer 1745 nach Hamburg zurück, nur für kurze Zeit, denn er fand Anfang des folgenden Jahres endlich ein feste Anstellung als Sekretär des Herzogs von Mecklenburg-Schwerin. Ein oder zwei Jahre später übernahm er eine Tätigkeit in England, über die sein Biograf Alfred Dreyer nichts Näheres herausfinden konnte. Wichtiger als diese Tätigkeit war, dass Dreyer in England viele Anregungen für seine weitere schriftstellerische Arbeit erhielt.

Ende der 1740er Jahre war er zurück in Hamburg und nahm den Brand der *St. Michaeliskirche* 1750 zum Anlass für ein langes Gedicht, das mit dem Wunsch schloss, Gott möge den Menschen „Religion, Vernunft und Menschenliebe" geben. Von 1748 an arbeitete Dreyer als Redakteur der Wochenschrift „Neue Beyträge zum Vergnügen des Verstandes und Witzes". Die Zeitschrift hat unter dem Kurztitel „Bremer Beiträge" einen festen Platz in der deutschen Literaturgeschichte und war vom Geist der Aufklärung geprägt. Dreyer war bis zur Einstellung der Zeitung 1759 verantwortlicher Redakteur, eine ehrenvolle, aber schlecht bezahlte Tätigkeit. Zudem konnte er ein Absinken der Qualität nicht verhindern, nachdem die meisten bisherigen Autoren nicht bereit waren, mit ihm als neuem Redakteur zusammenzuarbeiten.

Neben seiner Redakteurstätigkeit fand er Zeit für die Mitarbeit an anderen Zeitschriften und verfasste erneut bezahlte Gedichten für Hochzeits- und Trauerfeiern. Viele Zeitgenossen wären damit mehr als ausreichend beschäftigt gewesen, aber Dreyer verfasste zusätzlich eine große Zahl von – natürlich unbezahlten – Spottgedichten. Dass er drei Gedichte des berühmten Friedrich Klopstock parodierte, obwohl er gute Beziehungen zu dem Dichter unterhielt, trübte ihr Verhältnis. Das war nur eine von vielen beleidigenden Parodien und Spottgedichten, mit denen Dreyer seinen Ruf als Sonderling und Original festigte.

Ein Spötter im diplomatischen Dienst

Anfang 1753 fand Dreyer endlich eine halbwegs gut bezahlte Stellung, dazu noch eine Stellung, die mit recht wenig Arbeit verbunden war. Der Prinz Georg Ludwig von Holstein-Gottorp machte ihn zu seinem Depeschen-Sekretär mit Dienstsitz in Hamburg. Der Prinz war preußischer Offizier und kommandierte ein Kavallerieregiment in Ostpreußen.

Dreyer vertrat ihn und seinen Bruder Friedrich August, den Bischof in Eutin und Herzog von Holstein-Gottorp, in der Hansestadt Hamburg. Er musste sich unter anderem um die zügige Weiterleitung der Korrespondenz des Prinzen und dessen Zahlungsverkehr kümmern, wofür Hamburg ein guter Standort war. Außerdem hatte Dreyer die Aufgabe, den Bischof und in Personalunion Herzog regelmäßig mit Nachrichten aus Holstein und Hamburg zu versorgen.

Das neutrale Hamburg war damals ein wichtiger Begegnungsort von Diplomaten und Geheimdienstlern aller europäischen Mächte. Sie intrigierten je nach politischer und militärischer Großwetterlage in wechselnden Koalitionen mit- und gegeneinander. Die Konflikte zwischen dem preußischen König und der Kaiserin in Wien, die bald darauf in den Siebenjährigen Krieg mündeten, waren Anlass zu vielen politischen Ränkespielen in Hamburg.

Die Hamburger Kaufleute profitierten kräftig vom neutralen Status der Stadt, und der Senat tat alles, um keine der Großmächte zu verärgern und dadurch die lukrativen Handelsverbindungen zu stören. In Krisensituationen ermahnte der Rat die Zeitungsredaktionen, ja nicht zu deutlich für eine Seite Partei zu ergreifen und damit die Diplomaten der Gegenseite gegen die Stadt aufzubringen. Es gab also für Dreyer viel zu enthüllen und zu berichten. Seine Berichte füllten schließlich drei Bände und sind für Historiker eine lohnende Quelle.

Auch viele bissige Bemerkungen finden sich in seinen Berichten. Da sie nur den kleinen Kreis seiner Auftraggeber erreichten, lösten sie keinen Unmut in Hamburg aus. In den Berichten zeigte Dreyer eine scharfe Beobachtungsgabe und die Fähigkeit zu einer pointierten Entlarvung seiner Mitmenschen. Über eine Braut schrieb er: „Sie soll viel Geld haben und also sehr liebenswürdig sein."

Dreyer als gut informierter Diplomat und Redakteur

Dreyer hatte den Status eines Diplomaten im Dienste des Eutiner Bischofs. Mit diesem Status war allerdings nur ein recht bescheidenes Gehalt verbunden, das nicht ausreichte, um den aufwendigen Lebensstil Dreyers zu finanzieren. Geschickt baute er sich deshalb ein Netzwerk von Korrespondenten in verschiedenen deutschen Städten sowie in ausländischen Metropolen wie London, St. Petersburg und Amsterdam auf. Seinen Informanten zahlte Dreyer geringe Honorare und verkaufte die gesammelten Erkenntnisse teuer an diverse Diplomaten und Politiker. Hamburg war ein idealer Standort für solche Nachrichtengeschäfte und beseitigten Dreyers pekuniären Probleme vorerst.

Nachdem die „Bremer Beiträge" eingestellt werden mussten, suchte Dreyer ein neues publizistisches Organ. In Hamburg konnte der Spötter nicht auf eine Zeitungslizenz hoffen, aber der dänische König erlaubte ihm, im dänisch regierten Altona eine Staats- und Gelehrten-Zeitung herauszubringen, die dann auch in Hamburg eine Leserschaft fand. Wie zu erwarten, nutzte Dreyer seine Zeitung, um boshafte Texte und Spottgedichte zu verbreiten. Das brachte ihm zunächst viele Leser ein, aber auf die Dauer setzten sich die etablierten Zeitungen gegen das Blatt von Dreyer durch, das auch durch etliche Falschmeldungen allmählich die Reputation als zuverlässige Zeitung verlor.

Zudem gab es Streit zwischen Dreyer und dem Mitinhaber Schade, den die Zensoren in Altona für Gesetzesverstöße haftbar machten, während der Diplomat Dreyer unbehelligt blieb. Als Dreyer satirische Verse über den Herzog von Richelieu, einen bekannte Marschall der französischen Armee, in der Zeitung druckte, war der Protest des französischen Botschafters in Kopenhagen ein hinreichender Grund für den Altonaer Oberpräsidenten, das Blatt noch im ersten Jahr des Erscheinens zu verbieten. Dreyer verlor sein eingesetztes Kapital und verarmte.

Der Biograf Alfred Dreyer hat den Abstieg des Schriftstellers so beschrieben: „Wiederholt musste er wochenlang geradezu hungern. Langsam hob sich seine Lebenshaltung wieder, aber um welchen Preis! Um nur seinen Hunger stillen zu können, sank er zum Gelegenheitsdichter in des Wortes schlimmster Bedeutung, ja zum Possen- und Zotenreißer herab. Und als solcher nur war er in Hamburg und Umgebung bekannt, und lebt er weiter bis zum heutigen Tag."

Spottgedichte brachten Anerkennung, schafften aber auch Feinde

Seine Immunität als Diplomat schützte Dreyer lange Zeit vor juristischen Nachstellungen aufgrund seiner weiterhin öffentlich verbreiteten Spottgedichte. Vorerst genoss er es, sich in den Kaffeehäusern über Klatsch und Tratsch, aber auch politische Entwicklungen zu informieren und darüber Berichte zu verfassen. Mit witzigen Bemerkungen und Spottgedichten trug er zu lebhaften Gesprächsrunden in den Kaffeehäusern bei.

Allerdings machte er sich mit seinen launigen und oft bissigen Gesprächsbeiträgen und Gedichten auch viele Feinde, so Professor Dusch, den damaligen Rektor der *Altonaer Stadtschule*. Der hatte seinerseits Dreyer und andere Zeitgenossen heftig angegriffen und Dreyer antwortete mit dem Gedicht „An den Professor J. J. Dusch“:

Du, der Du wie ein Hund, grob, tückisch und voll Neid
Stets die Gelehrten Deiner Zeit
In Deiner Zeitung gern verrissest,
Beständig bellst und wenn Du könntest, bissest.
Dir sagt man: Herr Professor Dusch,
Auf allen Deinen Lärm nur dies: Kanaille, kusch!

Man ahnt, daraus konnte keine große Freundschaft werden. Auch der theologische Kandidat Flemming wurde zum Opfer des Spötters und nahm das Dreyer sehr übel. Flemming hatte in einem Gedicht anlässlich einer Hochzeit die Braut mit einem Apfel verglichen, worauf Dreyer dichtete:

Des Gipfels Scharfsinn zu erreichen,
Weiß er Braut, Hochzeitstag und Kuß
Mit einem Apfel zu vergleichen,
Fast scheint es, sein Gehirn sei Apfelmuß.

Flemming antwortete mit einem bissigen Gedicht über den Spötter Dreyer, das diese Zeilen enthielt:

Der Priester Feind, ein Frauenjäger,
Des Teufels treuster Waffenträger,
Für Geld ein Teufel und ein Christ,
Wer weiß nicht, daß es Dreyer ist!

Dreyer hat darauf mit einem geistreichen Gedicht geantwortet, durch das Flemming so blamiert war, dass er die Theologie aufgab und Jurist wurde. Leider habe ich dieses Gedicht nirgend finden können.

Langjährige Konflikte mit Pastor Melchior Goeze

Neuen und gefährlichen Ärger handelte Dreyer sich ein, als er Pastor Melchior Goeze mit Spottgedichten bedachte. Goeze war ein wortgewaltiger und streitbarer Theologe. Er war Senior des Geistlichen Ministeriums der Stadt, stand also an der Spitze des Gremiums der lutherischen Geistlichen.

Goeze ist durch seine Konflikte mit Lessing in die Literaturgeschichte eingegangen. Seine Auseinandersetzungen mit Dreyer jedoch waren weit heftiger. Ausgangspunkt war, dass Dreyer die christliche Religion schätzte, nicht aber das, was die Kirche und besonders die orthodox lutherische Kirche aus ihr gemacht hatte. Dies hat er in dem Gedicht „Die Religion" prägnant formuliert:

Sie war zuerst natürlich, leicht und rein,
Drauf drang die Schrift und der Gewinn hinein.
Die gaben ihr Geheimnis und Gebräuche,
Dem Volke Furcht, den Priestern dicke Bäuche."

Dreyer outete sich in seinen Gedichten als Anhänger der Aufklärung, zwar als gläubiger Christ, aber eben auch als Aufklärer. Goeze beschwerte sich beim Senat über Dreyer und seine Gedichte. Darauf reagierte Dreyer, indem er nun Goeze direkt attackierte. Im Jahr 1760 erschien das Gedicht „Der Hamburger Aaron":

Da steht er! Seine fette Wange
Färbt keine Scham mehr rot;
Und Hamburg, abergläubisch bange,
Horcht fromm auf sein Gebot;
Verehrt mit knechtischem Entsetzen
Den von ihm selbst erhöhten Mann.
So schuf sich Juda seinen „Goezen",
Ein goldnes Kalb, und betet's an!

Goeze seinerseits attackierte Dreyer von der Kanzel herab, ohne den Namen seines Widersachers in den Mund zu nehmen. Alle wussten trotzdem, wen er meinte, als er von Dreyers Gedichten als von „Teufelselaboraten" sprach und vor dem Umgang mit dem Verfasser warnte. Das zeigte Wirkung, und die Zahl der Einladungen an Dreyer zu Mittags- und Abendessen nahm drastisch ab. Das veranlasste Dreyer, den Senior mit noch böseren Schmähgedichten zu attackieren. Und einige in der Stadt kursierende anonyme gotteslästerliche Texte schrieben Dreyers Widersacher auch gleich diesem Spötter zu.

Der Senat hatte bisher das getan, was er in solchen Situationen häufig tat, er ignorierte die Konflikte und stellte sich taub. Aber im Oktober 1761 sah der Senat angesichts der Unruhe in der Öffentlichkeit keinen anderen Weg mehr, als sich der Sache anzunehmen. Man wollte Dreyer, der diplomatischen Schutz genoss, nicht direkt angreifen, sondern erließ ein „Mandat wider ausgestreute geschriebene gotteslästerliche Schriften". Wer solche Schriften verfasste, wurde mit einer hohen Geldstrafe bedroht. Es gelang Dreyers Gegnern allerdings zunächst nicht, ihn solcher Vergehen zu überführen.

Ein Buch mit Reimen löste heftige Reaktionen aus

Aber Dreyer hätte gewarnt sein müssen und sich, so sein Biograf Alfred Dreyer, „tunlichst Zurückhaltung" auferlegen sollen: „Aber das Gegenteil trat ein, unser Dichter schien das Schicksal geradezu herausfordern zu wollen." Hatte er bisher seine kurzen Spottgedichte mündlich vorgetragen oder einzeln in unterschiedlichen Zeitungen und Zeitschriften veröffentlicht, so gab er im Frühjahr 1763 eine Sammlung dieser Epigramme heraus. Immerhin verzichtete er auf eine Autorenangabe und gab dem Buch den unverfänglichen Titel „Schöne Spielwerke".

Deshalb dauerte es drei Monate, bis Senior Goeze auf den schmalen Band aufmerksam wurde. Auch der Rat der Stadt unternahm zunächst nichts, sei es, dass er das Buch übersah, sei es, dass er es bewusst ignorierte, um keinen neuen Ärger mit Dreyer zu haben.

Denn dass Dreyer die Sammlung von 216 Reimen herausgegeben hatte, daran hegte nicht nur Senior Goeze keinen Zweifel. Manche Verse waren so anstößig, dass der Biograf Alfred Dreyer sie nicht in seinem Buch wiedergeben mochte, sondern empfahl, sie selbst im Buch nachzulesen. Nachdem Goeze das Buch gelesen hatte, ging er umgehend zum Angriff über. Er forderte den Senat auf, das Werk sofort zu verbieten, was am 16. Juni 1763 auch geschah.

Das genügte Goeze allerdings nicht. Er verfasste für das Geistliche Ministerium eine Eingabe an den Senat, die mit diesen Worten begann: „Es ist abermals, und zwar, Gott sei es geklagt, in Hamburg eine Schrift verfertigt, verlegt und gedruckt worden, vor welcher der Himmel schwarz werden und die Erde erbeben mögte, eine Schrift, welche mit solchen Gotteslästerlichkeiten, die auch die Frechheit des Teufels übersteigen …" Goeze zitierte einige der Verse, die uns auch der Dreyer-Biograf überliefert hat, von denen hier dieser wiedergegeben werden soll:

Trinkt, als ein Deutscher trinkt,
Lacht, als ein Weiser lacht.
Ahmt Gott als Christen nach,
Indem ihr Menschen macht.

Nicht ganz so anstößig mag für heutige Ohren klingen:

Trinkt hier, so viel ihr könnt,
Thut, was das Fleisch euch heißt;
Dort habt ihr keinen Durst,
dort seyd ihr lauter Geist.

Mit diesem Vers bewies Dreyer, dass er die theologischen Auseinandersetzungen seiner Zeit kannte und in seiner Dichtung thematisierte. Während orthodoxe Lutheraner wie Goeze überzeugt waren, dass am Jüngsten Tag der Mensch in seiner ganzen Körperlichkeit auferstehen würde, bis hin zum letzten Härchen, erwarteten die von den Gedanken der Aufklärung beeinflussten Theologen und Gläubigen eine geistige Auferstehung. Sie stellten den Glauben an die Auferstehung also nicht infrage, interpretierten die biblische Verheißung aber anders.

Darüber ließ sich debattieren, und das taten orthodoxe Prediger wie Goeze auch, wenn es sein musste mit harten Bandagen. Aber es war etwas ganz Anderes und vollkommen Verwerfliches für die orthodoxen Theologen, diese Glaubensfrage zum Gegenstand eines Spottgedichtes zu machen.

Die Ahndung für die „Schmähschrift“ scheiterte zunächst einmal

Goeze bemühte sich, die Obrigkeit gegen Dreyer und sein Buch zu mobilisieren, und bezog sich dabei auf das Ratsmandat gegen Schmähgedichte. Goeze verkündete: „Nicht nur die Ehre Gottes, zugleich die Ehre der Obrigkeit ist frech mit Füßen getreten worden.“ Der Senat wurde aktiv und zwar zur Überraschung Goezes nicht nur gegen Verfasser, Verleger und Drucker der Schmähgedichte, sondern auch gegen den Senior, der aufgefordert wurde, hinfort „eine gemäßigtere Ausdrückung“ zu verwenden, „so wie es wahren Dienern unseres Heilandes anständig ist“.

Die juristische Verfolgung der Verantwortlichen des heftig attackierten Buches erwies sich als langwierig und schwierig. Dreyer konnte nachweisen, dass nicht alle abgedruckten Epigramme von ihm stammten, sondern dass er der Herausgeber des Werkes war, in dem er neben eigenen auch fremde Texte veröffentlicht hatte. Gerade die am heftigsten kritisierten Epigramme stammten gar nicht von ihm, behauptete Dreyer, und das Gegenteil war ihm nicht zu beweisen. Hinzu kam, dass er als Diplomat Immunität genoss.

Der als Verleger Angeklagte konnte erfolgreich argumentieren, dass er gar nicht der Verleger war, sondern sich nur um den Vertrieb des Buches gekümmert hatte und daher keine Verantwortung für die Inhalte trüge. Der Drucker kam mit einer milden Bestrafung davon, weil er ins Feld führte, Dreyer hätte ihm das Manuskript mit etlichen kleineren Lieferungen zur Verfügung gestellt und er hätte keinen Überblick über die Inhalte des Werkes gehabt. Der Senat nahm die Schutzbehauptung hin, wollte er doch die Angelegenheit rasch zu den Akten legen, da man den Hauptverantwortlichen ohnehin nicht belangen konnte.

Der Senat ließ die wenigen Exemplare des Buches, deren er noch habhaft werden konnte, beschlagnahmen. Nach dem Verbot des Buches waren viele Exemplare unter der Hand verkauft oder nach Altona geschafft worden. Von dort aus kehrte so manches Exemplar heimlich nach Hamburg zurück. Verständlicherweise war Goeze enttäuscht und wütend angesichts des Vorgehens des Senats. Er griff nun mit heftigen Worten nicht nur Dreyer, sondern auch die städtische Obrigkeit an. Dass er die

Gläubigen gegen den Senat aufhetzte, war eine Sache, aber Goeze ging so weit, zu fragen, was der Kaiser in Wien wohl von dem Verhalten des Senats halten würde, wenn er davon erführe.

Der Senat sah sich unter diesem Druck gezwungen, gegen Dreyer vorzugehen. Der war inzwischen nicht nur mit Goeze und seinen Amtsbrüdern konfrontiert, sondern ebenso mit den von dem Senior in Predigten aufgehetzten Gläubigen. Der Senat, stets an Ruhe und Ordnung interessiert, wollte den Spötter so rasch wie möglich aus der Stadt vertreiben.

Auf den ersten Blick mag es so scheinen, als habe Dreyer sein Unglück selbst heraufbeschworen, und so ist er auch in die Hamburger Geschichte eingegangen. Aber: Irgendeine Bedeutung besaß er in der Stadt nur als dichtendes Original. Ohne seine Verse war er lediglich eine kleinwüchsige, „verwachsene“ alternde verkrachte Existenz.

Er besaß zwar einen diplomatischen Status, der ihm als Spötter nützlich, aber nur mit einem geringen Status als Sekretär eines vergleichsweise kleinen Herzogtums verbunden war. Zudem wurde er nur schlecht bezahlt. Dreyer konnte keinen Berufsabschluss vorweisen, war als Zeitungsherausgeber gescheitert und als Journalist wegen seiner Reputation als Aufrührer nicht gefragt.

Umso entschlossener verfasste er spöttische Gedichte, die ihm zumindest eine gewisse Anerkennung in Teilen der Bevölkerung und eine beachtliche öffentliche Aufmerksamkeit einbrachten. Er schrieb sich allerdings, so wissen wir im Nachhinein, gradlinig in sein Unglück.

Der Spötter wurde aus der Stadt vertrieben

Nachdem ihn Goeze in einer Predigt als „frechen Seelenmörder“ gebrandmarkt hatte, gefährlicher als Mörder und Räuber, bedrohten aufgebrachte Menschen wiederholt den Poeten auf der Straße. Parallel dazu entschloss sich der Senat, Schritte zu unternehmen, um Dreyer aus der Stadt zu vertreiben. Die Sache musste vorsichtig angegangen werden, denn die fürstlichen Herrscher in Holstein waren eng mit der russischen Zarenfamilie verwandt und die wollte der Senat nicht verärgern.

Anfang September 1763 nutzte der Senatssyndikus Schuback einen Besuch von Herzog Georg Ludwig in Hamburg, um zu versuchen, den Arbeitgeber Dreyers davon zu überzeugen, den Sekretär aus Hamburg abzuziehen. Aber das lehnte der Herzog kategorisch ab. Dreyer wäre bereit, auf weitere Entgleisungen zu verzichten, erklärte sein Arbeitgeber, aber angesichts seiner Verdienste beharrte der Herzog darauf, ihn in Hamburg zu belassen.

Zwei Tage nach der Unterredung starb der Herzog am 7. September 1763 in Hamburg nach einem Schlaganfall. Die Situation nutzte der Senat, um gegen Dreyer vorzugehen. Die konfiszierten kaum mehr als zwei Dutzend Exemplare seines Buches wurden im Beisein einer größeren Menschenmenge spektakulär auf dem „ehrlosen Block“ zerrissen und die Reste verbrannt.

Dreyer sollte eine Strafe von 500 Reichstalern für seine Vergehen zahlen, eine so hohe Summe, dass er sie auf keinen Fall aufbringen konnte. Auch forderte der Rat Dreyer auf, die Stadt in Zukunft zu meiden. Dreyer, der nun ohne den Schutz des Herzogs dastand, verließ am Tag der Verbrennung seines Buches die Stadt.

Die Rückkehr des bei der Obrigkeit unbeliebten Dichters Dreyer

Dreyer bemühte sich mehrfach, nach Hamburg zurückzukehren, aber das verhinderte der Senat. Der Bischof von Eutin und Herzog von Holstein teilte diese Haltung und selbst aus St. Petersburg war zu hören, Dreyer sollte nicht versuchen, nach Hamburg zurückzukehren. Dreyer übernahm nun drei Jahre lang Aufgaben für den Herzog und Bischof in Eutin und Kiel.

Immerhin besaß Dreyer noch einen Förderer, den holsteinischen Minister Caspar von Saldern. Und der reiste 1766 in einer für Hamburg wichtigen Mission in die Hansestadt. Er war beauftragt worden, die dänischen und die russischen Interessen in Holstein auf diplomatischen Wege zu klären. In diesem Zusammenhang hoffte der Senat auf eine Anerkennung des Status der Hansestadt Hamburg als selbstständige Reichsstadt. Der Senat war also auf das Wohlwollen des Unterhändlers von Saldern angewiesen und der beharrte darauf, dass der erfahrene Diplomat Dreyer als Teil seiner Delegation mit nach Hamburg kam.

Von Saldern konnte erreichen, dass der Senat anschließend hinnahm, dass Dreyer auf Dauer in Hamburg blieb. Von Saldern sagte zu, dass Dreyer sich verpflichten würde, „literarisch zu schweigen“. Der Senat nahm die Rückkehr Dreyers notgedrungen hin, wollte ihn aber umgehend ausweisen, wenn er „seine vorigen Wege gehen“ sollte.

Dreyer genoss als herzoglicher Sekretär erneut diplomatische Immunität. Er hätte friedlich in seiner Heimatstadt leben können, zumal Goeze bei erneuten Attacken auf Dreyer keinerlei Unterstützung seiner Amtsbrüder fand. Aber Dreyer war entschlossen, seine publizistische Arbeit wieder aufzunehmen. Kurz nach seiner Rückkehr erschien die erste Ausgabe einer neuen Wochenzeitschrift mit dem langen, programmatischen Titel „Beytrag zum Nachttische, für muntere und ernsthafte Gesellschaften, bestehend in einer Sammlung von Marimen, Gedanken, Erzählungen, witzigen Einfällen, poetischen Kleinigkeiten und Rätseln; eine Wochenschrift, Hamburg, zu bekommen bey Gottfried Dalencon“. Dass Dreyer an diesem Projekt beteiligt war, blieb nicht lange verborgen, und nach einer Weile übernahm er auch offiziell die Aufgabe eines Herausgebers.

Die Zeitschrift verzichtete zunächst auf jede Polemik und fand mit Texten und Gedichten zu Lebens- und Liebesthemen viele Leserinnen und Leser. Überliefert ist dieses auch heute noch lesenswerte Epigramm Dreyers mit dem Titel „Die Wahrheit“:

Die Wahrheit mag man niemals hören,
Und hält die Schmeichelei an ihrer Statt in Ehren,
Die täuscht den Sinn durch eine süße List.
Wie kömmt es denn, daß man die Wahrheit scheuet,
Und ihr fast nie das schuldge Recht verleihe?
Man schämet sich für sie, weil sie stets nackend ist!

Hätte sich Dreyer auf solche Verse beschränkt, er wäre vielleicht doch noch als angesehener Poet in die Hamburger Kulturgeschichte eingegangen. Er veröffentlichte bald aber wieder satirische Texte, allerdings weniger aggressiv als in der Vergangenheit. Das hielt Senior Goeze nicht von weiteren heftigen Angriffen auf Dreyer ab. Gleichzeitig erschienen in der Zeitschrift immer wieder Texte, die von der tiefen Gläubigkeit Dreyers zeugen.

Sein Biograf Alfred Dreyer hat das so gedeutet: „Tiefe Religiosität und starke Neigung zur Satire, also Gottesfurcht und Menschenverachtung, Demut vor dem Höchsten, und ein loser Spott für die Mitmenschen, vermögen wohl nahe beieinander zu wohnen; auch schließt die Gegnerschaft zur herrschenden Kirche, die doch immerhin eine menschliche Einrichtung bleibt, ein starkes Empfinden für das Göttliche keineswegs aus."

Die Reputation Dreyers in der Stadt war eine solche, dass man seine Altersmilde kaum wahrnahm und er erneut zum Ziel polemischer Attacken wurde, angeführt von Pastor Goeze. Im April 1767 muss Dreyer resigniert haben und gab die Herausgeberschaft der Zeitschrift auf. Auch schrieb er nur noch selten Beiträge für diese oder andere Publikationen. Er lebte nun, von Krankheit gezeichnet, zurückgezogen mit seiner Frau und seiner 16-jährigen Tochter. Über beide haben wir von ihm nichts erfahren, aber einige Gedichte zeugen von seiner tiefen Liebe zu seiner Frau.

Am 20. Juni 1769 ist Johann Matthias Dreyer gestorben im Alter von kaum 53 Jahren. In seinem Nachlass fand sich dieser resignative Satz: „Unser Leben ist eine Ebbe und Flut von lauter Fehlern." Das Hamburger Original hatte einen hohen Preis für seine Originalität bezahlt, und diesen Preis musste nach seinem Tod auch noch seine Familie bezahlen. Er hinterließ seiner Witwe und seiner Tochter nur Schulden, sodass sie in tiefe Armut gerieten. Der Schauspieler Brandes, der zu denen gehört hatte, die an Dreyers Publikationen mitgewirkt hatten, besuchte sie um das Jahr 1775: „Endlich fand ich sie, die Witwe meines Wohltäters, in einem versteckten, schmutzigen Winkel, in einer armseligen Hütte. Hier lebte sie, von ihren und seinen ehemaligen Freunden längst vergessen, in der bittersten Armut. Zur Vergrößerung des Elends ist sie fast gänzlich blind!“

Das letzte Wort in diesem Kapitel soll Johann Matthias Dreyer selbst haben. Bereits 1849 hatte er in einem Gedicht sein Gottvertrauen in diese Worte gefasst:

In Deiner Hand stehn meine Tage,
Ich halt‘ und küsse diese Hand;
Wenn ich der Welt den Abschied sage,
So führt sie mich ins Vaterland,
Wo, eh‘ Du diese Welt gemacht,
Du schon an mich, Dein Kind gedacht.

Heinz Erhardt

„Wenn es draußen hupte, stürmten wir alle raus. Jeder wollte der Erste sein. ‚Nicht so stürmisch, ihr schmeißt mich ja um', rief Mutti und herzte uns alle leidenschaftlich. Pappi dagegen ließ sich Zeit mit dem Aussteigen. Er notierte erst den Kilometerstand, um den Benzinverbrauch ausrechnen zu können. Wenn er dann endlich auch ausstieg, umschwärmten wir ihn wie ein Bienenscharm. ‚Hallo', sagte er leicht erschöpft. ‚Das war eine anstrengende Fahrt.' – Und wir wussten sofort, dass ein stürmisches Um-den-Hals-Fallen nicht angebracht war. So trugen wir brav die Koffer ins Haus. Mutti sah sich unauffällig um, ob auch alles ordentlich war, während Pappi schnurstracks an den Schreibtisch marschierte und die Post durchsah. Trotzdem war es für uns immer wunderschön, wenn wieder einmal die ganze Familie zusammen war."

So erinnerte sich die Tochter Marita an die Heimkehr der Eltern Erhardt von einer Tournee. Die Eltern waren oft auf Tournee, denn Heinz Erhardt hatte jedes Jahr zahlreiche Engagements. Im Durchschnitt soll er 6.000 Kilometer im Monat gefahren sein.

Fünfzehn Schulwechsel zwischen St. Petersburg und Hannover

Heinz Erhardt wurde am 20. Februar 1909 in Riga geboren und gehörte einer deutschbaltischen Familie an. Die Eltern trennten sich bald nach der Geburt des Sohnes. Der Vater machte in Deutschland als Kapellmeister Karriere, die Mutter zog nach St. Petersburg. Der Sohn wuchs zunächst bei den Großeltern mütterlicherseits auf. Sie betrieben ein Noten- und Musikhaus im Zentrum von Riga und gehörten dem Großbürgertum der Stadt an. 1916 holte die Mutter ihren Sohn Heinz zu sich nach St. Petersburg, aber er hatte so großes Heimweh, dass er nach Riga zurückkehren durfte.

Mit zehn Jahren kam Heinz Erhardt 1919 zu seinem wiederverheirateten Vater. Hintergrund war, dass nach der Oktoberrevolution 1917 in Russland auch in Riga gewaltsame Auseinandersetzungen drohten. Da der Vater als Kapellmeister häufig umzog, führte der Sohn ein unstetes Leben, bis die zweite Frau seines Vaters ihn bei sich in Hannover aufnahm – und ihn bald darauf in einem Internat ablieferte.

1924, da war Heinz Erhardt 14 Jahre alt, hatte sich die politische Lage im Baltikum beruhigt und er durfte zurück zu seinen Großeltern in Riga. Nach fünfzehn Schulwechseln in unterschiedlichen Orten war ihm die Lust an der Schulbildung vergangen. Wie sagte er doch später so treffend: „Das Lernen macht stets dann Verdruss, wenn man's nicht will, es aber muss." Er dichtete über den Ritter Fips, was er selbst erlebt hatte:

Was er schätzte selbst in Serien,
das waren jedes Mal die Ferien,
die er von sich aus noch ergänzte,
indem er gern die Schule schwänzte.

Heinz Erhardt fiel in der Schule in Riga nicht durch seine schulischen Leistungen, sondern durch seine spöttischen Gedichte über seine Lehrer auf. Er sorgte dafür, dass die Lehrer seine literarischen Werke zu lesen bekamen – was seinem schulischen Erfolg natürlich nicht förderlich war. Immerhin nahm ein Lehrer ihn in seine Laienspielgruppe auf. Dort fiel er rasch durch sein humoristisches Talent auf und hatte die Lacher stets auf seiner Seite. Er schwankte trotzdem, ob er Schauspieler oder Komponist werden wollte.

Nicht Musiker, sondern Verkäufer in einer Musikalienhandlung

Heinz Erhard schaffte 1926 das Abitur nicht. Später schrieb er: „In der Schule war kein Fortkommen, also machte ich, dass ich fortkam." Sein Großvater brachte ihn erst einmal zur Ausbildung in einer Musikalienhandlung in Leipzig unter. So viel Zeit wie möglich verbrachte der junge Mann am dortigen Konservatorium, wo er ein Klavier- und Kompositionsstudium begann. In Leipzig betätigte er sich zusätzlich als Unterhalter bei „Bunten Abenden" und verfasste humorvolle Gedichte. Schon damals entstand das Gedicht „Das Gewitter". Es beginnt dramatisch und endet mit diesem Vers:

Und wie es stürmt und brandet und kracht,
da, eine Jungfrau tritt hinaus in die Nacht
und ruft in die tosenden Winde hinaus:
„Na, das ist ein Dreckwetter, da bleib ich zuhaus!"

Heinz Erhardts künstlerische Arbeit endete nach zwei Jahren abrupt, als sein Großvater ihn zurück nach Riga holte. Dort arbeitete er in der Musikalienhandlung der Familie, war als Erbe vorgesehen. Später schrieb er über diese Zeit: „Im großväterlichen Musikgeschäft befand ich mich inmitten hehrster Kunst – dachte ich! In Wirklichkeit ist es völlig wurst, ob man mit Käse handelt oder mit

Musik. Immer kauft man billig ein, um teurer zu verkaufen.“ Das äußerte er auch gegenüber seinem Großvater, der spätestens dann geahnt haben muss, dass aus dem Enkel kein erfolgreicher Musikalienhändler werden würde. Lustlos verkaufte Heinz Erhardt Noten und Instrumente, trat daneben aber wieder als Humorist bei Feiern und Festen in Riga auf. 1932 reüssierte er im deutschen Theater der Stadt als Komponist und parallel als Schauspieler in Lustspielen. Die „Rigaer Rundschau“ würdigte ihn als „der immer heitere Heinz Erhardt“. Da konnte er allenfalls ahnen, dass er einmal als Humorist große Erfolge feiern würde.

Nicht nur im Fahrstuhl auf dem Weg nach oben

Im Frühjahr 1934 lernte er im Fahrstuhl seine zukünftige Frau Gilda Zanetti kennen. Beide stiegen im Erdgeschoss in den Fahrstuhl ein und er fragte sie: „Wollen sie auch nach oben?“ Das war vielleicht nicht der geistreichste Beginn eines Gesprächs, aber es war der Anfang einer Freundschaft. Sie endete auch nicht, als er sie zum Tanzen ausführte: „Die reizende Gilda Zanetti war nun die Erste, die überhaupt nicht schimpfte, wenn ich mehr auf ihren als auf meinen Füßen stand.“

Ein Jahr später wurde geheiratet, der Beginn einer 45 Jahre währenden glücklichen Ehe. Heinz Erhardt erinnerte sich später: „Als wir heirateten, langte das Geld gerade für einen Ausflug ins Grüne.“ 1936 kam die Tochter Grit zur Welt. Ihre Eltern waren finanziell arm und die erhofften Erfolge auf der Bühne blieben zunächst aus. Eine spätere Bühnen-Pointe von Heinz Erhardt wird ihn vielleicht damals selbst beschlichen haben: „Viele betreten ja die Bretter, die die Welt bedeuten – und merken nicht, dass sie auf dem Holzweg sind."

Ehefrau Gilda wollte nicht nur im Fahrstuhl „auch nach oben". Sie bestärkte ihren Mann darin, das provinzielle Riga mit seiner überschaubaren deutschen Minderheit zu verlassen und eine Karriere in Danzig und dann 1938 in Berlin anzustreben. Dankbar bekundete er später, er hätte es seiner Frau zu verdanken, dass er es gewagt hatte, Riga zu verlassen und den Erfolg in größeren Städten zu suchen. Nach zähen Verhandlungen in Berlin bekam Erhardt eine Chance. Als ein berühmter Kabarettist krankheitsbedingt ausgefallen war, vermittelte eine Berliner Agentur Erhardt zu einem mehrtätigen Gastspiel nach Breslau.

Aber das enttäuschte Publikum der *Kaiserkrone*, das den bekannten und beliebten Kabarettisten erwartet hatte, buhte Erhardt am ersten Tag aus. Was am nächsten Tag geschah, hat Heinz Erhardt so beschrieben: „Mir war alles egal. Und so schlich ich mich verschlafen, mit tieftraurigem Gesicht auf die Bühne und spulte mein Programm ab. – Die Leute schrien vor Lachen." Der Humorist hatte sein Erfolgsrezept gefunden und trat hinfort mit traurigem Gesicht auf, gekoppelt mit gespielter Hilflosigkeit und schelmischem Übermut.

Erste Erfolge als Kabarettist in Breslau

Die Direktion der *Kaiserkrone* engagierte Erhardt auf der Stelle für drei Monate, und er war in dieser Zeit auch in Programmen des *Reichssenders Breslau* zu hören. Zurück in Berlin erhielt er Engagements bei einem Kabarett und einem großen Varieté mit 3.000 Plätzen. Der Durchbruch war geschafft und die Familie mit inzwischen zwei Kindern konnte sich eine Wohnung leisten.

Aber dann brach am 1. September 1939 mit dem deutschen Überfall auf Polen der Zweite Weltkrieg aus. Zunächst konnte Heinz Erhardt seine Karriere fortsetzen und trat auch im Kabarett *Gondel* in Hamburg auf. Aber im November 1941 zog man ihn zum Militärdienst ein. Da er Klavier spielen konnte, bereicherte er das *Marinemusikkorps Stralsund* um einen Klavierspieler. „So kam ich als Nichtschwimmer und Brillenträger zur Marine." Später versetzte man ihn zur Truppenbetreuung, wo die Soldaten endlich wieder einmal etwas zu lachen hatten.

Als Vorbilder hatte Heinz Erhardt Dichter wie Morgenstern und Ringelnatz:

O wär' ich
Der Kästner Erich!
Auch wär' ich gern
Christian Morgenstern!
Und hätte ich nur einen Satz
Vom Ringelnatz!
Doch nichts davon! - Zu aller Not
Hab ich auch nichts von Busch und Roth!
Drum bleib' ich, wenn es mir auch schwer ward
nur Heinz Erhardt ...

Ein beliebter Komiker im Nordwestdeutschen Rundfunk

Das Kriegsende erlebte Erhardt als englischer Kriegsgefangener. Nach einem Jahr entließ man ihn, und er konnte zu seiner Frau und seinen inzwischen vier Kindern reisen, die auf einem Gutshof in der Nähe von Preetz untergekommen waren. Im Sommer 1945 engagierte ihn der von den britischen Besatzungstruppen aufgebaute *Nordwestdeutsche Rundfunk* in Hamburg. In der Sendereihe „So was Dummes“ unterhielt er die Zuhörer, die sich mit den humorvollen Beiträgen vom tristen Alltag ablenken lassen wollten. Spontan durfte nichts gesendet werden, jeder Satz musste von der Zensurbehörde genehmigt werden. Aber es gelang Erhardt, seine Beiträge trotzdem spontan erscheinen zu lassen.

Die britischen Besatzer, die Erhardt und seinen Humor sehr schätzten, sorgten dafür, dass er mit seiner Familie in einer herrschaftlichen Villa in Blankenese einquartiert wurde. Die Eigentümer der Villa waren alles andere als erfreut über die verordneten Mieter und es kam zu einem „zermürbenden Kleinkrieg“, wie Rainer Berg und Norbert Klugmann in ihrer sehr lesenswerten Erhardt-Biografie schreiben. Erhardt verarbeitete den Kleinkrieg zu einer bissigen „Satire der Woche“, wobei er den Namen des Vermieters nur leicht verfremdete.

Was dann geschah, haben die Biografen so beschrieben: „Heinz Erhardt erhielt mehrere hundert Briefe, in denen ihm Zuhörer für seine offenen Worte dankten und ähnliche Erlebnisse schilderten. Ein einziger Brief war nicht so nett: Er enthielt die gerichtliche Anklage von Erhardts Vermieter wider Willen in Blankenese. Der Mann fühlte sich beleidigt, beklagte die Ähnlichkeit der Namen – und hatte völlig recht, denn natürlich hatte ihn sich Erhardt zum Vorbild genommen.“

Es folgte ein Prozess, bei dem der Humorist zu einer Geldstrafe verurteilt wurde. Das nahm Erhardt zum

Anlass für eine weitere Glosse, die er aber vorsichtshalber so formulierte, dass sie nicht justiziabel war. Der Vermieter war blamiert und das Verhältnis zu den einquartierten Mietern dauerhaft eisig. Da war es günstig, dass die Familie Erhardt auf ein kleines Haus in Wellingsbüttel stieß, das sie erst mietete und später kaufen konnte.

Ein hart arbeitender Humorist

Heinz Erhardt war inzwischen nicht nur im *Nordwestdeutschen Rundfunk*, sondern auch in anderen Sendern zu hören. Daneben trat er erneut in Kabaretts auf, auch im Hamburger *Trichter*, einer Bühne, die er noch aus der Anfangszeit seiner Karriere kannte. Auch in Lustspielen war er zu sehen. Große Erfolge erzielte Erhardt mit Stegreiftheater-Aufführungen, wobei sich als Schwierigkeit erwies, dass er nicht nur das Publikum, sondern auch seine Mitspieler immer wieder zum Lachen brachte.

Für die in der Nachkriegszeit sehr populären „Bunten Abende" reiste er durch die Republik. Er war ein Gegenbild zum zackigen Deutschen, war der humorvolle, menschliche Bürger. Selbst wenn er den spießigen Bürger spielte, fiel er durch einen schalkhaften Nonkonformismus auf. Er nahm seine Arbeit sehr ernst, konnte aber über sich selbst verkünden: „Was bin ich heute wieder für ein Schelm!" Auch die nachfolgende Aussage bezog er auf sich selbst: „Wer sich selbst auf den Arm nimmt, erspart anderen die Arbeit."

Seine Biografen haben über Erhardts Auftritte als Humorist geschrieben: „Er schöpfte seine humoristischen Einfälle aus Beobachtungen, aus Alltäglichkeiten, denn er war ungewöhnlich interessiert und immer aufmerksam –

seine Fantasie schien immer zu arbeiten. Er hat ja nie Witze erzählt, nacherzählt. Was er auf die Bühne brachte, war immer ureigene Schöpfung. Dabei ist er nie über irgendwen hergezogen, nie hat er Böses über Kollegen gesagt oder aus Gerüchten Kapital geschlagen. Seine ureigene Art war immer liebenswert und geradeheraus, so war er zuweilen wie ein großes Kind. Und gearbeitet hat er wie ein Pferd – von 365 Tagen im Jahr sicherlich mehr als 360!"

Selbst wenn er, wie es schien, nicht arbeitete, stand er manchmal plötzlich auf, um eine Idee oder ein neues Gedicht aufzuschreiben. So entstanden Sätze wie dieser: „Paradox ist, wenn einer sich im Handumdrehen den Fuß bricht." Eines seiner beliebtesten Gedichte trägt den Titel „Warum die Zitronen sauer wurden". Die Zitronen forderten in diesem Gedicht von Gott groß und rot oder bläulich zu werden:

Gott hörte oben die Beschwerden
Und sagte: „Daraus kann nichts werden!
Ihr müsst so bleiben! Ich bedauer!"
Da wurden die Zitronen sauer.

„Mein Leben hat mir Spaß gemacht" – nicht trotz, sondern auch wegen der vielen Arbeit

Einen großen Freundeskreis hatte Heinz Erhardt nicht, wie auch, wo er fast immer unterwegs war oder zu Hause am Schreibtisch saß. Es kam etwas hinzu. Seine Tochter Grit hat ihn so erlebt: „Er zog sich zurück. Zwar war er kontaktfreudig, doch eine gewisse Distanz blieb spürbar. Wenn er zu Hause in Hamburg war, hat er sich im Haus verkrochen. Er war kein geselliger Mensch, der große

Gesellschaften liebte. Ich führe das auch darauf zurück, dass er eben so populär war, dass ihn jeder erkannte. Auch deshalb hat er sich wohl abgekapselt, als Abwehr, um sich nicht völlig in der Öffentlichkeit zu verlieren."

Aber humorvoll war er auch im privaten Leben und häufig das, als was er sich auf der Bühne immer wieder bezeichnete, ein Schelm. Er hat sein mit Arbeit gefülltes Leben genossen: „Mein Leben hat mir Spaß gemacht. Die großen Reisen und Tourneen ... anstrengend, aber schön. Beruf und Leben waren bei mir identisch. Es ist ein Glück, wenn einem solches gelingt ..."

Die „großen Reisen" führten immer auf die nächste Bühne. Urlaubsreisen haben Gilda und Heinz Erhardt höchst selten unternommen. Nicht einmal die Hochzeitsreise holten sie nach, als sie genügend Geld dafür hatten, denn nun fehlte die Zeit dafür.

Lampenfieber gehörte zu diesem Leben. So trug der Humorist bei seinen Bühnenauftritten eine Hornbrille mit Fensterglas, das seine Kurzsichtigkeit nicht korrigierte. Er nahm das Publikum nur verschwommen wahr und hatte weniger Lampenfieber. Auch ein Doornkaat half, ohne zu große Beklemmungen auf die Bühne zu gehen.

Aber war er erst einmal auf der Bühne, trug er mit trockenem Humor all die Gedichte vor, die ihn berühmt machten, so das Gedicht vom Tod des Ritters Fips, der sich leichtsinnig in voller Rüstung über die Brüstung seines Schlosses beugte, um den Ursprung eines Krachs zu erkunden:

Hierbei verlor er alsobald
zuerst den Helm und dann den Halt,
wonach – verfolgend stur sein Ziel –
er pausenlos bis unten fiel.
Und hier verlor er durch sein Streben
als drittes nun auch noch sein Leben,
an dem er ganz besonders hing ---
Der Blechschaden war nur gering ...

Auch wenn Heinz Erhardt nicht arbeitete, hatte er immer Situationen im Blick, die sich für ein Gedicht eignen würden. Als er einmal mit Frau und Kindern zu Hagenbeck ging, sahen sie dort ein Nashorn, das über einen Holzpflock stolperte. Das verarbeitete Erhardt zu einem seiner beliebtesten Gedichte:

Ein Nashorn und ein Trockenhorn
spazierten durch die Wüste,
da stolperte das Trockenhorn,
und's Nashorn sagte. Siehste!

Erhardt spulte keineswegs immer das gleiche Programm ab, sondern variierte es ständig und war auch offen für spontane Einfälle. Als 1948 bei einer Aufführung von Erhardt und Kollegen nur acht Personen im Publikum saßen, verkündete er spontan: „Ich warne Sie vor Missfallenskundgebungen – heute sind wir nämlich in der Überzahl."

Aufstieg zum erfolgreichen Humoristen und Filmschauspieler

In den ersten Jahren der Nachkriegszeit war Heinz Erhardt zwar als Künstler erfolgreich, aber finanziell stand die Familie schlecht da, wie sich die Tochter Marita später erinnert hat. Sie zeigte sich „inzwischen fest davon überzeugt, dass meine Eltern ernsthafte Existenzängste hatten und dass die Verbissenheit, mit der mein Vater seine Karriere vorantrieb, mit diesen Ängsten eng zusammenhing. Sie haben ihn sein ganzes Leben lang nicht mehr losgelassen." Dabei verbesserte sich die finanziellen Verhältnisse im Laufe der 1950er Jahre und auch danach stetig.

Unvergessen sind bis heute viele seiner Gedichte, zum Beispiel „Die Made". Eine Made ermahnte ihr Kind, in ihrer Abwesenheit zu Hause zu bleiben:

Also sprach sie und entwich. –
Made junior aber schlich hinterdrein;
doch das war schlecht!
Denn schon kam ein bunter Specht
und verschlang die kleine fade Made
ohne Gnade. Schade!

Auch in Filmen war Erhardt bald zu sehen. Er verkündete, dass er mit seinen Körpermaßen einfach ideal auf eine Breitwand passen würde. Zunächst erhielt er nur Nebenrollen, aber 1957 seine erste von 40 Film-Hauptrollen in der Komödie „Der müde Theodor", eine Produktion, die großen Erfolg hatte. In diesem und in weiteren Produktionen spielte er den „Film-Papa", zum Beispiel in „Vater, Mutter und neun Kinder". Die Tochter Marita behielt diese Filme so in Erinnerung: „Wir, seine echten Kinder, waren ebenfalls gerührt, wenn wir unseren Vater in dieser Rolle sahen. Vielleicht auch deshalb, weil wir selbst ihn nie in diesem Maße väterlich um uns besorgt erlebt haben."

Die Vernachlässigung des Familienlebens

Heinz Erhardt hat im Alter selbstkritisch geschrieben: „Mal was ganz Privates: Ich bin ein schlechter Vater gewesen. Nie habe ich mich um meine vier prächtigen Kinder gekümmert ... Ich bin ein noch schlechterer Großvater – oder Gropi, wie man mich nennt. Ein Wunder, dass meine Enkel immer sagen, wie lieb sie mich haben. Ich habe direkt ein ganz schlechtes Gewissen! Viele sagen, ich sei der Prototyp eines vorbildlichen Familienoberhauptes! Dabei bin ich ein ganz mieses!" Zur Ehrenrettung von Heinz Erhardt muss gesagt werden, dass sein umtriebiges Berufsleben ihm nur wenig Zeit für das eigene Familienleben ließ. Auch hat er nie gereizt auf die Kinder reagiert oder sie ausgeschimpft. Die Kindererziehung überließ er vollständig seiner Frau, den Haushalt auch. Sie war außerdem als seine Managerin tätig.

Die Ehefrau, die Kinder und auch Heinz Erhardt selbst schätzten es sehr, wenn der Schauspieler ein längeres Engagement in Hamburg hatte, zum Beispiel in der Komödie „Lieber reich, aber glücklich" in der *Kleinen Komödie* von Peter Ahrweiler. Gern spielte Heinz Erhardt auf einer Tournee immer das gleiche Stück, bis zu 500 Mal: „Wenn ich schon eine so lange Rolle auswendig lerne, dann soll es sich auch lohnen."

Meistens war er unterwegs, und seit Anfang der 1960er Jahre war er zusätzlich an diversen Fernsehproduktionen beteiligt, zeitweise sogar mit einer eigenen Produktionsfirma. Zu erwähnen sind auch seine zahlreichen Auftritte bei Verkaufsveranstaltungen von Möbelfirmen und seine Mitwirkung an Werbespots. Auch fand er noch Zeit, mehrere Bücher zu veröffentlichen, darunter „Das große Heinz-Erhardt-Buch“, das mehr als eine Million Mal verkauft wurde. Das Buch zeigt, wie kreativ der Humorist war. Dass auch ihm das Verfassen kurzer, pointierter Gedichte nicht zuflog, mag dieser Vierzeiler belegen:

In nur vier Zeilen was zu sagen,
erscheint zwar leicht, doch es ist schwer!
Man braucht ja nur mal nachzuschlagen:
die meisten Dichter brauchen mehr ...

Heinz Erhardt hat seine eigenen Werke so vorgetragen, dass sich viele Menschen vor Lachen bogen. Und immer hatte er „Noch'n Gedicht“.

Er war festgelegt auf das humoristische Fach. Hierfür erhielt er Engagements in Theater und Film. Als Klavierspieler klassischer Stücke und als Schauspieler in ernsten Rollen wählte man – zu seinem Leidwesen – andere. Und sein Traum einer Opernregie hat sich nie erfüllt. Gern hätte er auch einmal im Film einen Mörder gespielt, aber seine Frau und Managerin redete ihm das aus. Er blieb seiner Rolle als trottelig-liebenswürdiger Mann treu. Mit großem Erfolg, aber eben auch mit dem Verzicht auf die anderen Rollen, die er gern einmal übernommen hätte.

Die Sorge, vergessen zu werden

Heinz Erhardt arbeitete fast ständig, und seine Biografen Berg und Klugmann haben diese private Aufzeichnung von Heinz Erhardt aus dem Jahr 1971 als Beleg für sein Getriebensein und zugleich sein „groteske Fehleinschätzung“ in ihr Buch aufgenommen: „Ich arbeite fast pausenlos. Nicht, um Geld zu verdienen, seltsamerweise denke ich oft gar nicht daran, sondern weil ich arbeiten muss. Denn in keinem Beruf wird man so schnell vergessen wie in meinem. Also kann ich mir keinen Urlaub erlauben und vor allem, ich darf nicht krank werden.“ Das schrieb Erhardt fünf Monate vor seinem ersten Schlaganfall im November 1971.

Auf den ersten Schlaganfall folgte rasch ein zweiter. Seine rechte Körperhälfte war gelähmt und sein Wortfindungszentrum zerstört. Er verstand weiterhin alles, aber konnte nicht mehr antworten. Das war eine Katastrophe für den Komiker und Schauspieler. Er konnte sich nur noch in einer einfachen Zeichensprache verständigen. Kein Wunder, dass er öfter seinen noch immer lebendigen Humor verlor und in Depressionen verfiel.

Daran änderte auch nicht, dass Tausende Briefe und Karten mit Genesungswünschen eintrafen. Anlässlich seines 70. Geburtstages erhielt Heinz Erhardt das Große Bundesverdienstkreuz. Eine geplante Geburtstagsfeier im *Atlantic-Hotel* musste angesichts seines verschlechterten Gesundheitszustandes ausfallen. Grit Erhardt schrieb über die lange Zeit der Krankheit ihres Vaters: „Diese siebeneinhalb Jahre waren für ihn die Hölle.“

Wenige Tage nach seinem 70. Geburtstag starb er in der Nacht zum 5. Juni 1979. Im Nachlass des Humoristen entdeckten die Verwandten später die bis dahin unbekannte Komödie „Geld sofort“ und die Noten von Kompositionen Erhardts aus der Zeit vor dem Zweiten Weltkrieg. Die

Funde zeigten erneut, wie vielseitig Erhardt und wie umfangreich sein Oeuvre waren.

Als Heinz Erhardt 100 Jahre alt geworden wäre, erinnerte sich Hamburg an seinen berühmten Künstlers und benannte ein Jahr später, im Juni 2010, eine Parkanlage in Wellingsbüttel in Heinz-Erhardt-Park. Auf Tafeln sind einige seiner populärsten Gedichte zu lesen.

Ein Gedicht Heinz Erhardts zum Ende des Lebens soll hier nicht fehlen:

Du warst ein Musiker und Dichter
Ein Maler und Kaninchenzüchter
Doch trotzdem war's dir nicht gegeben,
den eigenen Tod zu überleben.

Jan Fedder

„… genau am Tag meiner Speditionskaufmannsprüfung kündigte ich. Weil sich mein Herz ja schon lange vorher für die Schauspielerei entschieden hatte. Alles auf eine Karte. Das gefiel meinem Vater aber ganz und gar nicht: ‚Wenn du deinen Job kündigst, dann ist dein Zuhause auch gekündigt.' Und so flog ich am gleichen Tag raus und musste sehen, wie ich klar komme."

So hat Jan Fedder beschrieben, wie er sich trotz aller Risiken dazu entschloss, Schauspieler zu werden. Die Lehrlingszeit betrachtete er später als dreieinhalb verlorene Jahre. Er hatte da schon eine bewegte Kindheit und Jugend hinter sich. Geboren wurde er am 14. Januar 1955. Sein Vater war Wirt und hatte als gelernter Tischler eigenhändig aus Brettern eine Seemannskneipe am Baumwall unterhalb der Überseebrücke zusammengezimmert. Im Erdgeschoss befand sich die Kneipe, darüber wohnte die Familie unter ziemlich primitiven Bedingungen. Der Sohn erinnerte sich später, dass er im Winter das Eis an den Wänden spüren konnte. Dafür genoss er das bunte Leben im Hafen und in St. Pauli.

Die Mutter des kleinen Jan war Revuetänzerin. „Liebe habe ich nicht gekriegt von ihr", erzählte Jan Fedder seinem Biografen Tim Pröse. Die Biografie „Jan Fedder. Unsterblich" hat der Schauspieler noch kurz vor seinem Tod autorisiert. Die Mutter hatte ein uneheliches Kind in die Familie mitgebracht, Oliver, den Halbbruder von Jan.

Die Mutter schickte den Sohn Jan zum Ballettunterricht, der Vater ihn mit sieben Jahren in den Kirchenchor des

Michels. Das erklärte sich daraus, dass der Vater im Kirchenvorstand dieser Kirche saß. Im Chor blieb Jan sieben Jahre, bis er in den Stimmbruch kam. In dieser Zeit fand er zum Glauben an Gott: „Für mich war immer völlig klar, dass er existiert. Der liebe Gott ist da und der liebe Gott lenkt die Sachen und macht noch viel mehr." Auch in späteren Jahren galt: „Für mich ist das eine große Selbstverständlichkeit, mit dem lieben Gott zu kommunizieren. Heute. Wie damals."

Mit sieben Jahren erlebten Jan und seine Familie Dramatisches, die Hamburger Sturmflut von 1962. Rasch stand die Kneipe an der Kaimauer unter Wasser. Aber auch in die darüberliegende Wohnung schwappte bald Elbwasser. Weil der Wasserspiegel gerade noch rechtzeitig wieder sank, überlebte die Familie. Jan Fedder sagte dazu seinem Biografen, dass er damals gelernt habe, dass nicht nur materielle Dinge wichtig sind: „Dass es noch was viel Wichtigeres gibt. Nämlich dein eigenes Leben." Einige Jahre später zogen Fedders in eine Wohnung auf St. Pauli, die mühsam wiederhergerichtete Kneipe blieb am Baumwall.

Die Entscheidung für den Schauspielunterricht

Den Ballettunterricht hatte Jan Fedder mit zehn Jahren begonnen, als einziger Junge unter lauter Mädchen. Nach zwei Jahren wechselte er zum Schauspielkurs im gleichen Haus. Den Wechsel hat er nie bereut: „Irgendwann sah ich die Kollegen von der Schauspielabteilung immer besoffen und lustig in der Eckkneipe sitzen und dachte, Schauspielerei ist wirklich angenehmer." Mit 13 Jahren stand er das erste Mal auf einer Bühne, im *Ernst-*

Deutsch-Theater in dem Stück „Unsere kleine Stadt". Danach trat er mehrere Jahre im Hamburger Kindertheater *Klecks* auf und war auch wieder im *Ernst-Deutsch-Theater* zu sehen. Als junger Mann hatte er eine ganze Reihe von Geliebten. Weil er „so geil aussah" (Originalton Fedder) „haben die Frauen mich damals reihenweise vernascht". Und er fügte hinzu: „Ich habe nicht die Frauen vernascht, die haben mich alle vernascht."

Als Matrose im Film „Das Boot"

Sein erstes festes Engagement erhielt Jan Fedder 1974 am Theater in Esslingen und blieb dort zwei Jahre. Es folgten kleinere Film- und Fernsehrollen. Seinen Durchbruch als Schauspieler erlebte er 1981 durch den Film „Das Boot", in dem er den Matrosen Pilgrim spielte. Er bekannte sich dazu, Volksschauspieler zu sein, aber er bedauerte in einem Interview 2016: „Schauspieler wie ich sterben aus, die gibt's bald nicht mehr. Volksschauspieler werden irgendwie nicht mehr hergestellt. Die jungen Kollegen heute ähneln sich alle sehr. Guck dir ‚Das Boot' an, die Mannschaft, diese Fressen kriegst du heute gar nicht mehr zusammen."

Trotz des Erfolgs von „Das Boot" musste Jan Fedder sich erst einmal gedulden und erhielt nur kleine Filmrollen. Er nutzte die Zeit, um einen Kindheitstraum zu verwirklichen, ein eigener kleiner Bauernhof. Der Schauspieler hatte wenig Geld, aber die Sparkasse war überzeugt, dass er in Zukunft genug Geld verdienen würde, und finanzierte den größten Teil des Kaufes. Eine solche Sparkasse wird man heute lange suchen. Ein Jahr später bekam Fedder die Rolle als Kommissar in der Serie „Großstadtrevier“ und hatte nun tatsächlich keine Probleme mehr, die Kreditraten zu tilgen.

Stolz führte Fedder seinen Biografen über seinen Bauernhof: „Dieser Hof ist mein Himmel auf Erden. Mein Paradies, das ich mir selber geschaffen habe.“ Unter den Reetdächern von Bauernhaus und Scheunen war viel Platz für all das, was Fedder sammelte. Am spektakulärsten war seine Sammlung von Oldtimern, darunter auch „schlafende Schönheiten“, völlig verrostete alte Fahrzeuge. Auch für viele Erinnerungsstücke aus dem bewegten Leben des Schauspielers war auf dem Bauernhof Platz, zum Beispiel für seine Rollschuhe aus der Kindheit, den Brautstrauß seiner Frau Marion und eine Polizistenmütze.

Der Junge aus St. Pauli als Polizist im „Großstadtrevier“

Die Polizistenmütze stammt aus seiner erfolgreichen Mitwirkung an der Vorabendserie „Großstadtrevier“ als Kommissar Dirk Matthies. Tim Pröse schreibt über den Anfang der fast dreißigjährigen Mitarbeit Fedders in dieser Serie: „Es funkte in der ersten Minute. Als Jan da so durch die Tür kam zum ersten Drehtag, war allen sofort klar, dass nicht ihm die Tür geöffnet wurde, sondern dass er dem Großstadtrevier eine Tür geöffnet hatte. Er zog die schwarze Lederjacke an und war Dirk Matthies.“

Zunächst hatte Fedder nur eine Nebenrolle in der gerade gestarteten Fernsehserie. Das war ihm recht, denn er fremdelte zunächst mit der Rolle als Polizist. 2017 sagte er rückblickend in einem „Abendblatt“-Interview: „Ich habe damals lange gebraucht, um mich selbst zu überzeugen, weil ich zu der Zeit sicherlich auf der anderen

Seite stand. Ich wohnte ja auch damals schon auf St. Pauli – und dann kriegst du als St. Paulianer plötzlich das Angebot, einen Bullen zu spielen. Da musst du sehr lange nachdenken. Auf St. Pauli haben sich viele über diese Idee kaputtgelacht, aber sie haben mich akzeptiert."

Jan Fedder freundete sich mit dieser Rolle an und war schon bald unangefochten der Star der Serie. Dieser Kommissar hatte durchaus Sympathie für Menschen, die zur Halbwelt gehörten. Fedder konnte diese Rolle deshalb so authentisch spielen, weil er in der Jugend diese Halbwelt auf St Pauli kennengelernt hatte. Selbstbewusst sagte er seinem Biografen: „Ich bin derjenige, der die längere Erfahrung hat, und ich spiele das so, wie ich denke, und nicht, wie der Regisseur das will und macht. Und dadurch wird das immer ein Erfolg, komischerweise."

Eine spektakuläre Hochzeitsfeier

Jan Fedders spätere Frau Marion hat sich so an ihr Kennenlernen bei einer Gala erinnert: „Er hatte diese einfach unglaublich sympathische, humorvolle Art. Wir hatten gleich das Gefühl zusammenzugehören, denn wir haben wirklich den gleichen Humor. Und wir haben sofort über die gleichen Sachen nachgedacht. Das war einfach der berühmte Funke, der übersprang. Es hat allerdings doch ein bisschen gedauert."

Die Hochzeit im Jahr 2000 war dann spektakulär: ein Autokorso mit Oldtimern des Bräutigams und zwei englischen Doppeldeckerbussen für die Hochzeitsgäste sowie eine Feier im *Erotic Art Museum*. Die Hochzeit war, bekannte Jan Fedder später, sicherlich der schönste Augenblick seines Lebens.

Jan Fedder und seine Frau haben bewusst in verschiedenen Hamburger Wohnungen gelebt und sich meistens an Wochenenden getroffen, öfter auch auf dem Bauernhof. Jan Fedder liebte die Ruhe, brauchte die Zeiten, in denen er allein war, und genoss sie. Ebenso schätzte er die Zeit gemeinsam mit seiner Frau sehr. Sie sagte dazu: „Wenn wir uns jetzt treffen, sprechen wir natürlich lange. Lachen uns tot über Sachen. Gucken uns manchmal Filme an. Planen etwas zusammen."

Als Bauer in der Serie „Neues aus Büttenwarder"

Nicht nur in der Fernsehserie „Großstadtrevier", sondern auch als Kurt Brakelmann in der Serie „Neues aus Büttenwarder" brillierte Fedder. Achtzehn Jahre lang spielte er den komisch-liebenswerten Bauern in einem fiktiven Dorf in Schleswig-Holstein. Bauernschlau entwickelte er immer neue Geschäftsideen, die sich aber alle irgendwie nicht verwirklichen ließen.

Folgen aus dieser Serie werden auch heute noch häufig vom NDR mit Erfolg ausgestrahlt. Produzent Markus Trebitsch nannte Fedder „die größte Symbiose aus einer ziemlich großen Klappe und einem großen Herzen".

Die Verfilmung von Siegfried-Lenz-Romanen

Als Filmschauspieler ist Jan Fedder als Matrose in „Das Boot" in Erinnerung geblieben, vor allem aber durch seine Hauptrollen in Verfilmungen von vier Lenz-Romanen, darunter „Der Mann im Strom" und „Das Feuerschiff". In diesen Filmen konnte er seine Fähigkeit, ernste Filmrollen zu spielen, sehr überzeugend beweisen. Er sagte damals über seine Mitwirkung als Hauptdarsteller im Film „Der Mann im Strom“: „Ich bin sehr froh, dass ich in dieser Produktion einmal eine andere Facette zeigen kann. Wenn man so intensiv mit einer Serie verbunden ist wie mit dem ‚Großstadtrevier‘, hat man nicht oft die Gelegenheit dazu.“ Für seine herausragende Leistung in diesem Film wurde er 2006 mit dem Deutschen Fernsehpreis ausgezeichnet.

Sicherlich noch wichtiger war ihm, dass Siegfried Lenz voll das Lobes dafür war, wie Fedder den Romanfiguren überzeugend Leben einhauchte. Siegfried Lenz bekannte: „Jan Fedder ist ein Schauspieler, den ich einfach gern habe. Das geht so weit, dass ich für den Rest meines Lebens das, was ich schreibe, insgeheim an ihn adressieren werde, in der Hoffnung, das kann nur Jan Fedder spielen.“

Dass Jan Fedder so beeindruckend die Roman-Charaktere darstellen konnte, liegt auch daran: „Hauptberuflich bin ich Mensch und nebenberuflich Schauspieler. Übrigens: Wenn man als Mensch nicht überzeugt, überzeugt man auch nicht als Schauspieler.“

Erwähnt werden soll an dieser Stelle auch seine Rolle in der Fernsehserie „Der Hafenpastor“. Die Rolle des Pastors von St. Pauli passte gut zu dem realen Jan Fedder. In einem der letzten Gespräche mit seinem Biografen Tim Pröse bekannte der gläubige Jan Fedder, dass er sich Gott als alten Mann vorstellte: „Und es ist ein gütiger älterer Herr. Vielleicht habe ich mir diesen Kinderglauben bewahrt, weil ich so früh anfing; mit fünf im Kinderchor im Michel.“

Als das Polizeirevier in die Luft flog

2018 hatte der NDR beschlossen, die Räumlichkeiten aufzugeben, in denen bis dahin das „Großstadtrevier" gedreht wurde. Es war eigentlich ein Bürogebäude, das inzwischen in die Jahre gekommen war. Vor dem Umzug in eine Halle von *Studio Hamburg* flog das Filmrevier in der Mendelssohnstraße in Bahrenfeld am Ende einer Folge spektakulär in die Luft. Fedder, der zu den Wenigen gehörte, die die fast drei Jahrzehnte hier ihr Revier hatten, bekannte vorher: „Es ist sehr viel Wehmut, die mich beschleicht. Ich werde wahrscheinlich noch ein paar Mal heulen. 27 Jahre in einem Gebäude, die wischt man nicht so einfach weg." Er hat tatsächlich geweint, als sein geliebter Arbeitsplatz „filmreif" vernichtet wurde.

Fedder, der langlebigste deutsche Serienstar, hat wegen seiner angegriffenen Gesundheit nur noch kurze Zeit im neuen Revier spielen können. Er, der zum Ehrenkommissar der Hamburger und auch der Bayerischen Polizei ernannt worden war, musste einen Ruhestand antreten.

Die geplante Show zum 65. Geburtstag fand nicht mehr statt

2012 hatten die Ärzte ein Mundhöhlenkarzinom diagnostiziert. Ein Drittel seiner Zunge musste entfernt werden; es war eine Strahlentherapie erforderlich. Trotz dieser und weiterer gesundheitlicher Probleme spielte er mit Unterbrechungen weiter im „Großstadtrevier": „Das ist wie Urlaub hier. Wenn ich nicht mehr drehen kann, falle ich tot um." Er benötigte die Atmosphäre am Drehort: „Ich bin einfach ein Zirkuspferd. Ich muss das haben." Er war nun häufig zwischen den Aufnahmen auf einen

Rollstuhl angewiesen. In der letzten Lebensphase hat er weder geraucht noch Alkohol getrunken.

Jan Fedder plante eine Show zu seinem 65. Geburtstag, aber diesen Geburtstag hat er nicht mehr erlebt. Gern wäre er Hamburger Ehrenbürger geworden, was man nur zu Lebzeiten werden kann, aber dieser Wunsch ist ihm nicht erfüllt worden. In mehr als 600 Produktionen, in denen er mitgespielt hat, und vielen Auftritten als Polizist und Pastor hat er seine Heimatstadt sympathisch repräsentiert, da wäre eine solche Ehrung angemessen gewesen. Stolz war er darauf, dass die „Deutsche Gesellschaft zur Rettung Schiffbrüchiger" ihn zu Lebzeiten geehrt und zu einem ihrer Botschafter gemacht hat.

Jan Fedder starb am 30. Dezember 2019 in seiner Wohnung. Die eigene Trauerfeier hatte er detailliert geplant. Am 14. Januar versammelten sich fast 2.000 Menschen im Michel, um Abschied von Jan Fedder zu nehmen. Für all jene, die keinen Platz in der Kirche fanden, übertrug der NDR die Trauerfeier auf eine große Leinwand vor der Kirche. Wunschgemäß erklang während der Feier der Song „Knockin on Heaven's Door" und ebenso das Hamburger Lied vom „Tüdelband".

Hauptpastor Alexander Röder lobte in der Traueransprache Fedders „großes Herz und seinen Sinn für Gerechtigkeit". Polizeipräsident Ralf Martin Meyer brachte seine Anerkennung für den Schauspieler mit diesen Worten zum Ausdruck: „So wünsche ich mir meine Polizisten. Mit Herz für die kleineren Leute, die Schwächeren." In die Kondolenzbücher, die in der Davidwache auslagen, trugen sich 3.000 Hamburgerinnen und Hamburger ein.

Seine letzte Ruhe fand Jan Fedder auf dem Ohlsdorfer Friedhof. Es kamen so viele Menschen dorthin, dass der Rasen rund um das Grab bald niedergetreten war und eine Absperrung mit Kette erforderlich wurde.

In Erinnerung an einen großen Schauspieler

Jan Fedder ist noch zwei Mal gestorben, nämlich in seinen Fernsehserien. Im Mai 2020 trauerten seine Film-Kolleginnen und -Kollegen im „Großstadtrevier“ um Dirk Matthies und Ende Dezember des selben Jahres fand in „Büttenwarder“ eine Trauerfeier für den verstorbenen Kurt Brakelmann statt. Der Schauspieler Peter Heinrich Brix, in der Serie der Bauer Adsche Tönnsen, wollte die Serie ohne seinen langjährigen Partner Jan Fedder nicht fortsetzen. Die Serie ist daraufhin 2021 eingestellt worden.

Marion Fedder hat mehrfach Gegenstände aus dem Nachlass ihres verstorbenen Mannes für kirchliche und wohltätige Zwecke versteigern lassen. Bei einer der Versteigerungen erzielte Fedders Küchenuhr einen Preis von 14.000 Euro. Sein letztes Auto, ein Ford Explorer, brachte 61.200 Euro für den *Michel* ein. Ein Mercedes erzielte 97.000 Euro, ebenfalls zugunsten seiner geliebten Kirche.

Im September 2020 platzierte diese Kirche eine „Michel-Platte“ für Jan Fedder auf dem Kirchenvorplatz, direkt neben der Platte für Helmut Schmidt, den der Schauspieler sehr geschätzt hatte. Auf Fedders Platte steht: „Hamburg war Dein Revier, und der Michel war Dein Anker“.

Was erinnert außerdem in Hamburg an Jan Fedder? Seit Ende Juni 2022 prangt eine Ehrentafel für ihn am Lokal

„Zur Ritze“ an der Reeperbahn, zur Freude von Marion Fedder: „Jan ist St. Paulianer. Er wohnte gleich um die Ecke, die ‚Ritze‘ war sein Lieblingslokal, er nannte sie sein Wohnzimmer. Er hat hier viele Abende und Nächte verbracht, mit Bier und Gin Tonic.“ Zu erwähnen ist auch, dass im Panoptikum auf St. Pauli eine Wachsfigur des Schauspielers steht.

Im November 2022 ehrte ihn endlich die Stadt, die ihn nicht zum Ehrenbürger gemacht hatte, und gab der Uferpromenade zwischen Überseebrücke und Baumwall den Namen Jan-Fedder-Promenade. Seine Witwe zeigte sich bei der Einweihungsfeier überzeugt: „Die Stadt Hamburg hat Jan mit der Benennung der Jan-Fedder-Promenade das schönste Geschenk gemacht und ihm damit ein großartiges Denkmal gesetzt. Der Hamburger Hafen war sein Leben, sein Zuhause. Jan verkörperte Hamburg wie kein anderer. Das ist der schönste Wanderweg, den ich kenne. Hier kann man auf seinen Spuren wandern. Jan wäre unglaublich stolz darauf.“

Helga Feddersen

„Also, ich heiße Helga Feddersen, bin Hamburgerin und zur Zeit 17.895 Tage alt. Denn am 14.3., morgens 9.30 Uhr, erblickte ich das Licht der Welt und meine Mutter mich: letztere unter stolzen Tränen lächelnd. Drei Stunden darauf gefror das erwartungsvolle Lächeln meines Vaters: Er hatte einen Sohn geplant. Nach zwei Tagen strenger Klausur bei härtesten Getränken kehrte er an das Bett meiner Mutter zurück und verkündete: ‚Deine Tochter wird Zahnärztin.' – Mutter jedoch bestimmte: ‚Deine Tochter Helga wird erst einmal groß.'" Das hat die Tochter zwar nicht selbst mitbekommen, hat es aber in ihr Buch „Hallo, hier ist Helga!" aufgenommen.

Helga Feddersen kam am 14. März 1930 zur Welt. Ihre Eltern besaßen eine Firma für Seemannsausrüstungen an der Deichstraße, die bis heute besteht. Die Tochter hatte einen Sinn für Komik, auch für unfreiwillige Komik. Als Achtjährige blieb sie allein zu Haus, während die Mutter unerwartet weg musste. Helga erwartete einen gleichaltrigen Jungen zum Rollschuhlaufen und bekam von der Mutter den Auftrag, beim Weggehen gut abzuschließen. Als die Mutter vor der Tochter zurückkehrte, fand sie an der Wohnungstür einen Zettel, auf dem in der Handschrift der Tochter stand: „Geheim! Liebe Muttie! Alles gut abgeschloßsen. Hauschlüsel ligt unter der Fußmatte."

Aus Helga Feddersens Lebenserinnerungen können wir entnehmen, dass sie in einer humorvollen Familie aufwuchs. Pfingsten ging es jedes Jahr nach Hagenbeck, und der Vater hielt angesichts des Gedränges im Zoo diese „Pfingstpredigt“: „Die Familie bleibt zusammen. Sollten wir uns trotzdem verlieren, keiner fährt ohne den andern nach Haus. Sammelpunkt: Bärenkäfig außen.“ Zum Pfingstfest gehörten außerdem das gemeinsame Schmettern des berühmten Couplets von Hein Köllisch „To Pfingsten, ach wie scheun“ und des Liedes „An de Alster, an de Elbe, an de Bill, dor kann jeder eener moken wat he will“.

Eine belastende Kindheit, erleichtert durch eine Drehorgel

Dass ihre Kindheit nicht immer heiter war, hat Helga Feddersen in ihrer autobiografischen Novelle „Amanda mit der Drehorgel“ der Nachwelt hinterlassen. Die Novelle veröffentlichte sie erst kurz vor ihrem Tod. Die Hauptfigur Amanda ist häufig mit ihrer Drehorgel Amandus unterwegs, die sie ihrem Großvater „abgebettelt“ hat. Amanda verlebt eine glückliche Zeit mit ihren Freunden, den „Waldkindern“, in einem Waldkindergarten.

Umso größer ist der Kontrast zum Unterricht in der Grundschule: „Zum ersten Mal eine Tür geschlossen, durch die man nicht hinausgehen konnte, wenn man wollte. Den ersten Tag ohne meine Freunde, die Waldkinder.“ Amandus wird ihr Trost in einer fremden Umwelt. „Ich bin ‚Amanda mit der Drehorgel‘, und wir möchten alle lieber wieder gehen.“ Aber: „Als die Lehrerin in diesem Augenblick die Tür schloss, wusste ich, dass ich bleiben musste, dass es einfach sein musste.“

Nachmittags findet Amanda Zuflucht in einer Fliederlaube, die ihr Vater ihr im Garten in eine Fliederhecke geschnitten hat. Die Mutter versucht, Freundschaften mit anderen Mädchen zu stiften, und unternimmt es, möglichst oft „zwei zarte lerneifrige Mädchen, Walla und Hella, zu uns einzuladen". Aber es entsteht keine Freundschaft, schon deshalb nicht, weil Amanda mithört, wie eine der Mütter der Mädchen zur anderen über sie sagt: „Die arme Mutter, was für ein grobes, merkwürdiges Mädchen." Amanda gegenüber geben sich die beiden Mütter betont freundlich, aber aus einer Mädchenfreundschaft wird nichts: „Ich setzte mich neben Amandus, der am Fußende der Betten stand, und wir waren uns einig. Ein wenig traurig für Mutter, aber wir wollten Walla und Hella nicht. Sie waren falsch wie ihre Mütter, nur noch ein wenig mehr."

Dafür schließt sie Freundschaft mit Edgar, dem Sohn eines Schokoladenfabrikanten, der in der Nachbarschaft wohnt. Ihn besuchte sie oft und war auch in der Fabrik willkommen. Die Leserinnen und Leser der Novelle erfahren zunächst nicht, dass Edgar einer jüdischen Familie angehört. Erst nach dem nicht direkt erwähnten Machtantritt der Nazis lesen wir: „Edgar habe ich nicht mehr gesehen. Mutter erzählte, die Golds machen eine Auslandsreise. Und Vater ersteigerte eines Tages einen riesenlangen Tisch für seinen Lagerraum, der war mir vertraut." Das kann als ein Hinweis darauf verstanden werden, dass der Vater von der Zwangsversteigerung der Schokoladenfabrik – wenn auch in kleinem Umfang – profitierte.

Amanda wechselt auf Initiative ihrer Mutter und gegen den Willen ihrer Lehrerin auf eine Oberschule. Dort wird sie wegen ihrer schlechten Handarbeitsleistungen vor der ganzen Schule bloßgestellt. Sie denkt nun häufig an

Edgar und erinnert sich: „Edgar hasste alle braunfarbenen Sachen …" Amandas Eltern und die Tochter passen sich an. Der Vater erwägt, mit braunen Hemden zu handeln, die Mutter geht zur „rechten Mutterschaft" und Amanda erscheint zu den „Abenden", gemeint sind die Abende der NS-Jugend.

Im Krieg verlässt Amanda mit ihrer Klasse im Rahmen der Kinderlandverschickung die Stadt, um vor Bombenangriffen geschützt zu sein. Jeden Morgen hilft ihr „ein anderes williges Händepaar, das mir die immer noch dünnen Zöpfe flocht … Die Zöpfe hingen merkwürdig verdreht über den Ohren, vergeblich nach hinten gezogen." Das ist vielleicht ein Symbol dafür, dass Amanda mit ihren widerspenstigen Haaren (und ihren unangepassten Gedanken) nicht zu den strohblonden Mädchen mit den schön geflochtenen Zöpfen gehört.

Nach dem Ende des Krieges kehrt Amanda mit ihrer Drehorgel in die Stadt zurück, die zerstört ist und in der ihre Eltern in einem Schrebergarten in einer kleinen Hütte leben. Der Vater baut seinen Laden „auf einem Trümmerhaufen" wieder auf. Die Vergangenheit wird verdrängt, Fragen der Tochter mit dem Satz beantwortet: „Befehl ist Befehl." Und als sie leise fragt „Und Edgar", da hören die Eltern sie nicht, wollen sie nicht hören.

Der schweiß- und tränentreibende Hindernislauf durch die Theater

Helga Feddersen schloss die Oberschule erfolgreich ab und besuchte anschließend eine Frauenfachschule. 1948 nahm man sie in eine private Schauspielschule auf. Sie hatte bereits 1949 ihren ersten Auftritt im *Theater im*

Zimmer, das damals Helmuth Gmelin leitete. Es wurde Strindbergs Drama „Ostern“ gespielt. Helga Feddersen hat ihre nächsten Schritte auf dem Weg zu einer Bühnenkarriere im Buch über ihr Leben so beschrieben:

„Als Schauspielerin mit beglaubigter Bühnenreife trat ich den schweiß- und tränentreibenden Hindernislauf durch die Theater an. Über die ‚Naive‘ durch den ‚Charakter‘ zur ‚Komikerin‘. Der ‚Charakter‘ brachte mich ans *Deutsche Schauspielhaus* in Hamburg, die ‚Komik‘ zu Film und Fernsehen. „Hier gewann sich meine Nase einen nicht unbedeutenden Verehrerkreis. Man bestaunte dieselbe in dem Film ‚Die Buddenbrooks‘ als ‚Klothilde‘ sowie in vielen Fernsehspielen.“

Dass man die eigene Berühmtheit nicht überschätzen sollte, erlebte Helga Feddersen während einer Flugreise: „Als ich beim Heimflug in München umstieg, stand auf dem Rollfeld ein Fotograf. Er riss die Kamera hoch und machte mir eine Handbewegung. Ich reagierte sofort. Ging zurück, um dann nochmals die Gangway herabzuschreiten. Im Innersten wunderte ich mich: ‚Woher weiß der, dass ich komme?‘ Unten angekommen, fragte er mich nach meiner Adresse. ‚Per Nachnahme, innerhalb acht Tagen, Weltpostkarte.‘ Es war der Flughafenfotograf.“

Ihr erster Mann, der NDR-Dramaturg Götz Kozuszek, ermutigte sie dazu, Drehbücher und Kurzgeschichten zu schreiben. Mehrere Filme und Serien entstanden auf der Grundlage ihrer Drehbücher und auch ein Buch mit ihren Kurzgeschichten erschien.

Ein Tumor veränderte das Leben der Schauspielerin

Helga Feddersen war auf dem Weg, als Schauspielerin und Autorin viel Anerkennung zu finden, und bewies ihre vielseitigen Fähigkeiten in einem breiten Spektrum von Rollen. Aber dann entdeckten die Ärzte 1955 einen Tumor an ihrer Ohrspeicheldrüse. Der Tumor konnte entfernt werden, aber durch die Operation wurde ihr Gesicht entstellt, und sie konnte zeitweise nicht mehr sprechen. Helga Feddersen zog sich daraufhin aus der Öffentlichkeit zurück. Ihre Familie überzeugte sie, im Laden in der Deichstraße zu arbeiten. Sie beschränkte ihre Tätigkeit zunächst auf das Lager, aber mit der Wiedergewinnung ihrer Sprachfähigkeit bediente sie bald auch Kunden im Laden.

Mit neugewonnenem Selbstbewusstsein kehrte Helga Feddersen auf die Bühne und in die Filmstudios zurück. Die Vielseitigkeit der Schauspielerin sollte es verbieten, sie darauf zu reduzieren, sie wäre ausschließlich eine „Ulknudel" gewesen. In den folgenden Jahren spielte sie zum Beispiel in der Krimiserie „Stahlnetz" mit. Daneben war sie in Peter Ahrweilers *Kleiner Komödie*, im *Ohnsorg Theater* und in Filmkomödien sowie der Fernsehreihe „Ein Herz und eine Seele" zu sehen. Auch als Synchronsprecherin war sie gefragt.

Als Schauspielerin konzentrierte sich nun auf ihre komische Seite und übernahm Rollen in humoristischen Filmen und Fernsehsendungen. Die Schauspielerin Helga Feddersen hatte die innere Kraft, sich zu ihrer Behinderung zu bekennen und aus der Situation das Beste zu machen.

1978 erschien ihre erste Schallplatte mit eigenen Liedern und Gedichten. Gemeinsam mit Dieter Hallervorden nahm sie das Nonsenslied „Du, die Wanne ist voll“ auf, das es unter die Top Ten der deutschen Schlagerparade brachte.

In der Öffentlichkeit nahm man sie als extrovertierte, laute Frau wahr, aber privat war sie introvertiert und eher ruhig. Ole von Beust, der wie sie in der Deichstraße wohnte und mit dem sie befreundet war, sagte über die Schauspielerin: „Helga war eine sehr nachdenkliche, belesene Frau. Sehr gastfreundlich und empathisch. Sie fühlte mit anderen Menschen.“

Große Erfolge im eigenen „Theater am Holstenwall“

1983 eröffnete Helga Feddersen gemeinsam mit ihrem Partner Olli Maier das *Theater am Holstenwall.* Sie ließen einen alten Ballsaal zu einem Theater mit 250 Plätzen umbauen. Olli Maier war ein durchaus umstrittener Künstler, was sich auch am Titel seiner Lebenserinnerungen ablesen lässt: „Ich, der Buhmann der Nation“. Aber es gibt auch diese Beobachtung von Ole von Beust: „Ich fand, dass die beiden immer sehr liebevoll miteinander umgegangen sind, und sie haben viel zusammen gelacht.“

Ihr Boulevard-Theater fand mit Komödien und Schwänken ein großes Publikum und die Aufführungen waren häufig ausverkauft. Das lag vor allem an der populären Schauspielerin Helga Feddersen. Die Erfolgskomödie „Die Perle Anna“ wurde im *Theater am Holstenwall* mehr als 400 Mal vor vollen Haus gespielt. Dass Popularität relativ ist, erlebte die Schauspielerin in Kiel. Ein 12-Jähriger erbat sich gleich sieben Autogramme. „Aha“, sagte sie, „für alle deine Freunde?“. Der Junge antwortete: „Nee. Zum Tauschen. Für sechs Feddersen kriege ich einen Otto.“ Da tat es dem Ego von Helga Feddersen gut, was sie auf einem Flohmarkt erlebte: „Von Kindern umringt schrieb ich, was die Finger hergaben. Da schiebt sich ein Mann in die Kinderrunde und erbittet sich gleichfalls mein Konterfei. ‚Nö‘, sagt da eine kleine Hamburger Deern. ‚Sie kriegen kein Autogramm. Helga ist nämlich Kinderliebhaberin und keine Männerliebhaberin.‘“

Schwere Schicksalsschläge und der erneute Rückzug aus der Öffentlichkeit

1985 musste Helga Feddersen mit dem Tod ihres Mannes Götz Kozuszek fertig werden, der sie immer wieder ermutigt und gefördert hatte. Im Alter litt er unter Alzheimer und wurde in dieser Zeit zu einer großen Belastung für seine Frau. Außerdem musste sie selbst zwei Mal wegen neuer Tumore operiert werden.

Als wären dies nicht genug Belastungen, erzwang dann auch noch eine Kiefervereiterung die Entfernung aller Zähne. Die Schicksalsschläge lösten eine Medikamentenabhängigkeit aus, die zur Folge hatte, dass Helga Feddersen zeitweise nur noch 32 Kilogramm wog. Als Helga Feddersen nicht mehr in ihrem Theater auftreten konnte, verlor es einen großen Teil seines Stammpublikums. 1989 musste Insolvenz angemeldet werden. Es kam zu mehreren Besitzerwechseln, aber das Theater war nicht mehr zu retten. Im Februar 2008 fand die letzte Aufführung mit einem Sartre-Stück statt. Es hatte den beziehungsreichen Titel „Das Spiel ist aus“.

Die Öffentlichkeit hörte in den Jahren nach der Erkrankung Helga Feddersens nur noch von ihren Erkrankungen und ihren finanziellen Schwierigkeiten. Sie wählte Nieblum auf Föhr zum neuen Wohnort und lebte dort zurückgezogen mit ihrem Lebensgefährten Olli Maier. Helga Feddersen starb am 24. November 1990 im Alter von 60 Jahren. Kurz vor dem Tod hatte sie Olli Maier geheiratet. Beigesetzt wurde sie auf einem Friedhof in Stuttgart, der Heimatstadt ihres zweiten Ehemannes.

Am Haus Deichstraße 39, in dem sie viele Jahre im ersten Stock gewohnt hatte, erinnert keine Tafel an die Schauspielerin. Immerhin gibt es in Altona seit 2016 eine Helga-Feddersen-Twiete. Eine späte Ehrung. In Stuttgart erinnerte damals bereits seit zwei Jahren eine Straße den Namen Schauspielerin. Karl Dall sagte voller Anerkennung über sie: „Helga hatte den Mut, sich über sich selber lustig zu machen."

Käppen Haase

„Käppen Haase stand stets hemdsärmelig in seiner Klause. Ein strammer, aber nicht übermäßiger Bauch gab seiner Figur Wuchtigkeit. Ein schöner eisgrauer Admiralsbart zierte sein Gesicht. In seinen Augen flimmerte der Schalk, saß die berstende Lebensfreude." So hat Carl Thinius, der Chronist des alten St. Pauli, das Original Haase beschrieben:

August Emil Theodor Haase kam 1867 in Bergen auf Rügen zur Welt. Er fuhr in seiner Jugend zur See und stieg zum Kapitän auf, so hat er es jedenfalls später erzählt. 1894 eröffnete er ein Seemannslokal in der Erichstraße auf St. Pauli. Und wie andere damalige Kneipenbesitzer in der Gegend staffierte er sein Lokal mit Objekten aus aller Welt aus, um ihm einen maritimen und exotischen Charakter zu verleihen. Er habe viele der Ausstellungsobjekte selbst von seinen Seereisen rund um den Globus mitgebracht, verkündete Haase bei einem Glas Grog. Aber die meisten Ausstellungsstücke hatte der Wirt von Seeleuten und anderen weitgereisten Besuchern seines Lokals erhalten. Bald war seine Sammlung so groß, dass er seine Kneipe ein Museum nennen konnte.

Objekte aus aller Welt, vorgestellt vom Wirt mit fantasievollen Geschichten

Haase machte gar nicht erst den Versuch, sein Museum systematisch und nach wissenschaftlichen Maßstäben zu präsentieren und alle Objekte entsprechend zu beschriften. Im Gegenteil. Erst das Nebeneinander von Elefantenfuß, Maske, Sägefisch und Südseeungeheuer machte erst den Reiz der Sammlung aus. Es soll nicht verschwiegen werden, dass Haase auch Aktfotos von Afrikanerinnen in seiner Sammlung hatte, von denen er behauptete, es wären seine Schwiegermutter und deren Nichte. Die Tiere der Sammlung hatte Haase selbst präpariert, betätigte er sich doch auch als Tierpräparator. Auch Objekte aus der näheren Umgebung bereicherten das Museum, darunter eine Reihe alter Gewehre. Für viele Hamburg-Besucher bildete die kunterbunte Mischung bei Haase eine willkommene Abwechslung zu den wohlgeordneten, aber nach einer Weile vielleicht doch etwas langweiligen städtischen Museen der Stadt.

Die bunte Mischung seiner Sammlung allein hätten Käppen Haase nicht bekannt und ihn selbst nicht zu einem Original gemacht. Es waren seine fantasiereichen Geschichten, die ihn, den „Professor der unentdeckten Wissenschaft", berühmt machten. Dass er manche Objekte mit lateinischen Namen versah, sollte seinen Ruf als Professor unterstreichen. Aber Käppen Haases Präsentation der Museumsobjekte entbehrte jeglicher wissenschaftlicher Genauigkeit. Dafür verbreitete er zu jedem exotischen Objekt eine launige Geschichte.

Wenn er den Grog vor sich stehen und die Pfeife gestopft hatte, erzählte er über eine kleine ausgestopfte Giraffe: „Sie bringt in Hamburg die Kinder, weil es hier keine Störche mehr gibt." Zwei japanische Vasen waren nach Angaben des Käppen sechstausend Jahre alt, jede von ihnen etwa dreitausend Jahre. Eine der beiden Vasen, versicherte Haase, wäre vor der Sintflut entstanden, die andere bald darauf. Auch über eine Kette aus Holzringen hatte der Wirt etwas zu erzählen: „Dieses hier sind die

Verlobungsringe von Adam und Eva.“ Und da war dann auch noch ein Holzstock, mit dem Zar Nikolaus II. angeblich die Revolution niedergeschlagen hatte.

Ein faszinierendes „Sammelsurium“

Käppen Haase duzte alle Besucherinnen und Besucher. Er sprach alle Männer einheitlich mit Heinrich und alle Frauen mit Mariechen an. Der Kneipenwirt und Museumsdirektor erlangte in den 1920er Jahren eine beträchtliche Berühmtheit. Seine Sammlung firmierte nun als „Museum für Kolonie und Heimat“, zu einer Zeit, als es die deutschen Kolonien gar nicht mehr gab. Der bekannte Journalist Egon Erwin Kisch schrieb eine Reportage über das „Sammelsurium“ in dem Lokal. Der Schriftsteller Hans Leip hat die Seemannskneipe häufiger besucht und beschrieben. Wenn jemand den Käppen zu einem Grog einlud, war regelmäßig seine Antwort: „Ich habe noch keinen gehabt seit dem Letzten.“ Carl Thinius betont aber: „Niemand kann sich jedoch erinnern, ihn jemals betrunken erlebt zu haben.“

1930 hat Hans Harbeck in seinen Reiseführer „Hamburg. Was nicht im Baedeker steht“ ein Porträt des Kneipen- und Museumsbesitzers aufgenommen, das so beginnt: „Der rasende Zahn der Zeit hat die gemütvollen althamburgischen Straßenfiguren hinweggerafft. Die Gegenwart schwärmt für Tempo und Gleichmaß. Als eine Art von letztem Mohikaner haust in seinem Museum für Kolonie und Heimat (Erichstraße 46) der alte A. E. Th. Haase, Kapitän a.D. und Professor der unentdeckten Wissenschaft. Eine tolle Type und – nach Hans Leips Meinung – vielleicht das letzte große Original Europas. Jedenfalls ein echtes Hamburger Hafengewächs und wert, von allen Reisenden besichtigt zu werden, obwohl seine Redeweise eine fröhliche Unbefangenheit verrät und nicht für zimperliche Ohren bestimmt ist."

Gefragt nach der Zukunft seiner Sammlung, wenn er sie selbst nicht mehr betreuen könne, antwortete Haase: „Überhaupt, wer sollte sich meine Sammlung in seinem Gesamtbestand zulegen und die Schau so zelebrieren, wie ich es mache!" Und nachdem er seinen Blick über seine Sammlung schweifen ließ, sagte er resigniert: „Nee, lot man, Heinrich, dat blivt besohm, so lang ich lev. Mi kümmert nich, wat no mi kümmt."

Was aus der einmaligen Sammlung geworden ist

Käppen Haase starb 1934. Danach wurde sein Lokal geschlossen und das gesamte Inventar verkauft. Auch Museen sollen einzelne Objekte erstanden haben. Einen großen Teil der Museumsbestände erwarb der Gastronom Paul Wetzel, der sein Lokal an der Reeperbahn damit ausstattete. Er versuchte, von der Berühmtheit des Vorbesitzers zu profitieren, und nannte das Lokal *Kapitän Haase's Museum* und verkürzt *Käppen Haase*. Aber es fehlte der Namensgeber, das Original Haase. Außerdem beging Wetzel den Fehler, die Objekte in seinem Lokal gut geordnet wie in anderen Museen zu präsentieren und dem Museum damit den Charme der chaotischen und immer wieder überraschenden Präsentation von Haase zu nehmen.

1952 erwarb Harry Rosenberg das, was von den Schätzen von Käppen Haase übrig geblieben, und das, was von Paul Wetzel hinzugefügt worden war. Er machte diese

Objekte zum Grundstock von *Harrys Hamburger Hafenbasar.* Rosenberg erweiterte das originelle Museum schrittweise auf 2.600 Quadratmeter und nahm Eintritt für die Besichtigung. Er erwarb zusätzlich viele neue Objekte und erlangte mit seinem Museum weit über Hamburg hinaus Beachtung.

Das originelle Museum von Harry Rosenberg und seiner Nachfahren musste mehrmals in St. Pauli umziehen, wird inzwischen von einer Stiftung getragen und hat in einem Schwimmkran am Sandtorhafen eine neue Heimat gefunden. Das Museum *Harrys Hamburger Hafenbasar & Museum* wirbt im Internet so: „Reise in eine Welt aus Schätzen, Kuriositäten, Kostbarem und vielen Überraschungen – von allen Kontinenten der Welt - Entdecke spannende Geschichten wie die Kostbarkeiten des Hafenbasars ihren Seeweg nach Hamburg fanden."

Käpp'n Herbert

Als „wandelnde Bruttoregistertonne" hat er Rundfunkgeschichte geschrieben: Karl Herbert, besser bekannt als „Käpp'n Herbert". In den 1930er Jahren war er der Muntermacher im *Hamburger Hafenkonzert*. Jeden Sonntag um sechs in der Frühe schallte seine Stimme laut durch den Äther:

Wacht auf, ihr Schläfer groß und klein.
Es wacht schon längst der Kapitein.
Er ruft euch „Guten Morgen!" zu.
Wacht auf, wacht auf, aus Euer Ruh.
Reise! Reise!
Jeder weckt den Nebenmann,
Der letzte stößt sich selber an!

Manchmal musste Käpp'n Herbert selbst nicht geweckt werden, denn der Umtrunk am Abend vor der Sendung ging dann gleitend in den Morgen und den Weckruf über. Der Käpp'n brauchte auch die Menschen rund um den *Michel* nicht zu wecken, das erledigten die Kirchenglocken. Damals konnten die Radiosendungen und die einzelnen Beiträge noch nicht aufgezeichnet werden, sodass alles live gesendet werden musste. Das galt auch für das Glockengeläut, mit dem das *Hafenkonzert* jede Woche begann. Weil Glocken erst nach zehn Minuten gut klingen, begann man schon zehn vor sechs mit dem Läuten.

Dafür hörte man die Michelglocken dann nicht nur in Deutschland, sondern via Kurzwelle auch in China und Südafrika. Der maritime Charakter der Sendung kam dadurch zum Ausdruck, dass nach dem Glockenläuten das Horn des Schiffes ertönte, von dem live gesendet wurde.

Eine Sendung, die nach Tang und Teer riecht

Das *Hafenkonzert* ging am 9. Juni 1929 erstmals auf Sendung. Der Intendant des *Nordischen Rundfunks* hatte seinem Mitarbeiter Kurt Esmarch den Auftrag erteilt, ein neues Programm für den erst fünf Jahre alten Rundfunksender zu entwickeln. Wenn die Überlieferung stimmt, tat er das mit diesen Worten: „Schaffen Sie etwas ganz Neues, eine Sendung, die nach Tang und Teer riecht, eine Sendung, in der die See zu den Hörern spricht, die See und die Männer, die sich ihr verschrieben haben. Nutzen Sie alle Möglichkeiten, die Ihnen die Technik bietet. Stellen Sie die Technik vor neue Probleme. Kurz und gut: Schaffen Sie eine einmalige Sendung für den frühen Sonntagmorgen."

Kurt Esmarch entwickelte das Konzept einer Sendung, die jeden Sonntag von einem anderen Schiff im Hamburger Hafen oder auf der Elbe übertragen wurden und neben viel Musik auch informative und unterhaltende Beiträge aus der Welt der Seefahrt bieten sollte.

Gleich die erste Sendung löste allerdings bei der Hörerschaft Unmut aus. Zum Auftakt spielten die Altonaer Sinfoniker, die extra mit an Bord des Ozeandampfers „Antonio Delfino" der *Hamburg Süd* gekommen waren, die Ouvertüre der Oper „Die lustigen Weiber von Windsor". Die Streichinstrumente müssen aus den damaligen recht primitiven Radioempfängern kläglich geklungen haben und von Tang und Teer war auch nichts zu spüren. Fortan erklang Blasmusik, vorzugsweise Stücke aus der Welt der

Seefahrt. Gelegentlich bereicherten Kurt Esmarch und Käpp'n Herbert das Programm mit eigenen Gesangsnummern.

Das *Hamburger Hafenkonzert* war trotz der „Lustigen Weiber" von Anfang an ein großer Erfolg und wurde auch von anderen deutschen Sendern übernommen. Damals gab es immerhin bereits eine knappe halbe Million Rundfunkgeräte in Norddeutschland, und viele davon waren sonntags bereits um 6 Uhr morgens eingeschaltet. Besonders beliebt war sehr rasch Karl Herbert, neben Kurt Esmarch der Ko-Moderator der Sendung. Er trug in der Sendung den Titel Käpp'n Herbert, obwohl er nie Kapitän gewesen war.

Warum er von Freunden die „wandelnde Bruttoregistertonne" genannt wurde? Das lag zunächst einmal an seinem beeindruckenden Gedächtnis für Schiffsdaten, und da war dann auch noch sein beachtlicher Leibesumfang. Der hinderte ihn jedoch nie daran, eine Jakobsleiter zu erklimmen oder sich durch einen Maschinenraum zu zwängen.

Kurt Grobecker, der später die Sendung moderierte, hat betont, dass Käpp'n Herbert nicht nur wegen seiner Wendigkeit in Erinnerung geblieben ist: „Mehr noch aber beeindruckte er seine Umwelt durch eine nie versiegende Fröhlichkeit und sein immenses Gedächtnis für Ereignisse, Daten, Namen und Zusammenhänge der christlichen Seefahrt. Karl Herbert war von explosivem, unbezähmbarem Temperament und steckte voller lustiger Geschichten, die er ohne lange nachzudenken aus dem

Ärmel schütteln konnte.“ All das war für die Livesendung von enorm großem Wert.

Damit die Sendung nicht zu lang wurde und die Mischung aus Wort und Musik stimmte, lief der Käpp'n immer mit einem riesigen Wecker durch die Sendung, der an einer Kordel über seinem Bauch hin- und herpendelte. Wenn das *Hafenkonzert* von Bord eines Luxusdampfers oder eines Frachters kam, der gerade im Hafen lag, musste das Orchester mit an Bord, ebenso die Technik. Zunächst gab es nur ein einziges Mikrofon, das sich Musiker und Sprecher weiterreichten. Vieles musste improvisiert werden und Pannen waren nicht zu vermeiden. Entstand eine Pause, hatte der Käpp'n immer eine Geschichte parat. Und seine Beiträge rochen wirklich nach Tang und Teer. Nach jeder Sendung machte er sich auf den Weg zu einem seiner Lieblingslokale wie zu Alma Büngers *Köminsel* in Blankenese, wo er all jene Geschichten zum Besten gab, für die im *Hafenkonzert* keine Zeit gewesen war.

Als Käpp'n Herbert die Ankunft einer Viermastbark ankündigte, die tatsächlich vor Holland dümpelte

Unvergessen ist eine Live-Übertragung im Januar 1938 vom Feuerschiff „Elbe 1“. Es war windstill und weit und breit kein Schiff in Sicht. Aber Käpp'n Herbert machte auch aus dieser Situation etwas, und das hörte sich so an: „Wir haben hier einen phantastischen Ausblick auf die sturmzerfurchte, hochgehende See, welche herrlichen Naturgewalten. Diese Gischt: weißer Schaum und graublaue Wellen ... Aber was erspäht mein waches Seemannsauge? Dort am Horizont, wo das Meer an der Erdkugel herunterzurutschen scheint, offenbart sich uns ein an Schönheit nicht zu übertreffendes Bild. Die stolze Padua nähert sich uns unter vollen Segeln."

Die „Padua" war tatsächlich mit Salpeter aus Chile auf dem Weg nach Hamburg, aber sie dümpelte noch in einer Flaute vor der holländischen Insel Texel. Käpp'n Herbert stiftete große Verwirrung, als er seine fantasievolle Reportage so beendete: „Liebe Bräute in Hamburg und anderswo - macht euch schon mal bereit, eure Janmaaten in die Arme zu schließen. In ein paar Stunden habt ihr eure Jungs bei euch!"

Die Viermastbark „Padua" gehörte zu den berühmten *Flying-P-Linern* der *Laeisz-Reederei* und bot einen prächtigen Anblick, wie man im Hans-Albers-Film „Große Freiheit Nr. 7" sehen kann, und sie segelt auch heute noch als russisches Schulschiff „Kruzenshtern" auf den Weltmeeren. Damals, als Käpp'n Herbert das schöne Schiff angekündigt hatte, kamen alle an die Landungsbrücken - nur die „Padua" nicht. Unruhe machte sich breit, man befürchtete ein Unglück auf der Elbe.

Die *Laeisz-Reederei* sah sich Fragen und Verdächtigungen ausgesetzt. Was hieß da Flaute? Im Radio war von stürmischer See und prallgefüllten Segeln die Rede gewesen! Schließlich blieb der Reederei nichts übrig, als einen Bananendampfer umzuleiten, damit dieser die „Padua" nach Hamburg schleppte.

Aber Käpp'n Herbert war auch bei Reedern eine solche Institution, dass die *Laeisz-Reederei* den teuren Zwischenfall mit Fassung trug. Kurt Grobecker hat seine Beschreibung der Ereignisse mit diesem Satz beendet: „Und der ‚Käpp'n' versprach, dass er niemals in seinem Leben wieder eine Jungfrau enttäuschen wollte ..."

Die Zeiten hatten sich 1933 geändert. Die Naziherrschaft machte auch vor dem *Hafenkonzert* nicht halt. Käpp'n Herbert und sein Kollege Karl Esmarch weigerten sich beharrlich, in die Partei einzutreten oder die Sendung politisch „gleichzuschalten". Kurt Esmarch hat später betont und sicher auch für seinen Kollegen Käpp'n Herbert gesprochen, der zu dieser Zeit bereits verstorben war: „Nun wollte man mich 1933 propagandistisch-politisch einfangen. Ich habe allen diesen Versuchen mit dem mir eigenen – sprich schleswig-holsteinischen – Dickkopp widerstanden. Ins Hafenkonzert kam keine Politik."

Aber Kurt Esmarch und Käpp'n Herbert mussten die Hörer nun als „Volksgenossen" ansprechen und jedes neue „Kraft durch Freude"-Schiff mit einer Sendung würdigen. Bei der Taufe des Schiffes „Wilhelm Gustloff" musste im Mai 1937 die Rede von Robert Ley, der die *Deutsche Arbeitsfront* leitete, gesendet werden. Das blieb die Ausnahme. Im Krieg wurden die *Hafenkonzerte* jahrelang aus einem zerstörten Hafen gesendet, aber das hat Käpp'n Herbert nicht mehr erlebt.

Trauer um die „wandelnde Bruttoregistertonne"

In seinem Buch „Hamburger Hafenkonzert" hat Kurt Grobecker den Abschnitt über Käpp'n Herbert so beendet: „Dieses einzigartige Original des Hamburger Hafenkonzerts mit dem nie versiegenden deftigen Humor starb so, wie es sich Karl Herbert vielleicht selbst gewünscht hätte: überraschend und friedlich. Vor allem aber in der Umgebung, die er am meisten geliebt hatte. Im Oktober 1938 ließ er sich nach dem Hafenkonzert in sein gemütliches Stammlokal ‚Op'n Bull'n' fahren. Dort hat sein Herz ganz plötzlich zu schlagen aufgehört. Um kaum ein Rundfunk-Original haben die Hörer jemals so getrauert wie um die ‚wandelnde Bruttoregistertonne'."

Bedauernd stellte Kurt Grobecker fest: „Mit Karl Herbert war die erste Epoche des Hamburger Hafenkonzerts zu Ende gegangen. Ohne den Käpp'n und dazu noch im Krieg musste die Sendung im wahrsten Sinne des Wortes ihren Geist aufgeben. Denn nach dem Zusammenbruch gab es keine deutschen Schiffe mehr, von denen man senden konnte, und im Hafen gab es nichts mehr, über das zu reden lohnte."

Noch vor Kriegsende war vorerst das Ende des *Hafenkonzerts* gekommen. Zuletzt sendete die *Hafenkonzert*-Mannschaft nicht von Schiffen, die gab es im Hafen kaum noch, sondern aus einem Bunker. Und angesichts der vielen Bombenangriffe zeichnete man die Sendung vorab auf.

Aber bereits 1947 wurde die beliebte Sendung neu belebt und wird auch heute noch jeden Sonntagmorgen ausgestrahlt. Etliche Jahre hat Kurt Grobecker zum Erfolg der Sendung beigetragen, und mit Heidi Kabel kam auch erstmals eine Frau in der Sendung zu Wort. Das *Hafenkonzert* gilt heute als älteste Rundfunksendung der Welt, die immer noch ausgestrahlt wird. Bisher ist sie mehr als 3.000 Mal gesendet worden.

Tante Hermine

Unter ihrem Namen Hermine Brutschin-Hansen kannte sie kaum jemand. Ihre Freunde und die Gäste ihres Lokals nannten sie respektvoll „Tante Hermine". Mehr als vier Jahrzehnte lang saß sie neben dem Tresen der Hafenkneipe *Zur Kuhwerder Fähre* in der Hafenstraße 108 gleich gegenüber den Landungsbrücken, wo die Fähre VII täglich viele Hundert Hafenarbeiter, Werftarbeiter und Seeleute an Bord nahm und abends wieder ablieferte. Es war ein idealer Standort für eine Hafenkneipe. Das Lokal hatten ihre Eltern bereits seit 1923 betrieben.

Die Tochter, die 1905 geboren wurde, übernahm die Herrschaft über den Tresen, ihre „Kommandobrücke", schon als junge Frau und übte sie viele Jahre aus. 1931 heiratete sie den Steuermann Martin Brutschin, der zunächst weiter zur See fuhr. 1939 unternahm das Ehepaar eine gemeinsame Schiffsreise in die Karibik, die beim Ausbruch des Zweiten Weltkriegs abrupt endete. Hermine konnte über Norwegen in die Heimat und in ihre Kneipe zurückkehren, ihr Mann wurde auf Jamaika interniert. Nach seiner Rückkehr stand er in der Kombüse des Lokals.

Zu Gast bei der „Mutter der Seeleute"

Einen Blick auf die Speisekarte der Kneipe konnten die Gäste sich sparen, denn es gab jeden Tag nur ein Gericht, und das bestellte man, wenn man sich keinen Ärger einhandeln wollte. Es gab häufig Labskaus, aber auch schon Mal exotische Gerichte wie Nasi Goreng, die der Koch in seiner Fahrenszeit kennengelernt hatte. War für ihn nichts zu tun, saß der Koch unauffällig im Lokal und las die Zeitung. Für die Unterhaltung der Gäste und die Stimmung im Lokal war seine Ehefrau, die „Mutter der Seeleute", zuständig.

Kapitän Jochen Pahl erinnerte sich an die originelle Art der Bezahlung der Zeche in dieser Hafenkneipe: „Tante Hermine begrüßte auch an diesem Abend ‚ihre Jungs' direkt an der Eingangstür hinter einem kleinen Holztisch sitzend. Den Bierausschank besorgten derweil Besucher ihres Vertrauens. Die Buchführung wiederum war Sache jedes einzelnen Gastes selber – und die Abrechnung erfolgte auf Treu und Glauben bei der Verabschiedung am besagten kleinen Tisch. Ich glaube nicht, dass auch nur einer ihrer Seelords ohne Bezahlung den Laden je verlassen hat."

Hermine – ein bekanntes Hamburger Original

Es kann nicht überraschen, dass Hermine zu den beliebtesten Gästen des *Hamburger Hafenkonzerts* und der Weihnachtssendung *Gruß an Bord* zählte. Der NDR-Redakteur Kurt Grobecker hat 2019 in einem *Deutschlandfunk*-Beitrag daran erinnert, „dass sich die Seeleute zu Weihnachten über keine andere Stimme so sehr gefreut haben wie über die von Hermine Hansen. Sie war ein Original, eines der wenigen weiblichen in der Schifffahrt und keineswegs nur in der ‚Branche' bekannt. Als Seeleute im südamerikanischen Santos einmal auf die Idee kamen, ihrer Hamburger Wirtin einen Gruß zu schicken, schrieben sie auf einem Bierdeckel nichts weiter als ‚Hermine Hamburg' und klebten eine Briefmarke darauf. Für die Post war das kein Problem." Grobecker bezeichnete Tante Hermine als „eines der ganz großen Originale".

Ihr Lokal war, wie der St. Pauli-Pastor Sieghard Wilm es in einer Gedenkfeier für die Wirtin formulierte, „für viele Paulianer und Seeleute ein feucht-fröhlicher Heimatort". Hier trafen sich Seeleute und Studenten, Hafenarbeiter, Prominente aus Politik und Wirtschaft. Auch der berühmte Musiker Louis Armstrong war hier einmal zu Gast. Sonntags kamen auch viele Fischmarkt-Besucher und natürlich die Mannschaft vom *Hafenkonzert*. Die kam gewissermaßen dienstlich. Der Redakteur Kurt Grobecker erinnerte sich: „Man kam schnell miteinander ins Gespräch, und wenn wir die Ohren spitzten, was da so alles am Tresen gesprochen wurde, hatten wir schnell Stoff für ein paar Sendungen ‚im Sack'." Nur Prostituierte und ihre Zuhälter waren bei Hermine unerwünscht. Die setzte die resolute Wirtin binnen kürzester Zeit vor die Tür.

Wie in ähnlichen Seemannskneipen hingen an den Wänden die Seeleute Hermine mitgebracht hatten. Berühmt war ein 1,5 Meter langer Walpenis, der auf dem Klavier lag, wenn er nicht gerade herumgereicht wurde. Er gehörte später zu den Attraktionen der *Övelgönner Seekiste*. Im Mai 2022, als dieses Museum aufgelöst werden musste, erzielte der Auktionator für den Walpenis die stattliche Summe von 3.000 Euro.

Der Kiez-Schriftsteller Konrad Lorenz hat sich so an die Wirtin erinnert: „Hermine war sehr beleibt und etwas asthmatisch. Von ihrem Platz aus hatte sie sowohl die Fähre VII wie auch die Hafenstraße im Blick. Deshalb konnte sie jeden, der reinkam, gleich mit Namen begrüßen.“ Die Wirtin hatte ein beeindruckendes Personengedächtnis, und wer neu im Lokal war, bekam zu hören: „Wo kommst Du denn her, di kenn ick noch nicht?“ Stammgäste begrüßte sie mit „Wo geiht?“ und erwartete erst einmal die Antwort „Muss ja“, worauf sie begann, den Gast gründlich auszufragen. Sie war stets bestens informiert und genoss den Ruf als „Tageblatt des Hamburger Hafens“.

Als aus dem Seemannslokal eine Szenekneipe wurde

Wer am Tresen stand, hat sich Lorenz erinnert, musste damit rechnen, von Hermine mehr oder weniger herrisch zum Gläserspülen rekrutiert zu werden. Einer ihrer Sprüche lautete: „Hassu nix zu tun? Komm rüber und trockne ab!“ Genug zu tun gab es in der Kneipe bis in die 1950er Jahre, als noch Tausende Männer im Hafen arbeiteten. Mit dem Werftensterben und der stark abnehmenden Zahl der Seeleute folgte eine Flaute, die Hermine tapfer durchstand. Aber dann mutierte die Seemannskneipe *Zur Kuhwerder Fähre* zur Szenekneipe.

Der Schriftsteller Bern Hardy hat diesen Wandel miterlebt: „Sie wurde bei Jungakademikern immer beliebter, während die Seeleute allmählich wegblieben. Denen wurde es zu laut, seit Hermine einen Plattenspieler angeschafft hatte.“ An guten Abenden und Nächten flossen mehr als 700 Liter Bier durch die Zapfhähne. Und die bedienten nun junge Männer, die sich geschmeichelt fühlten, von Hermine für würdig befunden zu werden, hinter dem Tresen zu stehen und die kein Geld dafür erhielten.

Hermine starb am 20. August 1971. Sie fand ihren letzten Liegeplatz auf dem Ohlsdorfer Friedhof. An der Hauswand in der Hafenstraße erinnert eine Gedenktafel an das Seemannslokal und seine Wirtin Hermine. Der Text lautet: „Zur Kuhwerder Fähre. Bis 1971 legendäre Seemannskneipe, Filmkulisse, Ankerplatz für Matrosen und Künstler. Hinter der Theke stand 40 Jahre lang Hermine Brutschin-Hansen. Hamburgs Original ‚Tante Hermine' wurde wegen ihrer Redlichkeit, ihrer Fürsorge und ihres Witzes von Teerjacken aller Nationen geschätzt." Der Schriftsteller Bern Hardy hat ihr das Gedicht „Epilog für eine Seemannswirtin" gewidmet, das diese Zeilen enthält:

Du bist ein echtes Kind der Zeit gewesen
als es an Bord noch Segelmacher gab,
doch viel zu früh verholtest Du vom Tresen
an Deinen letzten Liegeplatz im Grab.
Trauert mit mir auch dieser oder jener
Seemann um Dich, den Du bemuttert hast,
die Zeit der Supertanker und Container
hat einfach nicht mehr recht zu Dir gepaßt.

Wilhelm Hocker

Hamburg, Stadt der mächt'gen Hanse,
frei und arg beschränkt zugleich,
Hamburg, Stadt der mächt'gen Hänse,
schaue auf Dein reiches Reich!
Schmück' die morsche Mauerkrone
einmal noch mit ed'lem Stoffe,
daß Dein Haupt sich hebe
und Dein Herz Verjüngung hoffe!

So begann ein 1835 erschienenes Spottgedicht mit dem Titel „Der Maskenzug, eine Vision". Das Gedicht des Poeten Wilhelm Hocker präsentierte die Regierenden Hamburgs als maskierte Mitwirkende an einem Karnevalsumzug – was diese durchaus nicht schätzten.

Wilhelm Hocker wurde am 28. Dezember 1812 als Sohn eines Handwerkers in Boizenburg geboren und kam mit neun Jahren nach Hamburg, wo sein Vater einen Weinhandel und eine Gastwirtschaft betrieb. Schon früh zeigte der Sohn großes Interesse daran, Verse zu schmieden. So hat er bereits im Alter von zwölf Jahren das Vaterunser in Reime gebracht.

Trotz seiner Intelligenz konnte Wilhelm Hocker keine höhere Schule besuchen, sondern musste mit 15 Jahren in den elterlichen Betrieben mithelfen. In der Gastwirtschaft lauschte er aufmerksam den Gesprächen der einfachen Leute und lernte ihre Weltsicht kennen. In seiner knappen Freizeit schrieb Hocker erste Gedichte. Die Hamburger Schriftstellerin Amalie Schoppe half ihm dabei, diese Gedichte in Zeitschriften unterzubringen.

Die Bestrafung des Verfassers von Spottgedichten

Die Obrigkeit wollte Hockers Spottgedichte nicht hinnehmen, angefangen mit dem Gedicht vom „Maskenzug". Die liberal eingestellte Altonaer Zeitschrift „Der Freihafen" schrieb über diesen Konflikt: „Zu Anfang des Jahres 1835 entstand sein ‚Maskenzug', der ihn zuerst mit der Polizei in Verbindung brachte. Während das Publicum das Gedicht mit Enthusiasmus aufnahm, verurtheilte der damalige Polizeiherr Hudtwalcker den Verfasser zu 14 Tagen Arrest." Es war die erste von diversen harten Strafen. „Der Freihafen" schrieb über den Verfasser: „Hocker ist mehr Gefühls- als Verstandesmensch, lebhaft und feurig, von Witzen sprudelnd, freimüthig, offen und wahr – *offener,* als es für sein eigenes Heil ersprießlich ist."

Es blieb nicht bei dem einen obrigkeitskritischen Gedicht:

Die großen Herrn verspeisen unsere Kirschen
und spucken uns die Steine ins Gesicht.

Solche Verhältnisse beklagte der Poet immer wieder in Spottgedichten und verschwieg nicht, dass er vor allem den mächtigen Senator Merck meinte, der durch ein zwielichtiges Grundstücksgeschäft ins Gerede gekommen war. Ein auf Merck gemünztes Gedicht Hockers begann mit diesen Zeilen:

Merk auf, mein Sohn
Ich will dir was erzählen …

Senator Merck wollte nicht zuhören und viele andere gutbetuchte Hanseaten auch nicht. Also zerrten sie den Poeten wiederholt vor Gericht und ließen ihn ob seiner kritischen Verse ins Gefängnis werfen. Der Popularität

Hockers tat das lange Zeit keinen Abbruch, im Gegenteil, er brachte in Versform, was die einfachen Leute in Hamburg dachten.

Spott über die Träume von der Südsee

Wie im Kapitel über Matthias Claudius erwähnt, gab es im 18. und 19. Jahrhundert unter den Intellektuellen romantische Vorstellungen vom Leben in der Südsee und den Wunsch, dort eine Dichterkolonie zu gründen. Auch der Syndikus Karl Sieveking, also der höchste Jurist im Dienste der Stadt, war von dieser Südseebegeisterung angesteckt worden und versuchte 1841 vergeblich, auf den Chatman Inseln in der Nähe von Neuseeland eine deutsche Siedlerkolonie zu gründen.

Ein Werbebroschüre für die Südseekolonie trug den Titel „Warrekauri", also den Namen der Hauptinsel der Chatman Inseln. Das nahm der Spötter Hocker zum Anlass für sein Gedicht „God Save the Sieveking!". Darin machte er sich lustig über die Vorstellungen von einer „Insel der Glückseligkeit" und die angebliche Begeisterung der Massen für eine Auswanderung in dieses Paradies:

Schon brüllen Hamburgs Rammer „Gottverdauri!"
Wi got mit Fro un Kind na Warrekauri.

Zu den euphorischen Beiträgen über die angeblich paradiesischen Aussichten für deutsche Siedler dichtete Wilhelm Hocker:

Schön muss sie sein; denn sie ist transatlantisch,
Und in der Ferne blüht allein das Glück;
Die Fahrt dahin, wie reizend, wie romantisch,
Legt kaum in sieben Monden man zurück.

Ein Gedicht über die verschlafenen Oberalten

Der Spott von Wilhelm Hocker in dem nun zitierten Gedicht zielte auf die Oberalten der Stadt, und es traf sie hart. Um das zu verstehen, muss man die Rolle dieses Gremiums in der ersten Hälfte des 19. Jahrhunderts kurz darstellen.

Die Oberalten waren Vertreter der Hamburger Kirchspiele und sollten die Interessen der Bürger gegenüber dem Senat vertreten. Aber die Oberalten waren meist betagte wohlhabende Herren, die den Senat nicht kontrollierten, sondern schon um des Friedens willen dessen Vorlagen zustimmten.

Zum Ärger der Bürger, die Reformen zugunsten der Bevölkerungsmehrheit forderten, nickten die Oberalten alles ab, was ihnen ihr Präses auf Geheiß des Senats vorlegte. Im Senat saßen nur reiche Kaufleute und einige Juristen, die auf Lebenszeit gewählt worden waren und die Interessen der Reichen der Stadt rücksichtslos vertraten.

Bis zu seinem Tod im Januar 1841 nahm Georg Nikolaus Mohr das Amt des Präses der Oberalten wahr. Aber noch ein Jahr später verkündete ein aus dem Schlaf gerüttelter Oberalter das, was er schon so oft gesagt hatte: „Ich bin derselben Meinung, wie mein Kollege Mohr!“

Dieses Vorkommnis sprach sich in der Stadt herum und bestätigte den unzufriedenen Bürgern, dass ihre Anliegen bei den Oberalten nicht gut aufgehoben waren. In Anspielung auf den Oberalten Mohr dichtete Hocker eine Fabel vom Mohrenland, die so beginnt:

O Stadt des Mohrenlandes, gerühmt in Bild und Wort,
O Stadt des Mohrenlandes am lichtbeglänzten Port.
Was hast Du noch verschuldet, wodurch jemals gefehlt,
Daß so viel dunkle Häupter man Dir zu Häupten zählt?
Es sitzen Deine Aelt'sten, wie Mumien zu Gericht,
Beharren wie im Traume, ob Dir das Herz auch bricht
Und einer raunt dem Andern schlaftrunken in das Ohr:
„Ich bin derselben Meinung, wie mein Kollege Mohr!"

Die Vertreibung des Spötters aus Hamburg

Hocker attackierte mit diesem und anderen Gedichten den politischen Status quo der Stadt, was wie zu erwarten den Mächtigen nicht genehm war. Dem Spötter wurde vorgeworfen, ein „Pasquillant" zu sein, also der Verfasser von Schmähschriften. Das Wort soll auf einen italienischen Schneider namens Pasquino zurückgehen, der Spottverse an eine antike Statue heftete. Auch nannte man Hocker einen „Libellisten", die Bezeichnung für Verfasser von Pamphleten vor der Französischen Revolution, in denen das Königshaus angegriffen wurde. Hier die Antwort des Satirikers auf die Vorwürfe:

Ich weiß es längst: man ist ein Pasquillant,
wenn öffentlich den Schuft man Schuft genannt.
Ein Libellist, wenn man von Recht erfüllt,
die Streiche dieser hohen Herrn enthüllt.
Jedoch zum Ruhm des menschlichen Geschlechtes
lebt auch noch heut die Poesie des Rechtes.
Wer gut, wer tugendhaft, wer sittlich rein,
wird stets vor dem Pamphlet gesichert sein.
Hart aber straf' es den, der unberechtigt
sich fremden Glückes, fremden Guts bemächtigt.

Vernichtend treff es ihn wie Dolch und Gift,
weil das Gesetz ihn eben niemals trifft.

So etwas schrieb man im Biedermeier-Hamburg nicht ungestraft. Dass Hocker im Volk viel Beifall fand, wenn er sich über die Obrigkeit lustig machte oder sie bissig attackierte, kam erschwerend hinzu. Um weiteren Strafen zu entgehen, emigrierte Hocker 1835 nach Berlin und arbeitete dort als Handwerker. Nach drei Jahren kehrte er zurück in die Stadt, die er liebte. Den von Zensoren bedrängten Zeitungsmachern der Stadt rief Hocker zu:

Reiß' Dich viel gepreßte Presse los von allen Deinen Bengeln,
die die Urteilskraft der Leser nur nach ihrer Willkür gängeln!

Der Angriff Hockers auf den „Mäßlgkeitsverein"

Immer wieder wurde Wilhelm Hocker zu Geld- und Haftstrafen verurteilt. Sogar einen richtigen Volksaufstand sollte er angestiftet haben - behauptete das Establishment. Jedenfalls stürmte eine aufgebrachte Menge am Abend des 18. Januar 1841 die Gelehrtenschule Johanneum und beendete gewaltsam eine Versammlung des sogenannten „Mäßigkeitsvereins".

Mit der Mäßigung des Volkes war es nämlich vorbei, nachdem bekannt geworden war, dass dieser Verein wohlhabender Bürger den Schnapskonsum der einfachen Leute einschränken wollte, aber den Wein„genuß" der „besseren Kreise" guthieß. Einer der Hauptakteure war der Getreidehändler (Kornumstecher) Ehlers, mit dem sich auch das Original Vetter Kirchhoff angelegt hatte. Angeblich hatte Hocker die Unruhen mit solchen Versen angezettelt:

Wo Helden weilen, die als Zecher,
Als Weinvertilger längst bekannt,
Ich mein' die Herren Kornumstecher,
Da ist der Fusel schnell verbannt!

Mit der Mäßigkeit im Sinne der Oberen der Stadt wurde es nichts, Grund genug für die einfachen Leute, auf das Wohl Wilhelm Hockers anzustoßen. Der hatte auch gedichtet:

Was soll der Zwang? – Warum den Armen
Entzieh'n die tröstende Tinctur?
Sein Festgericht, sein Hochzeitscarmen
Ist oft die Brandweinflasche nur.
Auf! Sucht Madeira ihm zu schaffen,
Canariensect und Pararet,
Der manchen Ratsherrn, manchen Pfaffen
Tagtäglich zu Gebote steht.

Hocker kam durch diesen Konflikt eine Geschäftsidee: Um die Weinliebhaber zu verspotten, lud er alle Weinfreunde ins *Belle Alliance-Lokal* in Eimsbüttel ein, angeblich um den *Europäischen Verein für Weintrinker* zu gründen. Der Andrang derer, die den Aufruf ernst genommen hatten, war so groß, dass sich der Poet 1844 entschloss, in der Poststraße eine Weinhalle zu eröffnen. Es war ein elegantes Lokal mit großen Spiegeln und Gasbeleuchtung, damals noch eine Seltenheit. Aber Hocker war Dichter und nicht Kaufmann, und so musste er mit seiner Weinhalle nach eineinhalb Jahren Konkurs anmelden. Es ging von nun an steil bergab mit ihm. Er hatte bald keine

Bewunderer mehr und war in einem bemitleidenswerten Zustand. In einem seiner letzten Gedichte schrieb er:

Ich habe die Freuden des Himmels gefühlt
Und getragen die schmerzlichsten Joche;
Ich habe auf seid'nen Matratzen gewühlt
und gelegen im Kellerloche.

Unterschiedliche Auffassungen über einen Dichter

1849 musste er ins Gefängnis, dieses Mal nicht wegen seiner „Schmähgedichte", sondern wegen hoher Schulden. Er infizierte sich dort mit Tuberkulose, an der er am 7. Juli 1850 im Alter von erst 38 Jahren im Krankenhaus starb. Was die Obrigkeit von dem Poeten dachte, brachte der Stadthistoriker J. G. Gallois zu Papier:

„Jener Dichterling, nicht ohne eine gewisse Gewandtheit im Reimen, aber ein ebenso charakterloser wie feiger und wüster Geselle, suchte in seiner maßloser Eitelkeit sich zum Wortführer der ... öffentlichen Unzufriedenheit zu machen."

Ganz anders wurde der Dichter im Juli 1843 in der Zeitschrift „Der Freihafen" gewürdigt: „Man hat Hocker oft vorgeworfen, daß die Ergüsse seiner Muse nur ein Gifthauch wären, daß er nur niederreiße, heruntermache, mit einem Worte, daß er ein Pasquillant sei, weshalb denn auch alle besseren Literaten sich von ihm abwendeten; aber keine Verurteilung ist wohl ungerechter als diese. Seine Gedichte sind zwar oft beißend, anzüglich und geradezu persönlich, aber was ist die Ursache davon? Der Mangel an Öffentlichkeit und Freiheit in dem freien Staate! Das tiefe Rechtsgefühl, das Hocker's ganzes Wesen durchdringt, darf sich nicht offen aussprechen über Gebrechen eines Staates, dessen Freiheit lediglich darin besteht, dass seine Bürger auf der Bierbank politisieren dürfen ..."

Hans Hummel

„Hummel, Hummel! – Mors, Mors!“ lautet der deftige Gruß traditionsbewusster Hamburger und Hamburgerinnen. Aber Hans Hummel stieg erst nach seinem Tod zum populärsten Hamburger auf und dazu noch zu einer komischen Figur, die er zu Lebzeiten nie war. Manche deuten bis heute das Hamburger Autokennzeichen „HH“ als „Hummel, Hummel“.

Paul Möhring, der ein Theaterstück über Hummel verfasste, hat die zeitgenössischen Quellen über das heute so berühmte Hamburger Original studiert und kam zu einem ernüchternden Ergebnis: „Die Chroniken und die verschiedenen geschichtlichen Darstellungen erwähnen das populäre Hamburger Original nicht. Hummel hat nach Auffassung der Historiker keinerlei Verdienste, die ihn dazu berechtigen, in die Stadtgeschichte einzugehen. Er war kein Wissenschaftler, kein Gelehrter, kein Kriegsheld, kein Künstler, kein Wirtschaftsführer, kein Politiker – er war eben nur ein ‚Kind des Volkes‘, ein Mann der Straße, der zur volkstümlichen Figur wurde.“

Wenigstens ist inzwischen vieles über seinen Beruf als Wasserträger bekannt. Dass es in Hamburg bis Mitte des 19. Jahrhunderts so viele Wasserträger gab, ist das Ergebnis einer völlig verfehlten städtischen Wasserversorgungspolitik der Stadt. In der Kaufmannsstadt Hamburg regierten über Jahrhunderte die „Pfeffersäcke“ (wie man im Volksmund die reichen Kaufleute spöttisch nannte), und die wollten staatliche Ausgaben und Steuern möglichst niedrig halten. Also überließ die Stadt die Wasserversorgung der Privatinitiative.

Vom 14. Jahrhundert an bildeten wohlhabende Kaufmannsfamilien sogenannte *Interessentschaften*. Sie ließen hölzerne Rohrleitungen bauen, durch die das Wasser von Quellen außerhalb der Stadtwälle zu ihren Häusern floss. Für alle, die genügend Geld hatten, war das eine ideale Wasserversorgung.

Was aber taten die, denen das Geld für die Beteiligung an einer solchen *Interessentschaft* fehlte? Die Armen schöpften das Wasser aus den Fleeten, eine sehr ungesunde Sache, denn in diesen Alsterarmen und Kanälen landeten auch die Abwässer der Stadt. Verschiedene Cholera-Epidemien wurden durch diese Form der Wasserversorgung verursacht oder begünstigt.

Wer etwas Geld erübrigen konnte, ließ sich sauberes Trinkwasser von einem Wasserträger oder einer Wasserträgerin ins Haus bringen. Manche Wasserträger verminderten ihren Zeitaufwand allerdings dadurch, dass sie das Wasser heimlich aus den Fleeten statt von weiter entfernten Quellen oder Brunnen holten.

Ein mürrischer Wasserträger

Einer der Wasserträger war in der ersten Hälfte des 19. Jahrhunderts Johann Wilhelm Bentz (oder Benz), geboren am 21. Januar 1787. Er soll nach zeitgenössischen Beschreibungen ein etwas griesgrämiges Original gewesen sein. Dass er griesgrämig war, dafür gab es der Überlieferung nach einen triftigen Grund. Er soll zunächst ein lebenslustiger junger Mann gewesen sein, der als Wasserträger auch zu etwas Geld kam. Nach dem Tod seines Vaters erbte er eine goldene Tabakdose und etwas Geld.

Er verliebte sich in eine junge Schenkmamsell und die beiden verlobten sich. Sie machten Pläne für ihre Heirat und Bentz übergab seiner Freundin die goldene Tabakdose und das Geld, damit sie Anschaffungen für den zukünftigen Hausstand tätigen konnte. Sie verschwand aber mit einem Seemann und mit ihr die goldene Tabakdose und das Geld. Sie ließ einen trübsinnigen und verbitterten Bentz zurück.

Vielleicht ist die Geschichte erfunden, aber wenigstens gut erfunden und erklärte den Zeitgenossen des Wasserträgers, warum dieser auch bei kleinen Anlässen so aufbrausend und zornig werden konnte.

Jahrelange Auseinandersetzungen mit den Jungen der Stadt

Es gibt aus seinen Lebzeiten keine einzige Abbildung des Wasserträgers und er wird auch in keiner der damaligen historischen Darstellung erwähnt. Es blieb aber in Erinnerung, dass Hamburger Jungen ihn mit dem Ruf „Hummel, Hummel!“ neckten, was ihn maßlos ärgerte. Nach einer Überlieferung hatte Bentz die Wohnung des 1836 verstorbenen Stadtsoldaten namens Daniel Christian Hummel im Hinterhaus des Gebäudes Große Drehbahn 36 übernommen. Der Stadtsoldat war - im Gegensatz zu Bentz - bei den Jungen sehr beliebt gewesen. Er erzählte ihnen nämlich viele wahre und erfundene spannende Geschichten von Kriegserlebnissen. Die Jungen brachten Bentz in Zorn, wenn sie ihm den Namen dieses Vormieters nachriefen.

Da Bentz zwei schwere Eimer an einer „Tracht" (einer Art Joch) trug, konnte er die Jungen nicht vertreiben und beantwortete die ewigen Neckereien mit dem Ausruf „Mors, Mors!". Der Mors ist auf Plattdeutsch der Hintern, und Bentz verkürzte mit seinem Ausruf den Spruch „Klei mi an Mors", was dem Götz von Berlichingen-Zitat recht nahe kommt. Bentz soll über die Wortwechsel mit den Jungen gesagt haben: „Jä, ick kann dat nich loten, ick mutt nu mol dat letzte Wort hebben! De Krieg mit de Jungs duert nu all'n lange Tied, und ick gleuw, he duurt noch öber mien Grav rut!"

Über sein Grab hinaus hat der „Krieg" mit den Jungen nicht gedauert, aber doch so lange, dass Bentz zum bekanntesten Original der Stadt wurde. Einige Hamburger Bürger nahmen Anstoß an den lautstarken Wortwechseln zwischen Bentz und den Jungen. Sie fanden Bentz offenkundig weder witzig noch komisch. Diese Bürger beschwerten sich bei der Obrigkeit, und der Wasserträger wurde vom zuständigen Senator vorgeladen.

Nach Vorhaltungen und seinem Versprechen der Besserung ging das Gespräch einvernehmlich zu Ende und der Senator wollte den Gast verabschieden. In diesem Augenblick fiel ihm der Familienname des Wasserträgers nicht ein, und deshalb sagte er ihm zum Abschied: „Hummel, Hummel". Bentz behielt wieder einmal das letzte Wort und rief im Hinausgehen: „Mors! Mors! Herr Senator!"

Wie die Wasserträger ihre Arbeit verloren

Johann Wilhelm Bentz und die anderen Wasserträger wurden für ihre schwere Arbeit schlecht bezahlt, denn die Konkurrenz unter den Trägern war groß und die Zahlungsfähigkeit ihrer Kunden gering. So musste Bentz oft lange mit dem Ruf „Woter! Woter!" durch die Straßen ziehen, bis er Kunden für sein Wasser fand. Er war so arm, dass er dankbar die Essensreste annahm, die ihm wohlwollende Hausgehilfinnen reicher Bürger zusteckten. Er wickelte die Reste vom Tisch der Reichen in Zeitungspapier und verstaute sie in seinem hohen Zylinder, um sie später zu essen.

Es gab in Hamburg auch viele Wasserträgerinnen. Die berühmteste von ihnen war Mutter Blohm, die noch als alte Frau die Eimer voll Wasser über schmale Treppen auch in die obersten Etagen schleppte. Ihr Wahlspruch lautete: „Langsam un wiß!" – langsam, aber sicher. Die Wasserversorgung in Hamburg blieb bis in die 40er Jahre des 19. Jahrhunderts in dem desolaten, aber für Leute wie Bentz immerhin etwas einträglichen Zustand. Als 1842 ein Brand ausbrach, zeigte sich ein weiterer Nachteil dieser privatisierten Versorgung. Es fehlte an Löschwasser, und die Holzleitungen der privaten Wasserversorger wurden rasch ein Opfer der Flammen. Nachdem große Teile der Stadt niedergebrannt waren, konnte der aus England stammende Ingenieur William Lindley sich erfolgreich für eine öffentliche Wasserversorgung einsetzen.

Mit der Eröffnung der Stadtwasserkunst 1848 verlor Johann Friedrich Bentz seine Arbeit. Der Wasserträger Hans Hummel hatte seine Schuldigkeit getan und starb am 15. März 1854 im *Werk- und Armenhaus* der Stadt. Man beerdigte ihn auf Kosten der *Allgemeinen Armenanstalt* in einem Armengrab. Er wurde wie die anderen Armen in einer sehr flachen Kiste beerdigt, die im Volksmund „Nasenquetscher" hießen. Am Begräbnistag erschien in den „Hamburger Nachrichten" die folgende Notiz: „Eine fast in der ganzen Stadt, und vornähmlich in der Neustadt, bekannte Persönlichkeit, der Arbeitsmann und Wasserträger Wilhelm Hummel, ist in diesen Tagen gestorben."

Ein bis heute berühmtes Original

Hummel ist vor allem durch Geschichten und Beschreibungen von Zeitgenossen in Erinnerung geblieben. Emilie Weber hat Bentz in ihren „Jugenderinnerungen" so beschrieben: „Er war ein Wasserträger, ein unschädlicher, harmloser Gemütskranker. Er ging immer mit seiner Tracht auf dem Rücken und schlenkerte mit seinen beiden Eimern hin und her. Diese Bewegungen begleitete er mit lautem Gesang, und es kümmerte ihn wenig, ob er dabei die Hälfte des Wassers verschüttete. Hochvergnügt zog er durch die Straßen, begleitet und geneckt von unserer lieben Straßenjugend." War Bentz also hochvergnügt und nicht griesgrämig? So genau kann das niemand mehr sagen. Aber ein Original, das war er auf jeden Fall.

Nach seinem Tod brachte das *Varieté-Theater* ein Volksstück über Hummel auf die Bühne. Mit dem echten Wasserträger hatte dieser Theater-Hummel nicht viel gemein. Der Theaterhistoriker Paul Möhring hat über die Aufführungen dieses Stücks geschrieben: „Der beliebte

Volkskomiker Charles Schultz soll als der populäre Wasserträger allabendlich Lachstürme hervorgerufen haben." Dem echten Hummel ist das nie gelungen und er hat es wahrscheinlich auch nicht angestrebt. Das Stück war so erfolgreich, dass es mehr als 400 Mal gespielt wurde.

Jahre später kam ein neues Hummel-Volksstück zur Aufführung. Paul Möhring hatte es sich zur Aufgabe gemacht, „ihn lebenswahr ins Rampenlicht zu stellen". Sein Volksstück „Hummel! Hummel!" beginnt so:

In Hamborg an de Waterkant
Bin ick bi jerdereen bekannt!
Ich bin een echt Hamburger Bloot.
Bin Hummel mit dem hogen Hoot!
Mien Slachtroop is jo grood nich fein
Und ook gewiß nich stubenrein,
doch jeder hier in Hamburg weet
mien Antwort. Wenn de Gören schreet:
Hummel! Hummel! – Mors! Mors!

Die Uraufführung im Ohnsorg-Theater war ein großer Erfolg, und Paul Möhring war mit der Leistung des Hauptdarstellers Ernst Grabbe sehr zufrieden, das Publikum auch. Von dem Möhring-Biografen Joachim Redetzki erfahren wir allerdings: „Der ‚Hummel' ist seit dieser Serie nicht wieder gezeigt worden. Es schien tatsächlich so zu sein, dass das Publikum den Hummel als eine der volkstümlichen Hamburger ‚Typen' sehen wollte und nicht als tragikomische Figur." Demgegenüber hat das Stück „Zitronenjette" von Paul Möhring bisher weit mehr als 1.000 Aufführungen erlebt, allerdings entgegen den Intentionen des Autors häufig in einer ins Komische verzerrten Version. Mehr dazu im Kapitel über Zitronenjette.

1938 ließ der *Verein geborener Hamburger* auf einem Platz am Rademachergang in der Neustadt ein Brunnendenkmal für Hummel aufstellen. An einem angrenzenden Wohnhaus wurde die Skulptur eines Jungen angebracht, der Hummel sein Hinterteil entgegenstreckt. Hummel-Denkmal und Junge hat Richard Kuöhl gestaltet.

2003 tauchten mehr als hundert lebensgroße Hummel-Figuren aus Kunststoff in der Hamburger Innenstadt auf. Sie waren von Künstlern bemalt worden und so populär, dass sie bis 2006 zu bestaunen waren und nicht wie ursprünglich geplant nur bis zum Oktober 2004. Am 23. Juni 2006 versteigerte man die Figuren zugunsten der Initiative „Ein Dach für Obdachlose". Es kamen 343.000 Euro zusammen. Einzelne der Kunststoff-Hummel sind noch in der Stadt zu entdecken.

Heidi Kabel

„Am Tode von Heidi Kabel erkennt man, was uns fehlt: Künstlerpersönlichkeiten, mit denen sich die gesamte Bevölkerung identifizieren kann. Das nennt man Volksschauspieler. Es scheint immer schwieriger zu sein, Menschen mit solcher Lebensnähe und einem solchen Humor anzutreffen. Vielleicht hat das mit einer veränderten Zeit zu tun, in der solche Gestalten kaum mehr ermöglicht werden.“ So hat Joachim Lux, Intendant des *Thalia Theaters,* an die Frau erinnert, die viele Rollen spielte und sich dabei stets treu blieb. Und nicht zu vergessen: Sie gehört zu Hamburgs bekanntesten Originalen.

Heidi Bertha Auguste Kabel wurde am 27. August 1914 geboren. Ihr Geburtshaus lag an der Straße Große Bleichen – gegenüber der *Niederdeutschen Bühne Hamburg,* später *Ohnsorg-Theater,* wo sie später als Schauspielerin große Erfolge feierte. Ihr Vater war Besitzer einer Druckerei und des *Ernst Kabel Verlages.* Zeitweise war er Vorsitzender des *Vereins geborener Hamburger* und engagierte sich im Theaterverein *Urania.* Gelegentlich trat er als Alleinunterhalter im Freundes- und Bekanntenkreis auf.

Die Tochter Heidi besuchte das *Emilie-Wüstenfeld-Lyzeum,* das sie mit der Mittleren Reife verließ. In dem Erinnerungsband an Heidi Kabel „In Hamburg sagt man Tschüss“ ist über ihre Schulzeit zu erfahren: „Sie soll durchaus strebsam, jedoch nicht überaus ehrgeizig gewesen sein. Ausnahme: In musischen Fächern blühte die Deern aus der Innenstadt auf. Im Nachhinein alles andere als ein Wunder. Mittlerweile leider gleichfalls verstorbene Mitschülerinnen berichteten den Medien einst von geradezu begeisternden Darbietungen des blonden Teenagers in der Theatergruppe des Lyzeums. Wer Heidi Kabel damals in der Aula beobachtete, wird die bewundernswerte Anlage bemerkt haben. Nur eine Petitesse wirkt rückblickend erstaunlich: In der Schule durfte kein Plattdeutsch gesprochen werden. War es nicht fein genug? Hinderte es die Pennäler am reinen Hochdeutsch?"

Durch Zufall und Hartnäckigkeit kam Heidi Kabel ans Theater

Die Tochter wollte gern Konzertpianistin werden, aber dafür besaß sie nicht genügend Talent. In ihrer Autobiografie „Das Leben macht mir Freude" schrieb Heidi Kabel über ihre Situation im Frühjahr 1932: „Längst schon hatte ich die Hoffnung aufgegeben, eine erstklassige Konzertpianistin zu werden. Mir fehlte einfach der Funken Talent, um aus dem Klavier das herausholen zu können, was die Zuhörer in den Bann schlägt. Mein ständiges, stundenlanges Üben nützte da wenig. Nur wollten meine Eltern das nicht wahrhaben. Sie hatten viel Geld und Hoffnung in meine Ausbildung gesteckt, und ich war dabei, alles hinzuwerfen."

Im März 1932 begleitete Heidi Kabel eine Freundin zum Vorsprechen bei der *Niederdeutschen Bühne*. Die Mutter gab ihr mit auf den Weg: „Heidi, du nicht!" Aber das blieb wirkungslos. Zwar war der Theaterintendant Richard Ohnsorg gerade nicht da, aber der Schauspieler Hans Mahler verhinderte, dass die beiden Mädchen gleich an der Tür abgewiesen wurden, indem er seinem Kollegen sagte: „Nu lot jem doch wenigstens ers mol rin." Sie durften eine Probe miterleben und erhielten von Mahler den Rat: „Am besten ist es, wenn Sie morgen noch einmal zur Probe kommen ..."

Heidi Kabel und ihre Freundin erschienen am nächsten Tag erneut. Sie durften noch immer nicht vorsprechen, aber wo sie nun schon einmal da waren, konnten sie sich in der nächsten Zeit als Anziehhilfen, Souffleusen und als Requisiteurinnen nützlich machen. Heidi Kabel gab die Idee einer Karriere als Konzertpianistin endgültig auf, zumal sie es genoss, mit Hans Mahler zusammen zu sein, denn sie hatte sich in ihn verliebt. Sie konnte Richard Ohnsorg von ihren schauspielerischen Fähigkeiten überzeugen und erhielt eine Rolle in dem Stück „Ralves Carstens". Heidi Kabel erhielt parallel zu ersten Rollen am Theater von zwei Schauspielern des *Ohnsorg-Theaters* Schauspielunterricht. Sie trat anschließend mehr als sechs Jahrzehnte in diesem Theater auf.

In schweren Zeiten in heiteren Stücken auf der Bühne

1937 heiratete Heidi Kabel ihren Kollegen Hans Mahler. Das Ehepaar hatte bald drei Kinder, und Heidi Kabel musste von nun an Beruf und Familienverpflichtungen miteinander verbinden. Ihre Tochter Heidi erinnerte sich später so an ihre Eltern: „Ich hatte ein sehr liebevolles und sehr liberales Elternhaus. Nur wenn meine Mutter mit mir schimpfte, dann auf Plattdeutsch. Das nahm dem Gesagten gleich die Spitze."

Dass Heidi Kabel Familie und Berufstätigkeit verbinden konnte und zur erfolgreichen Schauspielerin wurde, lag auch an der Unterstützung durch ihren Mann, damals alles andere als eine Selbstverständlichkeit in der deutschen Gesellschaft. Sie wollte ihrerseits ihren Mann bei seiner Karriere fördern.

Gern hätte er 1936 die Leitung der Bühne in Lüneburg übernommen, aber dort machte man die Mitgliedschaft in der NSDAP zur Voraussetzung für eine Berufung. Heidi Kabel überzeugte ihren Mann, in die Partei einzutreten und wurde selbst Mitglied der NS-Frauenschaft. Beide haben das bald bereut, aber einfach rückgängig machen ließ sich eine Mitgliedschaft nicht. Sie hatte nicht einmal die erhoffte Wirkung. Hans Mahler bekam die Stelle nicht, sondern ein Bewerber, der schon länger in der Partei war.

Während der schweren Bombenangriffe auf Hamburg im Juli 1943 lebte Heidi Kabel in der Lüneburger Heide. Bei ihrer Rückkehr in die zerstörte Stadt bald nach den Angriffen konnte sie mit dem Zug nur bis Wilhelmsburg fahren und musste den Weg zu Fuß fortsetzen: „Es wurde der schmerzlichste Fußweg meines Lebens. Selbst wenn ich heute, mit dem Zug von Süden kommend, nach Hamburg hineinfahre, habe ich noch das Grauen vor Augen, das sich mir damals ins Gedächtnis prägte." Diese Erlebnisse haben Heidi Kabels Leben verändert und dazu beigetragen, dass sie keine oberflächlich humoristische Schauspielerin wurde.

Die *Niederdeutsche Bühne* hat die Bombardierungen der Stadt überstanden, ebenso die Wohnung der Familie in der Binderstraße. Es folgte ein Umzug in ein gemietetes kleines Haus in Bahrenfeld, wo Heidi Kabel und ihre Familie die Schrecken der weiteren Bombenangriffe auf die

Stadt erlebten. Sie schrieb in ihren Lebenserinnerungen, dass sie oft in letzter Minuten mit ihren Kindern in einen Luftschutzbunker gerannt war, während erste Flugzeuge die grellen Leuchtbomben warfen, die die Flächen der vorgesehenen Bombenabwürfe markierten. „Und die Angst, die mich damals befiel, spüre ich noch heute, wenn ich unfreiwillig ein Feuerwerk mit ansehen muss".

Im unbeschädigten Theater führte das Ensemble trotz aller Bombenangriffe weiterhin Stücke auf – vor vollbesetztem Haus. Aber Schauspieler und Publikum wussten nie, wann der nächste Fliegeralarm kam und ob das Theater am folgenden Tag noch stehen würde. „Jede Vorstellung spielten wir in dem Bewusstsein, es könnte die letzte sein, und das brachte eine Intensität in unser Spiel, die wir vorher nicht erreicht hatten. Unbewusst erarbeiteten wir einen Stil, der uns alle prägte." Heidi Kabel hat diesen intensiven Stil auch in den folgenden Jahrzehnten bewahrt.

Ein abendlicher Besucher – Wolfgang Borchert

In dieser schweren Zeit klingelte ein junger Mann an der Tür des Hauses in Bahrenfeld. Es war Wolfgang Borchert, der mit Hans Mahler beruflich zu tun gehabt hatte und nun ihn und seine Frau besuchte. Borchert sprach sehr offen über die Gräuel der Naziherrscher. Es wurde ein langer Abend und der Schriftsteller verließ seine Gastgeber erst, als morgens die ersten S-Bahnen fuhren. Heidi Kabel erinnerte sich in ihren Lebenserinnerungen so an den Besuch von Wolfgang Borchert: „In dieser Nacht hatte ich einen Freund gewonnen." Der Dichter war seinerseits sehr beeindruckt von der Gastgeberin und schrieb nach dem Besuch das Gedicht „Bitte“, das er so beendete:

Schön bist du, Elfenkönigin –
so schlank und edel
und so zart …
Ich bitt' dich Wind:
Zerbrich sie nicht.“

Solange das Theater stand, waren Schauspieler wie Hans Mahler vor einer Einberufung zum Militär bewahrt, weil die Nazis es wichtig fanden, an der „Heimatfront“ für Unterhaltung zu sorgen. Allerdings war bei einer Zerstörung des Theaters mit einer sofortigen Einberufung zu rechnen. Das Theater entging den Bomben, aber am 1. September 1944 ließ Goebbels, der den „totalen Krieg“ verkündet hatte, alle Theater schließen. Hans Mahler musste wie viele andere Schauspieler an die Front.

Von den Kollegen vom Theater vertrieben

1945 verhinderte ein Komitee von Kollegen der *Niederdeutschen Bühne,* dass Kabel und Mahler wegen ihrer Vergangenheit in der Nazizeit weiter in dem Theater spielen durften. Es wird vermutet, dass auch Konkurrenzdenken und Neid der Kollegen eine große Rolle spielten, geklärt wurde das nie. Richard Ohnsorg sagte den beiden am Eingang des Theaters: „Kinders, es tut mir furchtbar leid, aber ihr könnt nicht proben. Die Kollegen haben sich geweigert, sie wollen nicht mehr mit euch auf der Bühne stehen.“ In die eingetretenen Stille hinein sagte Heidi Kabel: „Na ja, denn nicht. Dann müssen wir eben nach Hause gehen.“ In ihren Lebenserinnerungen schrieb sie:

„Ich war durch diesen Schock endgültig erwachsen geworden."

Christian Seeler, seit 1982 Schauspieler und später Intendant des *Ohnsorg-Theaters*, hat in Gesprächen erfahren, wie sehr dieser Rauswurf Heidi Kabel gedemütigt und gekränkt hat: „Das hat ihr sehr zugesetzt über viele, viele Jahre. Da saß ein Stachel im Fleisch, das hat sie nie verwunden. Sie hat ein bisschen den Glauben an das Gute im Menschen verloren." Richard Ohnsorg verlor ein Jahr später seinen Leitungsposten aus nicht ganz geklärten Gründen. Offiziell schied er aus gesundheitlichen Gründen aus, und als kleine Entschädigung erhielt die *Niederdeutsche Bühne* den Namen *Ohnsorg-Theater*.

Heidi Kabel stand erst einmal ohne festes Engagement da. Um das Überleben ihrer Familie zu sichern, schloss sie sich einer Unterhaltungstruppe an und tingelte in einem heiteren Programm mit Akkordeon durch die norddeutsche Provinz. Mit einer Mischung von Operettenliedern sowie plattdeutschen und hochdeutschen Geschichten erfreute sie das Publikum in schweren Zeiten. Dafür bezahlten die Zuschauer mit Naturalien, die den Künstlerfamilien das Überleben sicherten. Der Ehemann Hans Mahler war schlechter dran, weil er kein Talent als Entertainer besaß. Ohne zu murren, übernahm er deshalb die Aufgaben eines Hausmanns. Zusätzlich betätigte sich Heidi Kabel als Schwarzmarkthändlerin und beim Kohlenklau von Güterwagen.

Es blieb ihr Groll über den Rauswurf aus dem geliebten Theater: „Für mich sind die Machenschaften des Ensembles bis heute undurchsichtig geblieben, aber damals musste ich darunter leiden, weniger zwar als Hans Mahler, aber das lag wohl daran, dass ich, durch den Alltag abgelenkt, weniger grübelte." Im Entnazifizierungsprozess stuften die Engländer Heidi Kabel als „Nichtbetroffene" ein, ihren Mann wegen seiner Parteimitgliedschaft als „Mitläufer".

Sie erhielten nie ein offizielles Auftrittsverbot und gingen im Frühjahr 1947 mit der Frage, ob sie nun wieder spielen dürften, zur britischen Militärverwaltung. Dort trafen sie auf John Olden, der mit großem Verständnis und Engagement die Aufgabe übernommen hatte, Rundfunk- und Kultureinrichtungen in Hamburg neu aufzubauen. Er sagte den beiden Schauspielern: „Gehen Sie ruhig sofort wieder in ihr Theater. Sie können beide wieder arbeiten, es liegt überhaupt nichts gegen sie vor."

Als sie daraufhin das *Ohnsorg-Theater* betraten, sagte der neue Leiter der Bühne Rudolf Beiswanger lediglich: „Ihr dürft also wieder. Wie schön. Ich freue mich." Eine Aussprache über das Geschehene fand nicht statt – wie so oft im Nachkriegsdeutschland. Die beiden Schauspieler mussten nun wohl oder übel mit denen zusammenarbeiten, die sie aus dem Theater vertrieben hatten.

Der Neuanfang am Ohnsorg-Theater

Hans Mahler wurde 1949 zum künstlerischen Leiter des *Ohnsorg-Theaters* berufen. Es waren schwere Zeiten für das Privattheater angebrochen. Vor der Währungsreform war das Theater stets voll gewesen, aber nachdem jede und jeder am 20. Juni 1948 lediglich 40 Deutsche Mark erhalten hatte und es einen großen Nachholbedarf gab, die wieder verfügbaren Waren zu kaufen, sparten viele bei den Theaterkarten. Gleichzeitig musste das Theater nun die Gehälter und alle anderen Ausgaben in DM bezahlen. Von den fast 20 Privattheatern in Hamburg überlebten nur sechs die Währungsreform.

Dass das *Ohnsorg-Theater* zu den Überlebenden gehörte, lag vor allem am Engagement der Beschäftigten. Sie mussten zusätzlich zu den Proben und Aufführungen die früheren Abonnenten besuchen und zu einer Erneuerung ihres Abonnements motivieren. Dazu Heidi Kabel später: „Da wir alle wussten, dass unser Wohl und Wehe davon abhing, wuchsen wir über uns hinaus. Wir stiegen treppauf und treppab ..." Die Aktion hatte Erfolg und bald füllten sich wieder die Reihen im *Ohnsorg-Theater*. Dazu trug auch bei, dass das Theater dem Unterhaltungsbedürfnis des Publikums Rechnung trug und viele Komödien ins Programm aufnahm. Angesichts des wieder gestiegenen Zuspruchs des Publikums erhielt die Bühne dann auch die erhofften Zuschüsse von der Kulturbehörde.

Große Erfolge seit den 1950er Jahren

Heidi Kabel stand von den 1950er Jahren an nicht nur als Schauspielerin auf der Bühne des *Ohnsorg-Theaters*, sondern war auch als Hörfunksprecherin und Filmschauspielerin gefragt. Die ersten Gageneinahmen flossen in dringend nötige Haushaltsinvestitionen wie neue Gardinen, die alten waren im Zerfallen. Heidi Kabel wirkte auch an den inzwischen zur Legende gewordenen NDR-Schulfunksendungen „Neues aus Waldhagen" mit. Ein weiterer Sprecher war Henry Vahl.

Bundesweit bekannt wurde Heidi Kabel vom März 1954 an durch die Übertragungen von *Ohnsorg*-Aufführungen im Fernsehen. Um ein breites Publikum zu erreichen, ersetzte man dabei das Plattdeutsch durch Missingsch. Damals gab es nur ein Fernsehprogramm, aber 70 bis 80 % aller Fernsehgeräte waren eingeschaltet, wenn ein Stück aus dem *Ohnsorg-Theater* übertragen wurde, zeigte die große Popularität dieser Aufführungen und vor allem auch der Hauptdarstellerin Heidi Kabel. Sie war gern Volksschauspielerin und spielte ihre Rollen mit großer Ernsthaftigkeit und großem Engagement: „Boulevard ist sehr schwierig. Die meisten verwechseln Heiterkeit mit Oberflächlichkeit."

Christian Seeler erinnerte sich später so an seine Kollegin: „Sie war wunderbar. Sie war warmherzig, offen und hilfsbereit. Sie legte immer großen Wert auf ein harmonisches Ensemble, und es war ihr wichtig, dass auch die anderen gut waren und reüssieren konnten. Ich bin ihr mein Leben lang dankbar dafür, wie sehr sie mich gefördert und unterstützt hat."

Insgesamt hat Heidi Kabel in mehr als 160 plattdeutschen Stücken gespielt, oft gemeinsam mit Henry Vahl. Stücke wie „Tratsch im Treppenhaus" und „Die Kartenlegerin" erreichen auch heute noch hohe Einschaltquoten im Fernsehen. Das Stück „Tratsch im Treppenhaus" spielte Heidi Kabel im *Ohnsorg-Theater* mehr 500 Mal zusammen mit Henry Vahl. Dass sie und ihr Mann nun höhere Gagen bekamen, erwies sich 1960 als Segen, weil ihr Mietvertrag des Hauses in Bahrenfeld wegen Eigenbedarfs gekündigt wurde und sie es sich nun leisten konnten, ein kleines Haus in Nienstedten zu erwerben.

Der Tod von Hans Mahler nach 38 Ehejahren

1969, als sowohl das Theater als auch die Familie alle finanziellen Sorgen hinter sich gelassen hatten, erkrankte Hans Mahler schwer. Am 25. März 1970 starb er, als seine Frau auf der Bühne stand. Sie erfuhr in der Pause vom Tod ihres Mannes. Es wurde überlegt, die Aufführung abzubrechen, aber Heidi Kabel zeigte auch jetzt die große Disziplin als Schauspielerin, die sie immer ausgezeichnet hat: „Wir spielen den dritten Akt auch noch. Lasst wieder einklingeln, damit wir das hinter uns bringen."

Nach 38 Ehejahren stand sie nun ohne ihren Mann da. „Er war meine erste und einzige große Liebe." Sie schrieb in ihren Lebenserinnerungen über die Zeit nach seinem Tod: „Mein einzuübendes Alleinsein wurde mir allerdings durch meinen Beruf erleichtert." 1975 starb auch ihr langjähriger Theaterpartner Henry Vahl. Heidi Kabel trat nun seltener im *Ohnsorg-Theater* auf und übernahm immer wieder Rollen in Fernsehserien wie „Der Sonne entgegen" und „Die Erbin". Die berühmte Schauspielerin erhielt viele Ehrungen. Das Bundesverdienstkreuz lehnte sie ab, da war sie ganz traditionsbewusste Hanseatin: „Hamburger nehmen keine Orden an!"

Im Januar 1979 verabschiedete sich Heidi Kabel wegen der permanenten Auseinandersetzungen mit dem Intendanten Günther Siegmund vorübergehend vom *Ohnsorg-Theater*. Kolleginnen und Kollegen hatten von einer „vergifteten" und „unerträglichen" Situation gesprochen. Aber auch solche Krisen meisterte sie mutig. Sie pflegte dann zu sagen: „Dor möt wi dörch!"

Ein großes soziales Engagement und ein ruhiger Lebensabend

Heidi Kabel war für ihr großes soziales Engagement bekannt. Sie unterstützte zum Beispiel die „Aktion Sorgenkind" und setzte sich für Kriegsflüchtlinge aus dem zerfallenden Jugoslawien ein. Ein großes Anliegen war ihr auch die Förderung von Obdachlosenprojekten. Auch zählte sie zu den Unterstützerinnen der „Babyklappe" und des Hospizes *Hamburger Leuchtfeuer*. Ihre Tierliebe fand darin einen Ausdruck, dass sie die Stiftung des *Tierparks Hagenbeck* unterstützte. Unvergessen ist ihre Rezitation von Texten Wolfgang Borcherts bei einem Benefiz-Konzertes anlässlich des 50. Jahrestages der Bombardierung Hamburgs im Juli 1993.

Als sie im August 1994 80 Jahre alt wurde, überlegte Heidi Kabel: „Wo sind nur die Jahre geblieben? Sie sind im Flug vergangen, wahrscheinlich, weil ich immer gearbeitet habe. Ich hatte gar nicht die Zeit, über Vergangenes nachzudenken, ich musste mich immer auf die nächste Aufgabe vorbereiten, und meine eiserne Gesundheit hat das zugelassen. Sie ist das größte Geschenk meines Lebens."

Ende 1998 beendete Heidi Kabel mit dem Stück „Mein ehrlicher Tag" ihre insgesamt 75-jährige Schauspielkarriere. Nachdem sich ihre gesundheitliche Situation verschlechtert hatte, zog sie 2003 in eine Seniorenwohnanlage in Othmarschen. Am Ende ihrer Lebenserinnerungen hatte sie geschrieben, dass ihr vergönnt sein möge, bis zum letzten Atemzug auf der Bühne zu stehen: „Und wenn dann mit dem Schlussapplaus der letzte Vorhang fallen soll, ist es auch nicht so schlimm. Was mir vom Schicksal beschieden war, habe ich mit Anstand zu leben versucht."

Heidi Kabel starb am 15. Juni 2010 im Alter von 95 Jahren. Die Trauerfeier fand unter großer Anteilnahme im Michel statt. Ihre letzte Ruhe fand sie auf dem Nienstedtener Friedhof. Die frühere Kultursenatorin Karin von Welck hat sie so gewürdigt: „Für viele Menschen war Heidi Kabel weitaus mehr als eine Schauspielerin. Sie war ein Hamburger Original. Mit Heidi Kabel verbinden wir nicht nur die plattdeutsche Sprache, die sie mit dem Ohnsorg-Theater über Jahrzehnte in deutsche Wohnzimmer brachte. Heidi Kabel, das war und bleibt Hamburg: Hafen, Michel, Reeperbahn, unnachahmlich bodenständig, mit einem ausgeprägten Sinn für Gerechtigkeit und mit großem sozialem Engagement."

Im September 2011 benannte die Stadt den Platz vor dem neuen Standort des *Ohnsorg-Theaters* in Heidi-Kabel-Platz um. Seither steht eine lebensgroße Bronzestatue der Schauspielerin auf diesem Platz gegenüber vom Hauptbahnhof. Die Tochter Heidi Mahler gehörte Jahrzehnte lang zu den bekanntesten Schauspielerinnen des *Ohnsorg-Theaters*. Anlässlich ihres 80. Geburtstags spielte sie im Mai 2023 noch einmal die Rolle, mit der ihre Mutter in Erinnerung blieb und die auch sie oft gespielt hatte, den „Putzteufel" Meta Boldt in „Tratsch im Treppenhaus", Plattdeutsch „Tratsch op de Trepp".

Vetter Kirchhoff

„Unser Weten is doch man blots Stückwark, un veel Weten makt dumm un trurich, un ick will vergnöggt leben, solang dat Leben duurt." Jacob Friedrich Kirchhoff hat sich an sein Lebensmotto gehalten und sich nicht viel um die Anhäufung von Wissen geschert, besaß aber trotzdem eine beachtliche Bildung. Er kam am 13. Februar 1791 zur Welt. Über seine Kindheit und Jugend hat er offenbar nie gesprochen und auch aus anderen Quellen ist darüber nichts zu erfahren.

Als Makler hatte Kirchhoff in Hamburg einen gewissen Erfolg, ging seinem Beruf aber nicht mit großem Ehrgeiz nach. Hans-Heinrich Rottgardt schreibt dazu in seiner Biografie über Vetter Kirchhoff: „Von Beruf war er vereidigter Makler. Doch gehörte er nicht zu jener Sorte arbeitswütiger Börsenjobber, denen einzig und allein das Trachten nach Geld und Vermögen innewohnt. Im Gegenteil ..." Dafür wurde der charmante Spötter eine der beliebtesten Hamburger Persönlichkeiten des 19. Jahrhunderts.

Anders als die meisten anderen Originale lebte er in einer wirtschaftlich sehr soliden Situation. Auch genoss er die Gesellschaft anderer Menschen, die ihn achteten und wegen seine Originalität und seines Humors schätzten. Er war eloquent und besaß großen Wortwitz. Viele Kaufleute, Dichter und Künstlern schätzten deshalb seine Gesellschaft.

Nach dem ersten Kennenlernen sprach er alle mit „Du" und „mien Jung" an. „Er war der netteste Hamburger

Jung, der mir im Leben vorgekommen ist", hat der Schriftsteller Johann Peter Theodor Lyser in der ersten Kirchhoff-Biografie geschrieben. Und so ähnlich haben auch viele andere Zeitgenossen das vergnügte Original Vetter Kirchhoff erlebt.

Das angesehene und geschätzte Original

Der Schriftsteller Paul Möhring schrieb über ihn: „... ihm saß der Schelm im Nacken. Was ihm seine Originalität verschaffte, was ihn zum Original stempelte, das waren nicht seine gutbürgerlichen Eigenschaften und Vorzüge, das war vielmehr seine Neigung, den Schalksnarren zu spielen, allerlei Streiche auszuführen, die von seinen Mitmenschen belacht wurden, brave und biedere Bürger an der Nase herumzuführen, Respektspersonen höchst respektlos gegenüberzutreten ... Kirchhoff war trotz aller Streiche und Narreteien bei seinen Mitmenschen angesehen und geachtet; man lachte zwar über ihn, aber man respektierte ihn als Persönlichkeit, als Mann von Bildung, als humor- und witzbegabten Bürger der Stadt."

Vetter Kirchhoffs Tag begann mit einem Dampfbad. Er wohnte bei St. Annen in der heutigen Speicherstadt und ging von dort aus mit einem riesigen Tuch bekleidet zur Badeanstalt Wilhelminenbad an der Kehrwiederspitze. Die Möglichkeit, sein beachtliches Gewicht so zu vermindern, schwand schon beim anschließenden üppigen Frühstück mit Austern und Champagner im Hotel *König von Hannover* in der Dammtorstraße.

Leisten konnte Kirchhoff sich ein solches Leben auch deshalb, weil er – hartnäckigen Gerüchten zufolge – als Liebhaber sehr begehrt war und von den Damen großzügig finanziell bedacht wurde. Sie gehörten zu den sogenannten „Eckhäusern“, also zu den Einwohnern der Stadt, die sich repräsentative Eckhäuser leisten konnten.

Lassen wir hierzu einen anonym gebliebenen Zeitgenossen zu Wort kommen: „Die Liebschaften des Vetter Kirchhoff waren Legion! Wollt‘ ich von allen erzählen, es gäbe einen starken Beitrag zur Chronique scandleuse mancher sogenannter Eckhäuser. Kirchhoff war durchaus kein Kostverächter und man bezeichnete mir mehrere Damen, die ihm an Körperfülle nicht nachstanden, an Jahren aber bedeutend voraus waren, als seine erklärten Priesterinnen, von denen er ansehnliche Schürzenstipendien bezöge.“

Berühmt geworden ist Vetter Kirchhoff durch seine spitze Zunge. Gern setzten sich Heinrich Heine, der Komponist Albert Methfessel und andere Persönlichkeiten des Hamburger Kulturlebens im Lokal an seinen Tisch, weil dort immer für gute Stimmung gesorgt war. Dabei schätzten seine Gesprächspartner auch Kirchhoffs beachtliche Allgemeinbildung. Besonders in Musik, Malerei und Theater kannte er sich gut aus.

Häufiger kommentierte Kirchhoff bei solchen Treffen den Körperumfang seiner Zeitgenossen. Bei einem Paganini-Gastspiel in Hamburg genoss Kirchhoff dessen virtuoses Spiel, kommentierte aber auch: „Aber Gott! Wie mager de arme Mann is!“ Den Tenor Breitung lobte er hingegen wegen dessen Leibesfülle: „Datt is doch’n Kerl, de sick sehen laaten kann.“

Der ungeliebte Dienst bei der Bürgerwehr

Vetter Kirchhoff musste wie andere Männer der Stadt auch regelmäßig in der Bürgerwehr Dienst tun. Das fiel ihm wegen seines Volumens schwer, besonders das Exerzieren und die Teilnahme an Manövern. Mehrmals stellte er Anträge auf Befreiung von der Bürgerwehr, aber sie wurden abgelehnt. Er wehrte sich dadurch, dass er beim Marschieren nie Schritt hielt. Wenn der Kommandierende ihn daraufhin anfuhr, antwortete er seelenruhig: „Jo, sehn Se, davör kann ick nix!, bi en so dicken Mann as ick bün, geiht dat nich so gau, as bi den Andern!"

Bei Paraden ließ er sich von seinem Laufburschen einen Feldstuhl bringen, auf den er sich niederließ und die Kommandos wie „Gewehr bei Fuß" ignorierte. Dieses Verhalten löste, so hat es ein Zeitzeuge berichtet, beim Publikum großes Ergötzen aus, wobei die Jugend ein ohrenbetäubendes Gejohle anstimmte. Das wirkte, und Kirchhoff brauchte von nun an nicht mehr an Paraden teilnehmen.

Wie Vetter Kirchhoff eine Gefängnisstrafe vermied

Häufiger geriet Vetter Kirchhoff in Konflikt mit der Polizei – und mehr als einmal konnte er sie übertölpeln. Als zwei Polizisten kamen, um ihn zu einer Haftstrafe wegen nächtlicher Ruhestörung zur Gänsemarktwache abzuholen, lud er einen befreundeten Maler ein, ihn zu begleiten. Er hätte ihm etwas Wichtiges mitzuteilen, und weil das so wichtig wäre, wollte er es schriftlich tun. Mit Papier, Feder und Tinte machten sich Kirchhoff und der Maler begleitet von den beiden Polizisten auf den Weg. Die Gesellschaft stoppte in einem Lokal, wo Kirchhoff ein

Frühstück für die Gesellschaft bestellte. Die Polizisten war zunächst gegen diesen Abstecher gewesen, aber Kirchhoff antwortete: „Eile mit Weile! Mit nüchternem Magen kann ich nicht brummen und mein Geschäft muss ich erst in Ordnung bringen."

Das angebliche „Geschäft" war über dem üppigen Frühstück rasch vergessen. Die beiden Polizisten konnten der Versuchung nicht wiederstehen und langten kräftig zu. Auch die Liköre, die Kirchhoff ihnen aufdrängte, genossen sie reichlich. Ein Zeitzeuge wusste zu berichten, die Polizisten „... nachdem sie einmal in Zug gekommen waren, soffen mit Vehemenz drauf los". Nach einer Stunde waren die beiden Polizisten so betrunken, dass Kirchhoff und der Maler sie auf dem weiteren Weg zur Wache stützen mussten. Dort angekommen, befassten sich die wachhabenden Polizisten mit ihren beiden betrunkenen Kollegen und nicht mit Kirchhoff. Er konnte unbehelligt nach Hause zurückkehren und musste – da die Angelegenheit der Polizei wohl zu peinlich war – die Strafe nicht mehr antreten.

Als Vetter Kirchhoff ein Wettrennen auf einem Esel gewann

Vetter Kirchhoff liebte es, Maulhelden und selbstgerechte Bürger lächerlich zu machen. Einmal verspotteten ihn einige junge Schnösel, die sich als Herrenreiter bezeichneten. Das waren damals junge kaufmännische Angestellte, die ihre Zugehörigkeit zu den „besseren Kreisen" dadurch beweisen wollten, dass sie sonntags ausritten. Einer von ihnen verkündete: „Mein lieber Kirchhoff, Sie sollten man einmal mit uns ausreiten! Allerdings werden Sie wohl Schwierigkeiten haben, in Hamburg ein Pferd aufzutreiben, das Ihre Pfunde zu tragen in der Lage ist!“ Vetter Kirchhoff antwortete lächelnd: „Oh, ich würde sogar mit Ihnen am nächsten Sonntag um die Wette reiten, und wenn ich kein Pferd finde, so tut's ein Esel auch; ich wiege zwei tüchtige Mehlsäcke.“

Die jungen Schnösel waren sich ihres Sieges sicher und schlugen eine hohe Summe als Wetteinsatz vor. Kirchhoff stimmte zu, bestand aber vorsichtshalber auf einer schriftlichen Fixierung der Wette und des Wetteinsatzes. Groß war das Gelächter der Reiter, als Kirchhoff tatsächlich auf einem Esel erschien. Das Lachen erstarb, als die jungen Reiter rasch ins Hintertreffen gerieten. Kirchhoff hatte die Route für das Rennen mit Bedacht vorgeschlagen: Sie führte mitten durch eine Kiesgrube. Während der Esel seinen Reiter behände zum Ziel trug, blieben die Pferde im Mahlsand stecken.

Begegnung mit einem schießwütigen Advokaten

Vetter Kirchhoff verspottete viele hochnäsige Bürger. Sie verziehen ihm das meist rasch, aber einmal wurde es gefährlich für ihn. Er hatte sich im Theater mit einem schmächtigen Advokaten angelegt, der hinter ihm saß und sich darüber beschwerte, dass Kirchhoff ihm den Blick auf die Bühne versperren würde.

Der Advokat war so zornig, dass er Kirchhoff zum Duell herausforderte. Der ließ dem schießwütigen Advokaten ausrichten, er könnte sich beim besten Willen nicht mit ihm duellieren, solange der Advokat so dünn wäre, er aber eine große Zielfläche böte. Das Duell müsste deshalb verschoben werden, bis der Advokat so dick wäre wie er selbst oder er selbst so dünn wäre wie der Herausforderer.

Alle lachten über den Advokaten, aber es hieß auch, Kirchhoff habe keinen Mut. Das ließ der nicht auf sich sitzen. Als ihn zwei kräftige junge Leute im Gedränge des Weihnachtsmarktes anrempelten, wurde er laut: „Ick mutt ju beiden Lümmels wull mol Anstand beibringen, wat?“ Die Kraftprotze drehten sich um und riefen höhnisch: „Dat versöök man mol!“ Und tatsächlich, mit ungeahnter Schnelligkeit verteilte Kirchhoff zwei kräftige Faustschläge. Die Männer gingen zu Boden, und der Ruf des Spötters war wiederhergestellt. Er blieb es auch, als sich herumsprach, dass Kirchhoff die beiden für den Auftritt engagiert hatte.

Der blamierte Zeitungsverleger

Kirchhoff war ein regelmäßiger Theaterbesucher und ärgerte sich immer wieder über einen Verleger, der gewohnheitsmäßig zahlreiche Aufführungen in seiner Zeitung negativ bewertete. Deshalb wollte Kirchhoff ihm eine Lektion erteilen. Er wählte dafür das Gastspiel einer französischen Schauspieltruppe in Altona. Deren erste Aufführung verlief so enttäuschend, dass auf die geplanten Auftritte an den folgenden Tagen verzichtet wurde.

Das machte sich Kirchhoff zunutze. Er benutzte einen älteren Verriss einer anderen Theateraufführung des Zeitungsverlegers und fügte lediglich an den passenden Stellen den Namen des französischen Stücks und der Schauspieler ein. Diese Theaterkritik einer gar nicht stattgefundenen Aufführung bot er dem Verleger an, der sie arglos in seiner Zeitung abdruckte. Es sprach sich allerdings rasch herum, dass die Vorstellung ausgefallen war und Kirchhoff eine ältere Kritik des Verlegers nur leicht abgewandelt hatte. Der Verleger stand blamiert da und soll keine Theaterkritiken mehr verfasst haben.

Wo Kritik angezeigt war, zögerte Kirchhoff allerdings nicht, sie zu äußern. Der Freiherr von Malnitz, ein Dichter von durchaus begrenztem Talent, las bei einer Abendveranstaltung unter großem Stimmaufwand sein neues Theaterstück „Hans Kohlhas" vor. Beim anschließenden Beisammensein im Austernkeller wurde Kirchhoff von Malnitz gefragt, wie ihm das Stück gefallen hatte. Darauf hätte er besser verzichten sollen, denn er bekam zu hören: „Na weest du, mien Jung, du hest jo schreen, dat dovon en Kacheloben infalln kunn!"

Die Verspottung des „Mäßigkeitsvereins"

Kirchhoffs Lebenswandel machte ihn nicht zum Freund des *Mäßigkeitsvereins*, in dem reiche Bürger sich zusammengeschlossen hatten, um gegen den Schnapskonsum der armen Leute zu wettern. Sie selbst tranken „in gepflegter Atmosphäre" gern einige Gläser Wein, aber das sahen sie als Mäßigkeit an. Kirchhoff war diese Scheinheiligkeit zuwider.

Eines Nachts sah er einen total betrunkenen Mann in der Gosse liegen. Schnell rief er einige Arbeitsleute herbei: „Verdammich! Dor liggt jo Kornümsteker Ehlers sein Knecht! Gau Lüüd, haalt 'n Koor un bringt den armen Stackel nah Huus! Hier hebbt ji ok 12 Schilling!" Zwölf Schillinge waren ein beachtlichen Betrag, und so waren die Arbeitsleute gern bereit, den Betrunkenen auf einer

Karre zum Haus des Kornumstechers (Kornhändlers) Ehlers zu bringen.

Am Ziel angekommen, weckten die Arbeitsleute den Hausherrn, der äußerst erbost war. „Mien Knecht? Dat is nich mien Knecht! Wat schall ick mit den Swienegel vör min Döör?! Glieks bringt ji den Kerl wedder dorhen, wo ji em herhaalt hebbt!“ Aber die gewitzten Träger beharrten darauf, Kirchhoff hätte nur für den Transport zu Ehlers bezahlt, nicht für den Weg zurück. Um den unbekannten Betrunkenen loszuwerden, blieb dem Kornhändler nichts übrig, als den Trägern seinerseits zwölf Schillinge zu zahlen. Als Vorsitzender des *Mäßigkeitsvereins* wollte Ehlers keinen Betrunkenen vor seinem Haus liegen haben.

Am nächsten Tag stellte er Kirchhoff zur Rede. Der antwortete seelenruhig: „Ick weet gor nich, warum Se sick so opregen, Ehlers! De Besopene hett mi doch seggt, dat he geern in den Mässigkeitsvereen opnohmen warden wull – na, und dor weur he doch bi Ihn an de richtige Adress!“

Eines Tages beorderte man Kirchhoff wegen groben Unfugs in das Stadthaus, wo ihn der Polizeiherr zur Rede stellte: „Sie werden in Ihrem Leben wohl nicht mehr vernünftig, Kirchhoff!“ Der antwortete: „Was nützt denn alle Vernunft? Hat sie Ihnen vielleicht was geholfen? Nee – Sie sind ein vielgeplagter Polizeiherr, und ich bin und bleibe der dicke, lustige Kirchhoff – ick will gor nicks anners as vergneugt leben, so lang dat Leben duert – ob mit Vernunft oder ohne Vernunft, dat is mi egool!“

Kirchhoff besuchte ein Theaterstück über Kirchhoff

Vetter Kirchhoff war ein so berühmtes Hamburger Original, dass schon zu seinen Lebzeiten das Theaterstück „Kirchhoff oder Das lustige alte Hamburg. Hamburger Original-Volksposse in acht Bildern von Chr. Bischoff" im *Steinstraßen-Theater* auf die Bühne kam. Kirchhoff konnte mit der Darstellung seiner Person durchaus zufrieden sein, etwa mit diesem Dialog: „Kirchhoff ist doch nun einmal ein rechter Eulenspiegel." – „Eulenspiegel – so nennt man ihn in Hamburg, aber unter dieser spaßigen Maske schlägt das beste, edelste Herz! Wie manche Träne hat er heimlich schon getrocknet!" Damit wurde Kirchhoffs großzügige, aber dezente Unterstützung von Menschen in Not gewürdigt.

Ein Kritiker schrieb nach der Uraufführung in der Zeitung: „Wenn der alte Schwerenöter vom St.-Annen-Kirchspiel selbst unter den Zuschauern im Theater gewesen wäre, er hätte sein Freude an der geradezu meisterhaften Kopie seiner Person gehabt!" Kirchhoff besuchte tatsächlich eine der späteren Aufführungen und war mit den Leistungen des Bühnen-Kirchhoff ebenfalls sehr zufrieden. Er schickte ihm am nächsten Tag ein kleines Päckchen mit einem Paar mit Brillanten besetzten Knöpfen für sein Oberhemd. In einem Begleitbrief zollte er dem Schauspieler seine Anerkennung. Aber wenn er echt wirken wollte, sollte er bei seinen Hemdknöpfen auf Imitate verzichten und die beigefügten Knöpfe tragen. Das tat der Schauspieler dann auch gern.

Später übernahm ein Vorstadttheater das Stück, und Kirchhoff war Gast einer Aufführung. Er war aber entsetzt über das stümperhafte Spiel dieses Theater-Kirchhoffs. Der Schauspieler hatte Kirchhoff im Publikum entdeckt und freute sich darauf, ein ebenso großzügiges Geschenk wie sein Kollege zu erhalten. Tatsächlich traf am nächsten Tag ein kleines Päckchen von Kirchhoff ein, das aber nur ein Paar wertloser Imitate enthielt. Im Begleitbrief musste der Schauspieler lesen, dass es sich bei seinem Spiel um eine miserable Nachahmung handeln würde, zu der die Knopf-Imitationen passten.

Das Original bleibt in Erinnerung

Am 14. Mai 1844 ging das Leben von Vetter Kirchhoff zu Ende. Der Kirchhoff-Biograf Hans-Heinrich Rottgardt hat Vetter Kirchhoff auf eine Ebene mit Eulenspiegel gestellt. Er schrieb über Kirchhoff: „Auch dieser benutzte nämlich die ihm in die Wiege gelegten Gaben, sei es Schnellzüngigkeit, Spottlust, Humor und dergleichen, um damit gegen Dünkel, Heuchelei, Kastengeist und Bürokratismus zu Felde zu ziehen."

Die Geschichten vom dicken, vergnügten Kirchhoff sind auch dank des Buches „Drei Hamburger Originale" von Paul Möhring unvergessen. So auch diese: Der Bürgermeister war irritiert. Was wollten all die Menschen, die sich vor dem Rathaus versammelt hatten. Ein Ratsdiener konnte den Auflauf erklären: „Herr Bürgermeister, der Kirchhoff ist oben auf dem Dach des Rathauses und geht da immer auf und ab!"

Der Bürgermeister ließ ihn herunterholen und stellte ihn zur Rede: „Was haben Sie auf dem Dach vom Rathaus zu suchen? Solche Streiche verbitte ich mir! Aber verlassen Sie sich darauf, dieser Spaß wird Ihnen teuer zu stehen kommen!“ Kirchhoff belehrte ihn: „De Spooß kost mi gor nicks. Da – dor steht dat swatt up witt.“ Er reichte dem Bürgermeister das Schreiben, und da stand: „Sie werden hiermit aufgefordert, morgen früh zwischen zehn und elf auf dem Rathaus zu erscheinen!“

Kirchhoff blieb seinen Zeitgenossen in guter Erinnerung. Ein halbes Jahrhundert später entstand dieses Gedicht (Kneep bedeutet hier etwa Schelmenstücke):

In olen scheunen Tiden
leevt een vergneugter Mann,
vun dem manch oler Börger
goar veel vertellen kann;
een slichter Linwandmakler
weer he, doch kugelrund,
bi den sein Kneep kunn lachen
een Kranker sik gesund.
Gewiß hest, leve Leser,
villicht du mol von Kirchhoff heurt?,
de selbst den argsten Griesgram
to’n Lachen hett verfeuhrt.
Wat de von Kneep vullbröckt hett,
in’n Volksmund levt dat fort;
de Uhlenspeegeleen
bedreeft hin in Accord!

Hein Köllisch

Hein Köllisch war Ende des 19. Jahrhunderts der erfolgreichste Volkssänger von St. Pauli und weit über Hamburgs Grenzen hinaus berühmt. Mehr als 150 plattdeutsche Lieder sind von ihm überliefert, viele davon sangen die Leute auf der Straße oder in der Kneipe. Einige werden heute noch bei plattdeutschen Liederabenden vorgetragen. Köllisch schöpfte dabei aus dem Alltag. So entstand seine berühmte „Pingsttour" nach einer Landpartie mit Frau und fünf Gören. Hier eine Kostprobe aus dem Couplet, also dem Lied mit gereimten Strophen. Sie erzählt vom matschigen Ende eines Ausflugs in das Rodenbeker Quellental:

Op eenmol, wie gemeen, ehr eener sick verseh'n,
Dor kummt vun boben dohl een Regen kolossol.
De ganze Minschenschwarm, de kummt nu in Marm,
De Froonslüd kriescht un jucht, de Mannslüd flucht.
De Vadder springt nu opp, glitscht ut un fallt darop
Grood opp denn Kinnerwogen, de kippt un fallt in Groben.
He mit sien witte Büx recht in son deepe Pfütz,
Mit samt datt lüttje Göör, wat een Malheur.

Minna Köllisch, die älteste Tochter von Hein Köllisch, hat 1958 dem *Hamburger Abendblatt* bestätigt: „Es war alles genauso, wie Vater es in der ‚Pingsttour' geschildert hat … Wie das in Hamburg nun einmal so üblich war: Die ganze Familie wurde zu Pfingsten neu eingekleidet. Vaters witte Maibüx leuchtete unternehmensfreudig." Aber, sie blieb nicht lange weiß: „Wir hatten auf den

Wiesen gelagert, den Proviant verzehrt, glücklich und zufrieden den strahlenden Pfingstsonntag verbracht. Da öffnete der Himmel seine Schleusen …“ Wie die Tour zu Ende ging? Das hat Hein Köllisch so überliefert:

Na endlich, no den Suus,
dor geiht dat nu to Huus,
de Vadder un sien Söhn
sünd nüdlich antosehn,
de scheune witte Büx
süht ut wie Stebelwix,
de Strohheud sünd so slapp
wie oles Papp.
De Brögam un de Brut,
de seht erst lecker ut!
De harr'n, wat sull'n se mooken,
sick beid' in't Hei verkropen.
Dat allerlüttste Göör weur
dorch natt dör un dör,
de Mudder weur so natt
as wie so'n Katt.
De een schuwt achtern annern her
grood wie de Geus, se könt nich mehr!
Un dorbi alle Ogenblick
verswind mol eener achtern Knick.
Grood wie gerädert un half dood
kummt se denn endlich an de Bood.
So ward in Hamborg Pingst'n
fiert un sick fein amüsiert.

„Ein rundum fröhlicher und herzensguter Mann“

Heinrich Köllisch war ein Junge von St. Pauli, geboren am 19. September 1857 am Paulsplatz, heute Hein-Köllisch-Platz. Sein Vater besaß eine kleine Fabrikation von „Buddelwichse“, also Schuhcreme in Flaschen. Hein trat nicht sofort in des Vaters Fußstapfen, sondern ging nach einer Schlosserlehre als Geselle auf Wanderschaft. Doch nach dem plötzlichen Tod des Vaters musste er die Fabrik übernehmen. Aus Ruß, Zuckersirup, Bier und Schwefelsäure wurde dort „Köllisch Glanzwichse“ gebraut, aber vielleicht ist die originelle Mischung auch eine von den Geschichten von Hein Köllisch.

Er schrieb gereimte Werbesprüche für die Glanzwichse und brachte das Produkt selbst zu seinen Kunden. Nebenbei verfasste er humoristische Texte und Lieder, die er in seiner Stammkneipe auf St. Pauli zum Besten gab. 1890 heiratete er Marie Meyer, die Tochter eines Königlichen Musikmeisters. Bald gehörten fünf Kinder zur Familie. Der Enkel Heinz Köllisch erinnerte sich so an seinen berühmten Opa: „Mein Großvater war ein rundum fröhlicher und herzensguter Mann. Er soll der erste Hamburger gewesen sein, der mit seiner ganzen ‚Belegschaft‘ einen Betriebsausflug machte, einen Tag nach Pfingsten und natürlich ins geliebte Quellental.“

Ein erfolgreiches „Universum“

1892 wurde Hein Köllisch von einem Theaterdirektor entdeckt, als er in seiner Stammkneipe in der Bartelsstraße plattdeutsche Lieder vortrug. Sein erstes Lied war „De Orgel kummt“, und wie spätere Lieder beruhte es auf eigener Beobachtung des Alltagslebens in Hamburg. In diesem Fall hatte er die damals großen Zahl der Orgelmänner auf den Straßen der Stadtbeobachtet. Dieses Lied, das Hein Köllisch noch oft gesungen hat, endet mit diesen Zeilen:

De Orgel fangt kum an to spel'n,
dor gröhlt dat all ut hundert Kehl'n:
De Orgel kummt, de Orgel kummt!
De ganze Klick, de dreiht sick rund.
De Deerns de kriescht, de Jungs de jucht,
de Kinner schreet, de Nobern flucht!
Und alles rennt in'n hell'n Galopp
De Orgel achder rop!

Hein Köllisch konnte als Sänger im *Etablissement im Sieben Himmel* auftreten und auf der Stelle war er im Sieben Himmel. Donnernder Applaus verhalf ihm zu Höhenflug und festem Engagement. Marie Köllisch betrachtete die Karriere ihres Mannes als Volkssänger zunächst wohl etwas skeptisch, schließlich war sie die Tochter eines Königlichen Musikmeisters. Aber der Erfolg des Sängers überzeugte sie, und bald trug sie geschäftstüchtig zu dessen Karriere bei. Sie überzeugte einen Drucker, ein Blatt mit dem Lied „De Pingsttour" zu produzieren. Entgegen den Erwartungen des Druckers fand das Blatt reißenden Absatz und trug zur Bekanntheit des Volkssängers bei. Weitere Blätter mit Liedern von Hein Köllisch folgten.

Als Sänger und Humorist war Hein Köllisch so erfolgreich, dass er bereits 1894 am Spielbudenplatz ein eigenes Theater eröffnen konnte. *Heinrich Köllisch's Universum* bot eine Mischung aus Varieté und Volkstheater. Neben eigenen Liedern gehörten plattdeutsche Parodien, Tanzdarbietungen und kleine Theaterstücke zum Repertoire. Das erste Stück hatte den vielversprechenden Titel „Adam und Eva, oder hier dorff keener bi de Appeln gehen". Ein Werbespruch des *Universums* lautete: „Täglich urdrastische Komödien. Hoch und platt? Für jeden wat. Hierzu erstklassige Spezialitäten."

Mit eigenen Liedern und Couplets trug Hein Köllisch zum Erfolg seines Theaters bei. Die Premiere der „Pingsttour" im *Universum* kam so gut an, dass er das Lied gleich ein zweites Mal singen musste. Köllisch war ein volkstümlicher Sänger, der aus dem Volk kam und dem Alltagsleben der Menschen humorvolle Seiten abgewinnen konnte, zum Beispiel einer stürmischen Überfahrt nach Helgoland in „De Reis' no Helgoland":

Bald de Menschen legen
Op Deck rum wie de Flegen,
Kunn' nicht leben, kunn' nicht starb'n
Mancheen stöhnt: Och, wie sall dat ward'n.
Nu erst de Berliner,
De vertrock keen Mien mehr.
So käm'n se denn no Helgoland,
Wer Lust hatt, gung an' Strand.

Paul Möhring hat in seinem Buch über Hein Köllisch geschrieben, dass dessen Lieder und Couplets nicht am Schreibtisch entstanden sind: „Er fand seine Stoffe im hamburgischen Volksleben, auf der Straße, in der Familie, in seiner Stammkneipe. Er besang eigene Erlebnisse, er machte Menschen seiner täglichen Umgebung zum Mittelpunkt seiner Verse, er schöpfte aus dem Humor des hamburgischen Alltagslebens. Und alles in einer

Sprache, die jeder verstand ... Hein Köllisch erweckte die plattdeutsche Parodie zu neuem Leben. Der drastische Humor seines ‚Wilhelm Tell' und der ‚Loreley' rissen die Zuhörer zu lautem Lachen hin."

Wie der Direktor ein Trinkgeld erhielt und sich dafür bedankte

Auch als berühmter Mann blieb sich der Volkssänger treu. Einmal kam ein neuer Artist mit großem Gepäck ins Theater und rief im herrischen Ton einem etwas schäbig gekleideten Mann, den er für einen Laufburschen hielt, zu: „Tragen Sie mal den Koffer hinein!" Köllisch verzog keine Miene, nahm den Koffer und bedankte sich artig für das Trinkgeld. Als der Artist begriff, wer ihm das Gepäck getragen hatte, war ihm die Sache äußerst peinlich und er stammelte zahllose Entschuldigungen. Aber Hein Köllisch beruhigte ihn, es sei doch alles in Ordnung, schließlich hätte er ein gutes Trinkgeld erhalten.

Auf der Bühne trat Hein Köllisch nicht in schäbiger oder komischer Kleidung, sondern in Frack und Zylinder auf: „Für meine Muttersprache ist mir der beste Anzug gerade gut genug." Seine Frau Marie brachte den Zylinder vor jedem Auftritt auf Hochglanz. Abends saß sie hinter der Theke des *Universums* und überwachte den Lokalbetrieb. Wenn ihr Mann nach dem Ende des Programms an die Theke kam, stand sein geliebter Tee mit Rum schon für ihn bereit. Und wenn Hein Köllisch wieder einmal fragte, ob er heute gut war, lautete ihre Antwort: „Das hest du man wedder gut macht, mien Jung."

Auch vor einer Anpassung klassischer Themen an das Niederdeutsche und an den Humor seines Publikums scheute Hein Köllisch nicht zurück. Die Geschichte von Wilhelm Tell parodierte er so:

Wilhelm Tell, dat weer en Schweizer
un en Schütz von Profeschon,
hauptsächlich mit sien Flitzebogen,
dor wuß he umtogohn.
Jo, scheten kunn he bannig,
wat, weer em ganz egol,
wenn he nich grod vorbischeut,
dann dreup he jedesmol.

1901 erkrankte Hein Köllisch und entschloss sich, zur Linderung der Leiden – und um einen Jugendtraum zu erfüllen – nach Italien und Ägypten zu reisen. Er kam in Ägypten nie an, sondern starb bereits kurz bevor er Rom erreicht hatte am 18. April 1901 im Alter von 43 Jahren. Sein Leichnam wurde nach Hamburg überführt, wo eine unübersehbare Menschenmenge seinem Sarg vom Spielbudenplatz bis zum *Ohlsdorfer Friedhof* folgte. Seine Witwe und mehrere Kinder sorgten dafür, dass seine Bühne, das *Universum*, weiterbestehen konnte.

Der unvergessene Volkssänger

Besondere Verdienste erwarb sich die älteste Tochter Minna, die Jahrzehnte lang als Sängerin, Schauspielerin mit plattdeutschen Texten und als Verwandlungskünstlerin auf der Bühne des *Universums* und auf anderen Bühnen im In- und Ausland stand. Dabei hatte ihr Vater nicht gewollt, dass sie und ihre Geschwister Schauspieler oder Sänger würden. So stand Minna Köllisch erst nach seinem Tod das erste Mal in einem plattdeutschen Einakter auf der Bühne des *Universums* und arbeitete mit großer

Energie daran, das Theater zu erhalten. Da sie sowohl die Stimmlagen Sopran als auch Alt beherrschte, konnte sie mit sich selbst Opernduette singen. Ihr Mann war ein bekannter Zauberkünstler und so gestalteten sie gemeinsam ein vielfältiges Kulturprogramm.

1943 ging die Hamburger Institution *Universum* im Bombenhagel unter. Zu Ehren des Volksdichters und Sängers benannte die Stadt den Paulsplatz 1949 auf St. Pauli in Hein-Köllisch-Platz um. In der *Niederdeutschen Bibliothek* in der Peterstraße 36 wird seit 2023 in einer Dauerausstellung an Hein Köllisch erinnert.

Zum Abschluss eine Kostprobe aus der Köllischen „Loreley“:

> *Ick weet nich, wat sall dat bedüden,*
> *dat ick so gnadderich bin!*
> *So'n Quatschkrom ut urollen Tieden,*
> *de will mi gor nich mehr ut'n Sinn.*

Das Gedicht endet mit diesen Zeilen:

> *Wenn den Schipper die Wellen wegsnappen*
> *is gor nich to bedur'n de Mann.*
> *Wat geiht den dösigen Knappen*
> *dat Froonsminsch dor boben an?!*

Lord von Barmbeck

„Ich büße so, wie ich gefehlt habe, kühn waren meine Handlungen, ohne Murren ist meine Buße. Menschenleben habe ich nicht auf dem Gewissen; meine Handlungen kann ich restlos mit meinem Körper quittieren, und das wird jedem einleuchten, wenn er hört, ich habe keinem Armen nach seinem Hab und Gut getrachtet, sondern lediglich der reichen Klasse ihr Eigentum gesetzwidrig geschmälert, die ihren Schaden längst verschmerzt hat, wofür ich mein halbes Leben hier hinter Gittern vertrauern muss ... Nicht daß ich mich dessen rühmen will, darf es aber erwähnen, daß ich den Armen mit vollen Händen brachte von dem, was ich den Reichen entwendete."

Julius Adolf Petersen war der bekannteste und auch erfolgreichste Einbrecher und Ausbrecher Hamburgs im ersten Drittel des 20. Jahrhunderts. Gern wäre er als Helfer der Armen und Hüter der Moral in einer bösen Welt in die Geschichte eingegangen. Er hat seine Lebenserinnerungen auf 717 Seiten aufgeschrieben. Noch umfangreicher sind die Gerichtsakten – etwa zwanzig laufende Meter, wo unter anderem zahlreiche Eigentumsdelikte, das Verprügeln eines Polizisten und illegale Spielhöllen aufgeführt sind. Seinen Beruf übte Petersen in Frack und Zylinder aus und ist deshalb als „Lord von Barmbeck" (damals mit ck geschrieben) in die Kriminalgeschichte eingegangen.

Eine Kindheit in tiefer Armut

Der Lord von Barmbeck hatte berufsbedingt mehr als einmal mit der Polizei zu tun. Ähnliches lässt sich auch von seinem Vater sagen, allerdings aus anderen Gründen. Wilhelm Jasper Martin Petersen war Sozialdemokrat und wurde 1882 des Landes verwiesen. Bilder von Lassalle und Bebel sowie eine Flugschrift, die bei einer polizeilichen Hausdurchsuchung konfisziert wurden, reichten aus, um ihn nach Dänemark zu vertreiben. Nur gelegentlich kehrte er heimlich aus dem Exil nach Hamburg zurück. Seine Frau musste sich mit den Kindern in Hamburg durchschlagen, war eine „Arbeitsbiene", die sich für ihre Kinder aufopferte, schrieb der Sohn in seinen Lebenserinnerungen. Der am 7. Oktober 1882 geborene Julius Adolf war auch deshalb lange kränkelnd und schwach, weil die sechsköpfige Familie in tiefster Armut lebte. Die Ärzte hielten das Kleinkind nicht für lebensfähig, aber er überstand alle Krankheiten. Der Vater durfte zwar nach einigen Jahren zurückkehren, aber als Zigarrenmacher verdiente er wenig Geld.

Der kleine Adolf war ein ängstliches Kind, ließ sich aber nicht kleinkriegen, sondern entwickelte einen beachtlichen Widerstandsgeist. In der Schule galt er eigentlich als ruhig und still, aber nachdem der Dreizehnjährige von einem Lehrer einige Schläge mit dem Rohrstock auf den Hintern bekommen hatte, warf er diesem ein gutgefülltes Tintenfass ins Gesicht.

„Diesmal floss Tinte statt Tabaksauce über seinen Vollbart ... Während der Lehrer mit seinem Mohrenantlitz die Wirkung meiner Handlung noch im Begriffe war zu begreifen, war ich aus der Tür gerannt, hatte meine Mütze auf dem Korridor vom Garderobenhaken genommen und über den Schulhof hinweg fluchtartig das Weite gesucht."

Danach schwänzte Petersen vier Wochen lang die Schule und tauchte unter in jener Welt, die den braven Bürgern als Halb- oder Unterwelt galt. Er konnte sich danach mit seinen Eltern versöhnen und eine andere Schule besuchen. „Aber in diesen 4 Wochen hatte ich Gift getrunken, Gift in vollen Zügen. Eine ganze Reihe Streiche und Untugenden hatte ich in meine Seele gebrannt." Bald darauf stand Petersen 1896 das erste Mal vor einem Richter. Er hatte eine Geldbörse entwendet und erhielt eine Gefängnisstrafe von fünf Tagen.

Als die schiefe Bahn immer steiler wurde

Wirklich erfolgreich verlief die Schulkarriere auch danach nicht und der Junge beteiligte sich an einer „Reihe loser Streiche". Nach Abschluss der Schule begann er auf Vermittlung seines Vater eine Töpferlehre. Aber Adolf Petersen verlor seine Stelle durch Streiche bald wieder. Bei einer Ofenreparatur verschloss er ein Feuerloch mit Lehm und Steinen und schärfte den Besitzern ein, sie müssten eine Stunde bis zum Benutzen des Ofens warten. Nach einem weiteren Streich war der Meister zornig und der Lehrling bockig. Er gab die Stelle auf. Der arbeitslose Jugendliche tat sich mit zwei Gleichgesinnten zusammen, und gemeinsam stahlen sie Zinkrohre eines Klempnermeisters. Sie wurden erwischt und Petersen landete vor Gericht. Wegen seines Alters und nur einer kleinen Vorstrafe kam er dieses Mal mit einem Verweis davon.

Der Vater war entschlossen, seinen Sohn aus dem kriminellen Milieu herauszuholen, und sorgte dafür, dass er eine Lehre in einer Mühle in Dänemark beginnen konnte. Diese Ausbildung nahm nach drei Monaten ein abruptes

Ende, als Petersen das Pony der Müllerstochter misshandelte. Er kehrte nach Hamburg zurück: „Aller Fesseln ledig tauchte ich wieder in einem gleichgesinnten Freundeskreis unter ... Allerlei Unfug waren die nächsten Erscheinungen, und als Bombe kam die Polizei ins Haus."

Der Vater gab nicht auf und verschaffte dem Sohn eine Stelle auf einer Werft. Fast drei Jahre ging das gut, aber dann verlor Adolf Petersen wegen eines derben Streiches seine Arbeit. Er war nun wieder häufig in den Kaschemmen an der Peterstraße und am Neuen Steinweg zu finden und begann eine kriminelle Karriere mit allen Höhen und Tiefen – es waren mehr Tiefen. Nach einem Einbruch mit zwei Kumpanen fahndete die Polizei nach Petersen, und er floh nach Dänemark. Die Liebe zu einer dänischen Gutsbesitzertochter hätte eine Wende im Leben des jungen Mannes bedeuten können, aber er machte durch den Diebstahl eines Pferdes ihrer Eltern alles zunichte. „Liesbeth sah ich im Leben nicht wieder, mein Weg wurde ein abenteuerlicher."

Der elegante Herr im Schaufenster des Modegeschäfts

In einer Kaschemme in der Peterstraße nahm die Polizei Petersen fest, er konnte aber auf dem Weg zur Wache fliehen und war kurz darauf an dem Einbruch in ein Geschäft in der Spitalerstraße beteiligt. Reglos stand der Mann im Frack neben schön dekorierten Wachsfiguren im Schaufenster eines Herrenkonfektionsgeschäftes, so als gehörte er zum Ensemble. Er war nur vorübergehend im Schaufenster zu besichtigen, denn er stand Schmiere, während sein Kumpan „Lockenfitsche" sich am Tresor des Geschäftes zu schaffen machte. Ein Udl, der sich langweilte, stand dösend vor diesem Schaufenster. Udl (oder Udel) war im damaligen Hamburg der Spottname für Polizisten, die wie Eulen nachts unterwegs waren, um für die Sicherheit der Bürger zu sorgen. Nicht selten suchten sie sich irgendwo eine ruhige Ecke und dösten vor sich hin.

Dieser Udl döste vor dem besagten Schaufenster, und der Mann im Smoking wurde immer nervöser. „Meine wenige Beherrschung als Neuling ließ mich im aufgeregten Tempo aus dem Ausbauer springen, um Lockenfitsche in Kenntnis zu setzen, wobei ich selber ein Puppe anrannte, die umfiel und im Fallen mehrere Puppen mitriss."

Der Udl schreckte auf und ließ seine Alarmpfeife ertönen. Von überall her stürzten nun Polizisten herbei. Es begann eine wilde Verfolgungsjagd über die Dächer der Innenstadt. Der elegante Herr aus dem Schaufenster und sein Kumpan konnten über die Dächer fliehen und an einem Blitzableiter hinabsausen – allerdings nicht auf Nimmerwiedersehen, wie sich bald zeigen sollte. Aber erst einmal genossen Petersen und Lockenfitsche die Anerkennung der Boulevardpresse. „Verwegene Einbrecher und Kletteraffen" lautete eine der Schlagzeilen.

Harte Strafe, Reue und der Versuch eines Neuanfangs

Es folgten weitere Einbrüche und ein erneuter Polizeieinsatz, dieses Mal ohne Flucht, aber mit Festnahme und Untersuchungshaft. Petersens Kumpane standen mit ihm vor Gericht. Das Plädoyer des Staatsanwalts ließ nichts Gutes erwarten. Nach der Erinnerung Petersens erklärte er: „Meine sehr geehrten Herren, in dieser

Bande haben wir es zweifellos mit außergewöhnlichen Verbrechern zu tun, bei denen eine exemplare Strafe am Platze ist. Wie ein Hohn auf die Gesellschaft würde hier die Milde eines Gerichtshofes klingen." Und Milde gab es dann auch nicht. Petersen erhielt eine Gefängnisstrafe von vier Jahren, auf die die Untersuchungshaft von einem Jahr angerechnet wurde.

Nicht ohne Selbstmitleid schrieb Adolf Petersen später in seinen Lebenserinnerungen: „Beschäftigt wurde ich mit Strümpfestricken. Mein ganzes Tun und Treiben ließ ich im Geiste Revue passieren, bitter war die Erkenntnis. Jetzt erst dachte ich an meine Eltern und Geschwister, sah ein, was ich denen bereitet hatte. So oft benetzten Tränen die Strümpfe, die halbfertig in der Strickmaschine hingen."

Nach insgesamt drei Jahren im Gefängnis entließ man Petersen 1904 aufgrund der Fürsprache des Anstaltsgeistlichen. Der Exhäftling unternahm vergeblich den Versuch, ins bürgerliche Leben zurückzukehren. „Die Vorstrafen bleiben für den Deklassierten ein Strick, die ihm bei seinen besten Absichten Senat und Staatsanwaltschaft wie die Direktion der Strafanstalt und sonstige liebe Menschen jeden Moment drehen. Diesen Herrschaften fehlt eben das Verständnis für die seelische Auferstehung eines Gefangenen."

Petersen fand eine Anstellung bei einem Fuhrmann. Nach neun Monaten kam ein Kriminalbeamter mehrmals zu seiner Arbeitsstelle, um sich quittieren zu lassen, dass Petersen bei seiner Entlassung aus dem Gefängnis sechs Mark ausgezahlt bekommen hatte. Dadurch wurden

Fuhrmann und Kollegen auf die frühere Gefängnishaft aufmerksam und behandelten Petersen nun so, dass er nach einigen Tagen von sich aus kündigte.

Petersen erwarb anschließend mit finanzieller Unterstützung seines älteren Bruders eine Kneipe in Barmbek, die sich nachts in eine illegale Spielhölle verwandelte. „Die Einnahmen in der Wirtschaft erlaubten mir Ausgaben, die über das gewöhnliche Maß hinausgingen; besondere Verdienste hatte ich aus meiner Spielklubtätigkeit, die ich nach Wirtschaftsschluss abwickelte. Nur Geschäftsleute, die mir und denen ich bekannt waren, hatten Zutritt, um meistens bis in den hellen Morgen hinein zu spielen."

Die Heirat einer „Zauberfee" und die Folgen

Eines Nachts betrat eine junge Frau von der *Heilsarmee* das verdunkelte Lokal in Barmbek, um einige „Kriegsrufe" zu verkaufen. Petersen verliebte sich auf der Stelle in die bildhübsche Frau und kaufte der „Zauberfee" an diesem und den folgenden Abenden alle „Kriegsrufe" ab, die sie bei sich hatte. Daraus wurde die große Liebe und dann 1911 die Ehe.

Glaubt man Petersen, so verfiel seine Frau dem Luxusleben: „Dieser anspruchsvolle Lebenswandel meiner Frau kostete viel Geld, was ich mit ehrlicher Hände Arbeit nicht erreichen konnte. Ihre Wünsche aber zu erfüllen, war mir jedes Mittel recht." Er sah sich gezwungen, zur Geldbeschaffung immer neue Einbrüche zu organisieren, schrieb er in seinen Lebenserinnerungen, aber wahrscheinlich hätte sich die Geschichte aus der Perspektive seiner Frau ganz anders angehört. 1921 wurde die Ehe geschieden.

Die Gründung einer „Einbrechergesellschaft"

Das Alleinsein war nicht von Dauer. Petersen verliebte sich in Frieda Goedje und finanzierte ihr eine Pension in den Colonnaden. Von diesem zentral gelegenen Standort aus organisierte er die Aktivitäten der *Barmbecker Einbrechergesellschaft*, an denen einschließlich der Hehler über 200 Personen mitwirkten. Vor jedem Einbruch verschaffte die Bande allen Beteiligten fingierte Alibis für den Fall, dass sie festgenommen werden sollten. Als Petersen einmal verhaftet worden war, meldeten sich zehn Zeugen, die ihm ein Alibi für die Tatzeit gaben und auch durch Verhöre von diesen Behauptungen nicht abzubringen waren.

Petersen erreichte auf diese Weise einen Freispruch. Der vornehm gekleidete Herr stand erneut als verwegener Lord in der Öffentlichkeit da, dessen Treiben in Frack und Zylinder die Polizei anscheinend nicht beenden konnte. Nach einer weiteren Verhaftung konnte Petersen dank der Unterstützung seiner Bande aus dem Untersuchungsgefängnis flüchten. Zwar nahm die Polizei ihn drei Monate später erneut fest, aber trotz aller Sicherheitsmaßnahmen gelang ihm ein weiteres Mal die Flucht.

Der Ruhm des vornehm gekleideten Bandenchefs

Der Lord von Barmbeck genoss nun seinen Ruhm als Ein- und Ausbrecher. Er war aber bemüht, in der Öffentlichkeit als Ehrenmann dazustehen. Helmut Ebeling zufolge druckte die Tageszeitung „Hamburger Fremdenblatt" am

7. September 1920 die Vermutung, Petersen könnte für einen Raub in Uhlenhorst verantwortlich sein. Daraufhin erschien der Lord von Barmbeck in der Redaktion und verlangte eine Berichtigung: „Ich will Ihnen eins sagen: Ich bin kaufmännischer Angestellter, bin am Pulverteich 25 polizeilich gemeldet und habe mit der Sache nichts zu tun. Und wenn es Sie interessiert: Ich bin überhaupt kein Einbrecher, sondern höchstens Ausbrecher! Das sollten Sie wissen!"

Gern stilisierte sich Petersen zum Verfechter der Anliegen der Armen, und es ist überliefert, dass er mit einigen Barmbeker Straßenjungen in ein Kaufhaus zog und sie auf seine Kosten neu einkleiden ließ. Er raubte nie armen Leute etwas, schon deshalb nicht, weil dort nicht viel zu holen war. Er schoss nie auf seine Verfolger, auch wenn er manchmal damit drohte.

Unvergessen ist eine Szene auf den Dächern der ABC-Straße. Die Polizisten riefen Petersen zu: „Kommen Sie runter, sonst schießen wir rauf!" Petersen rief geistesgegenwärtig zurück: „Kommen Sie ja nicht rauf, sonst schieße ich runter!" Danach setzte er sich über das nächste Dach ab und ward nicht mehr gesehen.

Verhaftung in der Wohnung seines Verhältnisses

In der Pension seiner Freundin verhaftete ihn die Polizei 1921. Im Polizeibericht lesen wir: ,,Am 29. Juni abends gegen 8.30 Uhr wurde der Beschuldigte Adolf Petersen in der Wohnung seines Verhältnisses Frieda Goedje, Colonnaden 21, angetroffen. Bei Betreten der Wohnung leugnete die Goedje die Anwesenheit des Petersen ab. Als wir trotzdem die Zimmer durchsuchten und eines der

Zimmer öffneten, sahen wir, wie Petersen gerade einem Kleiderschrank entstieg ..."

1922 kam es zu einem spektakulären Prozess. Der Untersuchungsrichter machte Petersen in einem Bericht dieses Kompliment: „Seine Einbrüche und Überfälle sind in geradezu bewundernswürdiger Weise organisiert. Soweit bekannt, ist es in der letzten Zeit noch nie gelungen, die Täter in flagranti abzufassen." Aber die Bewunderung ging selbstverständlich nicht so weit, den Bandenchef mit Milde zu behandeln. Da kam es dem Gericht zugute, dass Petersen ein Geständnis über 49 Einbrüche und Raubdelikte ablegte. Nach eigenen Angaben verließ er sich dabei auf die Zusage des Richters, er würde durch das Geständnis eine milde Strafe erhalten.

So viele Zuschauer wollten den Prozess miterleben, dass Eintrittskarten ausgegeben werden mussten. Die Zeitungen waren voll von Berichten über die Taten der *Barmbecker Verbrechergesellschaft*. Im März 1924 verurteilte das Gericht Petersen entgegen aller Zusagen zu 15 Jahren Zuchthaus, aber 1932 entließ man ihn vorzeitig auf Bewährung. Er zog wieder zu seiner Freundin Frieda Goedje, setzte seine kriminelle Karriere fort und wurde im Juni 1933 erneut festgenommen.

Das Ende eines sehr bewegten Lebens

Als Petersen am Abend des 21. November 1933 im Untersuchungsgefängnis saß, war seine Berühmtheit bereits im Schwinden. Neue Herren regierten das Land. Er wusste, dass die Räuber- und Gendarmzeit vorbei war, und er hatte keine Aussicht mehr, seine Freiheit jemals zurückzuerlangen. Er nahm sich in der Nacht das Leben.

Der Schriftsteller Jürgen Ehlers, der sich intensiv mit dem Leben des Lords von Barmbeck befasst und dessen Lebenserinnerungen veröffentlicht hat, kam im März 2022 im NDR zu einem ernüchternden Ergebnis: „Petersen hat sich bemüht, als Gentleman aufzutreten, aber er war kein Gentleman. Er war ein Verbrecher durch und durch."

Das letzte Wort in diesem Kapitel soll Adolf Petersen selbst haben: „Nicht das Leben eines Grandseigneurs noch jenes, welches berufen ist, in dem Ahnensaal seiner Väter zu glänzen, kann ich schildern, sondern ein Leben, das mit seinen Erlebnissen weit über das Maß des Gewöhnlichen hinausgeht, aber nach unseren kulturellen Begriffen ein gescheitertes ist."

Schöne Marianne

Johanna Maria Carolina Ruaux, geboren am 2. Juli 1802, war die Tochter einer französischen Einwandererfamilie in Altona. Ihr Vater Jean Francois Ruaux war 1797 vor der Gewaltherrschaft nach der Französischen Revolution an die Elbe geflüchtet, seine Frau Louise Henriette gehörte ebenfalls zur großen Gruppe der Exilfranzosen im Hamburger Raum.

Die Familie war katholisch und ließ die Tochter Marianne in der St. Josephskirche an der Großen Freiheit taufen. Der Vater betätigte sich als Wäscher und Bleicher, aber trotz harter Arbeit lebte er mit Frau und zwei Kindern in Armut. Die französische Herrschaft in Hamburg ab 1806 löste eine Wirtschaftskrise aus, die auch das dänisch regierte Altona traf. Die Familie Ruaux verlor ihr kleines Haus und den größten Teil ihrer Habe. Sie musste ihr bisheriges Haus anschließend mieten. Zusammen mit seinem Sohn baute Jean Ruaux nach dem Ende der Franzosenzeit 1814 ein kleines Fuhrgeschäft auf.

Als die Männer zum Lokal „Mariannenruh" pilgerten

In den 1820er Jahren erholten sich Hamburg und Altona wirtschaftlich, und wie so häufig nach Krisen wollten sich die Leute wieder vergnügen. Davon profitierte auch das damals noch ländliche Eimsbüttel. In einem zeitgenössischen Bericht heißt es: „Es herrscht eine große Genuß-, Vergnügungs- und Schaulust. Jede Schenkwirtschaft, wo sich eine gefällige Schenkjungfer zeigt, wird stark besucht."

Hier eröffnete Marianne Ruaux 1824 das Wirtshaus *Mariannenruh*. Genau genommen lag das Lokal schon in Langenfelde, wurde aber vor allem von den Besuchern Eimsbüttels frequentiert. Die junge Wirtin zog von Anfang an die Männer der weiten Umgebung in ihren Bann.

In der Ausgabe von 1826 des Fremdenführers „Hamburg und Hamburgs Umgegenden“ wird das Lokal so beschrieben: „Seit einiger Zeit ist Eimsbüttel auch noch durch das am andern Ende des Dorfes liegende Gasthaus der sogenannten schönen Marianne, der Tochter eines Franzosen Ruaux, zu einer der beliebtesten Landpartien des Hamburgischen und Altonaischen Publikums, wie aller nach Hamburg kommenden Fremden, geworden. Das Lokal besteht nur aus einem kleinen Haus und Garten, aber die Besitzerin, die zugleich auch eine sehr angenehme und gefällige Wirtin ist, zeichnet sich in der Tat durch eine seltene, in keinem der beiden von ihr bis jetzt erschienenen lithographischen Bildnisse erreichten Schönheit ihrer Gestalt und Gesichtsbildung aus.“

Auch Berühmtheiten wie der Dichter Ludwig Börne pilgerten nach Langenfelde. Heinrich Heine beschrieb Marianne als „ein außergewöhnlich schönes Frauenzimmer“. Auch viele Maler scharten sich um sie, und es sind einige Porträts der schönen Frau erhalten geblieben.

Die Polizei musste für Ordnung sorgen

Groß war die Zahl der Artikel und Gedichte, die der Schönen Marianne gewidmet wurden, aber nicht immer entsprach die Dichtkunst ihrer Schönheit:

O Göttin, blumenreiche Schöne!
Zauberin am Herzaltar!
Sieh versammelt Teutos Söhne,
Eine ganze Heldenschar!
Bei Dir zu schlürfen den Nektar.
****
Welche Wonne, welch Entzücken,
Solch ein Wesen an das Herz zu drücken.

Und auch dieser Vers ist überliefert worden:

Amor kam, riß sie zu sehen
Sich die Binde vom Gesicht,
Plötzlich von dem Glanz entzündet,
der aus ihren Augen bricht,
Ruft er: Grazien verbindet
Hurtig wieder mein Gesicht,
Wahrlich im Olympus findet
Man so eine Schönheit nicht!

So oder so ähnlich schwärmten Hunderte Hamburger Männer von der schönen Wirtin Marianne. Heiraten durfte sie keiner von ihnen, jedenfalls lange Zeit nicht. Und als sie heiratete, war der „Mariannen-Kult“ bereits Geschichte.

Aber zunächst kamen so viele „Helden“, dass das Lokal einen stattlichen Eintrittspreis verlangen konnte und trotzdem so viel Publikum herbeiströmte, dass zeitweise die Polizei für Ordnung sorgen musste. „La belle Marianne" war über die Landesgrenzen hinaus eine Berühmtheit.

Die Traurigkeit der schönen Marianne

Das Geheimnis der schönen Marianne war wahrscheinlich ihr melancholisches Lächeln und ihre hinter der Freundlichkeit durchschimmernde tiefe Traurigkeit, die so ganz dem Zeitgeist entsprach. Zu ihrer Traurigkeit gab es auch eine Geschichte, die - wenn auch nicht wahr - so doch schön erfunden ist: Eines Tages brachte man der schönen Marianne ein Ölgemälde von einem Jüngling, der seinen Namen verschwieg, aber ihr mitteilen ließ, er liebe allein sie auf der Welt. Sie verliebte sich in das Bild und hoffte inständig, dass der Jüngling bald zu ihr kommen möge.

Umso größer war ihr Schrecken, als eben dieser junge Mann, ein neapolitanischer Edelmann, auf einer Bahre in ihr Haus getragen wurde. Er war bei einem Pistolenduell schwer verletzt worden, und die Wirtin räumte sofort ihr Schlafzimmer für ihn. Dort starb er. Zurück blieb ihre unendlich große Traurigkeit. Der Lokalhistoriker Armin Clasen, der 1972 die Biografie „Die schöne Marianne“ veröffentlicht hat, fand bei seinen akribischen Archivstudien keinen Hinweis darauf, dass ein solches Duell in Eimsbüttel damals tatsächlich stattgefunden hat.

Sechs Jahre währte die öffentliche Anbetung Mariannes, deren Augen, so ein Bewunderer, „wie der Plöner See schmachtend dalagen“. Sie war mit ihrem Lokal so erfolgreich, dass eine ganze Reihe von konkurrierenden „Mariannen-Wirtschaften“ in Eimsbüttel und Hamburg entstanden, Wirtshäuser, in denen Frauen hinter der Theke standen. Marianne selbst geriet allmählich in Vergessenheit, begleitet vom Spott von Zeitgenossen wie Heinrich Heine, der über sie schrieb, dass „der Zahn der Zeit“ an ihr „kaut“. Das provozierte auch andere zu herabwürdigender Kritik an der Wirtin. Schöne Frauen, die älter wurden, verloren rasch ihren Reiz für die Männerwelt.

Es kam noch schlimmer. Als Marianne ein uneheliches Kind erwartete, schloss sie ihr Lokal 1830, brachte ihre Tochter heimlich zur Welt und musste sie in Pflege geben. Der Vater, ein junger Hamburger Kaufmann, entzog sich jeglicher Verantwortung und wanderte in die Vereinigten Staaten aus. In Eimsbüttel eröffnete die immer noch Schöne Marianne ein kleineres neues Lokal, konnte aber nicht an ihre früheren Erfolge anknüpfen.

Das belastete Alter einer berühmten Frau

1836 heiratete Marianne Ruaux den Hamburger Kaufmann Robert Schindler. Gemeinsam eröffneten sie ein Lokal in Hamburg, aber der Ehemann war so ungeeignet für diese Aufgabe, dass auch seine tatkräftige Frau den raschen Niedergang des Lokals nicht verhindern konnte, sodass 1842 Konkurs angemeldet werden musste und die Familie das Haus zu räumen hatte. Freunde von Marianne aus besseren Zeiten halfen der Familie und 1844 konnte ein neues Lokal eröffnet werden. Allerdings war die geistige Umnachtung von Robert Schindler so weit fortgeschritten, dass er arbeitsunfähig war. Freunde versuchten, erneut zu helfen, aber im August 1848 war die Familie zahlungsunfähig. Im folgenden Jahr starb Robert Schindler in einer Klinik.

Er hinterließ die Mutter von inzwischen fünf Kindern in tiefer Armut. Und wieder waren Freunde zur Stelle und ermöglichten es, dass sie ein kleines Hotel an der Großen Theaterstraße eröffnen und später ihren Lebensabend in Eimsbüttel verbringen konnte. Als würdige alte Dame sprach sie mit Freunden gern darüber, wie früher die Leute Schlange gestanden hatten, um ihre schönen Augen zu sehen. Am 4. Juli 1882, zwei Tage nach ihrem 80. Geburtstag, starb Marianne Ruaux. Sie hatte ihren eigenen Mythos um ein halbes Jahrhundert überlebt, aber bewiesen, dass eine Frau mit großem Erfolg ein Lokal führen kann.

Ihr Biograf Armin Clasen schrieb am Ende seines Buches: „Von Schriftstellern gepriesen, von Malern und Lithographen porträtiert, von den Zeitgenossen in den Himmel gehoben, ist uns die ‚Schöne Marianne' als ein strahlender Stern am Himmel hamburgischer Gastlichkeit bekannt geworden. Aus höchsten Höhen überirdischer Schönheit stürzte sie, verraten von ihrem Liebhaber ... in das schwere Schicksal, das sie an einen lebensuntüchtigen und ihrer nicht würdigen Mann band, dem sie auch dann noch, als er völlig irre und kindisch wurde, eine treusorgende Ehegattin blieb. Mit welch beispielloser Energie war sie nach seinem Tod ihren Kindern die fürsorglichste Mutter."

Die *Patriotische Gesellschaft* hat am Eimsbütteler Marktplatz einen Gedenkstein für die Schöne Marianne aufstellen lassen, dort, wo ihr Ausflugslokal zum Anziehungspunkt für viele Hamburger Männer wurde. Die Inschrift des Gedenksteins lautet:

„Sie bediente schon in jungen Jahren die Gäste in der väterlichen Wirtschaft ‚Mariannenruh', die sie später übernahm. Das hier in der ehemaligen Emmausbleiche gelegene Lokal wurde wegen der Schönheit der Wirtin berühmt. Sie wurde weit über die Grenzen Hamburgs hinaus bekannt. Auch Heinrich Heine zählte zu ihren zahlreichen Bewunderern. ‚Mariannenwirtschaft' wurde in der Folgezeit ein Begriff für ein Lokal mit weiblicher Bedienung."

Wilhelm Marr

„Marr ist größer als Gastwirt denn als Dichter und die Schellfische, welche man bei ihm ißt, sind bei weitem besser als seine Poesie!" Das schrieb ein Zeitgenosse über Wilhelm Marr (geboren 1769). Heinrich Heine nahm „Marrs Tragödien" unter die zehn „Merkwürdigkeiten Hamburgs" auf.

Ein anonym gebliebener Zeitgenosse Marrs schrieb über den dichtenden Gastwirt: „Zu den Hamburger Originalen zählte damals auch der alte Marr, der Gastwirt und Volksdramendichter par exellence. Ich habe freilich den Dichtungen Marr's, trotz ihrer unleugbaren Originalität und Kühnheit der Konzeption, nie einen besonderen Geschmack abgewinnen können, desto besser ließ ich mir die Beefsteaks, die Mockturtle-Ragouts, Oxtail-, Krebs- und Aal-Suppe im ‚Alten König von England' schmecken."

Der erfolgreiche Hotelier und Gastronom

Hätte Marr sich auf die Leitung seiner beiden Hotels beschränkt, auf das *Hotel zum Russischen Kaiser* und das Hotel *König von England*, so wäre er allenfalls wegen seiner viel gerühmten Küche in Erinnerung geblieben. Auch dass Lord Nelson und Lady Hamilton im Jahr 1800 im *König von England* logierten, ist weitgehend in Vergessenheit geraten. Mit seinen Dichtungen und seinem Lebensweg zählt Marr noch immer zu den originellsten Originalen der Stadt.

Der Theaterhistoriker Paul Möhring hat über das Hotel *König von England* und seinen Besitzer geschrieben: „Es war ihm gelungen, dies Hotel zum Verkehrsmittelpunkt der Hamburger Theaterleute sowie auch der auswärtigen bedeutenden Schauspieler zu machen, die auf Hamburger Brettern gastierten. Man stieg bei Marr ab, weil man hier vortrefflich wohnte, ausgezeichnet speiste, vorbildlich bedient wurde und der Wirt sich alle erdenkliche Mühe gab, seinen Gästen den Aufenthalt so angenehm wie möglich zu machen. Schauspielern gegenüber war Marr großzügig; manchen Minderbemittelten unter ihnen unterstütze er finanziell oder ließ ihn unentgeltlich an seiner Mittagstafel teilnehmen."

Ein freigiebiger Hotelier fördert Schauspieler

Wilhelm Marr gebührt also ein ehrenvoller Platz unter den Hamburger Originalen, dem ein trauriges Alter erspart blieb, sondern dessen Leben mit einem furiosen Theatererfolg dem Ende entgegenging. Oft saß Wilhelm Marr an der Spitze der langen Mittagstafel und unterhielt die Gäste mit Geschichten, meist den immer gleichen Geschichten. Der großzügige Hotelier und Gastwirt lud auch arme Mitbürger zum Mittagessen ein. Er erwartete von ihnen kluge Beiträge zum Tischgespräch sowie am Ende jeder seiner eigenen Geschichten die Bestätigung dieser Gäste mit dem Satz: „Jo, so weer dat." Wenn ein Freigast eine Geschichte zum Besten gab, kommentierte der Wirt dies seinerseits mit dem Satz: „Jo, so weer dat."

Gern begrüßte Marr auswärtige und hiesige Schauspieler und Musiker in seinem Hotel *König von England* und in seiner Gaststube. Er bewirtete sie besonders zuvorkommend, sodass sein Hotel rasch zum Treffpunkt der Schauspieler der Stadt wurde. Auswärtige Schauspieler mussten allerdings über „eine gefüllte Börse disponieren“, erfahren wir von einem Zeitgenossen, der in diesem Zusammenhang über den Hotelbesitzer schrieb, „gute Rechnungen verstand er zu schreiben“.

Diese Auffassung teilte der englische Dichter Coleridge, der kurz vor Lord Nelson nach Hamburg kam und einem Freund, der ebenfalls die Stadt besuchen wollte, riet: „Willst Du aber in einen englischen Gasthof gehen, so meide um Gottes willen das Haus ‚Shakespeare‘ in Altona und den ‚König von England‘ in Hamburg. Ich gebe ihnen eher den Namen Neppbuden als den Namen anständiger Häuser.“

Lord Nelson und seine Gesellschaft wohnten also nicht erstklassig, aber teuer im Hotel *König von England*. Es muss aber hinzugefügt werden, dass Coleridge große Vorbehalte gegen deutsche Hotels hatte und nicht überliefert ist, dass Lord Nelson und Lady Hamilton sich über ihre Hotelunterkunft beschwert haben, aber teuer, das war sie schon.

Der dichtende Hotelbesitzer

Marr hatte eigene Ambitionen und wollte selbst in der Theaterwelt reüssieren. Da er seine berufliche Laufbahn als Schlachter begonnen hatte, nutzte er seine Kenntnisse in diesem Milieu und verfasste das Theaterstück „Der Schlachter auf Reisen oder das totgeglaubte Kind“. In das Stück nahm er eigne Erlebnisse als Wandergeselle und Geschichten aus seiner Fantasie auf und soll das Ergebnis als überaus gelungen empfunden haben. Deshalb war er hoch erfreut, dass die Uraufführung des Stücks im Juni 1808 im *Steinstraßen-Theater* stattfand. Das

Publikum war begeistert, und die Hamburger strömten in Scharen in die Aufführungen.

Das bewahrte Marr nicht davor, dass Theaterkritiker heftig über sein Stück herfielen, allein schon deshalb, weil er nicht vom Fach war. Johannes Sass hat diese Kritik in seinem Buch „Hamburger Originale und originelle Hamburger" so zusammengefasst: „Die Schauspieler mögen dem Stück zu einigem Erfolg verholfen haben, aber der Dichter erntete keine Lorbeeren. In Broschüren und Flugblättern, in Zeitschriften und Zeitungen fielen die Kritiker über ihn her und suchten, den Schlachterpoeten lächerlich zu machen Witzbolde dichteten in ‚Schlachtermanier' und verhöhnten den Verfasser des reisenden Schlachters."

Ein großzügiges Angebot an die Kritiker

Wie Marr auf diese heftige Kritik reagiert hat, wird von Chronisten unterschiedlich dargestellt. Sicher ist, dass er in einer Zeitungsanzeige den Kritikern seinen Dank aussprach. Zukünftigen Kritikern machte er in den „Gemeinnützigen Unterhaltungsblättern" in der Ausgabe vom 30. Juli 1808 folgendes Angebot:

„Jeder der künftig etwas gegen mich schreibt, bringe mir den ersten Abdruck seiner Schrift und legitimiere sich bei mir als der wirkliche Verfasser. Er soll dann drei Tage hintereinander in meinem Gasthof zum Russischen Kaiser in der Dammtorstraße Nr. 30 mit den ausgesuchtesten Speisen und den feinsten Weinen unentgeltlich bewirtet werden, zum Beweise, dass ich erkenntlich gegen diejenigen sein kann, die zu meinem Vergnügen etwas beigetragen haben."

Zunächst wagte kein Kritiker, dieses Angebot anzunehmen, stand der ehemalige Schlachter doch im Ruf, sehr schlagkräftig zu sein. Es war nicht sicher, ob die Kritiker nicht doch seine Fäuste zu spüren bekommen würden. Nach einer Weile war es ein gewisser J. John, der den Mut fand, das Angebot anzunehmen und ein Gedicht über Marr zu veröffentlichen. Das Gedicht zeugte mehr vom Mut des Verfassers als von seinen Fähigkeiten als Poet. Es sollen hier drei Verse als Beispiel für Schmähgedichte zu dieser Zeit wiedergegeben werden:

Schweig, schweig Herr Marr! Wenn dir noch ist zu raten
Und meid doch Komödi
Treib' was du kannst, so hast du keinen Schaden
Und wirst bezahlt für deine Müh!

Du kannst doch nur für nied're Geister denken,
Wirst stets den aufgeklärten Mann
Mit dem Geschmier und schlechten Stücken kränken,
Die er durchaus nicht leiden kann.

Die kluge Welt wird Dich dafür verfluchen,
Die Deine Schrift mit Ekel sieht,
Wer hieß dich, sie mit Schauspiele heimzusuchen
Für die der Teufel selber flieht?

Wonach stand Wilhelm Marr nach solchen Versen der Sinn, nach festlichen Essen oder Faustschlägen? Wir werden es nie erfahren. Zwar lud Marr den Schreiber des Schmähgedichts zu sich ein. Albert Borcherdt hat die Antwort in seinem Buch „Das lustige alte Hamburg“ so zusammengefasst: „Als Marr dieses Machwerk zu Gesicht bekam, verfehlte er nicht, ein ironisches Dankesschreiben an Herrn John zu erlassen, in welchem er dem genialen Dichter über das gelieferte Meisterwerk seine höchste Bewunderung aussprach, die Kraft und Reinheit seiner Poesie, sowie die originelle Rechtschreibung pries und innig wünschte, die Bekanntschaft seines gelehrten Gegners zu machen."

Es kam trotzdem nicht zu der Begegnung. Denn vorher meldete sich der Schneider und Dichter Erbshäuser bei Marr und wies ihn darauf hin, dass das Gedicht von ihm stamme. Es wäre in einem seiner Bücher erschienen. Erbshäuser schrieb daraufhin ein Schmähgedicht gegen John. Ob Marr danach Erbshäuser eingeladen hat, lässt sich nicht mehr feststellen. In jedem Fall ging Marr als Sieger aus der Auseinandersetzung mit John hervor.

Ein folgenreicher Scherz von Vetter Kirchhoff

Marr focht die Kritik an seinem Stück nicht an. Nachdem es eine Weile im eher volkstümlichen *Steinstraßen-Theater* gespielt worden war, strebte er nun an, dass es auch im prestigeträchtigen *Stadttheater* in der Innenstadt zur Aufführung kommen sollte. Er muss dieses Anliegen wohl zu oft bei seinen Gästen angesprochen haben; jedenfalls erlaubten sich einige Schauspieler und andere Freunde einen Scherz mit Marr. Darunter war Vetter Kirchhoff, der bereits in diesem Buch vorgestellt wurde und der die exzellente Küche im *König von England* und die munteren Tischgespräche sehr schätzte.

Zu dieser Zeit spielte gerade der bekannte Schauspieler Wagner von der Dresdner Hofbühne in Altona. Er konnte von Kirchhoff dafür gewonnen werden, Marr aufzusuchen und ihm zu übermitteln, die Dresdner Hofbühne wolle sein Stück aufführen. Er bat um eine Abschrift des Textes, die Marr eilfertig anfertigen und in Leder binden ließ. Zum Dank lud er den Schauspieler ein, für den Rest seines Aufenthalts kostenlos im feinsten Zimmer seines Hotels zu wohnen und fürstlich zu dinieren, was der Schauspieler dann auch genoss.

Marr war mächtig stolz und dies noch mehr, als ihm eine Weile später ein gefälschter Brief der Hofbühne zugesandt wurde, in dem von einem ungeheuren Beifall bei der Aufführung des Stücks die Rede war. Dem Brief lag ein ebenfalls gefälschter Theaterzettel bei, aus dem zu entnehmen war, dass bekannte Schauspieler an der Aufführung mitgewirkt hatten.

Marr war glückselig und ließ den Theaterzettel in einen wertvollen Rahmen fassen. Die Freude währte allerdings nur kurze Zeit. Denn bald darauf kam der Schauspieler Devrient, der angeblich die Hauptrolle gespielt haben sollte, nach Hamburg und logierte wie viele auswärtige Schauspieler im *König von England*. Nach einer anderen Überlieferung war es der Schauspieler Ludwig Ferdinand Pauli, aber der Name tut nicht viel zur Sache.

Jedenfalls wusste der Dresdner Schauspieler nichts von dem Scherz und war total überrumpelt, als Marr ihn begeistert begrüßte, ihm um den Hals fiel und den gerahmten Theaterzettel präsentierte. Der Schauspieler war so überrascht, dass er die Sache nicht durchschaute, sondern statt mitzuspielen, dem Hotelier sagte, es müsse ein Irrtum vorliegen und der Theaterzettel wäre eine Fälschung. Der Schauspieler Wagner soll nach diesem Eklat bei Gastspielen in Hamburg nie wieder im *König von England* gewohnt oder auch nur gespeist haben.

Erfolg mit dem Stück „Der Sieg der Tugend"

Der Gastwirt Marr erfuhr nie, dass Vetter Kirchhoff hinter dem Scherz gesteckt hatte. Tief enttäuscht ließ er längere Zeit von seinen Theaterambitionen ab. Aber dann schrieb er doch ein neues Stück mit dem Titel „Die Vorfälle beim Fallissement oder die Tugend siegt". Das Stück kam im April 1837 im *Steinstraßen-Theater* zur Aufführung. Die Freunde, die ihm den üblen Streich gespielt hatten, waren offenbar zum Ergebnis gekommen, dass Marr eine Wiedergutmachung verdient hatte, und feierten ihn nach der Uraufführung des neuen Stücks begeistert. Albert Borcherdt hat dies so beschrieben: „Nachdem das Stück unter großem Beifall zu Ende gespielt war, ist Marr von seinen Freunden hervorgerufen worden, und als er strahlend vor innerer Genugtuung auf der Bühne erschien, hat man ihn mit Lorbeerkränzen, Lobgedichten, Hurras und Tuschblasen überaus gefeiert."

Das hat auch Paul Möhring in seinem Theaterbuch „Bühne frei" bestätigt, allerdings hinzugefügt: „Das Stück erwies sich als recht belanglose Angelegenheit ohne dichterische Tiefe, dafür aber mit vielen Phrasen und moralischen Gemeinplätzen. Dem Publikum jedoch gefiel es, und die Darsteller waren mit Liebe und Eifer bei der Sache." Paul Möhring berichtet davon, wie sich nach Schluss der Veranstaltung eine unübersehbare Menschenmenge vor dem Theater versammelte und Marr hoch leben ließ. Anschließend gab es eine große Feier im

König von England. Marr erklärte an diesem Abend wiederholt: „Das war der schönste Tag meines Lebens!"

Der Erfolg seines Stückes soll Marr seinen inneren Frieden und seinen Humor zurückgegeben haben. Er wird mit großer Freude erlebt haben, dass sein Sohn Heinrich große Erfolge als Schauspieler feiern konnte. Paul Möhring schrieb über ihn, dass er „einer der ganz Großen des deutschen Schauspiels" im 19. Jahrhundert war, der „erste Mephisto der deutschen Bühne".

Drei Jahre nach der Uraufführung seines zweiten Stücks starb Wilhelm Marr im Alter von 71 Jahren. Sein letzter Wille war, dass ihm alle Schlachter der Stadt ein letztes Geleit geben sollten. Und tatsächlich waren unter der Trauergesellschaft für dieses Hamburger Original zahlreiche Hamburger Schlachter.

Emil Naucke

Emil Naucke kam am 2. Mai 1855 auf der Insel Poel zur Welt. Sein Vater betrieb dort eine Tabakhandlung. Emil soll schon als Säugling ein Gewicht von 14 Kilogramm erreicht haben und war bald übergewichtig, wie wir es heute nennen würden. Trotzdem war er gelenkig und versuchte sich sogar als Seiltänzer. Der Junge war fasziniert von Artisten und Komödianten. Heimlich schloss er sich noch als Heranwachsender einer Zirkusgesellschaft an und reiste mit ihr kreuz und quer durch Europa. Seine Eltern starteten eine Suchaktion und konnten ihn unter Mühen in die Heimat zurückholen. Was dann geschah, hat Lars Amenda in seiner Biografie Nauckes („Der schwerste Radfahrer der Welt!“) so beschrieben:

„Im Gegensatz zu ihrem Sprössling waren seine Eltern ganz und gar nicht angetan von der brotlosen Kunst der Unterhaltungsbranche. Sie bestimmten, dass Emil eine Lehre als Bäcker machen musste. Immerhin konnte er die Zeit mit – in seinen Augen – sinnvollen Dingen nutzen und trainierte sich mit ‚Exercitien mit Mehlsäcken‘ ganz nebenbei ‚zum künftigen Athleten‘. Wohl auch wegen dieses Mehlsack-Workouts entwickelten sich seine Muskeln im Alter von 15 Jahren recht erheblich.“

1873 setzte Emil Naucke sich durch und wurde Artist. In Hamburg fand er eine Anstellung im *St. Georg-Theater*. Genaueres über seine artistische Arbeit in diesem Unterhaltungstheater ist nicht bekannt. Anschließend trat er in einem Lokal in Eimsbüttel als Berufsringer auf. Das Ringen war damals eine Mischung von sportlichem Ringen und Show. Naucke trat nun auf Bühnen und in Zirkussen sowohl als Artist als auch als Ringer auf.

Ein schwergewichtiger Artist löste Begeisterung aus

Später konzentrierte er sich wieder ganz auf die Artistik. Er lebte in Hamburg, unternahm aber viele Tourneen in andere deutsche und europäische Städte. Zwischen St. Petersburg und Bordeaux beeindruckte er das Publikum mit seiner Kraft und seinen artistischen Fähigkeiten.

Die „Hamburger Freie Presse" beschrieb damals seine Auftritte so: „Emil Naucke schleuderte eine eiserne Kugel von ungefähr 70 Pfund, welche an einer Kette befestigt ist, durch die Luft, um sie dann mit seinem Genick aufzufangen. Zweitens streckte er eine Hantel von 212 Pfund mit einer Hand."

Naucke war aber nicht nur ein gewichtiger „Kraftmensch" von zeitweise 230 Kilogramm Gewicht und 190 Zentimetern Bauchumfang, sondern gleichzeitig ein behänder Artist mit erstaunlicher Gewandtheit und viel Humor. Auch abseits von den Bühnen der Welt soll er ein vergnügter Mensch gewesen sein.

„Pauline vom Ballett" und der Partner Peter Hansen

Naucke gründete 1880 ein eigenes Unternehmen, die *Tournee Naucke*. Selbstverständlich trat er selbst dort auf, engagierte aber auch andere Artisten, um eine abwechslungsreich Show anbieten zu können. Großes Aufsehen erregte Naucke in Frauenkleidern als „Pauline vom Ballett" und wurde ob seiner Beweglichkeit trotz großen Gewichts bestaunt. Er war jetzt regelmäßig auf dem Hamburger Winterdom zu sehen.

Naucke fand einen für seine zunehmend von Komik geprägten Auftritte einen idealen Partner, den Gastwirt Peter Hansen. Dieser war nur 98 Zentimeter groß und sehr dünn. Lars Amenda schreibt über ihre Auftritte: „Naucke und Hansen bildeten damit ein ungleiches Paar, das ihre jeweiligen körperlichen Besonderheiten durch ihr Gegenüber noch einmal verstärkten.

Das damalige Publikum belustigte bereits der Anblick des schwergewichtigen Naucke und des leichten und kleinen Hansen ... Sie traten aber darüber hinaus als Akteure, als Darsteller von selbst geschriebenen ‚Burlesken' auf, wie die derb-komischen und teilweise improvisierten Stücke seinerzeit genannt wurden." Man feierte Naucke und Hansen als Erfolgsduo.

Carl Thinius hat in seinem St-Pauli-Buch die Auftritte Nauckes beschrieben: „Wenn er als ‚Pauline vom Ballett' im kurzen Röckchen süß lächelnd auf der Bühne tanzte und sich von dem 80 Zentimeter kleinen Peter Hansen, einem Mitglied des Ensembles, den Hof machen ließ, erntete er jedesmal im Zuschauerraum Lachstürme. Neue Besucher wurden von der Grazie und der Beschwingtheit des Athleten-Tänzers geradezu überrascht."

Von Anfang 1887 bis Ende 1888 unternahm Naucke mit seiner Truppe eine sehr erfolgreiche Tournee durch die USA. Nach der Rückkehr von der anstrengenden Reise suchte Naucke erst einmal Ruhe und erwarb eine Villa in Bad Oldesloe. Hamburg war nahe genug, um dort seine künstlerische Karriere fortzusetzen.

War Naucke nur ein „aufgeblasener" Artist?

Es gab gelegentlich Zweifel, ob Naucke wirklich einen solchen gewaltigen Körperumfang hatte. Johannes Sass hat in seinem Buch über die Hamburger Originale eine solche Begebenheit überliefert. Zwei Bauern besuchten das Varieté, und bei der Ballettnummer kamen einem von ihnen Zweifel: „Du, Hinnerk, weetst wat? De Kerl is nich echt, de is oppust." Sein Reisegefährte wollte die Vermutung des aufgeblasenen Artisten aber nicht übernehmen und verkündete seinem Nachbarn: „De is echt, Willem, dor kannst die op verloten, dat heff ik swatt op witt in't Programm leest." Aber das überzeugte Willem nicht, und sie wetteten um eine Flasche Wein.

Nach dem Ende der Aufführung begaben die beiden sich hinter die Bühne, wo sie auf den Inspizienten trafen. Sie gaben vor, Herrn Naucke einmal guten Tag sagen zu wollen, und der Inspizient wies ihnen den Weg zur Garderobe Nauckes. In der Aufregung verwechselten die beiden aber rechts und links. Sie klopfen deshalb an die Tür von Hansen, der die Besucher hereinbat. Willem kam gleich zur Sache: „Seggen Se mol, Herr, sünd se Emil Naucke?"

Der humorvolle kleine Hansen durchschaute die Situation sofort und immer zu einem Spaß aufgelegt antwortete: „Jo, de bün ik, wat kann ik for Se doon?" Willem sah seinen Mitreisenden triumphierend an und verkündete: „Wat heff ik seggt, Hinnerk? De Kerl weer doch oppuust!" Die Sache endete damit, dass die beiden Besucher in einer nahe gelegenen Bodega die Flasche Wein tranken, die Hinnerk ohne zu murren bezahlte.

Wahrscheinlich ist die Geschichte erfunden, aber sie zeigt, wie sehr die Verbindung von großem Körpergewicht und Behändigkeit, die Naucke zur Schau stellte, seine Zeitgenossen zum Staunen und ins Grübeln brachte. Naucke und Hansen werden in ihrer Kindheit und Jugend häufig ob ihrer von der Norm abweichenden Körpermaße gehänselt und verspottet worden sein. Aber sie besaßen das Selbstbewusstsein, als Erwachsene ihre Körper dem staunenden Publikum zu präsentierten – und das wirkte natürlich besonders bei ihren gemeinsamen Auftritten.

Eröffnung eines eignen Varietés in St. Pauli

1896 kaufte Naucke ein Varieté am Spielbudenplatz und benannte es in *Emil Naucke's Varieté* um. Neben Auftritten des Duos Naucke und Hansen bot der Direktor dem Publikum auch die humoristischen und artistischen Auftritte anderer Künstler. Das Publikum und auch die Presse waren begeistert. Die „Altonaer Nachrichten" berichteten: „Groß und Klein amüsirt sich dabei auf das Köstlichste." Von 1897 an nahm Naucke auch die gerade erst entstandenen Kurzfilme in sein Unterhaltungsprogramm auf.

Als Ende des 19. Jahrhunderts erlebte Hamburg einen Fahrradboom, und auch Naucke kaufte sich ein Rad. Mit seinem beträchtlichen Gewicht radelte er durch die Stadt und fand wieder einmal viel Beachtung. Naucke erkannte sofort das humoristische Potenzial des neuen Fortbewegungsmittels und übte mit Hansen einige Fahrradnummern ein, die, wie zu erwarten war, große Heiterkeit auslösten. Dazu noch einmal Lars Amenda: „Die Naucke wiederholt attestierte Beweglichkeit und überraschende Körperkontrolle wird ihm auch bei den Fahrrad-Aufführungen geholfen haben und ermöglichte ihm überhaupt erst, die körperlich sehr anstrengende Leistung auf dem Fahrrad zu erbringen. Auch als humoristischer Radartist verzichtete Emil Naucke nicht auf seine üblichen Marketingmaßnahmen. Als ‚schwerster Radfahrer der Welt' bewarb sich Naucke selber und machte sich damit abermals zur Marke."

Der Tod auf einem Wohltätigkeitsfest

Naucke und Hansen engagierten sich immer wieder für soziale Vorhaben, so auch am 25. Januar 1900 bei einem Fest in *Sagebiels Etablissement* zugunsten von Kindergärten. Ihr gemeinsamer Auftritt wurde mit „brausendem Beifall" quittiert. Aber der anstrengende Auftritt löste bei dem Artisten Naucke einen Herzinfarkt aus, der zum Tod des erst 44-Jährigen führte.

Drei Tage später fand die Beerdigung statt. Eine Zeitung berichtete am nächsten Tag, dass sich eine „förmliche Völkerwanderung nach St. Pauli" ergoss. Das Varieté des Verstorbenen diente als Trauerkapelle, erwies sich aber als viel zu klein für Tausende Hamburgerinnen und Hamburger, die Abschied von Emil Naucke nehmen wollten.

Nach der Trauerfeier formierte sich ein langer Trauerzug mit mehreren Zehntausend Menschen. Die Popularität Nauckes beruhte auch darauf, dass er sich immer wieder an Wohltätigkeitaktionen beteiligt und auch einzelnen Menschen in Not geholfen hatte. Das Familiengrab der Familie Naucke auf dem *Ohlsdorfer Friedhof* mit dem hohen dunklen Obelisk wurde später von vielen Hamburgerinnen und Hamburgern besucht.

Die Witwe Nauckes führte das Varieté gemeinsam mit Peter Hansen fort, unterstützt von vielen Freunden des Verstorbenen. Ein Jahrzehnt lang konnten Johanna Naucke und Peter Hansen das Varieté erhalten und ein vielfältiges Programm mit Artistik und komischen Nummern anbieten. Aber es fehlte der Artist und Komiker Emil Naucke, und 1911 musste das Varieté verkauft werden.

Oskar vom Pferdemarkt

„... so steht Oskar mit seinem Warenhaus und schmettert mit krähendem Organ seine ulkigen Redensarten in Hamburger Platt oder Missingsch in die Gegend. Unermüdlich sorgt er dabei für Umsatz, wirft Groschen auf Groschen in seine Zigarrenkiste, verkauft nach vorn, nach hinten und nach beiden Seiten. Denn ruhige Minuten kennt er nicht; er ist immer in Hochform – mit den Händen und mit dem Mundwerk. Seine Kundschaft betrachtet er als eine große Familie. Er kennt nur das vertrauliche ‚Du' als Anrede, wünscht aber auch selbst nur als ‚Oskar' angesprochen zu werden." So hat Paul Möhring, der eine Broschüre über „Oskar vom Pferdemarkt" verfasst hat, das Original in den 1930er Jahren erlebt.

„Eine Wucht in Tüten!" war einer der beliebtesten Sprüche von Oskar. Er hatte noch viele andere Sprüche drauf, zum Beispiel „Frech wie Oskar". Manche der Sprüche gingen in den Sprachgebrauch der Hamburgerinnen und Hamburger über. Auch wenn er die Sprüche vermutlich nicht alle erfunden hat, so machte er sie doch populär. Das kam gut an auf dem Pferdemarkt (heute Gerhard-Hauptmann-Platz), und der Stand des Straßenhändlers war meist umlagert. Er erhielt den Ehrentitel „König der Straßenhändler".

Der „Hamburger Anzeiger" schrieb über ihn: „Er ist gewissermaßen ein wanderndes Warenhaus ... Und dazu gibt's bei Oskar eine *Zugabe,* sein köstliches Missingsch, nämlich seinen *drögen Humor.* Er nimmt sich kein Blatt vor den Mund, dieser bewegliche, vierschrötige Kerl, und das mögen die Leute ... Wer lacht nicht gern mal am Straßenrande zwischen Sorgen und ernsten Geschäften. Oskar weiß schon, wo jedem der Schuh drückt."

Keine Karriere als Schauspieler, aber große Erfolge als begnadeter Straßenhändler

Oskar vom Pferdemarkt hieß mit bürgerlichen Namen Fritz Krüger. Er wurde am 11. April 1902 in Hamburg geboren und wuchs in St. Pauli auf. Gern wäre er Schauspieler geworden, aber das kam für die Eltern, der Vater war Schriftsetzer, nicht infrage. Der Sohn sollte etwas Solides lernen und machte eine Schlosserlehre. Er versuchte trotzdem, als Schauspieler zu reüssieren, musste sich aber damit begnügen, als Mitglied des Laien-Theatervereins *Thaliamund von 1911* auf der Bühne zu stehen. Später verkündete er stolz: „Ich hab früher mal im Zigeunerbaron mitgewirkt."

Er entschloss sich, sein Glück als Straßenhändler zu versuchen. Der Anfang war schwer nach dem verlorenen Ersten Weltkrieg angesichts einer hohen Inflation und Massenarbeitslosigkeit. Aber unter den sich allmählich verbessernden wirtschaftlichen Verhältnisse, und zunehmenden eigenen Erfahrungen im Straßenhandel konnte er seine Eloquenz und Witzigkeit zur Geschäftsgrundlage machen und als Oskar vom Pferdemarkt einen hohen Bekanntheitsgrad erreichen. War er zunächst mit einem Bauchladen unterwegs gewesen, konnte er nun einen Verkaufsstand auf dem Pferdemarkt eröffnen.

Der Pferdemarkt wurde seine große Bühne und das fast täglich. Seine Erkennungszeichen waren eine Schlägermütze, ein kariertes Tuch um den Hals und aufgekrempelte Ärmel. An seinem Stand hatte er ein Schild mit diesem Text angebracht: „Sogar dat Bäbi in Kinnerwogen wet, bi Oskar warst nich bedrogen.“ Paul Möhring schreibt zum Erfolg dieses begnadeten Straßenhändlers: „Oskar hat sich im Laufe der Jahre eine nach vielen, vielen Tausend zählende ‚Gemeinde‘ geschaffen. Leute aller Berufsschichten sind seine treue Kundschaft, Leute aller Bildungsgrade stehen an seinem Stand, zu jeder Tageszeit und bei jedem Wetter, um sich durch den Humor dieses urwüchsigen Hamburgers mal so richtig durchschütteln zu lassen. Zu seinen besonderen Lieblingen aber gehörten Kinder.“

Zum bunten Sortiment des Straßenhändlers gehörten Rasierklingen, Schnürsenkel, Taschenmesser und Suppenlöffel. Vor allem bot er nützliche Dinge für Hausfrauen an. Hatte er einmal eine Ware nicht im Angebot, so verwies er die Kunden auf seine „Filiale“, womit er das große Kaufhaus Karstadt nahe seinem Stand an der Mönckebergstraße meinte. Und wenn ein potenzieller Kunde bedauernd erklärte, er habe gerade nicht genügend Geld dabei, verkündete Oskar: „Wer kein Geld hat, langt dem Nebenmann in die Tasche, vielleicht hat der noch was!“

Der Straßenhändler musste Soldat werden

Zu seiner Entlastung stellte Oskar seinen Freund Heini ein, der einen eigenen Stil fand, um das Publikum anzulocken und zu unterhalten. Auch an den Tagen, an denen der Stand am Pferdemarkt von ihm betreut wurde, war er von Käufern umlagert. In seiner Freizeit war Oskar immer gern bereit, an wohltätigen Veranstaltungen mit lustigen Beiträgen mitzuwirken. In den 1930er Jahren ließ er sich auch für nationalsozialistische Vorhaben einspannen wie dem „Winterhilfswerk" und dem „Reichskolonialbund".

Der „König der Straßenhändler" musste seinen erfolgreichen Handel 1940 vorerst beenden, weil er zur Wehrmacht eingezogen wurde. Als er 1945 zurückgekehrt war, eröffnete er eine Kantine im Stadtpark, wo eine große Zahl von Behelfsheimen stand, sogenannte Nissenhütten, halbrunde Wellblechunterkünfte für Tausende Flüchtlinge und Ausgebombte. Als der Wirt 1951 einen handgreiflichen Streit zwischen Gästen schlichten wollte, traf ihn ein heftiger Handkantenschlag, der seinen Kehlkopf zertrümmerte. Dreizehn größere Operationen brachten ihm seine Stimme nicht vollständig zurück.

Der Prozess gegen Oskar und Heini

Sprachlos war Oskar nicht und Humor hatte er noch immer. Das zeigte sich im Dezember 1951, als er zusammen mit seinem Kollegen Heini im Ziviljustizgebäude erscheinen musste. Der Geschäftsführer des Tanzlokals *Café Keese* hatte ihn und seinen Kollegen auf einen Schadensersatz von 1.500 Mark verklagt. Hintergrund war, dass Oskar, Heini und dessen Frau versucht hatten, das Lokal zu betreten. Die beiden Straßenhändler waren in Berufskleidung erschienen: mit Riesenschirmmütze, blauer Arbeitsschürze, sauberem Hemd, Pulli und Halstuch. So wollte der Portier sie nicht hereinlassen. Er rief den Geschäftsführer, der die beiden fragte: „Na, ihr wollt wohl ein Klavier abholen?" Aber da kein Klavier abzuholen war, wollte er die beiden nicht ins Café lassen. Es kam zum Streit, bei dem eine wachsende Zahl von Passanten Partei für die stadtbekannten Oskar und Heini ergriff.

Oskar unterhielt die Anwesenden mit launigen Bemerkungen und Witzen, sodass die Zuhörerschaft immer weiter anwuchs und den Verkehr behinderte. Oskar sagte im Prozess zu seiner Verteidigung: „Wir sind zwei wunderbare Menschen, die auch in die Welt passen. Wir waren auch nicht total besoffen, und wenn so viele Menschen um uns herumstanden, dann liegt das eben an unserer Popularität."

Einige wütende Sympathisanten der Straßenhändler entschlossen sich zu handfesten Argumenten und warfen mit Steinen einige Fenster des Lokals ein. Die herbeigerufene Polizei forderte die beiden Straßenhändler auf abzuhauen. Das taten sie nicht, was Oskar im Prozess gegenüber dem Richter so begründete: „Ich bin doch kein Verbrecher, ich hau nich aff. Das war mein Trotz, Herr Rat."

Der Richter führte die Verhandlung mit Humor. Er habe kürzlich ein Paar Schnürsenkel bei Oskar kaufen wollen, und der hatte ihm geraten: „Nehmen Sie gleich zwei Paar, der Schiet hält ja doch nicht." Es gab Jubel im Zuschauerraum. Der Richter versuchte nun, die beiden Straßenhändler für eine Schadensersatzzahlung zu gewinnen. Lediglich 15 Mark sollten Oskar und Heini jeder zahlen. Der Café-Geschäftsführer, so war im „Hamburger Abendblatt" zu lesen, „wurde ernstlich böse". Die beiden Straßenhändler versuchten, den Richter auf jeweils 10 Mark herunterzuhandeln, aber der blieb bei 15 Mark. Oskar zahlte den Betrag, aber Heini legte Einspruch ein.

Vergeblich. Es blieb bei den 15 Mark. Immerhin erlebte das Publikum eine zweite unterhaltsame Verhandlung mit Heini als Beklagter und Oskar als Zeuge.

Erinnerungen an ein Originals mit großem Verkaufstalent

Trotz seiner Sprachprobleme konnte Oskar an seine großen Erfolge als Straßenhändler anknüpfen. Er war weiterhin schlagfertig und originell, aber die Umstehenden verstanden ihn kaum noch. Oskar vom Pferdemarkt starb am 18. Februar 1969. Aus der Todesanzeige erfuhr man, dass Oskar vom Pferdemarkt gestorben war, und nur in Klammern stand dahinter Fritz Krüger. Seinem Sarg folgten auf dem *Ohlsdorfer Friedhof* neben der Familie auch manche seiner früheren Kundinnen und Kunden. Zu den zufriedenen Kunden gehörte H. Brendel, der dieses Gedicht in der Zeitschrift „Hummel“ veröffentlichte:

Der „Oskar“ auf dem Pferdemarkt
das ist ein Unikum.
Auf seinem Platz umringt ihn stets
Ein lust'ges Publikum.

Er ist nicht nur ein Unikum,
auch ein Verkaufsgenie;
denn was er feilhält zum Verkauf,
verkauft er, wie noch nie.

Ja, er versteht sich auf den Dreh. –
Den Leuten, die da stehn,
versteht er mit Humor und Witz
die Ware anzudreh'n.

Zu seiner Ehre sei gesagt:
- das ist nicht mehr wie recht –
Was er da anpreist mit Humor
Ist billig und nicht schlecht.

Wer einmal was von ihm gekauft,
kommt immer gerne wieder.
Und darum blüht auch sein Geschäft
so wie im Mai der Flieder.

Es gibt von Händlern seiner Art
in Hamburg nur den einen.
Es gibt nur einen „Oskar" hier,
sonst gibt es weiter keinen.

So Oskar, so gefällst du mir,
denn du verstehst den Rummel.
Mach weiter so. – Ich grüße dich
Als Kunde. – Hummel! Hummel!

Noch ein Gedicht? Dieses schickte ein zufriedener Kunde aus dem fernen Bombay (heute Mumbai) an Oskar:

Aus Indiens heißen Gestaden
Denk ich an deinen Laden,
an dem so manche Stunde
stehend ich verbracht,
der Redeschwall aus deinem Munde
hat immer zum Lachen mich gebracht
reimt sich dieser Gruß auch schlecht,
er kommt von Herzen – er ist echt!

Leberecht Pankoken

Gern wäre Leberecht Pankoken ein Musiker im Orchester des Hamburger *Stadttheaters* geworden, einer angesehenen Bühne, auf der sowohl Schauspiele als auch Opern aufgeführt wurden. Pankoken war der Sohn eines Klarinettisten in Krempe und kam in den 1820er Jahren im Alter von zwanzig Jahren nach Hamburg.

Seine Bewerbung beim Stadttheater wurde abgelehnt. Daraufhin beschloss Pankoken, eine eigene kleine Musikgruppe aufzubauen und sich den Lebensunterhalt durch Straßenmusik zu verdienen. Damals konnte er noch nicht ahnen, dass er zum Urvater der Pankokenkapellen werden sollte.

Er suchte sich drei Mitspieler, die Geige, Posaune und Klarinette spielten, er selbst trat mit einer Schalmei auf, manchmal wechselten die Instrumente. Zwar hatte es auch schon vorher Straßenmusiker gegeben, aber die Pankokenkapelle erfreute sich bald einer beträchtlichen Beliebtheit, auch wenn die Herren Musikkritiker sie ignorierten. Sie berichteten über die Opernaufführungen und Konzerte für die reichen und wohlhabenden Kreise der Stadt.

Aber zu dieser Musik hatte die arme Bevölkerung keinen Zugang. Wenn Pankoken und seine Mitspieler mit ihren charakteristischen schwarzen Filzhüten auf einem Platz oder an einer Straßenecke aufspielten, sammelte sich rasch eine Menschenmenge und viele tanzten auch zu den munteren Melodien der Kapelle.

Beliebt auf Straßen und Plätzen

Die Pankokenkapelle besaß – als vermutlich erste Musikgruppe – eine städtische Genehmigung zum Spielen auf Straßen und Plätzen und war vor allem in der Neustadt rund um den Michel unterwegs. Eine Zeitung schrieb damals über die Auftritte von Pankoken & Co.: „Lassen sie ihre Weisen vor eines Handwerkers Haus ertönen, so ergreift Meister, Geselle und Lehrling das Werkzeug noch einmal so schnell. Sollte zwischen Mann, Weib und Kindern ein Donnerwetter im höchsten Grade entstanden sein, so vertreibt die ins Haus hineinströmende fröhliche Musik sogleich alle Gewitterwolken, und man fühlt sich augenblicklich von einem paradiesischen Geiste beseelt." Da machte es dann auch nichts, wenn einer der Musiker einmal nicht den richtigen Ton fand.

Wenn die Pankokenkapelle von manchen etwas spöttisch belächelt wurde, hatte das vor allem einen anderen Grund. Die Straßenmusiker waren auf Spenden der Zuhörerinnen und Zuhörer angewiesen. Hätten die Musiker mit dem Sammeln erst nach dem letzten Stück begonnen, hätte sich die Zuhörerschaft rasch verstreut und Pankoken und seine Musikerkollegen wären leer ausgegangen. Deshalb hörte schon vorher einer der Spieler auf zu spielen und sammelte Geld bei den Umstehenden und in den benachbarten Häusern ein.

Um höhere Einnahmen zu erzielen, unterbrachen auch schon mal ein oder zwei weitere Musiker der kleinen Musikgruppe ihr Spiel und sammelten Geld ein. Meist unterhielt „Direktor Pankoken" dann unverdrossen die Zuhörerschaft allein auf seiner Schalmei. Das soll noch recht gut geklungen haben, aber wenn Pankoken sich am Spendensammeln beteiligte und nur einer seiner Mitspieler allein für die Musik verantwortlich war, soll der Hörgenuss doch erheblich eingeschränkt gewesen sein.

Schräge Töne – und trotzdem erfolgreich

Aber auch, wenn alle vier Musiker spielten, müssen beachtlich viele schräge Töne zu hören gewesen sein, sodass später Musikgruppen mit wenig musikalischem Talent abschätzig als „Pankokenkapelle“ bezeichnet wurden. Albert Borcherdt hat sich in seinem 1912 erschienenen Buch „Das lustige alte Hamburg“ sehr negativ über die „Musikbande“ Pankokens geäußert.

Nachdem er die schlechten Leistungen der anderen Musiker bewertet hatte, schrieb er: „... so ruhte die ganze Last des Konzerts auf Pankoken, der aber seiner schwindsüchtigen Schalmei nur so schwache Töne abzuringen vermochte, dass bei dieser Kapelle die Hunde eine größere Freude als die Jungen empfanden, die für den Dreiling, den sie nicht bezahlt hatten, eine volle Musik verlangten und sich für ihre getäuschten Erwartungen durch Verspottung der biederen Musikanten rächten. Von dieser Kapelle her wird noch jetzt jede schlechte hamburgische Musikbande ‚Pankoken‘ gescholten.“

Beliebt war die kleine Kapelle von Pankoken trotzdem, besonders in der Neustadt. Pankoken und seine Mitspieler wurden immer wieder zu Hochzeiten und anderen Familienfeiern engagiert. Die Kapelle für einen ganzen Nachmitttag oder Abend zu beschäftigen, war für die meisten armen Familien viel zu teuer, aber wenn sie mit einigen Stücken zum Tanz aufspielten, war auch das schon eine große Bereicherung des Festes.

Der Schabernack der jungen Zuhörer

Die Musiker hatten nicht nur damit zu kämpfen, immer oder doch meistens den richtigen Ton zu treffen. Sie mussten auch vor Jungenstreichen auf der Hut sein. In dem Augenblick, wenn die Musiker ihre Instrumente an die Lippen setzten, holten die Jungen bis dahin verborgen gehaltene Zitronen hervor und bissen gut sichtbar für die Kapelle hinein. Daraufhin lief den Musikern das Wasser im Mund zusammen und an ein Spielen der Blasinstrumente war erst einmal nicht zu denken. Auch nutzten die Jungen unbeobachtete Augenblicke, um den Fiedelbogen mit Seife einzuschmieren und die Klarinette mit einem Korken zu verstopfen.

Die Straßenjungen liebten auch die Kapelle. Wenn Pankoken mit seinen Musikern auftauchte, wurde er lautstark mit „Hurra, Pankoken!“ begrüßt. Auch sollen die Jungen ihren Schabernack besonders gern mit neu entstandenen Konkurrenzkapellen getrieben haben, um sie aus dem Wirkungsbereich der Pankokenkapelle zu vertreiben.

Der unvergessene Pankoken

Als Leberecht Pankoken in den 1870er Jahren starb, hatte er mehr als vier Jahrzehnte lang auf Hamburger Straßen und bei Familienfeiern gespielt und besaß einen hohen Bekanntheitsgrad als origineller Begründer der nach ihm benannten Pankokenmusik.

Die große Zeit der Pankokenkapellen ging mit dem Ersten Weltkrieg zu Ende. Danach boten Radio und Film neue Unterhaltungsmöglichkeiten. Immerhin blieben diese Musiker bei vielen in guter Erinnerung. 1921 entstand die Komödie „Stratenmusik“ des Schriftstellers Paul Schurek. Das Stück von den Hoffnungen der „kleinen Leute“ auf Liebe und Wohlstand war so erfolgreich, dass es 1936 verfilmt wurde. Im gleichen Jahr eröffnete Richard Ohnsorg mit „Stratenmusiker“ das neue Haus seiner *Niederdeutschen Bühne* an der Straße Große Bleichen. Wer wollte dem Spruch des Tubabläsers in diesem Stück widersprechen: „Allens in düsse Welt is ünnerschiedlich.“

2010 hat das *Ohnsorg-Theater* mit diesem Stück die Theatersaison eröffnet und konnte sich über eine umjubelte Premiere freuen. Zu erwähnen ist auch, dass es in der Stadt weiterhin einzelne „Pankokenkapellen“ gibt, die in der musikalischen Tradition von Leberecht Pankoken stehen und die Menschen mit fröhlicher Musik unterhalten wollen – und das mit möglichst wenigen Misstönen.

Joachim Ringelnatz

„Dort trat ein Matrose aufs Podium, der sichtlich duhn war, ein kleiner Kerl mit einem vom Wind und Feuerwasser gegerbten Geiergesicht, die Haut spannte sich straff über die Backenknochen, die Wangen eingefallen, und unter einer großen messerscharf geknickten Nase sprang noch schärfer ein Kinn spitz hervor, darüber ein Seemannsmaul mit herabgezogenen Mundwinkeln und herabfallender, vorspringender Unterlippe. Es war die seltsamste Vereinigung von Sachse und Seemann, und dort oben stand er im blauen Tabakqualm und trug zuerst seine Turngedichte vor und bald darauf seine Balladen von Kuttel Daddeldu. Es wäre falsch, anzunehmen, daß diese Gedichte alle salonfähig gewesen wären, im Gegenteil ..." So hat Bruno E. Werner 1934 in einem Nachruf geschildert, wie er kurz nach dem Ersten Weltkrieg Ringelnatz erlebt hatte.

In Hamburg hatte Ringelnatz seine kurze Seemannslaufbahn begonnen und hier durfte er von 1933 an nicht mehr auftreten. Das, was dazwischen lag, war ein Leben mit vielen Aufs und Abs – eigentlich mehr Abs, aber Ringelnatz gab nicht auf und verarbeitete viele seiner Erlebnisse in Gedichten, die bis heute amüsiert und oder nachdenklich gelesen werden.

Kindheit in einer Künstler- und Literatenfamilie

Geboren wurde er am 7. August 1883 als Hans Gustav Bötticher in Wurzen bei Leipzig. Da war sein Weg zum witzig-skurrilen Schriftsteller, Kabarettisten und Maler natürlich noch nicht vorgezeichnet, aber die Voraussetzungen dafür waren günstig. Sein Vater Georg Bötticher war Zeichner und vor allem erfolgreicher Verfasser humoristischer Verse und Kinderbücher. Er konnte von seiner schriftstellerischen Tätigkeit leben, veröffentlichte vierzig Bücher und war - auf diesem Gebiet - das große Vorbild des Sohnes. Die Mutter Rosa Marie zeichnete ebenfalls und erstellte Muster für Perlenstickereien. Die Eltern waren mit ihrer künstlerischen und schriftstellerischen Tätigkeit so erfolgreich, dass sie zu Wohlstand kamen und zum Beispiel zwei Dienstmädchen hatten.

1886 zog die Familie nach Leipzig um, wo der Vater noch besser Kontakte für seine schriftstellerische Tätigkeit knüpfen konnte. So gab er nun zum Beispiel regelmäßig „Auerbachs Deutschen Kinderkalender" heraus, in dem dann auch die ersten literarischen Arbeiten des Sohnes erschienen, ein Märchen und zwei Gedichte.

Als ein Tattoo den Besuch des Gymnasiums beendete

In der Schule hatte der zukünftige Schriftsteller große Probleme, nicht nur mit den Lehrern, sondern auch den Mitschülern. Diese hänselten ihn wegen seiner mädchenhaften Frisur, seiner Vogelnase und seinem markanten Kinn. Später bekannte Ringelnatz: „Ich bin überzeugt, dass mein Gesicht mein Schicksal bestimmt. Hätte ich ein anderes Gesicht, wäre mein Leben ganz anders, jedenfalls ruhiger verlaufen." So aber flüchtete der Junge erst einmal in die Welt des Zeichnens und Schreibens. Über seine Schulzeit schrieb Bötticher später: „Das einzige Verlockende am Königlichen Staatsgymnasium waren Senfgurken, die der Pedell selber einlegte und davon er uns gegen geringe Bezahlung verkaufte. Sie zergingen auf der Zunge wie Butter und schmeckten ungleich köstlicher als die gewohnten Mahlzeiten daheim."

Die Gymnasialzeit ging abrupt zu Ende, nachdem Joachim Bötticher sich bei einer „Völkerschau" in Leipzig von einer Samoanerin ein Tattoo auf dem Unterarm stechen ließ und es stolz in der Schule präsentierte. Er wurde daraufhin mit sofortiger Wirkung vom Gymnasium verwiesen. Beim anschließenden Besuch einer Privatschule verbesserten sich seine schulischen Leistungen nicht, und er war nach eigenem Bekunden rasch wieder der „Haupthanswurst". Er musste zwei Schuljahre wiederholen und beendete mit der Obersekundarreife seine Schulzeit im Jahre 1901. Er schrieb später: „Keines der Lehrfächer regte mich an. Ich war in allen schlecht."

Die Flucht aus dem bürgerlichen Milieu

Zum Entsetzen seiner Eltern beschloss der Schulabbrecher, Seemann zu werden. Sein Biograf Herbert Günther schrieb über das Verhältnis des jungen Mannes zu seinen Eltern: „Das Leben von Ringelnatz war nicht zuletzt bestimmt durch seine Flucht aus dem bürgerlichen Milieu des Elternhauses." Die Beziehung zu den Eltern und besonders zum Vater war schwierig, das hat der Dichter Ringelnatz später nicht verschwiegen. 1905 schrieb er ein Gedicht zum Geburtstag des Vaters mit diesem Vers:

Daß ich so oft Dich kränkte
Und daß ich Dir heute nichts schenke
Mein lieber Papa, verzeih.
Mögst Du, Gott wolle es geben,
Gesund und glücklich verleben,
Den nächsten zwanzigsten Mai!

Alle Warnungen der Eltern halfen nichts, und als der Sohn sich 1901 von Leipzig auf den Weg nach Hamburg machte, um Seemann zu werden, da begleitete ihn sein Vater. Er war es, der beim „Heuerbas“ die 450 Mark bezahlte, die erforderlich waren, um den zukünftigen Seemann mit allem auszustatten, was er an Bord brauchen würde, von den Fausthandschuhen bis zur Tabakpfeife. Auch ein dolchartiges Messer samt Scheide gehörte zur Ausrüstung: „Das erschien mir das Wertvollste an der ganzen Ausrüstung. Meine achtzehnjährige Phantasie malte sich dabei abenteuerliche, wilde Szenen an fernen Küsten aus, wo dieses Messer eine Hauptrolle spielte.“

Bötticher heuerte auf dem Segelschiff „Elli“ an. Das Schiff lag nicht im Hamburger Hafen, sondern in Le Havre. Deshalb musste der zukünftige Matrose erst einmal an Bord eines französischen Dampfers zu diesem Hafen reisen. Hamburg verließ er, der zuletzt ohne seinen Vater in der Stadt gelebt hatte, in trüber Stimmung: „Mir war sehr beklommen zu Mute ... Bald kamen wir an das Freihafenviertel. Über Brücken hinweg. Links und rechts zeigten sich die für Hamburg charakteristischen Fleete. Vor den langen Lagerhäusern standen große, eiserne Kräne. Arbeiter, Packer, Kutscher, Zollwächter waren überall lärmend beschäftigt. Plattdeutsche Laute, Schimpfworte, Kommandos und Pfeifensignale drangen an mein Ohr. Aber alles, was ich sah, war mir fremd und abstoßend.“

Endlich an Bord der „Elli“, wurde der jugendliche Seemann gehänselt (allein schon wegen seines sächsischen Dialekts) und beleidigt, musste sogar körperliche Gewalt erdulden. Und trotzdem blieb Bötticher zunächst Seemann, eine Tätigkeit, die er in den Häfen immer wieder unterbrach, um für eine Weile Aushilfsjobs anzunehmen. „Ich fuhr als Schiffsjunge, Leichtmatrose und Matrose auf Seglern und Dampfschiffen einige Jahre lang nach Süd-, Zentral- und Nordamerika, Afrika, Spanien, Russland – nach etwa 22 außerdeutschen Ländern. Einige davon lernte ich näher kennen, indem ich mehrmals desertierte und mich dann, meist mittellos, herumtrieb, bis ich irgendwelche Beschäftigung fand."

Nach eigenen Angaben hat Bötticher an Land mehr als 30 verschiedene Tätigkeiten ausgeübt. Die Arbeit als Aushilfe bei einem Schlangenbeschwörer in der „Schlangenbude" auf dem Hamburger Dom gehört zweifellos zu den interessantesten dieser Tätigkeiten. Hier hatte er die Aufgabe, die Riesenschlangen zu ihrem Auftritt und zurück zu tragen. Seine Seemanns-Karriere beendete Bötticher 1905 bei der Kaiserlichen Marine in Kiel. Aber sein Traum, weiter als Seemann die Meere der Welt zu befahren, blieb lebendig, und er verarbeitete ihn später zu seinen berühmten „Kuttel-Daddeldu"-Versen. Auf der Bühne trat er passenderweise in Matrosenkleidung auf.

Lehrzeit in einer Dachpappenfirma in Hamburg

Es war in Hamburg, wo Bötticher 1903 ein Kabarett besuchte und eine ganz neue Welt für sich entdeckte: „Ich ging auch zum ersten Mal ein Kabarett, in der Wexpassage. Eine robuste Dame sang dort allabendlich ‚Ich bin a armer Bettelbuah.' Dem Zauber dieser Dame erlag ich eine Zeit lang." Anfang 1905 begann Bötticher eine Lehre bei der Hamburger Dachpappenfirma *Ruberoid*. In der zweijährigen Ausbildungszeit hat er sich dort wohlgefühlt: „Bald war ich eingelebt, kannte die Leute und ihre besonderen Eigenheiten. Es war ein großes Stück Gemütlichkeit in diesem Kontorleben. Die Firma war sowohl in ihrem geschäftlichen Gebaren als auch in ihrer Haltung zum Personal hamburgisch vornehm." Der Lehrling erhielt zwar kein Gehalt, aber zu Weihnachten eine Gratifikation. Als eine Zeichnung und ein Text des jungen Mannes geeignet befunden wurden, für die Reklame der Firma genutzt zu werden, erhielt er Sonderhonorare.

Weil sein Vater ihn jeden Monat finanziell unterstützte, konnte Bötticher sich ein Zimmer bei einer Wirtin in der Großen Reichenstraße leisten. Hier entstanden seine ersten Gemälde und er schrieb weiterhin Gedichte, die er an satirische Zeitschriften wie „Kladderadatsch" schickte - viele kamen allerdings unveröffentlicht zurück. Bötticher besuchte eine Handelsschule, wo er „allerhand Allotria" trieb, und nahm außerdem Klavierunterricht. Wie so oft, verbaute Bötticher sich auch diesen Klavierunterricht durch seinen Schabernack. Er zwickte den Schwanz der Katze seines Klavierlehrers, der ihn daraufhin zur Tür hinaus schob und dem Schüler bedeutete, er möge nie wieder kommen.

Ringelnatz tauchte in die Welt der Hamburger Bohème ein und war häufiger Gast des Juweliers Wilkens, dessen Haus am Jungfernstieg ein Treffpunkt der avantgardistischen Maler-, Musiker- und Literatenkreise war. Nach langen Abenden soll Ringelnatz sich in einen Teppich des Hausherrn eingerollt und geschlafen haben. Er nannte den Juwelier „Kapitän Muckelmann" und hat ihm 1923 in der Geschichte „Kuttel Daddeldu erzählt seinen Kindern das Märchen vom Rotkäppchen" ein literarisches Denkmal gesetzt: „Also Kinners, wenn ihr mal fünf Minuten lang das Maul halten könnt, dann will ich euch die Geschichte vom Rotkäppchen erzählen, wenn ich mir das noch zusammenreimen kann. Der alte Kapitän Muckelmann hat mir das vorerzählt, als ich noch so klein und so dumm war, wie ihr jetzt seid. Und Kapitän Muckelmann hat nie gelogen."

Erfahrungen im Militärarrest

Nachdem Bötticher zu einer vorgeschriebenen „Kontrollversammlung" des Militärs nicht erschienen war, erhielt er die schriftliche Nachricht, dass er sich zu einem 24-stündigen Arrest einzufinden hätte. Als er erschien, war aber gerade keine Arrestzelle frei, man „vertröstete mich auf andernmal". Für den zweiten Termin holte ihn ein Soldat ab.

Was dann geschah, hat Böttcher später so beschrieben: „Unterwegs beschwatzte ich ihn, mit mir in einer entlegenen Schenke einzukehren. Dort besoff er sich auf meine Kosten so sehr, dass er, nachdem er mich im Arrestlokal unter vorschriftsmäßigem Zeremoniell abgeliefert hatte, selbst abgeführt wurde. Man nahm mir die Hosenträger ab, damit ich mich nicht erhängen könnte. Ich verbrachte vierundzwanzig abscheuliche Stunden bei Wasser und Brot. Kaum erträglich, obwohl meine Phantasie viele Spiele in der kahlen Zelle erfand."

Die *Ruberoid*-Gesellschaft schickte Bötticher nach Abschluss seiner Ausbildung in Hamburg als Angestellten nach Leipzig und Frankfurt am Main. In den folgenden Jahren wechselte er die Arbeitgeber, aber seine Bemühungen, eine dauerhafte feste Anstellung zu finden, scheiterten immer wieder an seinen spontanen abenteuerlichen Reisen ohne ausreichend Geld.

Erfahrungen als Kabarettist in München und im Kriegsdienst in Cuxhaven

1909 begannen – etwas – bessere Zeiten für Bötticher. Er trat in der Künstlerkneipe *Simplicissimus* in München auf und stieg zu so etwas wie dem Hausdichter auf. Er bekam viel Lob, aber wenig Honorar. Zunächst erhielt er für jeden Auftritt lediglich ein Bier und etwas zu essen, dann zusätzlich zwei Mark. Davon konnte er nicht leben und ebenso wenig von den Honoraren der Zeitschrift „Simplicissimus". Er fühlte sich zu Recht ausgebeutet und machte sich wieder auf die Wanderschaft. Auf Meldezetteln schrieb er als Beruf „reisender Artist".

Bötticher kam weit herum und blieb bitterarm. Daran konnte auch sein erster schmaler Gedichtband im Jahre 1910 nichts ändern. Dass er von 1912 an zwei Jahre lang in den Bibliotheken von Adligen arbeiten konnte, war die große Ausnahme, änderte aber nichts an seiner insgesamt beklagenswerten Situation. 1914 meldete er sich freiwillig zum Kriegsdienst bei der Marine, wo er vergeblich auf einen Einsatz bei einer Seeschlacht hoffte. Er musste sich damit zufrieden geben, zum Kommandanten eines Minensuchbootes in Cuxhaven (damals ein Teil Hamburgs) aufzusteigen.

In all den Jahren schrieb und veröffentlichte er zahlreiche Gedichte, Geschichten und Novellen. Sie erschienen von 1919 an unter dem Pseudonym Joachim Ringelnatz.

Ich komme und gehe wieder,
Ich, der Matrose Ringelnatz.
Die Wellen des Meeres auf und nieder
Tragen mich und meine Lieder
Von Hafenplatz zu Hafenplatz.
Ihr kennt meine lange Nase,
Mein vom Sturm zerknittertes Gesicht
Daß ich so gerne spaße,
Versteht ihr das?
Oder nicht?

Als Offizier auf der Seite der Revolutionäre

1918 schloss Ringelnatz sich den aufständischen Matrosen an, beharrte aber darauf, mit der Offiziersmütze auf dem Kopf an der Revolution teilzunehmen. Bekanntlich scheiterten die aufständischen Matrosen mit ihren Vorstellungen von einer deutschen Revolution und Ringelnatz scheiterte auch. 1920 heiratete er die Lehrerin Leonharda Pieper, ein großer Glücksfall für ihn, denn sie wurde zum sicheren Hafen in seinem Vagabundenleben. „Muschelkalk“, wie er sie liebevoll nannte, unterstützte ihn intensiv bei seiner Arbeit. Er war inzwischen durch Auftritte in Kabaretts und Veröffentlichungen bekannt und anerkannt. Auch im neuen Medium Rundfunk war er gefragt. Unvergessen sein Gedicht „Im Park“:

Ein ganz kleines Reh stand am ganz kleinen Baum
still und verklärt wie im Traum.
Das war des Nachts elf Uhr zwei.
Und dann kam ich um vier
Morgens wieder vorbei.

Und da träumte noch immer das Tier.
Nun schlich ich mich leise - ich atmete kaum -
gegen den Wind an den Baum,
und gab dem Reh einen ganz kleinen Stips.
Und da war es aus Gips.

Erfolgreiche Jahre als Kabarettist und Dichter

Ringelnatz trat auch wieder als Kabarettist im Münchner *Simplicissimus* auf, ebenso in Hamburg. So erinnerte sich der Journalist und Kunsthistoriker Lovis H. Lorenz an die vielen Auftritte von Joachim Ringelnatz in der Hansestadt: „An seinen Vortragsabenden trug er Matrosenbluse und flattrige Seemannsbüx. Selten ließ er dabei das Glas aus der Hand, nahm zwischen den Zeilen einen stärkenden Schluck und schwankte gelegentlich auch bedenklich. Doch er fiel niemals aus der Rolle, auch bei einem anschließenden Zug über St. Pauli nicht.“

Daneben schrieb er zahlreiche Gedichte, darunter Tiergedichte, und Bücher, vor allem auch Kinderbücher. In einem dieser Kinderbücher steht dieser Vers:

Was du verschweigst,
Was du den andern nicht zeigst,
Was dein Mund spricht
Und deine Hand tut,
Es kommt alles ans Licht.
Sei ohnedies gut.

Der sich oft verschlossen gebende Ringelnatz, der vielen misstrauisch und scheu erschien, öffnete sich Kindern. Der befreundete Schauspieler Paul Wegener hat geschrieben: „Am schnellsten gab er sich Kindern, die hingen sofort an ihm. Wer sein köstliches *Kinder-Verwirr-Buch* kennt, diesen Schreck aller bürgerlichen Eltern, wird es verstehen. Meine Söhne und Neffe und Töchter und Nichten liebten ihn gleichermaßen."

Zu den Erwachsenen, zu denen Ringelnatz Vertrauen fasste, gehörte die berühmte Filmschauspielerin Asta Nielsen. Sie freundete sich mit ihm an, lud ihn in ihr Haus auf Hiddensee ein und beschrieb ihn so: „Ringelnatz war klein und unwahrscheinlich mager. Auf den ersten Blick schien sein Gesicht von einer mächtigen Don-Quichote-Nase beherrscht zu sein, sah man aber näher hin, wich alles in seinem großen Antlitz, ja beinahe seine ganze Gestalt, hinter ein Paar großer, dunkelblauer Augen zurück, die so schön waren, wie ich es kaum jemals erlebt habe."

1928 erschien Ringelnatz' Buch „Matrosen", das sein Biograf Herbert Günther uns so vorstellt: „In diesem Buch *Matrosen* tritt der Verfasser zurück, und doch trägt es seine persönliche Note. Ringelnatz erzählt hier in kurzen Kapiteln und einfachen knappen Sätzen von den Nöten und Freuden jener weltfahrenden Menschen voller Fernweh und Heimweh, von diesem gutmütigen, groben, sentimentalen und tapferen Volk, das wir Matrosen nennen ... Diese Berichte sind ehrlich, ungewollt, ungekünstelt, ohne Verzerrung und ohne Verklärung. Sie atmen den kräftigen Geruch von blanken Planken, braunen Mädchen, Branntwein, Apfelsinen, Schweiß. Wer sie liest, weiß mehr von der Welt."

Von den Nazis geächtet

Dann kamen die Nazis an die Macht, und Ringelnatz musste erleben, dass sein Humor bei den neuen Herren nicht gefragt war. Im Gegenteil. Er erhielt ein Auftrittsverbot und seine Bücher wurden verbrannt. Dem Verbot fiel auch die von Freunden geplante Veranstaltung zu seinem 50. Geburtstag in Hamburg zum Opfer. Es war vorgesehen, dass er selbst Gedichte vortragen würde. Als der *Rowohlt-Verlag* 1943 zwangsweise geschlossen wurde, war die Begründung, dass der Verlag die Werke von Ringelnatz und Fallada veröffentlicht hatte. Ringelnatz' Kommentar zu den unsicheren politischen Verhältnissen hatte er bereits 1931 so formuliert:

Wir haben keinen günstigen Wind.
Indem wir die Richtung verlieren,
Wissen wir doch, wo wir sind.
Aber wir frieren.

Das Ehepaar Ringelnatz verarmte, und dann erkrankte er zu allem Unglück auch noch an Tuberkulose. Joachim Ringelnatz starb am 17. November 1934 in Berlin. Seiner Frau Leonharda, „Muschelkalk", hatte er in einem Gedicht zugerufen:

Wenn ich tot bin, darfst du garnicht trauern,
Meine Liebe wird mich überdauern
Und in fremden Kleidern dir begegnen
Und dich segnen.

„Muschelkalk" und Asta Nielsen gehörten zu den wenigen Trauergästen, denn seine Frau hatte den Tod von Ringelnatz bewusst erst danach bekannt gemacht. Bei der Trauerfeier erklang noch einmal sein Lieblingslied „La Paloma". Dazu passen diese Zeilen seines Freundes, des Schauspielers Paul Wegener: „Es gibt Wanderer auf dieser Erde, die seelische Nomaden bleiben und als ewig fahrendes Volk durch die Wälder und Steppen des Lebens treiben und ohne Möbel in leichten Zelten flüchtig nächtigen. – So einer war Ringelnatz. Sein einzig fester Punkt, seine Heimat jenseits aller Dinge – Muschelkalk, seine Frau."

Als Dichter bis heute in Erinnerung

„Muschelkalk" wohnte bis zu ihrem Tod 1977 in Berlin. In der Nachkriegszeit erlebten die Gedichte ihres Mannes, nicht nur die humorvollen, eine Renaissance. Auch der Maler Ringelnatz wurde mit mehreren Ausstellungen gewürdigt. In Othmarschen gibt es eine Ringelnatztreppe. In Cuxhaven wurde ein *Joachim-Ringelnatz-Museum* eröffnet. Dabei hatte er über Cuxhaven geschrieben: „Eine Stadt, die mir gipsern, starr und unerträglich langweilig vorkam."

Dieses Porträt kann nicht abgeschlossen werden, bevor eines seiner berühmtesten Gedichte hier erscheint, wobei nicht unerwähnt bleiben soll, dass an der Ecke Liebermannstraße/Elbchaussee eine Bronzeskulptur mit zwei überlebensgroßen Ameisen steht (wenn sie nicht gerade wieder einmal gestohlen wurde):

In Hamburg lebten zwei Ameisen,
die wollten nach Australien reisen.
Bei Altona auf der Chaussee,
da taten ihnen die Beine weh,
und da verzichteten sie weise
dann auf den letzten Teil der Reise.

Hilde Rosenberg

„Mama Blume war nicht nur die bekannte Wahrsagerin vom Hamburger Dom, in deren kuschelig überheiztem Wagen sich unzählige Menschen in den letzten Jahrzehnten die Karten legen ließen. Mama Blume, die Sinteza, die mit bürgerlichem Namen Hilde Rosenberg hieß, war ein Kraftwerk. Ein Überlebenswunder. Ein winziges, zähes Persönchen mit Witz und unglaublicher Frechheit, eine Frau, die sich nie hat kleinkriegen lassen." Das schrieb Tania Kibermanis im Februar 2019 in einem Nachruf in der „Zeit".

Der *Zentralrat Deutscher Sinti & Roma* sprach nach ihrem Tod von „einer hochgeachteten Institution nicht nur für die Sinti und Roma". Mama Blume war ein beeindruckendes Hamburger Original, jedenfalls, wenn man unter einem Original nicht eine Witzfigur versteht, über die ihre Umgebung lacht.

Mama Blume kam 1928 im polnischen Lódź in einer Sinti-Familie zur Welt, unter deren Vorfahren mütter- und väterlicherseits viele Musiker waren. Ihr Vater war Kammerjäger, die Mutter eine bekannte Wahrsagerin. Gern erinnerte sich Mama Blume an die Zeit, als die Familie in einer Wohnung lebte, aber auch einen Wohnwagen und Pferde besaß: „... am Lagerfeuer schmeckt alles besser. Allein diese gemütliche Stimmung am Feuer. Stundenlang konnte ich in die Flammen schauen. Und wenn dann noch die Pferde hinter dem Wohnwagen standen, war alles irgendwie abenteuerlich und romantisch zugleich. Leider ist diese Zeit vorüber ..." Das hat sie ihrem Sohn

Tornado erzählt. Er hat 2019 die Lebensgeschichte seiner Eltern unter dem Titel „Vom Glück im Leben“ veröffentlicht.

Auf der Suche nach den Musikern im Radio

Mama Blume erinnerte sich im Alter an ein Erlebnis als Achtjährige. Ihr Vater hatte ein Radio gekauft, und als ihr Bruder und sie allein waren, stellten sie das Radio an und hörten schöne Musik: „Doch ich und mein Bruder wollten unbedingt wissen, wer diese Musiker sind. Also nahmen wir einen Hammer und haste nicht gesehen, das Radio war entzwei. Es schauten nur noch Federn heraus. Und von den Musikern? Natürlich keine Spur.“ Als der Vater nach Hause kam, schimpfte er die Kinder nicht aus, sondern lachte und versuchte, ihnen zu erklären, wie ein Radio funktioniert. Diese Geschichte sagt viel über den Erziehungsstil im Elternhaus von Mama Blume aus.

Bald darauf starb der Vater und die Mutter musste nun als Wahrsagerin die Familie allein ernähren. Die Tochter sah ihr dabei häufig zu. „Oft war ich überrascht, wenn ich hörte, was alles eingetroffen war, und wurde immer neugieriger.“ Die Tochter wollte nun auch selbst die Zukunft voraussagen. Sie sprach auf der Straße einen Jungen an und bot ihm an, ihm zu sagen, welche Zukunft er haben würde, wenn er ihr einen Pfennig zahlte. Er war einverstanden, und sie sagte ihm eine schöne Zukunft voraus. Daraufhin fand sie einige weitere Kinder, die für einen Pfennig etwas über ihre Zukunft erfahren wollten.

Als Hilde stolz ihrer Mutter von ihren Erfolgen erzählte, antwortete diese: „So mein Kind, höre jetzt immer gut zu und lerne.“ Die Mutter prägte Hilde ein, den anderen

Kindern nie etwas Schlechtes vorherzusagen. Die Tochter beobachtete ihre Mutter nun noch intensiver: „Ich war sehr oft davon berührt, wenn ich sah, wie die Menschen mit ihren Nöten zu ihr kamen. Oft weinten sie, aber sie gingen mit fröhlichen Gesichtern aus der Tür ... Sie sagte mir, dass sie die Gabe hat, Menschen in jeder Situation zu helfen."

Als die Tochter fragte, woher sie diese Gabe her habe, antwortete sie, dass es ein Geschenk wäre. Die Tochter solle ihr geduldig zuschauen, denn sie brauche viel Weisheit und habe eine große Verantwortung den Menschen gegenüber.

Leidenszeit in SS-Arbeitslagern

Nach dem deutschen Überfall auf Polen musste Hilde als Sinti-Mädchen im Alter von 11 Jahren die Schule verlassen. Als sie 13 Jahren alt war, verschleppten die Nazis sie in ein Arbeitslager. Später musste sie in Niederwiesa bei Chemnitz in einer Munitionsfabrik Zwangsarbeit leisten. Als Folge wiederholter Misshandlungen erlitt sie mehrere Knochenbrüche, verlor auf einer Seite das Gehör und litt zeitlebens unter den Folgen einer zertrümmerten Schulter.

Sie machte in diesen Jahren auch positive Erfahrungen, die ihr halfen, den Glauben an das Gute im Menschen nicht zu verlieren: „Unser Chef in der Munitionsfabrik, Herr Litke, war uns Frauen, die wir die Arbeit dort machten, immer gut gesinnt." Das zeigte sich auch, als Hilde ein defektes Kabel anfasste und mehrere starke Stromschläge erlitt. In dieser Situation war es der Chef, der den

Stromschalter rasch ausschaltete. „Ich habe ihm mein weiteres Leben zu verdanken.“

Im Arbeitslager lernte die Jugendliche im Juli 1944 ihren späteren Mann Lani Rosenberg kennen, einen Sinto. Er war im Mai 1940 im Alter von 17 Jahren in Hamburg festgenommen und in ein Arbeitslager verschleppt worden. In der Nähe des Arbeitslagers mussten die Häftlinge mitten im Winter Schützengräben ausheben. Lani Rosenberg bot dem Mädchen an, ihr bei der schweren Arbeit zu helfen und sie kamen einander näher.

Einmal arbeiteten sie auf einem Feld, und da sie an diesem Tag eine kleine Gruppe waren, bewachte sie nur ein einziger Soldat. Das machte Hilde sich zunutze. Zur Überraschung ihrer Mithäftlinge sprach sie den jungen Soldaten an und sagte ihm: „Hey du, du siehst aus wie eine Ziege.“ Der Soldat hatte tatsächlich einen Bart, der dem einer Ziege ähnelte. Die Bemerkung über den Bart hätte eine harte Bestrafung des Mädchens auslösen können. Aber wie später so oft, bewährte sich ihre beeindruckende Menschenkenntnis.

Der junge Soldat nahm die Bemerkung humorvoll auf und lachte. Sie fragte ihn daraufhin, ob sie zu dem Bauernhof in der Nähe gehen dürfe, um etwas zum Essen zu holen. Der Soldat lehnte das zunächst ab, aber sie konnte ihn für sich einnehmen und er schaute weg, als sie sich zum Bauernhof entfernte. Dort erhielt sie einen Topf mit Essen, den die Häftlingsgruppe noch auf dem Feld aß, ohne dabei von dem Soldaten gestört zu werden.

Das war eine große Ausnahme. Meistens behandelten die SS-Wächter die Häftlinge mit großer Brutalität. Hilde überlebte, weil sie den SS-Wachmännern aus der Hand las und ihnen eine gute Zukunft vorhersagte. Viele ihrer Angehörigen wurden ermordet. Ihr späterer Mann Lani überlebte, weil er für die SS-Leute auf der Gitarre spielte. Hilde Rosenberg erhielt für ihre Leiden im Konzentrationslager später eine Entschädigungsrente von 40 Euro im Monat.

Ein Neuanfang in Hamburg

Nach der Befreiung aus dem Konzentrationslager heirateten Mama Blume und Lani Rosenberg und ließen sich in seiner Heimatstadt Hamburg nieder. Dort wohnten sie zunächst in einem Wohnwagen, den der Ehemann selbst gebaut hatte. Er machte als Musiker Karriere, und die Familie konnte sich schon bald eine Wohnung leisten. Das Ehepaar bekam sechs Kinder. Der zweitälteste Sohn Tornado erinnerte sich später daran, dass es für ihn eine wunderbare Zeit war, in der er bereits als Kind mit dem Orchester seines Vaters auftreten konnte. Er behielt aber auch dies in Erinnerung:

„Wir sahen unseren Vater manchmal weinen, wenn er allein in der Essdiele saß. Er redete kein Wort. Zuerst wusste ich nicht, warum er ohne ein Wort nur dort saß. Erst später erfuhr ich, dass er wegen des Verlustes seiner Eltern und Verwandten durch die Nazis nachdachte. Er allein überlebte das KZ. Alle seine Brüder kamen um. Nur er und seine Schwester und einige Neffen und Nichten hatten es überlebt." Auch die Eltern von Lani Rosenberg und viele Familienmitglieder von Mama Blume waren ermordet worden. Tornado Rosenberg schrieb über die Trauerarbeit seiner Mutter Hilde: „Unsere Mutter steckte es irgendwie anders weg." Aber auch sie brauchte lange Zeit, bevor sie über ihre traumatischen Erfahrungen sprechen konnte.

Hilde Rosenberg war bald eine angesehene Wahrsagerin und arbeitete viele Jahre auf dem Hamburger Dom. Auch bildete sie andere Wahrsagerinnen und Wahrsager aus. Sie arbeitete bis ins hohe Alter, was angesichts ihrer geringen Rente auch geboten war. 2017 bekam sie eine Nachzahlung von 27 Euro Wiedergutmachung. Da war ihr Antrag auf Entschädigung für erlittenes Unrecht noch immer nicht abschließend bearbeitet, mehr als sechs Jahrzehnte nach dem Ende der Naziherrschaft. Ihre Familie sorgte für Mama Blume, aber das ersetzte nicht die Anerkennung und angemessene Entschädigung als Opfer des Naziregimes.

„Uns Sinti gibt es nicht allein"

„Mama Blume öffnete mir die Tür, schaute mich kurz an und lächelte: ‚Das ist scheen, du bist ja eine von uns. Du hast ein warmes Herz.'" So begrüßte die Wahrsagerin ihre Besucherin, die Journalistin Tania Kibermanis. Es entwickelte sich eine langjährige Freundschaft zwischen der Journalistin und der Sinti-Familie. Sie wurde auch eingeladen, zuzuschauen, wenn Mama Blume und ihre Tochter Esmeralda den Besuchern des Hamburger Doms die Karten legten oder aus der Hand lasen. Anita Kibermanis schrieb in der „Frankfurter Rundschau", dass Mama Blume den Besuchern auch unbequeme Wahrheiten sagte, so zum Beispiel mit donnernder, empörter Stimme: „Hör auf zu saufen, sonst wird dich deine Frau verlassen." In dem Beitrag heißt es weiter: „Auch mir hat sie ein paarmal die Karten gelegt. Dinge prophezeit, die mir ganz unglaublich schienen. Und sie hat immer Recht behalten."

„Uns Sinti gibt es nicht allein", sagte Esmeralda der Journalistin, und die schrieb: „Stimmt. Immer, wenn ich bei Rosenbergs zu Besuch bin, kommt spätestens nach zehn Minuten jemand aus der Familie vorbei, bleibt auf einen Kaffee, spielt vielleicht ein neues Stück auf der Gitarre vor ... Enkelkinder toben durch die Wohnung, dazwischen wuselt ein kleiner Hund. Und egal, um welche Uhrzeit ich auch vorbeischaue, immer köchelt in einem riesigen Topf irgendein stark fleischhaltiges Essen, falls vielleicht jemand auf der Matte steht, der noch Hunger hat. Immer ist noch Platz und ein Moment Zeit für einen, der gerade etwas braucht."

Die Tochter setzt die Hellseher-Tradition ihrer Mutter fort

Die jüngste Tochter Simona, genannt Esmeralda, hat das Wahrsagen in dem buntem Wagen auf dem Hamburger Dom fortgeführt. Sie war zunächst selbst skeptisch gewesen, wie sie 2021 in einem Interview der „Kreiszeitung-Wochenblatt" (Buchholz) einräumte: „Als junges Mädchen habe ich an die Hellseherei nicht geglaubt. Dann kam es aber zu einem Schlüsselerlebnis für mich: Ich habe meine Mutter gebeten, einem Bekannten aus der Hand zu lesen. Dem schuldete ich einen kleinen Geldbetrag. Mit der Sitzung sollten die Schulden beglichen werden. Ohne vorher mit ihm zu sprechen, sagte meine Mutter dem Mann, dass er große Angst vor Feuer habe. Das traf tatsächlich zu, denn mein Bekannter hatte sich als

Kind ganz fürchterlich verbrannt. Ich habe mich danach der Wahrsagerei geöffnet und entdeckte, das ich über die gleiche hellseherische Gabe wie meine Mutter verfügte.“ 2015 sagte sie in einem anderen Zeitungsgespräch über ihre Tätigkeit: „Man braucht viel Kraft für diese Arbeit. Aber es ist unsere Bestimmung. Wir versuchen, den Menschen zu helfen und ihnen den Weg zu weisen.“

Mama Blume starb am 1. Februar 2019 in Hamburg. Ihren Kindern hatte sie mit auf den Weg gegeben: „Der Sinn des Lebens ist, dass du einfach da bist und dich an dieser Welt freuen sollst.“ Zum Tod äußerte die tiefgläubige Frau: „Nur Gott zündet die Kerze an und pustet sie auch wieder aus.“

Der Sohn Tornado ist ein bekannter Musiker. Wie erwähnt hat er die Geschichte von Lani Rosenberg und Mama Blume unter dem Titel „Vom Glück im Leben“ veröffentlicht. Er bekämpft die Vorurteile gegen die „Zigeuner“ und fordert ihre Anerkennung als KZ-Opfer sowie endlich eine angemessene Entschädigung für erlittenes Unrecht. Über sich selbst schreibt er: „Ich fühle mich als deutscher Sinto, als Hamburger, und erwarte genau den Respekt, den die Menschen auch von mir erwarten können.“

Ein Platz oder eine Straße in Erinnerung an Mama Blume

2021 gab es eine Initiative, den Lohseplatz in Mama-Blume-Platz umzubenennen. Das würde sich anbieten, weil der Ehemann und Verwandte von Hilde Rosenberg vom Hannoverschen Bahnhof, der sich hier früher befand, in Konzentrationslager verschleppt wurden. Aber wie schon zu Lebzeiten, waren die Paragrafen auch diesmal gegen sie. Das zuständige Fachamt des Bezirksamtes Mitte lehnte den Antrag ab: „Eine Umbenennung ist in diesem Fall nicht möglich. Die Benennungsbestimmungen des Senats geben vor, dass Umbenennungen ausschließlich erfolgen dürfen, wenn diese der Beseitigung von Unklarheiten (Verwechslung, Änderungen des Wegeverlaufs) dienen. Zu Unklarheiten kam es beim Lohseplatz bisher nicht."

Immerhin schlug das zuständige Amt vor, die Bezirksversammlung möge den Vorschlag auf die „Warteliste" für die Benennung neuer Straßen setzen. 2022 gab es eine neue Eingabe, dieses Mal mit dem Vorschlag, eine Fläche an der Davidstraße als Mama-Blume-Platz zu benennen. Bis heute ist aber weder ein Platz noch eine Straße nach Mama Blume benannt worden.

Tania Kibermanis hat in einem Nachruf in der Wochenzeitung „Die Zeit" über die letzte Lebenszeit von Mama Blume geschrieben: „Am liebsten saß sie inmitten ihrer Familie, ganz still, und beobachtete lächelnd das Treiben um sie herum. Sie liebte Blumen. Und natürlich Gitarrenmusik. Sie konnte schimpfen, wenn einer mit ungebügeltem Hemd zu ihr kam. Noch an Silvester hat sie getanzt. Nie hat sie jemanden abgewiesen, der zu ihr kam. Sie war eine fürsorgliche und warmherzige Mama, weit über ihre eigene Familie hinaus. Wer diese wunderbare Frau mit der rauen Stimme jemals erlebt hat, kann dankbar sein. So ein großes Herz findet man nur alle 100 Jahre."

Harry Rowohlt

„Von allen Menschen, denen ich bisher begegnet bin, kommt Harry Rowohlt einem Genie am nächsten.“ Das schrieb der irisch-stämmige amerikanische Schriftsteller Roger Boylan über seinen Übersetzer, als dieser 60 Jahre alt geworden war. Boylan erinnerte sich an eine gemeinsame Lesereise im Jahr 2000. Sie führte auch nach Wien, wo „wir spätabends vor einem erschöpften Publikum lasen, das den ganzen Tag schon Lesungen über sich hatte ergehen lassen. Doch es hielt durch, mehr Harrys als meinetwegen, weil es in ihm ein Original erkannte, eine einzigartige Erscheinung mit jenem Maß an Unberechenbarkeit, das seiner Kunst einen Hauch von Gefahr und Aufregung verlieh. Das tun Genies eben: Sie bringen das Unerwartete in die Welt alltäglicher Gewissheiten, die wir übrigen bewohnen.“

Eine Kindheit mit „Pu der Bär“

Harry Rowohlt kam am 27. März 1945 in einem Luftschutzbunker in der Hamburger Hochallee zur Welt. Sein leiblicher Vater war der Verleger Ernst Rowohlt, seine Mutter die Schauspielerin Maria Pierenkämper, die bei der Geburt von Harry in dritter Ehe mit dem Maler Max Rupp verheiratet war. Der kam als Erzeuger von Harry nicht infrage, weil er sich zum fraglichen Zeitpunkt in russischer Kriegsgefangenschaft befand. In den ersten zehn Jahren trug Harry trotzdem den Nachnamen Rupp.

Die Mutter spielte weiter Theater, längere Zeit in Wiesbaden. In dem Interview-Buch „In-Schlucken-zwei-Spechte“ von Ralf Sotschek hat sich Harry Rowohlt so an diese Zeit erinnert: „Bewusst aufgewachsen bin ich in Wiesbaden im Alter von zwei bis sechs. Mit großem Genuss. Wir hatten einen wunderbaren Kindergarten. Lauter Schauspielerinnen und Künstlerinnen – also das, was man heutzutage als allein erziehende Mütter bezeichnen würde – haben zusammengelegt und eine Kindergärtnerin bezahlt, die wir alle sehr liebten ... Das war ein Kinderladen lange vor der Zeit."

Die Mutter nahm sich die Zeit, dem kleinen Harry „Pu der Bär" vorzulesen, und der Sohn lernte Lesen, um dieses Buch allein genießen zu können. Das war natürlich noch die ältere Übersetzung jenes Buches, durch dessen Neuübersetzung Harry Rowohlt später ge- und berühmt wurde.

Das „ausgelagerte" Kind

Nach der Wiesbadener Zeit wechselte die Mutter oft die Bühne und der Sohn Harry die Schule, „da bin ich ihr immer von Engagement zu Engagement nachgefolgt und war manchmal auch bei Freunden ausgelagert". Sechszehn oder achtzehn verschiedene Schulen besuchte Harry.

Auch nachdem die Mutter sich von ihrem dritten Mann hatte scheiden lassen und 1957 Ernst Rowohlt heiratete, war die „Bildungsreise" noch nicht zu Ende, weil der Vater aus gesundheitlichen Gründen mit seiner Familie ins Allgäu zog und erst danach nach Hamburg zurückkehrte. Von seinem Vater hatte Harry Rowohlt später keine hohe Meinung: „Meinen Vater habe ich als jemanden erlebt, der zu den seltenen Menschen gehört, die überhaupt nichts können. Das ist ja eine echte Begabung."

Harry Rowohlt als „Biedermann“

Trotz der nicht gerade günstige Bedingungen für den schulischen Erfolg schaffte Harry Rowohlt am *Walddörfer-Gymnasium* in Volksdorf das Abitur. Sein Abituraufsatz wurde als bester Aufsatz in Hamburg und seinem Umland ausgezeichnet. Der Klassen- und Deutschlehrer Horst-Jürgen Glockauer hat sich so an den Schulabschluss Rowohlts erinnert: „Der krönende Abschluss unserer gemeinsamen Oberstufenzeit war für mich das Musische Abitur, in dem die gesamte Klasse eine atmosphärisch dichte, geradezu unheimliche Aufführung von *Biedermann und die Brandstifter* ablieferte. In ihrem Zentrum stand – wen wunderte es - Harry Rowohlts schaurig-komische Verkörperung des negativen Protagnisten Biedermann (‚Zum Glück ist's nicht bei uns ... Zum Glück'). Ich schätze, es war seine erste große satirische Leistung.“

Die Leistung war noch bemerkenswerter, wenn man weiß, dass Harry Rowohlt im Anzug seines Vater, mit grauer Perücke und aufgeklebtem Schnurbart auftrat. „An der spannendsten Stelle ging immer der Schnurbart ab.“ Wer solche Kalamitäten souverän meisterte, den konnte auch später bei Auftritten nichts erschüttern.

Die Studienzeit Harry Rowohlts war sehr kurz: „Amerikanistik in München, zweieinhalb Stunden lang. Ich hab so kurz studiert, dass ich noch nicht einmal in der Mensa war, dabei war es Freitag, und es hätte Fisch gegeben. Weil ich aber wirklich etwas lernen wollte, habe ich ziemlich bald gemerkt, dass man an der Uni falsch ist. Da kann man zwar in mehreren Jahren mehrere Scheine machen, aber um etwas zu lernen, ist es der falsche Ort.“

Als der Sohn sich weigerte, mit dem Rowohlt-Verlag in Konkurs zu gehen

Es bestand in der Familie die Hoffnung, dass der Sohn Harry im *Rowohlt-Verlag* tätig werden würde. Er machte deshalb eine Lehre beim *Suhrkamp-Verlag*. In Frankfurt am Main. Dort lernte er seine spätere Frau Ulla kennen. Nach dem Abschluss der zweieinhalbjährigen Lehrzeit arbeitete Harry Rowohlt als Volontär im *Rowohlt-Verlag*, in dem sein Halbbruder Heinrich Maria Ledig-Rowohlt nach dem Tod des Vaters die Leitung übernommen hatte.

Harry Rowohlt war über die wilhelminischen Strukturen und den Umgang mit den Beschäftigten im Verlag entsetzt. Er äußerte später über den Verlag: „Ich kannte den ja vorher nicht. Da hab ich ihn dann kennen gelernt und gedacht: Womit habe ich dieses Straflager verdient? Ich hatte doch niemanden umgebracht." Er fasste den Entschluss, sich nicht an der Leitung des Verlages zu beteiligen. Sein Vater war mit dem Verlag fünfmal pleitegegangen, und der Sohn war überzeugt, „diese Tradition hätte ich als erstes wiederbelebt".

Harry Rowohlt heiratete seine Freundin Ulla und beide reisten in die USA. Der Verlegersohn war froh, jenseits des Atlantiks nicht ständig nach seiner Verbindung zum *Rowohlt-Verlag* gefragt zu werden, war dieser dort doch unbekannt. Er sammelte als Mitarbeiter des avantgardistischen New Yorker Verlages *Grove Press* weitere Erfahrungen in der literarischen Welt. Eineinhalb Jahre blieb er dort. „Das war eine wunderbare Zeit bei Grove", erinnerte er sich später, aber sie endete abrupt mit einer fristlosen Kündigung, als er sich für die Bildung einer Gewerkschaftsgruppe engagierte.

Ein begnadeter und fleißiger Übersetzer

In seiner Zeit in New York stieß Harry Rowohlt auf ein Kinderbuch von Alexander Sutherland Neill, der gerade als Leiter der alternativen englischen *Summerhill-Schule* in Deutschland viel Interesse fand. Harry bot seinem Bruder an, das Buch zu übersetzen, aber der erklärte es für nicht übersetzbar, weil so viel amerikanischer 40er-Jahre-Gangsterslang darin vorkomme. Harry Rowohlt gelang es trotzdem meisterhaft, das Buch ins Deutsche zu übertragen, und er begründete damit seinen Ruf als begnadeter Übersetzer. Das Buch „Die grüne Wolke" landete 1970 auf Platz Eins der Spiegel-Bestsellerliste.

Rowohlt Tätigkeit als Werbetexter endete rasch, die er nach der Rückkehr aus den USA übernommen hatte, rasch und er etablierte sich 1971 als freiberuflicher Übersetzer: „... weil ich ziemlich ungern vor die Tür gehe, bin ich beim Übersetzen geblieben, denn da muss man nicht vor die Tür gehen". Ganze Generationen hat Harry Rowohlt mit seiner Übertragung und seinen Lesungen des Buches „Pu der Bär" erfreut. Es hat auch heute noch einen festen Platz in Bücher- und Hörbuchregalen von Kindern und Erwachsenen. Daran anknüpfend hat Rowohlt unregelmäßig, aber dafür über etliche Jahre die Kolumne „Pooh'S Corner" in der „Zeit" veröffentlicht.

Im Laufe der Jahrzehnte hat Harry Rowohlt annähernd 200 Bücher übersetzt, darunter viele irische Romane und einige Comics. Wie hoch seine Übersetzungsleistungen geschätzt wurden, zeigte sich an mehreren Auszeichnungen, aber auch an einem pfiffigen Cartoon des Zeichner-Duos Hauck & Bauer mit dieser Zeile: „Das Buch musst Du in der Übersetzung von Harry Rowohlt lesen. Im Original geht da viel verloren.“ Auch fünf Theaterstücke und einen Film hat er ins Deutsche übertragen.

Wie gründlich Rowohlt als Übersetzer vorging, hat der amerikanische Schriftsteller Padgett Powell erlebt: „Als er um 1987 herum mein erstes Buch übersetzte, schickte er mir zwanzig oder dreißig Fragen über die genaue Bedeutung englischer idiomatischer Wendungen und Wörter. Ich erinnere mich, ihm zur Antwort sechs Seiten geschickt zu haben, die mir mehr Arbeit gemacht hatten als das ganze Buch.“

Als Obdachloser in der „Lindenstraße“

Durch einen Zufall geriet Rowohlt 1975 in die Fernsehserie „Lindenstraße“. Die Zeitschrift „Essen und Trinken“ veröffentlichte damals regelmäßig Beiträge über den gemeinsamen Besuch mit Prominenten in Restaurants irgendwo in Europa. Die Redaktion rief auch Harry Rowohlt an, der kein Interesse an der Mitwirkung an einem solchen Beitrag hatte und ablehnte. Seine Frau Ulla kritisierte ihn daraufhin, er hätte doch das Lokal „Akropolis“ in der Fernsehserie „Lindenstraße“ vorschlagen können. Dann hätte er seine Ruhe gehabt und es hätte höflicher geklungen. Harry Rowohlt rief auf der Stelle die Zeitschriftenredaktion an und machte diesen Vorschlag.

Wider Erwarten lud man ihn tatsächlich zur Mitwirkung an einer Folge der Fernsehserie in einer Nebenrolle im Lokal „Akropolis“ ein. Er schlug vor, die Rolle eines Obdachlosen im Restaurant zu übernehmen, „weil das die einzige Randgruppe ist, die bisher in der ‚Lindenstraße' etwas stiefmütterlich behandelt wurde. Und außerdem brauche ich dafür nicht viel Maske."

Harry Rowohlt spielte den Obdachlosen so überzeugend, dass er zwei Jahrzehnte lang in insgesamt 193 Folgen der „Lindenstraße" zu sehen war. Der Produzent dieser Fernsehserie, Hans W. Geißendörfer, erinnerte sich so an den Schauspieler: „Harry Rowohlt, unser intellektueller Penner aus der ‚Lindenstraße', war unvergleichlich naiv, schlau, schlitzohrig, charmant, klug und intellektuell, Dichter, Lesekünstler und Selbstdarsteller. Er war kein Schauspieler mit Fremdtext, er war immer er selbst und schenkte dem Publikum mit jedem Blick, Wort oder stummem Lächeln sein Herz."

In den 1970er Jahren engagierte sich Harry Rowohlt in der Regierungszeit von Willy Brandt in der SPD. Später kühlte sein Verhältnis zur Partei ab, aber ausgetreten ist er nicht. Zu seinem politischen Engagement hat stets die Teilnahme an 1. Mai-Demonstrationen gehört. Seine Ablehnung des zweiten Irakkrieges der USA veranlasste eine Redakteurin des WDR zu der Interviewfrage, ob er antiamerikanisch wäre. Er widersprach vehement: „Ich – antiamerikanisch?? Ich habe geweint, als Winnetou starb!"

„Der dröhnende Bass hinter einem Urwald aus Bart"

1982 verkauften Harry Rowohlt und sein Bruder ihre Anteile am *Rowohlt-Verlag* an die *Holtzbrinck-Verlagsgruppe*, womit Harry Rowohlt endgültig von der Sorge befreit war, vielleicht doch noch einmal Verleger werden zu müssen. Stattdessen eröffnete sich ihm mit Lesungen ein neues Tätigkeitsfeld. David Hugendick schrieb in der „Zeit“ in einem Nachruf: „Als Vorleser war Rowohlt der größte, den wir hatten. Der dröhnende Bass hinter einem Urwald aus Bart. Ein ganzes Stimm-Orchester kam da hervor, so nannte es der Kritiker Rolf Michaelis einmal, das seufzte, schmatzte, schnaufte, gluckste, zwitscherte und ja, so hat es Pu sicher gewollt: brummte.“

Ein Meisterwerk war zweifellos das Hörbuch „Pu der Bär“, dazu noch einmal David Hugendick: „Rowohlt in jeder Rolle, für Ferkel in der Kopfstimme, dem depressiven Esel I-Ah leiht er ein tranlges Näseln, das immer geschäftige und beschäftigte Kaninchen immer außer Atem, und selbstredend Pu, der summend umherwandert: ‚Der Schnee, der Schnee, in dem ich geh, tidelipom!‘“

Harry Rowohlt löste mit seinen Lesungen beim Publikum immer wieder Begeisterung aus, obwohl manch eine Veranstaltung vier oder auch sechs Stunden dauern konnte. Es waren nämlich keine Lesungen im engeren Sinne, weil Rowohlt das Lesen der Texte immer wieder für Abschweifungen unterbrach. Im Verlauf seiner Lesungen nahm er häufiger einen Schluck von einem alkoholischen Getränke zu sich, vorzugsweise irischen Whisky. Er war besonders stolz darauf, dass ihm der Titel „Ambassador of Irish Whisky“ verliehen wurde. Aber auch am fortgeschrittenen Abend und nach so manchem Whisky hielt er sich an seine Lieblingstugend: „Sagen, was man denkt. Und vorher was gedacht haben.“ Deshalb „geriet ihm jede Vorlesung zu einer abenteuerlichen Odyssee der Abschweifungen“, wie Arno Frank in einem „Spiegel“-Nachruf schrieb. Und auf dieser Odyssee spielten eigene literarische Texte immer eine große Rolle.

Gelegentlich hatte Rowohlt Mühe, zu den eigenen Lesungen hereingelassen zu werden, weil die Veranstalter ihn mit langer Mähne und ungezähmtem Bart für einen Obdachlosen hielten. „Ich bin so oft in meinem Leben, weil ich so aussah, wie ich aussah, irgendwo nicht reingelassen worden. Zum Beispiel im Hamburger Literaturhaus in meine eigene Lesung nicht." Eine studentische Hilfskraft erklärte ihm kategorisch: „Nee, das kann gar nicht sein, wir haben hier heute Abend Dichterlesung."

Erinnerungen an einen wunderbaren Übersetzer und humorvollen Menschen

2007 machte Rowohlt bekannt, dass er an Polyneuropathie litt, eine Erkrankung, die seine Gehfähigkeit stark einschränkte. Sein Trost: „Ich brauch' mich als passionierter Stubenhocker nicht groß umschulen zu lassen." Und in der Tat saß er viel öfter einsam am Schreibtisch und übersetzte, als er in Lesungen oder bei Fernsehaufnahmen zu finden war.

Der Literaturkritiker Hellmuth Karasek war gut mit ihm bekannt und hat gelegentlich Abende in Kneipen mit ihm verbracht. Er hat betont, dass Rowohlts Alkoholkonsum oft übertrieben dargestellt worden ist: „In Wahrheit verbarg sich hinter dem Porträt des großen Trinkers ein Mensch, der sehr scheu war. Und ein fast fieberhaft arbeitender Mensch. Deshalb ist er ein so wunderbarer Übersetzer geworden. Und in den Kneipen fiel er nur durch kurze Einwürfe trockenen Humors auf."

Im Alter lebte Rowohlt mit seiner Frau in Eppendorf. Am 15. Juni 2015 starb er an Lungenkrebs. Sein Grab befindet sich auf dem *Ohlsdorfer Friedhof*. Der Lindenstraßen-

Produzent Geißendörfer äußerte sich so zum himmlischen Leben Rowohlts: „Ich kann mir gut vorstellen, dass er jetzt neben Petrus im Himmel sitzt und sein Bier mit ihm teilt, während beide die Neuankömmlinge dort oben liebevoll willkommen heißen und ihnen (mit einem Schluck aus der Flasche) die Angst vor dem Neuanfang nehmen."

Johann Balthasar Schupp

Hier liegt Herr Doctor Schuppius.
Er war ein scharfer Critikus,
Mitunter auch ein sehr grober Gesell.
Ist leicht zu finden an seiner Stell.
Man rührt Grobheit und Dummheit zu Mut,
So haben wir einen neuen Schuppius.

Der Vers stand nicht auf dem Grabstein von Johann Balthasar Schupp. Aber er kursierte nach seinem Tod in der Stadt, verbreitet von den vielen Gegnern des Pastors von *St. Jacobi*. Es gab auf der anderen Seite zahlreiche Hamburgerinnen und Hamburger, die gern in seine Gottesdienste strömten. Es waren so viele, dass in *St. Jacobi* zwei neue Emporen eingebaut wurden.

Aber das besänftigte seine Kritiker in der Kirche nicht, am wenigsten seine Amtsbrüder in den anderen Kirchen der Stadt, die argwöhnisch beobachteten, dass ihre Schäfchen in die Gottesdienste Schupps strömten. Man kann Schupp ohne Weiteres zu den Hamburger Originalen zählen - und wie so viele Originale war er den Mächtigen unbequem, in diesem Fall besonders den Mächtigen in seiner Kirche.

Ein beeindruckender Bildungsweg in kriegerischen Zeiten

Johann Balthasar Schupp (später auch Schuppius genannt) wurde am 1. März 1610 in Gießen geboren. Sein Vater war Bürgermeister der Stadt, die Mutter stammte ebenfalls aus einer angesehenen bürgerlichen Familie. Der Sohn besuchte standesgemäß die Gelehrtenschule in

Gießen und begann bereits mit 15 Jahren ein Studium in Marburg. Er studierte zunächst Philosophie und wechselte dann zur Theologie. Mitten im Dreißigjährigen Krieg unternahm er von 1628 an eine akademische Reise in verschiedene deutsche Universitätsstädte und ebenso nach Livland, Estland, Polen und Dänemark. Die Kriegswirren brachten ihn mehrfach in Gefahr und zwangen ihn zur Flucht, aber er erlangte auf dieser Bildungsreise auch viele neue wissenschaftliche Einsichten.

Schupp schloss sein Studium 1631 in Rostock mit Auszeichnung ab. Er hielt nun Vorlesungen an dieser Universität. Als Folge der militärischen Auseinandersetzungen um die Stadt musste er allerdings noch im gleichen Jahr über Hamburg zurück nach Gießen flüchten. Sein Landgraf berief den 25-Jährigen zum Professor.

Er unterrichtete in Marburg und Gießen. Er war so beliebt, dass seine Kollegen und Studenten sich erfolgreich bei seinem Landesherrn für eine deutliche Erhöhung seines Gehalts einsetzten. Er konnte nun eine Familie gründen und heiratete 1636. Seine Frau Anna Elisabeth und er sollen eine glückliche Ehe geführt haben und hatten fünf Kinder.

1645 erreichte der Krieg auch Marburg. Schwedische Truppen eroberten und plünderten die Stadt. Auch das Gartenhaus und die ganze Habe der Familie Schupp gingen verloren. Da war es nur ein schwacher Trost, dass Schupp im gleichen Jahr zum Doktor der Theologie promoviert wurde. Im folgenden Jahr nahm Schupp die Berufung zum Hofprediger des Landgrafen von Hessen-Braubach an und zog mit seiner Familie nach Braubach um. Der Landgraf fasste rasch großes Vertrauen in seinen Hofprediger und ernannte ihn 1648 zu seinem Bevollmächtigten bei den Friedensverhandlungen zur Beendigung des Dreißigjährigen Krieges in Osnabrück und Münster.

Der populäre Pastor von St. Jacobi

Im gleichen Jahr trug man Balthasar Schupp die Stelle des Pastors der *St. Jacobikirche* in Hamburg an. Er hielt eine so beeindruckende Probepredigt, dass er einstimmig gewählt wurde. Gern hätten ihn die Verantwortlichen des *Hochstiftes Münster* stattdessen zum Generalsuperintendenten gemacht und boten ihm ein höheres Gehalt, als man ihm in Hamburg in Aussicht gestellt hatte. Schupp entschied sich trotzdem für Hamburg: „Wegen Education meiner Kinder und anderer Commoditäten halber deuchte mich, es sei ein Pastorat in Hamburg besser, als anderswo ein großer Titel."

Schupp wurde am 20. Juli 1649 in sein neues Amt eingeführt. Der weitgereiste Theologe war erfreut, in eine so international geprägte Stadt zu kommen. Er schrieb einem Freund, dass er vorher schon mehrmals in Hamburg gewesen war, „und habe nicht gewusst, was Hamburg war, dass Hamburg ist Klein Spanien, Klein Portugal, Klein Frankreich, Klein Schweden, Klein Dänemark, dass Hamburg eine kleine Welt ist." Auch über die „klugen Köpfe" in der Stadt zeigte er sich erfreut. „Hamburg ist gefüllt mit Doktoren, Lizentiaten, Magistern."

Über die Hamburger Gartenpracht äußerte er: „Hamburg ist ein irdisches Paradies. Ich weiß mich nicht zu besinnen, dass ich eine Stadt in Deutschland gesehen hätte, die so viele schöne Lustgärten hat wie Hamburg."

Schupp besaß im Vergleich zu seinen Amtsbrüdern eine sehr beeindruckende theologische und philosophische Bildung. Das hat ihn vermutlich davon befreit, hochgebildete, aber schwer verständliche Predigten in *St. Jacobi* zu halten. Mittwochs, freitags und sonntags war die Kirche stets gefüllt, weil Schupp einen volkstümlichen Predigtstil hatte, wenn er auf der Kanzel stand. Er vermittelte seine biblischen Einsichten mit Geschichten aus dem Alltag, Anekdoten und Witzen. Die Kirche soll häufig von Lachen erfüllt gewesen sein.

Von seinen Amtsbrüdern attackiert

Schupp schuf sich dadurch Gegner in der Stadt, dass er die Lebensweise mancher Gemeindemitglieder mit drastischen Worten anprangerte. So warf er den Kaufleuten vor, in der Kirche vor und sogar im Gottesdienst hinter vorgehaltener Hand leise über geschäftliche Angelegenheiten zu reden. Er sagte in einer Predigt: „Wann wird wohl größerer Wucher, größere Schinderei und Betrügerei in Hamburg getrieben als an dem Christabend in der Domkirche!"

Seine Amtsbrüder und manche Gemeindemitglieder empfanden seinen Predigtstil als nicht vereinbar mit dem Ernst einer Predigt. Schupp hatte nach dem Tod seiner Frau 1651 erneut geheiratet, und um dem populären Prediger zu schaden, verbreiteten seine Gegner falsche Gerüchte über die Zustände in seiner Familie und darüber, dass er keine glückliche Ehe führen würde.

Sein Amt ließ Schupp Zeit für schriftstellerische Arbeiten. Hatte er frühere Werke wie damals üblich auf Latein veröffentlicht, so schrieb er nun Bücher auf Deutsch. Er wollte damit auch weniger gebildete Menschen erreichen. Schupp war als orthodoxer lutherischer Theologe nach Hamburg gekommen, wandelte sich aber zu einem Reformtheologen.

Der Hamburger Historiker Franklin Kopitzsch hat in seinem umfangreichen Werk über die Aufklärung in Hamburg den Pastor von *St. Jacobi* so gewürdigt: „Der Gedanke der Bildung durch und für das Leben, die Neuerungen im Gottesdienst und die über die Fachdisziplin der Theologie hinausreichende literarische Tätigkeit – alle diese Fakten machten den aus Hessen, wo er immerhin Hofprediger gewesen war, nach Hamburg gekommenen Schuppius bei den Amtsbrüdern nicht eben beliebt. Vor allem Senior Müller machte ihm das Leben schwer."

Die judenfeindlichen Auffassungen Schupps

Nicht verschwiegen werden soll, dass es einen dunklen Schatten im Leben und Wirken von Pastor Schupp gab, seine Judenfeindlichkeit, die sich besonders gegen die sefardischen (aus Portugal eingewanderten) Juden und ihren zur Schau gestellten Reichtum richtete. Manche dieser aus Portugal und Spanien vor der Inquisition geflohenen Juden betätigten sich in Hamburg erfolgreich als Fernhändler und Bankiers. Besonders reich war Diego Teixeira, der in der Stadt als „der reiche Jude" galt. Schupp teilte die Auffassung vieler Christen, dass der jüdischen Bevölkerung lediglich eine untergeordnete Stellung in der Gesellschaft zukam. Er mokierte sich deshalb in einer Geschichte über den „reichen Juden“, dem sein Geld ermöglichte, wie ein Adliger in einer „schönen mit Sammet gefütterten Kutsche“ in Begleitung eines Dieners in Livree durch die Stadt zu fahren.

Schupp unterstellte in einer Veröffentlichung, dass der reiche Jude sein Vermögen durch Betrug „zusammen gescharret“ hatte. Um zu betonen, dass den Juden lediglich eine untergeordnete Stellung in der Gesellschaft zustand, erinnerte er am Ende seines Textes an die Zerstörung Jerusalems im Jahre 70. Dieses historische Ereignis galt in der Theologie zu Zeiten Schupps als göttliche Strafe dafür, dass die damaligen Juden sich nicht zum Christentum bekannt hatten.

Einem solchen Verständnis der Rolle der Juden stand, so werden es auch viele Leserinnen und Leser der Schrift Schupps gesehen haben, der Reichtum mancher Juden in der Stadt diametral entgegen. Schupp wollte den Juden in Hamburg mit fragwürdigen theologischen Argumenten lediglich niedrigste Tätigkeiten als „Holzhäuer“ und „Wasserträger“ zuweisen. Ein reicher Jude in einer prächtigen Kutsche passte ganz und gar nicht zu einem solchen Verständnis des Platzes der Juden in der Hamburger Gesellschaft.

Immer neue Angriffe auf den beliebten Prediger

Solche Auffassungen teilten Schupps Amtsbrüder, aber andere Schriften Schupps nahmen die orthodox lutherischen Pastoren in Hamburg zum Anlass, ihn vor eine Kommission des Geistlichen Ministeriums, dem Gremium aller lutherischen Pastoren der Stadt, zu laden. Es wurde 1657 von Schupp verlangt, keine theologischen

Schriften mehr zu veröffentlichen und alle Publikationen ohne ein Pseudonym herauszugeben. Das nahm Schupp hin. Er weigerte sich aber, seine Schriften vorab dem Senior, dem leitenden Pastor, zur Zensur vorzulegen.

Dass Schupp weitere Bücher veröffentlichte, ohne sie vorher zensieren zu lassen, verschärfte die Konflikte. Die volkstümlichen Schriften fanden reißenden Absatz. Sie befassten sich mit Fragen von Alltagleben und Pädagogik, aber zum Beispiel auch mit dem Gelehrtendünkel. Besonders in der Leserschaft beliebt und bei den Mächtigen verhasst waren seine satirischen Schriften. Schupp wurde vorgeworfen, seine Kollegen lästerlich anzugreifen. Seine Gegner attackierten ihn ihrerseits mit hässlichen Schmähschriften.

Das Geistliche Ministerium ließ von den theologischen Fakultäten in Straßburg und Wittenberg theologische Gutachten zu den Schriften Schupps anfertigen, deren Ergebnisse 1658 in eine Klageschrift gegen Schupp beim Senat einflossen. Vor allem forderte das Geistliche Ministerium vom Senat, er möge Schupp verbieten, Fabeln, Scherze, Satiren und Ähnliches in seine Predigten und Schriften einzubeziehen. Der Senat wollte sich verständlicherweise nicht in die Angelegenheit verwickeln lassen und gebot beiden Seiten, Stillschweigen zu wahren und die Konflikte hinfort nicht mehr öffentlich auszutragen.

Schupp publizierte weiter Schriften, vermied aber Themen und Formulierungen, die öffentlich Anstoß erregen konnten. Fabeln und Anekdoten bezog er aber weiterhin auch in seine religiösen Schriften ein. Der Senat verbot ihm daraufhin im Frühjahr 1658, weitere Schriften in

Hamburg zu publizieren. Viele der späteren Veröffentlichungen Schupps erschienen daraufhin in Wolfenbüttel. Der Streit ging weiter und der Senat wollte endlich Ruhe haben. Er verwarnte Schupp deshalb im Januar 1669.

Das reichte dem Geistlichen Ministerium nicht und es richtete kurz darauf eine Eingabe an den Senat, in dem gebeten wurde, „solchem ärgerlichen Wesen und großer Zerrüttung unserer Kirche, wie auch dem betrübten Zustand des Ministerii nicht länger zuzusehen". Der Senat unternahm zwar nichts, Schupp sah sich aber trotzdem genötigt, in einer Verteidigungsschrift die gegen ihn erhobenen Vorwürfe zu widerlegen. In einem biografischen Beitrag über Schupp hat der evangelische Theologe Carl Bertheau im 19. Jahrhundert geschrieben: „Die vielen Widerwärtigkeiten, die ihm zu Theil wurden, blieben nicht ohne Folgen; er starb frühzeitig an einer heftigen Krankheit in seinem 52. Lebensjahr am 26. October 1661 ..."

Ein „Eulenspiegel" auf der Kanzel

Schupp ist als bedeutender satirischer Schriftsteller in die Literaturgeschichte eingegangen. Wie beliebt seine Schriften waren, zeigt sich auch daran, dass man eine ganze Reihe von ihnen ins Dänische und Niederländische übersetzte. Er selbst wurde trotzdem als vermutlich erster – und wahrlich nicht als letzter – Satiriker der Stadt verspottet und verfolgt. Jemand, der Missstände in der Stadt und die Völlerei der Reichen anprangerte, war den Herrschenden ein Dorn im Auge.

Wie Till Eulenspiegel hielt Schupp seinen Zeitgenossen den Spiegel vor. Dass er sehr anschaulich und gut verständlich schrieb und predigte, machte die Sache nur noch schlimmer. Johannes Sass hat in seinem Buch über Hamburger Originale dem Pastor von *St. Jacobi* einen ehrenvollen Platz eingeräumt, und das soll auch hier geschehen. Er war ohne Zweifel ein besonders gebildetes Mitglied der Gruppe der Hamburger Originale – und das erklärt wahrscheinlich auch, warum er mit solcher Vehemenz bekämpft wurde.

Die in *St. Jacobi* wegen der großen Zahl von Besuchern in Schupps Gottesdiensten errichteten zusätzlichen Emporen hat man später wieder abgerissen – sie wurden nicht mehr benötigt. Schupp selbst hatte über seine Gottesdienste geschrieben: „Die Kirche ist so voll, dass ich mich durch das Volk auf die Kanzel drängen muss."

Emma Thiele-Lundershausen

Kaum ein in diesem Buch vorgestelltes Hamburger Original ist so sehr in Vergessenheit geraten wie Emma Thiele-Lundershausen. Dabei gehörte sie in der zweiten Hälfte des 19. Jahrhunderts zu den gefeierten Sängerinnen der Stadt und hatte beachtlichen Erfolg als Direktorin von Konzerthallen.

Im Alter von 19 Jahren trat sie 1856 erstmals als Sängerin in Konzerthäusern auf St. Pauli auf. Bald unternahm sie auch Auslandstourneen, kam aber immer gern wieder in die Heimat und besonders nach St. Pauli zurück. In ihren längst vergriffenen Lebenserinnerungen schrieb sie: „Wie war mir wohl, wie war mir wonnig, als ich nach langer Auslandsreise in Kiel landete und ein breitschultriger Mann mit den Worten ‚Sall ick Ihn ok den Koffer besorgen' auf mich zutrat. Es waren Heimatklänge, die ich lange entbehrt hatte, und ich weiß auch heute nicht, was mich damals hinderte, dem Verkünder dieser Heimatgrüße um den Hals zu fallen und zu küssen!"

Eine erfolgreiche und glückliche Sängerin

Sie trat danach zum Beispiel in der *Bazar-Halle* am Jungfernstieg auf. Dieser Saal gehörte zu *Sillems Bazar*, der ersten – prachtvollen – Einkaufspassage Europas. Die Sängerin konnte dort beliebig lange singen, musste danach selbst aber mit dem Teller in der Hand durch die Halle gehen und „den klingenden Zoll der Anerkennung" einsammeln. Emma Thiele-Lundershausen fand hier viel Anerkennung. Daraufhin erhielt sie im *Ludwig'schen Etablissement* ein festes Engagement mit festem Honorar. Das Haus lag am Spielbudenplatz und war eines der beliebtesten Konzerthäuser in Hamburg. Die Sängerin konnte hier ein ganzes Jahr lang auftreten. Sie schrieb in ihren Lebenserinnerungen:

„Es war die schönste Zeit meiner Gesangs-Carrière, die ich hier verbrachte. Von der Direktion aufs Freundlichste und Zuvorkommendste behandelt, verhätschelt vom Publikum, umgeben von Freunden und Gönnern, so schwand mir ein glückliches Jahr dahin. Ich will nicht verhehlen, dass es mir auch an Anbetern nicht fehlte, offenkundigen sowohl als auch stillen."

Das Konzerthaus mit der Plattdeutsch sprechenden Direktorin

Sie war inzwischen als Sängerin so wohlhabend geworden, dass sie 1882 ein eigenes Konzerthaus am Spielbudenplatz eröffnen konnte, dem sie den Namen *Casino, das Gesangs-Institut internationaler Prägung* gab. Das Unternehmen war so erfolgreich, dass sie drei Jahre später das Nachbargrundstück dazukaufen und ihr Konzerthaus erweitern konnte. Sie nannte ihr Haus nun *Die neue Welt*.

Carl Thinius, dem es zu verdanken ist, dass die Künstlerin nicht ganz in Vergessenheit geraten ist, hat in seinem Buch „Damals in St. Pauli" über diese Zeit geschrieben: „In ihrem eigenen Konzerthaus ‚Die neue Welt' war Frau Emma zum Original geworden. Sie sprach als echte Hamburgerin gern plattdeutsch und, wenn sie recht gute Laune hatte, auch missingsch. Alle ihre Inserate und Verlautbarungen unterzeichnete Emma Thiele-Lundershausen mit der stereotypen Schlussbemerkung: ‚Achtungsvoll: Die Direktion‘. Dieses geflügelte Wort machte sie bald ungemein populär. Wenn sie sich bei einem Rundgang durch das Lokal einer Gruppe jovialer Gäste näherte, dann schallte ihr der Gruß entgegen: ‚Achtungsvoll, die Direktion!‘.“

Die „Neue Welt“ musste aus finanziellen Gründen schließen

Leider hielt der finanzielle Erfolg ihrer Konzerthalle nicht lange an. Ein Grund soll gewesen sein, dass sie zu großzügig mit ihrem Geld umging, auch bei ihren Liebesabenteuern, über deren Einzelheiten sie in ihren Lebenserinnerungen schwieg. 1891 musste das Konzerthaus schließen. Die Direktorin verfasste aus diesem Anlass diesen Epilog:

> *Hier stand ich einst, vor kaum fünf Jahren,*
> *als dieses Haus war neu und schön,*
> *begrüßte froher Gäste Scharen,*
> *Erhoffend Glück und Wohlergehen.*
>
> *Mit freud'gem Eifer wollt' ich gründen*
> *Die lusterfüllte „Neue Welt“, -*
> *Und heute nah ich, zu verkünden*
> *Den Untergang, dem sie verfällt.*
>
> *Nicht, dass ich nach Verlorenem hasche*
> *Und klagend scheide, soll man sehn.*
> *Nein, wie ein Phönix aus der Asche,*
> *wird Emma Thiele neu erstehn!*

Dann grüß' ich meine Freunde wieder,
die treu und lieb mir lange schon.
So leg ich denn das Szepter nieder.
Hochachtungsvoll: Die Direktion!

Das Konzerthaus wurde von anderen Betreibern unter dem Namen *Im siebten Himmel* fortgeführt. Der später berühmte Sänger und Humorist Hein Köllisch erlebte hier sein erfolgreiches Bühnendebüt. Der *Siebte Himmel* musste trotzdem bald geschlossen werden, und hier eröffnete 1898 das Varieté *Apollo*. Es blieb ein kurzes Intermezzo. 1900 entstand unter dem Namen *Hamburg-America-Bar* die laut Eigenwerbung „größte Bar Deutschlands".

Es folgte die Nutzung des Grundstücks für ein Kino und dann für ein Gefrierfleisch-Geschäft. 1934 wurde an dieser Stelle ein Schwimmbad eröffnet. Das schloss 1980. Nach einem Dornröschenschlaf von über vier Jahrzehnten wurde auf dem Grundstück ein Weingarten eröffnet. Die erhalten gebliebene Gründerzeitfassade erinnert an die Geschichte eines Hauses, die fast so bewegt war wie die Lebensgeschichte von Emma Thiele-Lundershausen.

Henry Vahl

„Wenn ich gewusst hätte, wie das Leben so spielt und was es noch alles mit mir vorhatte, ich hätte vieles leichter genommen. Wenn ich aber gewusst hätte, dass ich erst fünfzig Jahre auf der Bühne stehen müsste, um mich dann im Rentenalter von 68 Jahren noch zu ‚Deutschlands Fernsehopa' zu mausern, so weiß ich heute gar nicht, ob ich die lange Wartezeit durchgestanden hätte." Das schrieb Henry Vahl in seinen Lebenserinnerungen. Nach all den Jahren ohne große Erfolge hatte er sich damit abgefunden, zu den vielen Schauspielern zu gehören, die „auch kleine Rollen mit Herzblut ausfüllen und den Weg freischaufeln für diejenigen, die das Publikum anlocken".

„Und was macht die Tante da unten?"

Henry Vahl stand bereits im Alter von vier Jahren auf einer Bühne. „Mama" sollte der kleine Junge rufen und dann auf seine Mutter zustürzen und sie umarmen. So hatte es Ibsen in seiner Tragödie „Nora" für den dritten Akt vorgesehen und so hatte es der kleine Henry mehrfach geprobt. Eigentlich konnte nichts schiefgehen, als er bei der ersten Aufführung des Stücks in seinem Matrosenanzug auf die Bühne trat. Aber was tat die Frau da in dem Kasten? Henry fasste sich ein Herz und fragte seine Schauspiel-Mutter laut: „Und was macht die Tante da unten?"

Die Schauspielerin blickte auf den Souffleusenkasten und antwortete geistesgegenwärtig: „Komm her, mein Kind, ich erkläre es dir später, jetzt sag mir erst einmal gute

Nacht.“ Henry kannte die Vertröstungen der Erwachsenen und sagte leicht resigniert „Na ja, dann gute Nacht.“ Das Publikum bog sich vor Lachen, das einzige Mal während dieser Aufführung. Henry durfte auch an den kommenden Abenden „gute Nacht" sagen. Jeden Abend wanderten 50 Pfennig in den Spartopf, damit zu Weihnachten ein Matrosenmantel für den jungen Schauspieler gekauft werden konnte. Jetzt konnte eigentlich eine traumhafte Theaterkarriere beginnen, aber im wirklichen Leben kam alles anders.

Wie Henry den Schuss von Wilhelm Tell überlebte

Henry Vahl (geboren 1897 in Stralsund) war der Sohn eines Seemanns und verdankte seinen Vornamen dem besten Freund des Vaters, einem englischen Seemann. Er bekam auch die Vornamen Adolf, Emil und Otto – Henry blieb sein Rufname. Der Vater wollte aus dem Sohn gern einen Seemann machen und nahm ihn schon im Alter von fünf Jahren mit auf See.

Die Schwiegermutter sah Henry bereits als Schauspieler. Sie setzte sich durch, und so stand Henry schon als Kind auf der Bühne, auch wenn der Vater von dem „Kasperkram“ nichts hielt. Nach Ibsens „Nora“ erhielt Henry eine gefährliche Rolle: Er spielte den Sohn, dem der Vater Wilhelm Tell den Apfel vom Kopf schießen sollte. Glücklicherweise wurde im Theater von Stralsund gemogelt. Der Apfel war bereits zerschnitten und Henry zog ihn im richtigen Augenblick mit Hilfe eines Bindfadens vom Kopf. Es klappte perfekt, und der kleine Henry wurde stürmisch gefeiert. Es folgten kleine Ballettrollen in Weihnachtsmärchen.

Der Schüler hatte nur im Betragen eine Eins

Zur Schule gehen musste Henry auch, ungern, wie er später bekannte. Er marschierte dann schon lieber mit der Großmutter auf den Friedhof, „auch kein reines Vergnügen, aber immer noch besser, als in der Schule die Stunden abzusitzen". Henry versuchte in der Schule, möglichst wenig aufzufallen und vom Lehrer in Ruhe gelassen zu werden. Da traf es sich gut, dass er wegen seiner schlechten Leistungen meist in einer der hinteren Bankreihen saß. Vor und nach der Schule trug Henry zum Familieneinkommen bei. Was er trug, waren Pferdeäpfel, die er morgens bei Fuhrbetrieben einsammelte. Nach der Schule lieferte er die gefüllten Eimer bei einer Samenhandlung ab.

Nachdem sein Fischkutter im Sturm gesunken war, fand der Vater 1905 eine Anstellung bei der *Kaiserlichen Werft* in Kiel. Henry sammelte und verkaufte auch in Kiel Pferdeäpfel, um etwas dazuzuverdienen. 1911 schloss er die Schule ab, mit mäßigen Noten. Nur im Betragen hatte er eine Eins. Zur Konfirmation schenkte die Mutter ihm das Buch „Der gute Ton in allen Lebenslagen". Schon länger hatte sie eigene Zukunftspläne für den Sohn gehegt: Er sollte herrschaftlicher Diener werden und schön gekleidet feine Leute bedienen. Deshalb sprach sie mit ihrem Sohn konsequent Hochdeutsch, während die Familie ansonsten Plattdeutsch sprach. Den Vater beeindruckte das mütterliche Bildungsprogramm für Henry nicht: „De Jung kümmt no See."

Aber der Junge wollte nicht zur See fahren, und so einigte sich die Familie auf einen Kompromiss. Henry kam als

Lehrling in die Druckerei der *Kaiserlichen Werft*. Aber er konnte am Druck von Verordnungen keinen Gefallen finden und am Dreck in dem Betrieb auch nicht: „Nee, meinen Beruf hatte ich mir ganz anders vorgestellt." Er kündigte und wechselte zu einer Molkerei. Viel wichtiger als diese Arbeit waren dem jungen Mann damals die ersten zarten Liebesbande.

Als Liftboy für das Theater entdeckt

Dann brachen zwei Katastrophen über die Familie herein. Die erste betraf das ganze Land, der Ausbruch des Ersten Weltkriegs. Mit der zweiten Katastrophe musste die Familie allein fertig werden: Der Vater starb durch einen Unfall. Die Witwe ergriff entschlossen die Initiative, die finanzielle Situation der Familie zu verbessern. Der Sohn erhielt einen Frack. Er sollte nun nicht mehr herrschaftlicher Diener werden, sondern einmal Hoteldirektor. Mutter und Sohn gingen zum Direktor des eleganten *Hansa-Hotels* in Kiel. Die guten Manieren des jungen Manns und sein exzellentes Hochdeutsch beeindruckten den Direktor. Er stellte Henry Vahl als Liftboy ein. Ein Gehalt bekam er nicht, aber es waren Trinkgelder zu erwarten. Kost und Logis stellte das Hotel.

Im Hotel begann sein Aufstieg, zunächst einmal nur in den zweiten Stock, denn dahin wollte der freundliche Herr, der ihm beim Singen zuhörte. Es war Karl Alving, der Direktor des *Stadt-Theaters* in Kiel. Er fragte den Liftboy: ,,Hättest Du Lust, abends Theater zu spielen?" Lust? Henry war begeistert, dass er im Kieler Schauspielhaus auf die Bühne durfte, zunächst allerdings nur in schwarzer spanischer Tracht im Gefolge von „Don Carlos".

Der junge Mann sah die Gefahr auf sich zukommen, zum Kriegsdienst eingezogen zu werden. Um dem zu entgehen, zog er die Liftboy-Uniform aus und arbeitete in der Stahlschmiede der *Howaldtswerft* in Kiel. Der schmächtige junge Mann erwies sich als ungeeignet für die Arbeit als Schmied. Er wurde nach draußen versetzt und war nun an der Reparatur von Schiffen beteiligt. Abends spielte er weiter Theater, und da viele Schauspieler eingezogen worden waren, bekam der Komparse Vahl nun erste Sprechrollen. In den Nachmittagsvorstellungen konnte er sogar die Titelrolle in „Peterchens Mondfahrt" spielen. Die Kritiken in den Zeitungen waren positiv, vom Direktor gab es einen Rüffel. Wie später so oft hatte Vahl den Text nicht auswendig gelernt, sondern improvisierte.

Erfolg in der Rolle eines tollpatschigen Seemanns

Als nach Kriegsende wieder herzlich gelacht werden konnte, begann Henry Vahls Karriere als Komiker. Als ein Kollege wegen einer Lebensmittelvergiftung ausfiel, übernahm Vahl die Rolle eines tollpatschigen Seemanns in einer Operette. In einer Szene sollte er feurig und verführerisch ins Publikum blicken. „Das Publikum lachte, weil mein Blick wohl mehr neckisch als verführerisch war." Er spielte nun komische Rollen, vor allem viel ältere Männer, etwa den Schweinefürsten Zupan im Zigeunerbaron. Er erhielt ein festes Engagement und gab seine bisherige Arbeit auf.

Mit 21 Jahren engagierte ihn das neu eröffnete *Hansa-Theater* in Lübeck. Henry Vahl reiste mit zwei Pappkartons in die Hansestadt und fragte ein 17-jähriges Mädchen nach dem Weg. Es war die Balletttänzerin Germaine

Koch. Erst gingen sie gemeinsam zum Theater und bald auch durchs Leben. Der Heiratsantrag kam von ihr – bühnenreif. Bei einer Probe rief sie quer durch den Raum: „Schieter, hör mal, wir müssen heiraten. Sofort und ganz schnell!“ Nein, ein Kind war nicht unterwegs, aber ohne Trauschein war an eine eigene Wohnung nicht zu denken. Am 31. Januar 1925 wurde geheiratet.

Gemeinsam zogen sie anschließend von einer Provinzbühne zur nächsten. Germaine übernahm oft die Aufgabe einer Souffleuse und Henry spielte komische Rollen, in denen er öfter aus der Rolle fiel, weil er den Text vergessen hatte. Er versuchte, auch ernste Rollen zu spielen, aber das Publikum sah in ihm den Komiker. 1931 wagte das Paar auf Initiative von Germaine den Sprung nach Berlin. Henry Vahl bekam ein Engagement an Max Reinhardts berühmtem *Deutschen Theater*, zunächst allerdings nur als Statist für drei Reichsmark pro Abend. Aber bald bekam er auch Rollen, in denen er sprechen konnte – und wieder vor allem komische Rollen. Gern ließ er sich von älteren Kollegen Ratschläge geben, vor allem von dem Schauspieler Albert Bassermann, der ihm zum Beispiel empfahl: „Henry, um Wirkung zu erzielen, musst du mehr Pausen einlegen. Die Leute brauchen Zeit zum Lachen.“

Schwere Zeiten während der Naziherrschaft

1933 änderte sich die Lebenssituation des Paars radikal. Germaine war evangelischen Glaubens, aber in den Kategorien der Nazis „Halbjüdin“. Die Vahls durften zunächst noch spielen, standen aber unter Beobachtung. In der Theaterkantine war Gesprächsstoff, welche Schauspielerinnen und Schauspieler gerade das Land verlassen hatten, weil sie Juden waren. Vor dem Machtantritt der Nazis wusste im Theater kaum jemand, wer Jude war; es hatte niemanden interessiert.

1940 wechselten die Vahls an das Theater im tschechischen Karlsbad, wo vom Krieg weniger zu spüren war als in Berlin. Germaine erhielt Auftrittsverbot, eine Verhaftung drohte. Ohne das Wissen ihres Mannes hatte sie sich mit Unterstützung ihrer Eltern auf diese Situation vorbereitet, tauchte unter und überlebte in einer Gartenlaube in der Nähe von Ratzeburg. Nicht einmal der Ehemann erfuhr ihren Aufenthaltsort.

So konnte er bei mehreren Verhören glaubhaft versichern, dass er nicht wüsste, wo seine Frau war. Henry Vahl erhielt einen Einberufungsbefehl und den Auftrag, als Komiker an der Truppenbetreuung mitzuwirken. Als es nichts mehr zu lachen gab und die deutschen Truppen auf dem Rückzug waren, steckte man Henry Vahl in eine Wehrmachtsuniform und machte ihn zum Flaksoldaten. Er geriet in amerikanische Kriegsgefangenschaft und wurde bereits nach einem halben Jahr wieder entlassen.

Engagements an mehreren Hamburger Theatern

Henry Vahl kehrte nach Berlin zurück. Die Berliner Wohnung war heil geblieben, und hier konnte der Schauspieler endlich wieder seine Frau in die Arme nehmen. Sie hatte schwere Zeiten erlebt, aber überlebt. Beide beschlossen, das zerstörte und geteilte Berlin zu verlassen und sich 1950 in Hamburg eine neue Existenz aufzubauen. Sie zogen in eine 2-Zimmer-Wohnung im Heußweg in Eimsbüttel.

Germaine Vahl nahm ihre künstlerische Arbeit nicht wieder auf und konzentrierte sich hinfort darauf, ihren Mann zu fördern. Aus dem Traum von der großen Karriere war bisher nichts geworden. Henry Vahl hatte sich inzwischen damit abgefunden nur „einer der vielen Schauspieler zu sein, ohne die das Theater nicht leben kann". Aber immerhin erhielt er gleich nach seiner Ankunft in Hamburg ein Engagement im *Flora-Theater* und stand in jeder Inszenierung auf der Bühne. Auch im kleinen *Theater im Zimmer*, im *Thalia-Theater* und im *Jungen Theater* (heute *Ernst-Deutsch-Theater*) trat er auf.

Große Erfolge als Schustergeselle im Stück „Meister Anecker"

1958 fragte das *Ohnsorg-Theater* Henry Vahl, ob er die Rolle des Schustergesellen Matten im Stück „Meister Anecker" übernehmen wolle. Er sagte sofort zu, ohne zu ahnen, dass damit für ihn eine ganz neue und sehr erfolgreiche Zeit seiner Schauspielerkarriere begann. Er war bereits 60 Jahre alt, als er nun seine erste plattdeutsche Rolle spielte. Und endlich hatte er mit dem Volkstheater die Bühne gefunden, für die er wie geschaffen war. Das Stück war von Anfang an ein großer Erfolg. Vahls Sprüche wie „Was ich trinke, das bringt keinen anderen um!" wurden legendär.

Das Fernsehen wurde auf das Stück aufmerksam und beschloss, eine Aufführung des Stücks am 13. November 1965 auszustrahlen. Die Resonanz war überwältigend. Henry Vahl erinnerte sich später: „Unser Telefon klingelte bis in den Sonntagmorgen. Kollegen, Freunde, fremde Menschen riefen mich an und gratulierten.

Telegramme kamen, Blumen. Ich wusste nicht, wie mir geschah."

Große Erfolge am Ohnsorg-Theater

Allerdings, seine Gedächtnisprobleme und Versprecher blieben bestehen. Als Schustergeselle sollte er sagen. „Meine Mutter war eine Frau, die konnte ihre Zunge nicht im Zaum halten ..." Daraus machte Henry Vahl: „Meine Mutter war eine Frau, die steckte ihre Zunge immer durch den Zaun." Das Publikum war begeistert über diese unfreiwillige Pointe. Aber bei anderen Hängern mussten seine Mitspieler spontan neue Texte finden, um die Handlung wieder in geordnete Bahnen zu lenken.

Heidi Kabel erinnerte sich so an die Auftritte Henry Vahls: „Wenn er die Bühne betrat, applaudierte das Publikum und lachte, bevor er einen Satz gesagt hatte. Es genügte, dass er zu sehen war. Seine Mitspieler allerdings brachte er oft in Verlegenheit. Schon immer war es ihm schwergefallen, Texte zu lernen. Deshalb wiederholte er stets seinen Spruch: ‚Die Souffleusen waren immer meine besten Freundinnen.' Aber manchmal verließ er sich doch lieber auf die anderen Schauspieler, die mit ihm auf der Bühne standen, und schob ihnen, wenn er nicht textsicher war, den Schwarzen Peter zu. Dann hieß es improvisieren und nochmals improvisieren."

Über Nacht war Henry Vahl zum Star und „Fernsehopa der Nation" geworden. Nur eine schien der Durchbruch Henry Vahls nicht zu überraschen – Germaine: „Ich hab es ja immer gewusst, es kommt einmal, mein Schieter." An der Seite von Heidi Kabel war Henry Vahl bald in allen Wohnzimmern zu Hause. In seinen Lebenserinnerungen schrieb er über diese Zusammenarbeit: „Heidi Kabel und das Ensemble des ‚Ohnsorg-Theaters' hatten eine so nahtlose Zusammenarbeit entwickelt, dass ich als Neuling mitgetragen wurde. Sie trugen mich zum Erfolg. So etwas hatte ich in meiner langen Bühnenlaufbahn noch niemals erlebt. Die Zuschauer nahmen Heidi Kabel einfach alles ab und bald darauf auch mir. Von ihr habe ich mehr gelernt als in den 50 Jahren meiner Laufbahn."

Auch als Filmschauspieler gefragt

Henry Vahl musste nun nicht mehr mit Schminke zum alten Mann gemacht werden, er war inzwischen ein alter Mann: „Die Schminke macht doch meine ganze Mimik kaputt. Meine Falten sind schließlich mein Kapital." Stücke wie „Opa wird verkauft" und „Tratsch im Treppenhaus" wurden zu Klassikern des niederdeutschen Theaters und bereichern bis heute das Fernsehprogramm.

Auch Filmrollen bot man Henry Vahl an, unter anderem im Fernsehkrimi „Die Rote Geldbörse". Von seinen ersten Filmgagen kaufte er seiner Frau einen Nerzmantel und sich ein Auto, einen Mercedes 230. Daran hatte er nur kurze Zeit Freude: „Damit fuhr ich genau 26 Kilometer. Dann kam ein Kombiwagen von rechts und knallte an die rechte Seite des neuen Wagens. Er hatte Vorfahrt." Danach gab er das Autofahren auf.

Zur Erholung fuhren die Vahls, die kinderlos geblieben waren, im Sommer nach Büsum und im Winter in die Berge. 1969 unternahmen Germaine und Henry endlich die immer wieder verschobene Hochzeitsreise. Sie fuhren auf einem Bananendampfer nach Honduras und zurück: „Sechs Wochen lang haben wir uns auf dem Schiff verwöhnen lassen und uns prächtig erholt."

Ein getrübter Abschied vom Ohnsorg-Theater

1970 ging Henry Vahls Arbeit für das *Ohnsorg-Theater* abrupt zu Ende. Nach dem plötzlichen Tod des Intendanten Hans Mahler übernahm Günther Siegmund die Leitung des Hauses. Er wollte das Programm modernisieren und dabei gab es keinen Platz mehr für Henry Vahl. An die Zusage Mahlers, dass Vahl sich als Schustergeselle Matten vom Publikum des Theaters verabschieden könnte, sah sich der neue Intendant nicht gebunden. Da traf es sich für den Schauspieler gut, dass Kurt Collien, der Leiter des *St. Pauli-Theaters*, anbot, dort den „Meister Anecker" in sein Programm aufzunehmen. Henry Vahl spielte wiederum den Schustergesellen. Das Stück kam an 93 aufeinanderfolgenden Abenden zur Aufführung – und jede Aufführung war ausverkauft.

Danach bot Collien dem beliebten Schauspieler an, die Hauptrolle in dem Stück „Zitronenjette" zu übernehmen. Paul Möhring hatte das Stück geschrieben, um das wahre Leben des Hamburger Originals auf die Bühne zu bringen. Dieses Leben war keineswegs komisch, sondern lange Zeit tragisch. Es erwies sich als Fehler, die Rolle der Zitronenjette immer wieder mit Männern wie Henry Vahl zu besetzen, die sehr begabte Komiker, aber nicht geeignet waren, die Tragik im Leben der Zitronenjette zu verkörpern.

Henry Vahl hatte die Ehre, die Zitronenjette bei der 1.000ten Aufführung dieses Stücks im *St. Pauli-Theater* zu spielen. Die Aufführung wurde vom Fernsehen übertragen. Germaine Vahl versuchte ihren Mann davon abzuhalten, einen Vertrag zu unterzeichnen und weiterhin Tag für Tag als Zitronenjette auf der Bühne zu stehen, aber er wollte noch einmal große Erfolge feiern. Seine Kolleginnen und Kollegen mussten wahrnehmen, dass „Old Henry“, wie er liebevoll genannt wurde, überfordert war und nicht zu seiner alten Form zurückfand.

„Peter drei, nun komm doch endlich!“

Da seine Gedächtnisprobleme im Alter weiter zugenommen hatten, bereitete es Henry Vahl immer mehr Mühe, sich an seine Texte zu erinnern. Ein Kollege kam auf die Idee, dass sich unter seiner blonden Zitronenjette-Perücke, die auch die Ohren bedeckte, gut ein Sendegerät verstecken ließ. Man lieferte ihm nun jeweils per Funk den Text, den er gerade zu sprechen hatte. Das funktionierte gut und gab Henry Vahl eine neue Sicherheit als Schauspieler.

Einmal kam es allerdings zu einer folgenschweren Panne. Bekanntlich liegt das *St. Pauli-Theater* neben der *Davidwache,* und mitten im zweiten Akt überlagerte der Polizeifunk die Ansagen für den Schauspieler. Henry Vahl hörte nun mehrfach „Peter drei bitte kommen! Peter drei bitte kommen!“ Schließlich platze dem Schauspieler die Geduld und er verkündete auf der Bühne: „Peter drei, nun komm doch endlich!“ Da er eine skurrile Person spielte, fiel das dem Publikum nicht weiter auf, aber seinen Helfern hinter der Bühne war sofort klar, was schiefgegangen war. Sie änderten daraufhin sofort die Frequenz.

Henry Vahl ignorierte die Warnsignale in seinem Körper und die Mahnungen seiner Frau. Am Neujahrstag 1975 standen gleich zwei Aufführungen der „Zitronenjette" auf dem Programm. Henry Vahl merkte, wie geschwächt es war, verheimlichte das aber vor seiner Frau. Er wollte noch an den vier ausverkauften Aufführungen in den ersten Januartagen mitwirken, aber am Vormittag des 3. Januar erlitt er einen Schwächeanfall. Er wurde in das Israelitische Krankenhaus eingeliefert.

Er musste sechs Wochen im Krankenhaus bleiben und nach der Rückkehr in die Wohnung in der Maria-Louisen-Straße seiner Frau versprechen, dass er keine Verträge über Aufführungsserien mehr unterschreiben werde. Er beschloss, nicht wieder auf einer Bühne aufzutreten, schließlich wäre er 77 Jahre alt.

Abschied von einem humorvollen, beliebten Volksschauspieler

Eine besondere Ehrung erlebte Henry Vahl 1974 zu seinem 77. Geburtstag. Die *Hamburger Schuster-Innung* ernannte ihn zum Ehrenmitglied. Bei der Ehrung fragte der humorvolle Vahl. „Bekomme ich nun meine Schuhsohlen künftig geschenkt?" Viele Schuhsohlen hat er nicht mehr benötigt.

Am 13. März 1975 starb Germaine Vahl plötzlich an Herzversagen und ihr Mann stand nun allein auf der Welt da. Am Ende seiner Lebenserinnerungen schrieb er: „Über 50 Jahre unseres Lebens hatten wir zusammen verbracht. Ich weiß gar nicht, was ich ohne Germaine anfangen soll." Henry Vahl erlitt im Februar 1976 einen Schlaganfall, von dem er sich nicht mehr erholte. Er starb am 21. Juli 1977.

Mehr als 8.000 Menschen versammelten sich auf dem Ohlsdorfer Friedhof, um Abschied von Henry Vahl zu nehmen. Der Journalist Horst Ebert sagte in einer Traueransprache: „Du spielst nicht nur die ‚Zitronenjette', dieses Hamburger Original, Du bist selbst ein Hamburger Original geworden ..." Die Orgel spielte Lieder, die Henry Vahl geliebt hatte wie „La Paloma" und „In Hamburg sagt man Tschüs".

Seine langjährige Schauspiel-Partnerin Heidi Kabel sagte unter Tränen: „Lieber Henry, gode oole Fründ! To 'n Lewen 'hört de Dod, so will 't de leve Gott. Fünfzehn Jahre durften wir zusammen auf unserer kleinen Bühne stehen. Du bist berühmt geworden an unserem Theater. Ach, berühmt! Dich, Henry, haben die Menschen geliebt ... Du hast ihnen das Lachen gegeben mit deinem schrulligen, kauzigen und so liebenswerten Humor ... Du bist immer jung geblieben, Henry. Im Herzen jung. Un so jung büs du nu ok von uns gohn. Sloop got, min Jung."

1992 benannte die Stadt Hamburg einen Park zwischen Heußweg und Emilienstraße nach Henry Vahl. In der Nähe hatte sich die erste Hamburger Wohnung von Germaine und Henry Vahl befunden.

Vogeljette

Unter ihrem Namen Lydia Adelheid Hellenbrecht kennt sie kaum noch jemand, aber als Vogeljette zählt sie zu den bekannteren Hamburger Originalen. Sie bot sogar den Stoff für ein Theaterstück, das 1961 im *Ohnsorg-Theater* seine Uraufführung erlebte. Lange Zeit hatte nichts darauf hingedeutet, dass sie einmal eine bekannte Person in St. Georg werden würde. Geboren wurde sie am 13. Dezember 1844 als Lydia Adelheid Köbner. Ihr Vater, ein Steuermann, starb bereits während ihrer Kindheit beim Untergang seines Schiffes. Im Alter von 30 Jahren heiratete sie den 20 Jahre älteren Schreiber und Boten Johann Hellenbrecht. Ihr geliebter Mann starb bereits nach neun Jahren Ehe 1883 an der Cholera.

Jeden Tag gab es Brotstückchen für die Vögel

Ihre Trauer war so groß, dass sie von da an stets Trauerkleidung trug. Bald kannte jeder in St. Georg die Frau mit dem schwarzen Kleid, dem weißen gehäkelten Umschlagtuch, dem Häubchen und dem weißen Schleier. Stets war sie mit einem Körbchen mit Brotstückchen und einem kleinen Emaileimer mit Wasser unterwegs. Da ihre Rente klein war, konnte sie nicht jeden Tag frisches Brot kaufen, sondern profitierte davon, dass die Bäcker ihr kostenlos altes Brot überließen. Den Spitznamen Vogeljette erhielt sie in Anlehnung an Zitronenjette. Manche Leute in St. Georg hielten sie für verrückt, aber sie war geistig völlig normal. Ihre einzige Auffälligkeit bestand darin, jeden Tag in Trauerkleidung die Vögel zu füttern. Sie wohnte im Haus Rostocker Straße 9 zur Untermiete.

Nicht nur die Bewohner, sondern auch die Vögel der Vorstadt St. Georg kannten bald die Frau in Schwarz und flogen herbei, sobald sie sie kommen sahen. Sie tunkte die Brotstückchen in das Wasser und verfütterte sie an die Vögel, vorzugsweise an Spatzen. Damals gab es noch keinen Hauptbahnhof, und in diesem Bereich der früheren Wallanlagen, zwischen den heutigen Straßen Glockengießerwall und Kirchenallee, befand sich eine Parkanlage. Ein tiefes Tal ließ noch ahnen, dass hier ein Festungsgraben zu der gewaltigen Wallanlage Hamburgs gehört hatte. Die Parkanlage mit ihren Baumgruppen, Büschen und Rasenflächen wurde sowohl von den Vögeln als auch von Vogeljette geschätzt. Sie war nicht die einzige, die hier Vögel fütterte, aber sie fiel durch ihre schwarze Kleidung und dadurch auf, dass sie jeden Tag hier erschien.

Hans Ross hat sie in seiner Kindheit erlebt und seine Erinnerungen 1978 in der Zeitschrift „Blätter aus St. Georg" veröffentlicht: „Dass wir Jungs von damals, wenn die Vogeljette ihrem Körbchen die sorgfältig geschnittenen Brotwürfel entnommen hatte, sie dann mit einigen Spritzern aus dem kleinen Eimer angefeuchtet hatte, alles jedenfalls meistens in Ruhe betrachteten, lag wohl an dem stillen Respekt, den die alte Frau genoss. Wenn es mal nicht so artig verlief und die Jungens die Spatzen verjagten, ging ein großes Donnerwetter über die Jugend los." Ansonsten war Vogeljette meistens wenig gesprächig.

Warum die Vögel gefüttert wurden

Die Vorübergehenden fragten sich, warum die Frau im schwarzen Kleid sommers wie winters jeden Tag unterwegs war, um Vögel zu füttern, und sogar mit ihnen sprach. Manche waren überzeugt, dass sie glaube, ihr Mann sei als Vogel wiedergeboren worden. Damit er immer genug zu essen hätte, mache sie sich jeden Tag mit den Brotstückchen auf den Weg. Da sie aber nicht wissen konnte, welcher von den Vögeln ihr früherer Mann wäre, würde sie alle Vögel füttern.

Menschen, die sie näher kannten, wussten, dass das Füttern der Vögel einen anderen Grund hatte. Ihr verstorbener Mann war tierlieb gewesen und hatte häufig Vögel gefüttert. In Erinnerung an ihn machte sich seine Witwe jeden Tag auf den Weg zu den Vögeln von St. Georg. Das war ihre Form der Trauerarbeit und des Andenkens. Dass sie mit den Vögeln sprach, war kein Zeichen geistiger Verwirrung, sondern Ausdruck ihrer Tierliebe. Vielleicht wusste die fromme Frau auch, dass schon Franz von Assisi mit den Tieren gesprochen hatte.

Es war ihr natürlich bekannt, dass das Füttern der Vögel von vielen belächelt wurde. Sie setzte es trotzdem mehrere Jahrzehnte lang fort. Hans Ross hat zu dieser Hartnäckigkeit geschrieben: „Sie kannte die Nachrede und Erzählungen der Leute genau, hat sich aber, auch gestützt auf eine schlichte Frömmigkeit, nicht beirren lassen und bei sparsamster Lebenshaltung, da sie nur sehr geringe Einkünfte hatte, ihre vielbespöttelte Tätigkeit zum Segen der gefiederten Natur durch Jahrzehnte ausgeübt."

Im Jahr 1915 musste sie das Füttern der Vögel einstellen, weil im Krieg das Brot knapp geworden war und nur noch gegen Brotmarken abgegeben wurde. Sie starb am 30. Januar 1920.

Johannes Sass schrieb in seinem Buch „Hamburger Originale und originelle Hamburger“ über sie: „Jedermann war der Spitzname ‚Vogeljette‘ bekannt. Es muss aber in ihrer Persönlichkeit eine gewisse Würde gelegen haben, denn niemals haben Straßenjungen es gewagt, ihr diesen Namen nachzurufen.“ Im Garten der Frauen auf dem Ohlsdorfer Friedhof erinnert ein gemeinsamer „Stein der Erinnerung“ an sie und an Zitronenjette.

Caspar Voght

„Caspar Voght war Kaufmann von Beruf und voller Humor, der allerdings nicht immer beabsichtigt, sondern einfach aus seiner derben Art entsprang." So hat Johannes Sass den Senator Voght in seinem Buch „Hamburger Originale und originelle Hamburger" vorgestellt, dem ich viele Informationen zu diesem Kapitel verdanke. Dass Voght einen Platz unter den Originalen der Stadt verdient hat, dafür soll hier eine Begebenheit erzählt werden.

„Wat gifft dat hüüt avend to eten, Liesbeth?" Die Frage war verfrüht, denn das Orchester spielte gerade erst die Ouvertüre, und Elisabeth wurde abrupt aus ihrem Kunstgenuss gerissen. Sie flüsterte ihrem Gatten zu: „Kramsvagels, Caspar!" Damit hätten die beiden zum Genuss der Musik zurückkehren können, denn Kramsvagels, also Drosseln, waren das Lieblingsgericht des Herrn Senator. Aber beim Gedanken an sein Leib- und Magengericht kam seine nächste Frage, die das ganze Unglück auslöste: „Ok Appelmoos dorbi?"

Das geflüsterte „Nee" brachte den Ehegatten in Zorn und er sagte mit allen Anzeichen der Empörung: „Denn schiet ik op de Kramsvagels!" Diesen Satz sprach der Senator laut in die Stille nach der Ouvertüre hinein, und sie war überall im Opernhaus am Gänsemarkt zu hören. Auch die Besucher, die den ersten Teil des Gesprächs nicht mitbekommen hatten, erfuhren rasch, was den Zorn des Polizeisenators ausgelöst hatte. Von nun an hieß er in der Stadt „Senator Appelmoos".

Heikle diplomatische Aufgaben des Polizeisenators

Caspar Voght „der Ältere" sollte nicht mit seinem Sohn gleichen Namens verwechselt werden, der zu den führenden Vertretern der Aufklärung in Hamburg gehörte. Der Vater wurde 1707 in Beverstedt bei Bremen geboren und hatte im Alter von 16 Jahren eine kaufmännische Lehre im Hamburger Handelshaus Jencquel begonnen. Seine Leistungen waren offenbar so beeindruckend, dass er mit 25 Jahren die Leitung der wichtigen Lissabonner Filiale des Handelshauses übernehmen konnte. Sechzehn Jahre lang handelte er erfolgreich mit Tuchen und Weinen, und wie in manchen Märchen durfte der Heimgekehrte dann die Tochter seines Dienstherrn heiraten.

Mit Geschick gelang es Voght, von 1748 an aus kleinen Anfängen ein eigenes erfolgreiches Handelsunternehmen für Seiden- und Leinenartikel aufzubauen. Der reiche Kaufmann besaß ein Landhaus in Hamm, und dorthin lud er einmal die Herzogin von Mecklenburg zu einem Mittagessen ein. Zur Begrüßung der Besucherin sollten die Wasserkünste spielen, auf die Voght besonders stolz war. Der Gärtnerbursche war instruiert worden, sie rechtzeitig in Gang zu setzen. Aber der Regieplan geriet durcheinander, als die Besucherin deutlich früher als geplant eintraf. Was dann geschah, hat Johannes Sass so beschrieben:

„Als Caspar Voght ihr aus dem Wagen half, fielen ihm plötzlich die Wasserkünste ein, die natürlich noch nicht zu spielen begonnen hatten. Er glaubte aber, die Situation noch retten zu können und rief mit lauter Stimme über alle Anwesenden hinweg: ‚Krischan, treck den Plack rut!', ein Ausruf, der sehr bald sprichwörtlich wurde."

Ein Original an der Spitze der Polizei

Sein Erfolg als Kaufmann prädestinierte Voght dafür, in den Rat der Stadt gewählt zu werden, und als Polizeisenator entwickelte er ein gewisses Talent, mit schwierigen Problemen umzugehen. Damals waren die Gassen der Stadt schmal und die Eitelkeiten der Herren Gesandten groß. Das führte zu einer kleinen diplomatischen Krise, als der Kaiserlich Österreichische Gesandte und der Kaiserlich Russische Gesandte mit ihren Kutschen aus entgegengesetzten Richtungen in die Brandstwiete einbogen. Die Gasse war so schmal, dass die zwei Kutschen beim besten Willen nicht aneinander vorbeikommen konnten. Trotzdem trieben die hohen Herren ihre Pferde an und standen sich dann Pferdenase an Pferdenase gegenüber. Die Kutscher der beiden Diplomaten beschimpften einander ganz undiplomatisch, und keiner der Gesandten wollte nachgeben. Schließlich entschlossen sie sich, den Polizeisenator einzuschalten.

Für Caspar Voght war das eine heikle Angelegenheit. Eine der beiden Mächte zu verärgern, konnte für die Hamburger Kaufleute teuer werden. Der schlaue Polizeisenator erklärte den beiden Kontrahenten, die Sache wäre so wichtig, dass sie vom ganzen Rat entschieden werden müsse. Der tage am kommenden Morgen wieder, und er werde höchstpersönlich dafür sorgen, dass diese wichtige Angelegenheit als erstes behandelt werden würde. Die Gesandten wollten dann doch lieber nicht in ihren Kutschen übernachten, und jeder ließ seine Kutsche rückwärts aus der schmalen Gasse herausbugsieren, um auf einem anderen Weg ihr Ziel noch am gleichen Tag zu erreichen.

Unkonventionell ging der Senator auch bei kleinen Streitfällen vor. Ein Schlachter klagte einen Berufskollegen an, seinen Hund gestohlen zu haben, und der Senator bestellte die Kontrahenten samt Hund ins Rathaus. Ein Wortwechsel zwischen den beiden Schlachtern führte zu nichts. Da lockte Caspar Voght den Hund zu sich und streichelte ihn eine ganze Weile, dann gab er ihm plötzlich einen Schlag. Der Hund jaulte und verkroch sich bei dem Schlachter, der den Diebstahl gemeldet hatte. Der Fall war aufgeklärt, und der Dieb nahm ohne Murren seine Strafe an.

Gesellschaftliche Verpflichtungen und ihre Risiken

Vielleicht wäre Senator Voght ausschließlich als kluger und weiser Staatsmann in die Stadtgeschichte eingegangen, hätte es nicht die vielen gesellschaftlichen Verpflichtungen gegeben ... Da war zum Beispiel die Geschichte mit der „Calla aethiopica". So war bei einer Gesellschaft nämlich eine Dame von ihrem Verehrer tituliert worden. Und da sie nicht genau wusste, um welch schöne Pflanze es sich handelte, mit der sie verglichen wurde, fragte sie den Senator.

Der hatte das Kompliment zwar nicht mitbekommen, hätte sich aber denken können, dass die schöne Dame ihn nicht aus botanischem Interesse nach der „Calla aethiopica" fragte. Hätte, wie gesagt, denn von Senator Appelmoos ist diese Antwort überliefert: „Die Calla aethiopica, meine Beste, das ist ein dummes Ding, sieht aus wie ein Besenstiel, dem man oben eine Nachtmütze aufgesetzt hat." Schweigend ging die schöne Dame von dannen und soll von da an eine Abneigung gegen die „Calla aethiopica" gehabt haben.

Einmal wollte der gutmütige Voght einem Bediensteten einen Gefallen tun. Der spielte Geige und wäre zu gern Ratsmusiker geworden. Der Senator sprach den Musikdirektor Carl Philipp Emanuel Bach darauf an, der sich bereit erklärte, sich das Geigenspiel des Bediensteten einmal anzuhören. Da dieser beim Vorspielen nur auf der Geige herumkratze, sah der Musikdirektor keine Möglichkeit, ihn als Ratsmusiker aufzunehmen. Unverblümt sagte er bei nächster Gelegenheit zu Voght: „Ihr Bediensteter, Herr Senator, ist ein elender Stümper auf der Geige und nicht zu gebrauchen." Der gutmütige Voght machte einen letzten Versuch, seinem Bediensteten doch noch einen Platz unter den Ratsmusikern zu sichern: „Na, wenn ji em bi de Vigelinen nich bruken kööntt, denn smiet em bi de Baß!"

Wie Zeitgenossen den Senator Voght sahen

Es kann nicht verwundern, dass der Senator als etwas derber Mann in die Stadtgeschichte eingegangen ist. Immerhin schrieb die Lessing-Freundin Eva König in einem Brief: „Voght ist doch ein braver Mann, wenn man sich auch über seine nicht ganz feinen Sitten lustig gemacht hat." Der Hamburger Diplomat und Publizist Piter Poel nannte ihn „einen groben Spießbürger, schlau, wo es um seinen Vortheil geht, und berühmt durch seine plattdeutschen Naivitäten". Poel fügte aber hinzu, Voght habe ein offenes, wohltätiges Herz besessen und unter anderem eine großzügige Spende für den Bau des Kleinen Michel zur Verfügung gestellt.

1781 starb Caspar Voght. In einer Zeitungsmeldung hieß es: „Sein Handlungshaus ist eines der ansehnlichsten unserer Stadt.“ Sein Sohn Caspar führte die Geschäfte weiter. Er war nicht nur ein erfolgreicher Kaufmann, sondern auch ein angesehener Sozialreformer und Aufklärer.

Zum Schluss zurück in die Welt der Musik. Bei einem Konzert fiel dem sparsamen Senator Caspar Voght „dem Älteren“ auf, dass zwei Musiker bei einem Stück nicht mitspielten. Nach dem Ende des Konzerts fragte er den Dirigenten: „Worum hebbt denn de bieden Kerls nich mitspeelt?" Höflich erklärte der Dirigent dem Herrn Senator, dass bei dem Satz ihre Instrumente nicht in der Partitur vorkämen und sie deshalb pausiert hätten. Damit zog er den Zorn Voghts auf sich: „Pauseert? Wat heet hier pauseert? Se kriegt jüst so goot betahlt as de annern, denn süllt se ok speeln!"

Agneta Willeken

Die Mühlen des Reichskammergerichts mahlten sehr langsam, zu langsam für Agneta Willeken, die starb, bevor ein Urteil erging. Auch ihre beiden Töchter, um deren schlechte Behandlung es in dem Prozess ging, waren verstorben – ebenso die Anwälte der Klägerin und der beklagten Stadt Hamburg. So erlebte Agneta Willeken nicht mehr den Triumpf, die Stadt Hamburg erfolgreich verklagt zu haben. Die Entschädigung kam den Erben der Klägerin und deren Töchter zugute.

Wer war die streitbare Frau, die gegen ihre Heimatstadt vor das höchste Gericht zog? Sie wurde etwa 1497 in Hamburg geboren. Ihr Vater war ein wohlhabender Brauer und besaß ein stattliches Haus am Hopfenmarkt. Seine Frau Margaretha und er hatten sechs Töchter, von denen Agneta die älteste war. In jungen Jahren heiratete sie Hans Willeken, einen Islandfahrer. Er betrieb also Handel mit Island, leider ohne Erfolg, sodass er 1527 zahlungsunfähig war und Hamburg verlassen musste. Er starb einige Jahre später verarmt in Lübeck.

Wie die ehrgeizige Agneta Willeken die Stadt Lübeck zu einem Krieg veranlasste

Agneta Willeken blieb in Hamburg und nahm nun entschlossen ihr Schicksal selbst in die Hand. Ihre beiden kleinen Töchter übergab sie ihrer Schwester, begann eine Beziehung zu dem Schmied Marx Meyer und stachelte dessen Ehrgeiz an. Der Historiker Heinrich Reincke hat dies in seinem 1928 erschienenen Lebensbild „Agneta Willeken“ so beschrieben: „Sie wollte ihn groß sehen und sich groß! So reizte sie in ihm den Wagemut und die Abenteuerlust und trieb ihn hinaus in die Welt zu Kampf und Sieg. Marx Meyer hat es frei und offen selbst anerkannt, was er ihr und ihrem Ehrgeiz verdankte."

Unter ihrem Einfluss gab er das Schmiedehandwerk auf und begann eine militärische Laufbahn in Lübeck. Agneta Willeken blieb in Hamburg, konnte aber seinen Ehrgeiz auch aus der Ferne wachhalten. Tatsächlich stieg er zum Feldhauptmann der immer noch ziemlich mächtigen Stadt Lübeck auf. Lang ist die Liste seiner militärischen Erfolge und sogar an einem Feldzug gegen die Türken war er beteiligt. Er genoss große Popularität in Lübeck und heiratete die Witwe eines angesehenen Bürgermeisters. Aber Agneta Willeken blieb eng mit ihm verbunden.

Sie soll ihren Einfluss dafür genutzt haben, dass Marx Meyer und über ihn der Lübecker Bürgermeister Jürgen Wullenwever die Hansestadt in die Erbfolgekonflikte am dänischen Königshof verwickelten. Zum Hintergrund: Lübeck hatte erleben müssen, dass seine wirtschaftliche Vormachtstellung im Ostseeraum schwand, seit sich der Handel im 16. Jahrhundert in den Nordseeraum und nach Übersee verlagerte.

Zudem tauchten immer mehr holländische Schiffe in der Ostsee auf und betrieben erfolgreich Handel. Die Lübecker begannen sogar unter Mitwirkung von Marx Meyer Kaperfahrten, um die holländischen Schiffe zu vertreiben, allerdings ohne den gewünschten Erfolg. Die letzte Hoffnung war, durch die Beteiligung an den dänischen Erbfolgekonflikten zu erreichen, dass ein neuer lübeckfreundlicher dänischer König den Holländern die Durchfahrt durch den Sund untersagen würde. Aber die Pläne misslangen und Herzog Christian von Schleswig-Holstein regierte als Christian III. das dänische Reich.

Die Plünderung des Schlosses in Trittau

Ohne Kriegserklärung begann Marx Meyer 1534 einen Feldzug in Holstein, um die Burgen der Familie Rantzau zu erobern, die in den dänischen Erbfolgeauseinandersetzungen auf der von Lübeck bekämpften Seite stand. Mit dem überraschenden Angriff erzielten die Lübecker zunächst einige militärische Erfolge. So konnte Meyer das Schloss der Rantzaus in Trittau erobern und plündern.

An dieser Plünderung beteiligte sich auch Agneta Willeken, die für sich und ihre Töchter größere Mengen teurer Kleidung sowie wertvollen Schmuck mit nach Hamburg nahm. Heinrich Reinecke schreibt: „Die Tage, da Marx Meyer auf Trittau saß, bildeten den Höhepunkt in Agnetas Leben. Fast täglich war sie mit ihrem Ritter zusammen und lebte herrlich und in Freuden."

In ihrem Roman „Agneta Willeken" hat Andrea Schampier diese Tage in Trittau so beschrieben: „... dort an der Seite von Marx hatte sie sich wie eine Schlossherrin gefühlt, und wenn es auch nur wenige Tage gewesen waren, die sie beide nach Marx' Übernahme des Schlosses dort hatte verweilen können ... die eroberten Räume hatten alles an Gütern und noch viel mehr geboten, dessen sie bedurft hatte, um mit Marx glücklich zu sein. Luxus, Luxus, Luxus, wohin man sich auch gewandt hatte. Kleider aus edlen Stoffen, auserwählte Mahlzeiten von Silberbesteck, Weine, von denen Agneta nicht gewusst hatte, das es sie gab, feine Tuche und Laken, warme Bäder und exotische Duftessenzen."

Eine Niederlage für Lübeck – und für Agneta Willeken

Allerdings währte das Luxusleben nur sehr kurz, denn rasch konnten die holsteinischen Gegner der Lübecker mit neuen Truppen den Kriegsverlauf zu ihren Gunsten verändern. Im Mai 1536 kämpften Marx Meyer und seine Mannen in Skandinavien auf verlorenem Posten. Er musste schließlich kapitulieren und wurde im Felsenschloss Warberg am Kattegat eingekerkert. Durch eine List und unter Mitwirkung der Frau des Schlossherrn gelang es ihm, sich zu befreien und das Schloss mit einer getreuen Truppe unter seine Kontrolle zu bringen. Dort belagerten ihn überlegene dänischen Truppen.

Es gelang Marx Meyer, einen Brief an Agneta Willeken zu senden. Ihren Antwortbrief vom 23. April 1535 an den Liebhaber konnten dänischen Truppen abfangen. In dem Brief ging es nicht nur um die Aufmunterung Meyers und Ratschläge für seine Kriegsführung, sondern auch um Details ihrer Liaison. Agneta Willeken bedauerte, dass Marx Meyer sie aufgefordert hatte, vorerst nicht zu ihm nach Warberg zu kommen.

Es war ihr bewusst, dass Marx Meyer nun nicht nur eine Frau in Lübeck, sondern auch die Frau des Schlossherrn von Warberg als Gefährtin hatte. Sie betonte aber ihre hervorgehobene Rolle als Liebhaberin des Feldherrn. Sie wählte für ihren Anspruch, letztendlich die Partnerin von Marx Meyer zu sein und zu bleiben, dieses Bild: „Wenn alle Kapellen besungen sind, so soll noch immer ich für Euch die rechte Hauptkirche bleiben."

Wir hören hier eine Frau, die trotz aller Widrigkeiten und Rückschläge an ihrem Lebensziel festhielt, an der Seite von Marx Meyer zu Macht und Einfluss zu gelangen. Die Tage im Schloss in Trittau sollten ein Vorgeschmack auf zukünftiges Glück sein. Als bürgerliche Frau im 16. Jahrhundert hatte Agneta Willeken nur an der Seite eines einflussreichen Mannes die Aussicht, ihre Ziele zu erreichen.

Der abgefangene Brief schadete ihrem Ruf nachhaltig. Das dänische Königshaus ließ den Brief vervielfältigen und weit streuen. In Hamburg ging der Senat so weit, den Brief öffentlich verlesen zu lassen. Diese Bloßstellung verfehlte nicht ihre Wirkung und isolierte Agneta Willeken weiter in der Stadt. Da das Original des Briefes nicht mehr existiert, muss offenbleiben, ob er von den Dänen um skandalträchtige Passagen ergänzt wurde.

Dass Agneta Willeken sich in dem Brief als „Hauptkirche“ bezeichnet hatte, nahmen ihre Gegner zum Anlass, von ihr höhnisch als von der „Hauptkirche“ zu sprechen. Den beteiligten Männern erging es noch wesentlich schlechter als ihr. Marx Meyer musste erneut kapitulieren und wurde hingerichtet. Der Lübecker Bürgermeister Wullenwever, der den missglückten Feldzug zu verantworten hatte, wurde gestürzt, festgenommen, gefoltert und ebenfalls hingerichtet.

Ein angesehenes Ratsmitglied stürzte ins Unglück

Agneta Willeken war nun mehr denn je in Hamburg isoliert und zudem hoch verschuldet. Sie musste ihr Haus verkaufen und hatte große Mühe, eine neue Bleibe zu mieten, weil niemand die Frau mit dem schlechten Ruf aufnehmen wollte. Heinrich Reincke schrieb über die nun entstandene Situation: „Mit Marx Meyer schien auch Agneta vernichtet: ihr brennender Ehrgeiz hatte sein Ziel verfehlt. Mit der Rolle, die sie spielen wollte, schien es endgültig aus zu sein. Aber – es schien nur so. Denn kaum war der erste Kummer verwunden, da wusste sie einen anderen hochgestellten Mann völlig zu betören, so dass er Ehre und Eid vergaß. Das war Joachim Wollenwever, der ältere Bruder Jürgens, des gestürzten lübischen Bürgermeisters."

Joachim Wollenwever genoss in Hamburg als Kaufmann und Ratsherr ein hohes Ansehen – jedenfalls bis zu dem Zeitpunkt, als seine Verbindung zu Agneta Willekes bekannt wurde. Man warf ihm nicht nur diese Liaison vor, sondern es entstand auch der Verdacht, er hätte die Hamburger Interessen in Zusammenarbeit mit seinem Bruder verraten. Man schloss ihn daraufhin 1536 aus dem Rat aus. Er verließ die Stadt und starb zwei Jahre später verarmt in Schweden.

Skandal bei einem Fest im Eimbeckschen Haus

Hamburg hatte sich wohlweislich aus den Erbfolgestreitigkeiten in Dänemark herausgehalten und konnte 1538 den neuen dänischen König Christian III. freundschaftlich in der Stadt begrüßen. Dabei scheute der Rat der Stadt keine Kosten, um den Gast zu beschenken und die Stadt herauszuputzen. Die Besucher wurde in das beliebte Eimbecksche Haus zu einem großen Fest eingeladen. Das hätte ungetrübt verlaufen können, wären nicht die 18 und 15 Jahre alten Willeken-Töchter durch einen Nebeneingang in den Saal gelangt, auf Geheiß ihrer Mutter.

In ihrem Roman schrieb Andrea Schampier: „Der Besuch des dänischen Königshofs in Hamburg war für Agneta eine ungeheure und angesichts der Situation, in der man sich befand, wohl einmalige Gelegenheit, ihre beiden heiratsfähigen Töchter in die Gesellschaft einzuführen ... Es sollte ein unvergesslicher Abend für die beiden Mädchen werden; ein Abend, der ihnen den Weg in eine unbeschwerte Zukunft ebnen sollte.“ Unvergesslich wurde der Abend für die beiden jungen Frauen tatsächlich, aber ganz anders, als die Mutter erhofft hatte.

Die wie adlige Fräulein gekleideten schönen jungen Frauen mit den von der Mutter geraubten Kleidern und dem Schmuck aus dem Schloss der Rantzaus in Trittau fielen den jungen dänischen Gästen gleich auf. Aber auch Melchior Rantzau erspähte die jungen Damen. Der holsteinische Ritter und Politiker im Dienst des dänischen Königs war erbost, als er erfuhr, wer diese beiden Damen waren und vor allem, wer ihre Mutter war. Er beschwerte sich beim Bürgermeister und der veranlasste, dass die Töchter Willeken von einem Ratsdiener aus dem Saal gewiesen wurden.

Andrea Schampier schrieb in ihrem Roman: „Und so mussten die Töchter der Agneta Willeken auf Geheiß des Hamburger Rats und unter den neugierigen, teils auch mitleidigen Blicken von zahlreichen Männern und Frauen, die mehr oder weniger beteiligt das Geschehen verfolgten und sich einen Reim darauf machten, das Tanzfest zu Ehren seiner Königlichen Majestät Christian III. verlassen. Ein schändliches Ereignis, das sich tief in die Geschichte Hamburgs einprägen sollte.“

Raubzüge auf Initiative einer Hamburgerin

Agneta Willeken war empört über die Behandlung ihrer Töchter und über deren durch den Skandal weiter gesunkene Heiratsaussichten. Es gelang der Mutter trotzdem, ihre Tochter Anna 1539 mit dem Mecklenburger Hans Kopeke, der als berittener Soldat im Dienste Hamburgs stand, zu verheiraten. Kopeke musste allerdings erleben, dass er in der Stadt, der er getreulich diente, nach dieser Heirat von vielen Bekannten gemieden und von anderen Hamburgern wegen seiner Verbindung zur Familie von Agneta Willeken verspottet wurde.

Die Verbitterung über diese Behandlung machte ihn zugänglich für die Bemühungen seiner Schwiegermutter, ihn dazu anzustacheln, sich gegen die Stadt Hamburg zu wenden. Er gab seine Tätigkeit als städtischer Soldat auf und schmiedete Rachepläne. Agneta Willeken veranlasste ihn, Hamburg am 1. Dezember 1540 die Fehde anzusagen. Das hätte wie bei Don Quichotte enden können, denn die Zeit der Ritterfehden war Mitte des 16. Jahrhunderts definitiv vorbei und ein einzelner Ritter der mächtigen Stadt Hamburg hoffnungslos unterlegen.

Die Geschichte nahm aber einen tragischen Verlauf. Kopeke überfiel zwei oder drei Jahre lang Hamburger Kaufmannswagen und machte zunächst reiche Beute. Heinrich Reincke schrieb über diese Zeit: „Immer mehr sank Kopekes Schar zu einer bloßen Räuberbande herab. Verwegene Gesellen aus aller Welt, die seit den nordischen Friedensschlüssen soldlos durch die Lande streiften, schlossen sich ihm an, heruntergekommene Adlige des südlichen Mecklenburg und der Provinz schämten sich nicht, Unterschlupf zu gewähren und an der Beute teilzunehmen.“ Agneta Willeken soll geeignete Gelegenheiten für Raubzüge erkundet und neue Räuber angeworben haben. Kopeke wurde schließlich 1542 festgenommen und hingerichtet.

Eine Entschädigungsklage gegen die Stadt Hamburg

Zehn Jahre nach dem Vorfall im Eimbeckschen Haus, im Jahre 1548, wählte Agneta Willeke eine neue Strategie, um sich an Hamburg zu rächen. Sie reiste nach Speyer, um die Stadt Hamburg vor dem Reichskammergericht auf eine Entschädigung dafür zu verklagen, dass ihre beiden Töchter aus dem Tanzsaal vertrieben worden waren. Sie erreichte, dass ihre Klage zur Verhandlung angenommen wurde. Sie forderte die Zahlung von 24.000 Gulden, das entsprach dem Jahreshaushalt der Stadt.

Die Hamburger Obrigkeit nahm die Klage zunächst nicht sonderlich ernst, sah sich aber dann doch gezwungen, Argumente zu finden, um die Klage als unberechtigt abzuwehren. Dabei ging der Rat ausführlich auf Verfehlungen der Klägerin ein. Aber das verfing nicht beim Reichskammergericht, das zur Auffassung gelangte, diese Einlassungen wären für den Prozess unerheblich. Nicht Agneta Willeken, sondern ihre Töchter seien des Saals verwiesen worden.

Der Prozess zog sich hin und das Urteil wurde erst 1583 gefällt, etwa zwei Jahrzehnte nach dem Tod der Klägerin. Der Klägerin sprach das Gericht 1.000 Gulden zu, die Gerichtskosten musste Hamburg ebenfalls zahlen. Anschließend gab es noch einen Rechtsstreit über Einzelheiten der Zahlung an die Erben und die Höhe der Kostenerstattungen. Erst 1590 konnte das Reichskammergericht den Vorgang nach 42 Jahren abschließen.

Die Romanautorin Andrea Schampier hat in einem Interview 2007 zum Charakter von Agneta Willeken gesagt: „Ja, sie ist kein linearer Charakter. Sie ist widersprüchlich und verhängnisvoll. Weil sie eine so attraktive Frau war – das ist keine Erfindung, das belegen die Prozessakten -, hat sie viele Männer in ihren Bann gezogen. Und ins Unglück gerissen."

Es sei hinzugefügt, dass sie auch sich selbst ins Unglück gestürzt hat. Sie ist als tragische Gestalt in die Hamburger Geschichte eingegangen. Sie war zweifellos eine außergewöhnliche Frau, für deren Streben nach Einfluss und Reichtum in der Hansestadt des 16. Jahrhunderts kein Platz war. Sie stellte sich außerhalb der Normen der damaligen städtischen Gesellschaft und kann als Original angesehen werden kann.

Dass in Hamburg kein Straßenname an Agneta Willeke erinnert, kann angesichts ihres Lebensweges nicht überraschen.

Zitronenjette

„Wat bin ick eemool for ne arme unglückliche Persoon, und ick heff in mien ganzes Leben noch ken Mensch wat doon!“ Diesen Satz hat Henriette (verkürzt: Jette) Müller des Öfteren vor sich hingesagt, wenn sie mit einem Korb Zitronen durch die Stadt ging und die Früchte mit dem Ruf „Zitroon! Zitroon!" anpries.

Die am 18. Juli 1841 unehelich geborene Johanne Henriette Marie Müller erlebte eine freudlose Kindheit. Ihre Mutter wohnte zunächst mit ihr in Dessau, bevor sie nach Hamburg zog. Dort heiratete sie und bekam mehrere weitere Kinder. Jette war in der Familie wegen ihrer geistigen und körperlichen Behinderungen isoliert. Über ihren Stiefvater behielt sie in Erinnerung: „Mein Vater hat mich nicht ausstehen können und deshalb die Straßenjungen auf mich gehetzt.“

Jette konnte nur ihren Namen schreiben und etwas lesen und rechnen. Nur ihre Halbschwester Anna hielt zu ihr. Nach dem Tod des Vaters nahm sie sie in ihre Wohnung im Gängeviertel auf. Es kam zwischen den Schwestern offenbar häufiger zum Streit. Paul Möhring hat in seinem niederdeutschen Theaterstück „Zitronenjette“, von dem noch die Rede sein wird, einen Dialog über den Alkoholkonsum der Zitronenjette aufgenommen. Anna sagte ihrer Schwester: „Jette, wenn du dat Drinken nich inschränken deist, nimmt dat mit di mool keen godes Enn! Denn bist du ganz bestimmt de längste Tied bi mi west.“ Anna wollte ihre Schwester nicht vertreiben, aber sah voraus, dass sie bald entweder auf dem Ohlsdorfer Friedhof oder in der „Irrenanstalt“ Friedrichsberg enden würde. Jette antwortet verzweifelt: „Ick will ober immer bi di blieben, Anna!“ Die beiden Schwestern versöhnen sich am Ende der Theaterszene, aber es wird deutlich, dass beide es im Leben nicht leicht hatten.

Der mühsame Verkauf von Zitronen

Als Erwachsene galt die geistig zurückgebliebene, aber keineswegs schwachsinnige Henriette Müller als eine Frau, über die Kinder und Erwachsene spotteten und mit allerlei derben „Späßen“ ärgerten. Die nur 1.32 Meter große Frau mit der eingedrückten Nase, dem kurzen Rock und der blauen Schürze galt als sehr gutmütig und betrieb ihren Handel mit Stolz und Ehrlichkeit, wenn auch ohne großen Erfolg. Aber das ging damals auch anderen Straßenverkäuferinnen so. Vom 13. Lebensjahr an kaufte sie von den Frachtschiffen im Hafen Zitronen minderer Qualität und versuchte, sie im Laufe des Tages auf den Straßen der Stadt zu verkaufen, wobei manche Kunden sie betrogen. Andere Hamburgerinnen und Hamburger kauften ihr aus Mitleid einige Zitronen ab oder schenkten ihr etwas Geld. Sie war stolz auf ihren Handel und hat nie gebettelt.

Arthur Schmidt, der in der Gegend des Hopfenmarktes aufwuchs, hat Zitronenjette in seiner Kindheit erlebt. Er erzählte Paul Möhring später: „Rückblickend fällt mir ihre Ehrlichkeit auf. Ich erinnere mich, dass ich einmal das eingewickelte Geld, das ich zum Einholen in Papier mit dem aufgeschriebenen Kaufauftrag mitbekommen hatte, auf den Steinklotz gelegt hatte und mich dann durch andere Buttjes davon wegspielen ließ. Die Zitronenjette fand das Geld und brachte es meinen Eltern." Der Junge nahm ihr das zunächst übel, weil er wegen seiner Vergesslichkeit zu Hause eine Tracht Prügel bekam. „Aber dieser Hass ist inzwischen verblasst und der Hochachtung vor der Ehrlichkeit der Jette gewichen."

Oft konnte Zitronenjette tagsüber nicht alle Zitronen verkaufen und zog abends durch Lokale und Spelunken, um ihre Ware anzubieten. Hier war sie noch mehr das Objekt von Spott und „Scherzen". Vor allem drängte man ihr immer wieder Schnaps und Bier auf, sodass sie schließlich alkoholkrank wurde.

Lebensabend in einer „Irrenanstalt"

Zitronenjette verdiente so wenig, dass sie sich keine eigene Wohnung leisten konnte, sondern weiterhin bei ihrer Schwester wohnen musste, zuletzt im Gängeviertel in der Nähe ihres heutigen Denkmals. Als sie immer häufiger so betrunken war, dass sie nicht nach Hause fand und auf der Polizeiwache landete, wies man sie 1894 in die „Irrenanstalt Friedrichsberg" ein.

So ähnlich erging es einer ganzen Reihe von Frauen, die als Originale galten, während Männern mehr „Narrenfreiheit" zugestanden wurde. Jette hatte nun endlich einmal Glück, denn *die Irren-, Heil- und Pflegeanstalt Friedrichsberg* war eine Reformeinrichtung, wo man auf Zwangsjacken und andere Zwangsmittel verzichtete. Auch gab es keine vergitterten Fenster. Die betreuten Menschen konnten sich frei auf dem weitläufigen Gelände bewegen. Henriette Müller lebte dort zwei Jahrzehnte lang recht zufrieden, schälte Kartoffeln und putzte Gemüse.

Paul Möhring schrieb über ihr Alter: „Zu ihrem siebzigsten Geburtstag im Jahre 1911 veröffentlichten einige Hamburger Zeitungen kurze Artikel über sie, welche man ihr zu lesen gab. Mit sichtbarer Freude las sie die Zeilen über sich und war erstaunt, dass sie in Hamburg so populär gewesen war. Eine Zeitung hatte geschrieben, sie sei schwachsinnig. Da protestierte sie energisch und sagte, sie sei nicht schwachsinnig und sei es auch nie gewesen."

Nach dem Ausbruch des Ersten Weltkriegs verschlechterte sich die Lage der Patienten in Friedrichsberg drastisch. Auf dem Gelände der Anstalt wurde ein Reservelazarett für verwundete Soldaten eingerichtet. Zugunsten dieser Soldaten erhielten die psychisch Kranken nur noch Hungerrationen. 40 Prozent der Patientinnen und Patienten sollen in dieser Zeit verhungert sein. Ob Jette Müller zu ihnen gehörte, lässt sich nicht mehr mit Sicherheit feststellen, ist aber zu befürchten.

Ein Theaterstück bewahrt Zitronenjette vor dem Vergessen

Als Jette Müller am 8. Juli 1916 starb, war sie immer noch eine Berühmtheit, deren Lebensgeschichte in einer Volksposse Anlass zum Lachen bot. Den Hamburger Theaterkenner und Autor Paul Möhring ärgerte es, dass Jette nur als komische Person erschien, und so verfasste er ein eigenes Stück. Darin hat er die Zitronenjette möglichst lebensecht auf die Bühne gebracht, nicht als komische Figur. „Der Zuschauer sollte den Eindruck haben: So war diese Volksfigur wirklich, so sah sie aus, so lebte sie und so war der Menschenkreis, in welchem sie sich täglich bewegte. Bei der dramatischen Gestaltung wurde vermieden, diese Frau als Karikatur darzustellen oder sie nur als ‚komische Person', die sie in Wirklichkeit gar nicht war, zu schildern."

1940 hatte das Theaterstück „Zitronenjette" Uraufführung. Dieses, sein erfolgreichstes Stück, hatte Möhring gründlich vorbereitet. So konnte er die Akte von Jette Müller in der *Irrenanstalt Friedrichsberg* einsehen. Diese Vorarbeiten und der Verzicht auf Klamauk zahlten sich aus.

Die erste Besetzung der Rolle der Zitronenjette mit dem Schauspieler Ernst Budzinski war ein Glücksfall. In einer Hamburger Zeitung war zu lesen: „Er hält dies merkwürdige Menschenkind abseits aller Übertreibungen und gibt ihm eine kindliche Einfalt und ehrliches Streben und Redlichkeit." Budzinski war so überzeugend, dass er 526 Mal hintereinander diese Rolle übernahm.

„Zitronenjette" wurde auch danach jeden Abend vor vollem Haus gespielt. Noch bis in die 70er Jahre ging das Stück 1.067 Mal über die Bühne eines einzigen Theaters, des *Ernst-Drucker-Theaters* (später *St. Pauli Theater*) am Spielbudenplatz. Das war ein Rekord in der Hamburger Theatergeschichte. Anlässlich der 1000. Aufführung ehrte der Intendant des *St. Pauli Theaters* Paul Möhring mit einem Lorbeerkranz. Das Stück zeigt sehr feinfühlig das Leben des Originals Zitronenjette, vor allem die ganze Tragik der Frau, die wegen ihrer geistigen Einschränkungen verspottet wurde.

Eine tragische, aber keine komische Person

„Zitronenjette“ hatte diese Ehrenrettung wahrlich verdient. Allerdings wurde die Theater-„Zitronenjette“ noch mehrmals von Männern gespielt, zuletzt von Henry Vahl, der aus der tragischen Gestalt eine komische Figur werden ließ. Das geschah mit Erfolg beim Publikum, war aber weit entfernt von der realen Henriette Müller. Die Schwierigkeiten begannen schon damit, dass das Publikum den Schauspieler Henry Vahl als komisch wahrnahm und man alle Rollen, die er spielte, so einordnete. Paul Möhring soll die Inszenierung mit Henry Vahl mehr oder minder entsetzt zur Kenntnis genommen haben – und Jette Müller hätte es sicher auch getan.

Vorher hatte die Schauspielerin Christa Siems diese Rolle so überzeugend gespielt, dass das „Hamburger Abendblatt“ damals schrieb: „Die sonst im derbkomischen Fach brillierende Schauspielerin Christa Siems hat es verstanden, aus dieser Rolle ein jedenfalls für St. Pauli theatergeschichtliches Ereignis zu machen. Ihre ganze aus dem mitleidenden Herzen hervorgeholte, von glücklicher Rollenversenkung und naiver Selbstverleugnung zeugende kleine Hökerin ist ein ans Herz greifendes darstellerisches Meisterwerk: eine hamburgische Sehenswürdigkeit.“ Jette Müller hätte diese Darstellung ihres Lebens gefreut.

Im Februar 2024 hat Marut Yeginer zu seiner Verabschiedung als künstlerischer Leiter des *Ohnsorg-Theaters* das Stück „Bittersüße Zitronen“ inszeniert. Es verbindet Gerhart Hauptmanns Sozialdrama „Die Ratten“ mit einer realistischen Darstellung der Zitronenjette. In einer Kritik des Portals „Die deutsche Bühne“ hieß es: „Es bleibt ein

Verdienst, dass Yeginer die Figur der kleinen Zitronenhändlerin mit dem großen Alkoholdurst der allfälligen lokalpatriotischen Verharmlosung entreißt und sie in ein Milieu transferiert, das ihrem traurigen Schicksal Gerechtigkeit widerfahren lässt." Allerdings sei ein Manko vorhanden: „Im dramaturgischen Gehege von Hauptmanns ‚Ratten' ist schlicht kein Platz für die biographische Wahrheit der Figur."

2007, mehr als 90 Jahre nach dem Tod der Zitronenjette, erhielt eine Straße in Ohlsdorf den Namen Jette-Müller-Weg. Im *Garten der Frauen* auf dem *Ohlsdorfer Friedhof* steht ein Erinnerungsstein für sie und Vogeljette. Zu erwähnen ist auch, dass eine zitronengelbe Rose den Namen „Rose Zitronenjette" trägt und dass an der Ludwig-Erhard-Straße/Ecke Krayenkamp eine Bronzeskulptur von Hansjörg Wagner an Zitronenjette erinnert. Die Inschrift im Sockel der Skulptur lautet: „Dien Leben wer suur as de Zitroonen, sall sick dat Erinnern an di lohnen? Dien Schicksol wiest op all de Lüüd, for de dat Glück het gor keen Tiet."

Es ist dem Alphabet geschuldet, dass dieses Buch mit einem Kapitel über Zitronenjette abschließt. Und es ist ein guter Anlass, erneut dem Irrtum entgegenzutreten, die Hamburger Originale wären komisch gewesen. Das trifft auf die wenigsten von ihnen zu. Viele Originale hatten Humor, andere waren tragische Gestalten, die von ihren Zeitgenossen verspottet und herablassend behandelt wurden. Zitronenjette selbst hatte nicht viel zu lachen. Andere Originale kehrten den Spieß um und verspotteten ihre Zeitgenossen, was manche von ihnen mit der Verfolgung durch die Obrigkeit bezahlten.

Was alle Hamburger Originale verbindet, ist die Tatsache, dass sie ungewöhnliche Menschen waren. Wir sollten sie in ihrer Individualität und mit ihrem Mut, ihren „abweichenden“ Lebensweg zu gehen, wahrnehmen und anerkennen. Wir sollten uns davor hüten, sie zu komischen Figuren der Lokalgeschichte umzudeuten und herabzuwürdigen. Ihr Schicksal kann uns lehren, Menschen, die anders sind als die Mehrheit, mit Achtung zu begegnen und sie nicht auszugrenzen oder zu verspotten.

Literaturauswahl

Ein Hinweis vorab: Eine ganze Reihe der aufgeführten Bücher ist vergriffen, aber oft noch antiquarisch erhältlich.

Lars Amenda: „Der schwerste Radfahrer der Welt!“, Emil Naucke und die Unterhaltungskultur im späten 19. Jahrhundert, Hamburg 2021

Rainer Berg/Norbert Klugmann: Heinz Erhardt, Eine Biografie, Oldenburg 2009

Albert Borcherdt: Das lustige alte Hamburg, Scherze, Sitten und Gebräuche unserer Väter, Hamburg 1912

Armin Clasen: Die schöne Marianne, Hamburg 1972

Alfred Dreyer: Johann Matthias Dreyer 1717-1769, Hamburg 1934

Helmut Ebeling (Hrsg.): Der Lord von Barmbeck, Das Leben des berüchtigten Ein- und Ausbrechers Julius Adolf Petersen, von ihm selbst erzählt, Hamburg 1999

Helga Feddersen: Hallo, hier ist Helga!, Hamburg o. J.

Kurt Grobecker: Hamburger Hafenkonzert, Geschichten um eine erfolgreiche Radiosendung, Hamburg 1996

Herbert Günther: Ringelnatz, Hamburg 1964

Heidi Kabel: „Das Leben macht mir Freude“, Erinnerungen einer lebensklugen Frau, Hamburg 1994

Konrad Lorenz: Rohrkrepierer, Eine Jugend auf St. Pauli, Roman, Bremen 2011

Ana Mikula/Peter Haag (Hrsg.): Harry Rowohlt, Der große Bär und seine Gestirne, Zürich 2005

Paul Möhring: Drei Hamburger Originale, Hamburg o. J.

Paul Möhring: Ein Hamburger Jung, Hein Köllisch – Der Sänger von St. Pauli, Hamburg 1975

Tim Pröse: Jan Fedder unsterblich, Die autorisierte Biografie, München 2020

Tornado Rosenberg: Vom Glück im Leben, Die Geschichte von Lani Rosenberg und Mama Blume, Berlin 2017

Hans-Heinrich Rottgardt: Vetter Kirchhoff, ein Hamburger Eulenspiegel, Neumünster 1979

Johann Sass: Hamburger Originale und originelle Hamburger, Hamburg o. J.

Andrea Schampier: Agneta Willeken, Ein historischer Roman, Hamburg 2007

Ralf Sotscheck: Harry Rowohlt, In Schlucken-zwei-Spechte, Berlin 2004

Carl Thinius: Damals in St. Pauli, Lust und Freude in der Vorstadt, Hamburg 1975

Henry Vahl: Wie das Leben so s-pielt, Hamburg 1977

Matthias Wegner: Hans Albers, Hamburg 2005